W9-DGN-489

Center Point

FOR RECOVERY PUBLIC LIBRARY WITHDRAWN

WITHIN MY
HEART

**Center Point
Large Print**

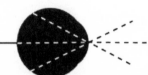

**This Large Print Book carries the
Seal of Approval of N.A.V.H.**

WITHIN MY
HEART

TIMBER RIDGE REFLECTIONS

TAMERA ALEXANDER

CENTER POINT PUBLISHING
THORNDIKE, MAINE

This Center Point Large Print edition
is published in the year 2010 by arrangement with
Bethany House Publishers,
a division of Baker Book Group.

Copyright © 2010 by Tamera Alexander.

All rights reserved.

Scripture quotations are from
the King James Version of the Bible.

The text of this Large Print edition is unabridged.
In other aspects, this book may vary
from the original edition.
Printed in the United States of America.
Set in 16-point Times New Roman type.

ISBN: 978-1-60285-902-9

Library of Congress Cataloging-in-Publication Data
Alexander, Tamera.
    Within my heart / Tamera Alexander. — Center Point large print ed.
        p. cm. — (Timber Ridge reflections ; 3)
    Originally published: Minneapolis, Minn. : Bethany House, 2010.
    ISBN 978-1-60285-902-9 (library binding : alk. paper)
    1. Self-actualization (Psychology) in women—Fiction. 2. Widows—Fiction.
    3. Colorado—History—19th century—Fiction. 4. Large type books. I. Title.
    II. Series.
    PS3601.L3563W58 2010b
    813'.6—dc22
                                                                2010022603

To my precious mother, June Gattis.
Heaven is sweeter still,
knowing you're there.

Keep thy heart with all diligence; for out of it are the issues of life.

PROVERBS 4:23

PROLOGUE

Half hidden beneath the bare-limbed canopy of a dogwood tree, the gravedigger kept a reverent distance, patiently waiting for the last whispered prayers to be uttered and for the final mourner to take her leave. Only then did he step into the fading light, a worn spool of string clutched tight in his gnarled hand. Not much time left. It would be dark soon. And the last grave still needed tending before the pewter skies let loose their winter white.

The distant squeak of wagon wheels and the clomp of horses' hooves faded into the night, leaving only the faint chirrup of crickets to companion the silence. Jessup Collum lifted the lid of the oblong pine box and with painstaking care, his arthritic fingers numb from the cold and marred with time and age, he tied a trailing length of string around the soldier's right wrist. Mindful not to tie the string overtight, he looped the other end through a tiny bell.

He stared for a moment at the soldier's face—the fallen Confederate a mere boy judging from his features—then he glanced around at the

7

freshly covered graves. Deep in his bones he knew what he was doing was right, even if a bit out of the ordinary. There was no malice in his actions, and no sin, most certainly. Nothing that would bring serious offense. Though folks would surely think him a touch senile, if they saw. If they knew . . .

So many ways for a man to die, yet only one was needed for the earth to cradle a body back from whence all life had come.

Jessup turned that thought over in his mind as he'd done countless times before, not indifferent to the shadows stealing across the graveyard as the December sun hastened its retreat. Nightfall brought bitter cold, but not a breath of wind stirred, and each snowflake lofted downward from heaven, unhindered in its journey. He worked hurriedly to cover the last grave, mindful of the trailing string.

After the last shovel of dirt, he straightened, slowly, his crooked spine bearing the brunt of forty-two years of tending this hallowed ground— and of the last few hours of burying the bloodied remnants the Federal Army had abandoned following their assault. If the once-valiant Tennessee Army had been crippled in the battle at Franklin two weeks ago, then the past two days of fighting had delivered a mortal wound.

Jessup lit a torch and stared over row after row of mounded earth, the light casting a burnished glow around him. Too many and too young were those who lay here, going before their time. Before their lives had been lived out. He thought again of the young woman earlier who'd been last to take her leave.

Dark-haired with skin pale and smooth as cream, she'd knelt for the longest time at the grave on the far end, one he'd taken care in covering not two hours earlier, as he'd done the one at his feet just now. She'd huddled close by that grave, weeping, arms drawn around herself, looking as if she'd wanted to lay herself down and mark an end to her own life, what little she had left after losing the man buried there—"a decorated lieutenant from the Tennessee regiment, and my only brother," she'd whispered through tears.

The wound on the lieutenant's neck had told Jessup how the man had died, and the sutures and bloodstained bandages told him how hard some doctor had fought to save him. Shame how fast these soldiers were buried. No proper funeral. No time for one—not with the Federal Army bearing down hard, void of mercy, bent on conquering what little was left.

He tugged the worn collar of his coat closer about his neck and begged the Almighty, again, to intervene, to put an end to this war. Surely it couldn't go on much longer.

A heavy mist crept over the rise from the creek, shrouding the stone markers. The fog seemed to deepen the pungent aroma of upturned earth, and a beguiling trace of honeysuckle clung to the cool night air, despite the wild vine not being in bloom. Jessup took a deeper whiff and could almost taste the sweet summer nectar. A smile pushed up his whiskered cheeks. Maybe folks were right. Maybe he was a touch senile after all. These days recent memories skittered off about as quickly as he reached for them, while others that should have been long gathering dust inched closer as the years stretched on.

He sat down against an ancient poplar, borrowing its strength. Still no wind, and the snow had ceased falling. He imagined the boy's face again, able to see it clearly in his mind's eye as he stared at the bell, willing it to move.

Even the slightest bit.

He put his head back, resting his eyes, only for a moment. But the moments lengthened and gathered and pulled taut, coaxing him along on a gentle wave, absent of the throb in his lower back and the ache across his swollen knuckles.

He was a boy again, running through fields knee-high with summer grass, the sun hot on his face, sweat from a humid Tennessee afternoon beading on his forehead and matting his hair to his head. Someone called to him in the distance. A voice so sweet . . . A lifetime had passed since he'd heard that voice. *Mother* . . .

He ran, youthful legs pumping hard, trying to

reach her, wanting to see her again. But the faster he ran, the farther away her voice seemed to—

Jessup awakened with a start, his breath coming in sharp staggers.

An uncanny sense of presence crowded the darkness around him, and he realized the torch had gone out. He sat straighter, head cocked to one side, and listened, straining to hear his mother's voice again.

But her voice was gone.

He wiped the telling moisture from his cheeks and rose, the joints cracking in his knees. In all his days, he couldn't recall so still a night. So loud a hush over the graves. With a sinking feeling, he looked down at the grave of the young boy. It was late now. Too late.

He prayed the boy was at peace, wherever he was. Same for the decorated lieutenant down the way. He didn't know much about the afterlife—not like folks expected him to—but he reckoned if God was as kind as he believed Him to be that there was some sort of special welcome going on right now for those men who'd laid down their lives in this terrible—

The distant tinkling of a bell brought Jessup upright.

A skitter shimmied up his spine. The air trapped viselike in his lungs. Praying he wasn't still dreaming, he searched the darkness at the end of the row where the woman had knelt earlier, and his skin turned to gooseflesh. If this was what some folks felt when they visited this place late at night, he knew now why they never ventured back.

He also knew why he would never leave.

1

TIMBER RIDGE, COLORADO,
ROCKY MOUNTAINS
APRIL 12, 1877

Rachel Boyd stood motionless in the main aisle of the general store, knowing she shouldn't eavesdrop. But heaven help her, she couldn't bring herself to move! Half afraid that Ben and Lyda Mullins would hear her if she *did* try to make a stealthy exit, she gripped the jar of molasses in her hand, unable to stifle a giggle. The only patron in the store, she was grateful for the lull in afternoon traffic and was more than a little amused—and surprised—by the affectionate whispers coming from beyond the curtained doorway.

A soft chuckle. "Ben Mullins, what's gotten into you? Someone could walk in on us."

A deeper laugh. "Who's going to come back here into the storeroom? All I want is a little kiss. Come here, woman, and let me . . ."

Rachel couldn't make out the low murmurs that followed, and didn't need to. Her imagination filled in the blanks just fine. Warmth rose to her face. Unbidden, her memory skimmed the past two years, and emotions long buried since Thomas's death, yet never forgotten, slowly reawakened inside her.

With them came bittersweet memories of the tender way her husband used to love her, and desires long dormant began to unfurl. She closed her eyes, recalling what it had felt like to be loved by a man. A shiver stole through her, though not an altogether pleasurable one. Her smile slowly faded.

While this wasn't the first time she'd remembered the intimacy she and Thomas had enjoyed in marriage, it *was* her first time to feel those intimate stirrings again. The desire for a man's touch, for that relationship. But the desire wasn't welcome. She would not—could not—ever again love a man the way she'd loved Thomas.

Following his passing, there had been moments when she'd questioned whether she would survive. It had taken so long to find her way out of that fog, that deep, dark place where she'd known she needed to start living again, if only for her boys, but couldn't. With the double-edged gift of time's passing, and the persistent encouragement of family and friends, she'd finally found her way back into the sunlight.

But loving someone so completely, giving herself to a man the way she'd done with her husband, it gave them the power to hurt you in a way no one else could, even when it wasn't their intention.

And she never wanted to hurt like that again. Ever.

More than once, she'd been told she needed to consider remarrying, if only for her boys' sake. But just as she wouldn't risk her heart a second time, neither would she risk her sons having to endure the same hurt they'd gone through with their father's passing. Besides, she and Mitchell and Kurt were getting along fine, just the three of them.

A not-so-gentle check tugged at her flagging confidence. She fingered the jar of molasses in her hand. Perhaps *fine* wasn't the best choice of a word, but the three of them were managing as best they could. She smoothed a hand down the front panel of her skirt and forced down a recurring tide of emotion. With effort, she refocused her thoughts.

School would dismiss within the hour, and she planned on dropping by to visit with the schoolteacher about Kurt. She didn't have an appointment—and it wasn't her first "meeting" with Miss Stafford over her younger son. She just wanted to make sure things were going smoothly and that Kurt hadn't done something else foolish. Again. Like the shenanigan he'd pulled two weeks prior involving the school's outhouse.

He hadn't been the only boy involved, she'd learned, but she had a feeling he'd been the instigator. And she cringed again just thinking about it, putting herself in Miss Stafford's place. Young and inexperienced, Judith Stafford was, from all accounts, being more than patient with Kurt. How embarrassing that must have been. Kurt had written a note of apology, and she'd written Judith Stafford a note too, offering her own expression of regret and thanking the teacher for her understanding. Hopefully a quick visit today would keep things moving in the right direction.

After dealing with that issue, endless chores awaited on the ranch, not to mention the meeting about the overdue loan payment. Mr. Fossey, the bank manager, had been more than lenient, but she sensed his patience waning.

She returned the jar of molasses to the shelf, considering it a luxury these days with funds on the scarce side. In the midst of everything, she was still determined to keep Thomas's dream alive for their two sons. It was what pushed her from bed each morning and what carried her through each day until she fell exhausted back into bed long after dark. That, and the pledge they'd made as a couple to give Mitchell and Kurt a heritage, a better life than the boys would have had if she and Thomas had stayed in Tennessee following the war.

She fingered a callus on her palm. Losing the ranch Thomas had worked so diligently to build wasn't an option, and it hardly defined giving their boys a "better life." She'd stood over her husband's grave and had given her solemn oath that she would see his dream—their dream—come to fruition. And that was a promise she intended to keep. *If* Mr. Fossey still considered her a worthwhile risk.

The intimate exchange behind the blue-and-yellow gingham curtain grew more ardent, and Rachel felt a blush, regretting not having left at the outset. She made her way to the door, hoping Ben had remembered to oil the squeaky hinge. Guilty as she felt, it was nice to know that after twenty-something years of marriage, Ben and Lyda's feelings for each other were still—

"Ben?"

Hearing the name, and catching the unmistakable alarm in Lyda's tone, Rachel paused, hand on the latch.

"Ben, what's—" A muted gasp sounded from the back storeroom. "Honey, what's wrong? Ben . . . are you all—"

A dull thud.

"Ben!"

Rachel raced to the curtain that separated the store from the back part of the building but stopped shy of continuing on. "Lyda, it's Rachel. Is everything all right?" She waited, impatient. "Lyda?"

"No, we're—Ben, can you hear me?" Anxiety constricted Lyda's voice. "Rachel! Something's wrong. I . . . I don't think he's breathing!"

Rachel whipped past the curtain and hurried down the hallway, and came to a stilting halt by the storage closet.

Ben lay crumpled on the floor, motionless, his complexion drained of color. Lyda knelt close beside him. Panic lined her features.

Instinct kicked in and Rachel squeezed in beside them into the cramped space. "What happened?" She checked Ben's pulse, first on the underside of his wrist, then on his neck.

Tears rimmed Lyda's eyes. Her hands shook. "We were . . ." She looked away and Rachel felt a pinch of guilt. "We were . . . kissing, and the next thing I knew Ben was clutching at his arm." Panic thinned her tone. "He acted like he couldn't catch his breath, and then he . . ." She bit her lower lip as tears spilled over. "He just went down."

Rachel closed her eyes and concentrated on finding a pulse, wishing she had her father's old stethoscope. "Has anything like this happened to Ben before?"

Lyda shook her head and nudged her husband's shoulder with a trembling hand. "Ben," she whispered, "can you hear me?"

Fingertips pressed against the underside of his wrist, Rachel stilled. There—finally, she felt something. A pulse. Thready and shallow. Too much so. "He needs Dr. Brookston," she whispered, touching Ben's brow to find it cool and clammy. "I'll go find him. You stay here."

Lyda reached for her hand. "You know what's happening . . ."

It wasn't a question and Rachel didn't answer. Before Timber Ridge boasted a physician of its own, she'd served as midwife to women in town. She'd also treated wounds and sewn up her share of cuts and gashes. People rarely called on her since the doctor arrived—maybe an expectant mother every now and then—but she had a fairly good idea of what was happening to Ben. Yet she wasn't about to state it aloud. It would only add to Lyda's worry, and her assumption could well be wrong. She wasn't a trained physician, after all. Medical schools were for men, not women.

"The important thing, Lyda, is that Ben is breathing and I can feel a pulse. Whatever you do, *don't* move him. If he comes to while I'm gone, make sure he doesn't try to get up. That's very important." She reached for a towel on a shelf, rolled it up, and gently slid it beneath Ben's head. "And keep his head elevated until I get back with the doctor." She stood.

Lyda stared up, fresh tears rising. "Is he . . . going to be all right?"

Rachel knelt again, on the verge of tears herself. At forty-nine, Ben Mullins was almost twenty years her senior—Lyda was half that. Yet in recent years the older couple had become almost like parents to her. Ben treated her much like a father would and was like an uncle to her sons. Lyda was

18

a trusted friend and filled the role of an indulgent aunt to the boys, which included sneaking them candy in church when they were younger, and occasionally even now. Yet Rachel still couldn't bring herself to answer Lyda's question.

She forced a smile she didn't feel. "Did you hear what I said? About making sure Ben stays still and about keeping his head elevated?"

Shadows of realization darkened Lyda's eyes. "Yes," she choked out, nodding. "I heard. It's just that—" She drew in a ragged breath. "Rachel . . . he's all I have now. I can't lose him too."

A horrible, suffocating wave of grief hit Rachel all over again. Only it wasn't from memories of Thomas. She knew that pain only too well. This was different, and it tore at her heart. She reached for Lyda's hand and gripped it tight, remembering a bitter wintry night eight years ago. A night she and Lyda had spoken of only a handful of times since.

Filling her lungs, she worked to steady her voice, the image of Ben and Lyda's children, their expressions so peaceful, so precious, even in death, making that nearly impossible. She squeezed her eyes shut, but the haunting images remained. "I'm going to go find the doctor—he'll know what to do. I won't be long, I promise."

Lyda nodded, her expression communicating what words could not. "Thank you, Rachel. And please . . . *hurry*."

• • •

Rachel ran the short distance to the doctor's clinic and entered without knocking. Angelo Giordano stood at a worktable inside, pestle in hand. "Angelo—" She paused to catch her breath, the chilled mountain air still burning her lungs. "Is Dr. Brookston here?"

The young man shook his head. "The doctor . . . he is at—" He lowered his head. "He is away, Mrs. Boyd." Though his Italian accent was thick and his word choices careful, Angelo Giordano's diction was flawless. "But if maybe . . . I could be of help—"

"I need Dr. Brookston, Angelo! I think Ben Mullins is having heart failure."

The boy's dark eyes went wide.

Rachel hurried to a bookcase crammed with bottles and metal tins, each neatly labeled. But the shelves were cramped, and numerous tins sat stacked on the plank-wood floor gathering dust. She scanned the labels, finding them a challenge to read in the poor light and with the containers stuffed in as they were. She exhaled. Could Dr. Brookston not afford a proper cabinet for his medicine? "Do you know if the doctor has any foxglove? It's a plant—an herb. It's used with patients who have heart ailments."

"I do not know, ma'am," Angelo said, joining her in the search.

Rachel shoved a tin aside to view another behind

it, and a bottle of laudanum slipped off the shelf. She tried to catch it, but the bottle hit the floor with a crack and shattered, splattering laudanum and sending glass shards in all directions. She bit back a harsh word. "I'm sorry, Angelo. I didn't mean to break—"

"Dr. Brookston will not be angry." The boy reached for a rag. "I will clean it."

Her panic mounting, Rachel spotted two wooden crates in the corner, but they held only bottles of lamp oil. Enough to last for an entire year! What did anyone need with that much oil? An unopened box on the examination table drew her attention.

Angelo gestured. "It is new medicine. It came today. That is why I am here. Maybe I should—"

She nodded, anticipating what he might say next. "Yes. Go through that box—quickly please, Angelo—and look for anything that has either of these words on it." She grabbed the fountain pen and a piece of paper from Dr. Brookston's desk and scribbled a note. She already knew firsthand from having assisted Dr. Rand Brookston last fall that he was an exemplary surgeon—she only hoped he was as conscientious about keeping medications ordered and in stock.

She pressed the paper into Angelo's hand. "Now, do you have any idea where the doctor might be? Who he was going to see?"

Angelo blinked, glancing downward.

"Angelo, *please!* There's little time."

21

Wincing, the young man reluctantly met her gaze. "He spoke of going to . . . to Miss Bailey's."

Rachel frowned, confused. "Miss Bailey's . . ."

He nodded once. "The woman, she has a house over on—"

"I know where Miss Bailey's *house* is."

Angelo swallowed and the sound was audible. "The doctor . . . sometimes he sees to the . . . boarders who live there."

Rachel felt the furrows in her brow. *Boarders* wasn't exactly the word she would have chosen to describe the women who lived under Miss Bailey's roof. Regardless, she needed the doctor, and if that's where he was, for whatever reason, then that's where she would go. "As soon as you find either of the items listed on that sheet of paper, bring them as *quickly* as you can to the mercantile, to the back storeroom. Will you do that, please?"

Angelo nodded, his chest puffing out. "Yes, Mrs. Boyd. If what is on this paper is in this box, I will find it. I will bring it."

She thanked him and took off down the boardwalk at a run.

The April air was brisk, burning her lungs. It held the promise of more snow, and Rachel pulled her winter shawl tighter around her shoulders, wishing she hadn't left her coat at the store. A gust of wind disturbed the layer of fresh-fallen snow lining the rooftops and sent it swirling downward.

Winter wouldn't leave the Rockies for at least

another month, maybe two, and she prayed the cold wouldn't cost her more cattle than it already had, or the calves due to drop any day. But especially the calf belonging to Lady. She'd bought Lady a year ago, her first major investment for the ranch, and a good one, for a change.

She turned at the next street. Thankfully, foot traffic on the boardwalk was scarce.

School hadn't dismissed yet but soon would—and she wouldn't be there to meet the boys, or to have that visit with their teacher. When she didn't show, she knew Mitchell and Kurt would walk to James's office and wait there until she arrived. The boys loved their uncle James and never complained about visiting the sheriff's office, but she worried about what they saw and overheard there. Still, some days it couldn't be helped.

Only last fall had she begun to allow Mitch and Kurt to walk to school on their own again. She still accompanied them in the wagon as far as Ben and Lyda's store each morning, unable to stomach the thought of them walking the distance from the ranch like they once had. Not after what had happened to Thomas, and with the recent reports of cougar sightings.

Winded, she struggled to maintain the hurried pace, her breath puffing white. Winter-shrouded peaks towered high above Timber Ridge and drew her gaze upward as thoughts of Ben pressed close. The rush of her pulse pounded hard in her ears.

If only Ben's heart could beat half as strong . . .

If Ben had a history of heart weakness, he'd never mentioned it. Neither had Lyda. And Rachel felt certain they would have, given her closeness to them.

A left at the next intersection led her into a part of town she didn't usually frequent. Saloons and gaming halls lined the thoroughfare. Even midday the smell of liquor was potent. She spotted Miss Bailey's establishment at the end of the street and made a beeline for it, wondering how she knew which building it was. She couldn't recall being told. It was simply one of those places everybody in town knew of, but most folks—at least in her circle—never spoke about.

Two women lazed against the railing of the wraparound porch, talking, dressed in a manner ill-advised for the cold and that might have been shocking had Rachel been naïve about their occupation. But she wasn't, and she raced up the porch stairs, the unease over having to visit a place like this paling in comparison to her concern for Ben. She never broke stride. "I've come to get Dr. Brookston. It's an emergen—"

The woman on the left, a blonde, stepped directly into her path, blocking the door.

Rachel stopped short.

"I think you mean *Rand,* don't you?" the woman said, looking her up and down and smiling, though not in a friendly way. "That's what we all call him." She crossed her arms over her chest and her ample cleavage lifted to threaten the already strained buttons of her thin shirtwaist. "He's inside, *visiting* with one of the girls. And I don't think he'll take kindly to being interrupted." She gave a throaty laugh. "I know Patricia won't. She's been waitin' for this all week." She tossed a wink at the woman beside her.

"Visiting with one of the girls." Fairly good at reading people, Rachel knew when she was being goaded. She had no qualms about the doctor seeing to the health of these women. Her father had been a physician, and she respected a physician's oath to care for the sick, regardless of person or circumstance. Yet Dr. Brookston's coming *here,* to this place, and his apparent familiarity with these women . . . Such behavior hinted at arrogance. An arrogance with which she was only too familiar when it came to men of his profession.

An arrogance that often led to their downfall.

"Like it or not—" Rachel squared her shoulders, finding boldness when picturing Lyda cradling Ben—"Dr. Brookston's *visit* here is about to be cut short." She pushed past the woman, yanking her arm free when the blonde grabbed hold. Once inside, she hustled to close the door and flipped the lock into place, knowing it wouldn't buy her much time.

The women pounded on the glass-paned door behind her, yelling obscenities. Surely the building had a back door, so Rachel knew she was only prolonging the inevitable, but she didn't need long.

The sickeningly sweet smell of perfume hit her full in the face. That, and stale liquor. It took a moment for her eyes to adjust to the dim light.

Laughter drifted down from the second floor, giving hint as to where she should begin her search. She hurried up the spiral staircase. The garish red carpet muted her boot steps. She instinctively reached for the handrail, then held back, thinking better of it.

Oversized oil paintings covered the walls, detailed in their renderings and advertising the services bartered in this place. After her gaze collided with a particularly graphic "portrait," she kept her eyes averted, but couldn't block out the disturbing memories that came with being inside a place like this. Not that she'd ever been inside a brothel before—

But her father had. On numerous occasions. With many women. For many years.

For the thousandth time, she questioned why doctors considered themselves more highly than they ought, more immune to weaknesses in character and less prone to fault—when based on personal experience, with few exceptions, she'd found quite the opposite to be true.

She reached the second-story landing, and the gravel of male voices blended with female laughter to paint a plurality of mental images Rachel tried in vain to block out. She looked down the long hallway. So many doors . . . and they were all closed.

The rush of footsteps sounded from downstairs. "She must have gone up there!"

Time running out, Rachel pounded on the first door.

2

Rand helped the young woman to a sitting position, ignoring how she held his hand a tad too long. What he had to tell Miss Bailey downstairs would not go over well. Not when it meant her *best girl* wouldn't be working for a while. But for Patricia, "working" wasn't an option, and he had a fairly good idea of how to ensure Miss Bailey's compliance. He crossed the room to wash his hands.

"Will it hurt like this for long, Doc?"

"For a few days, I'm afraid." He dried his hands on the clean towel he carried with him in his medical bag, hearing what sounded like pounding from down the hallway. Probably another fight, which would likely result in someone else needing to be sutured, same as the last time he was here. "I'll give you a salve to use and some herbs to be mixed with hot tea. Drink it twice daily, morning and night, until the herbs are gone." He packed his equipment back in his bag, aware of the young woman's continued stare.

Patricia would never be mistaken for subtle, but the way she perched on the edge of the wrought-iron bed—one leg drawn up beneath her while the other dangled off the side—was particularly unladylike. And held purpose.

"You're gonna say no again, Doc, because right now I'm ailin'. But maybe later, when I'm better . . ." Her shapely leg swung from side to side, keeping time with the clock's pendulum on the opposite wall. She patted the bedcovers beside her. "Miss Bailey wouldn't need to know. Nobody would. And I wouldn't charge you either." She fingered the lace ties of her shirtwaist, a pouty smile rising. "I guess you could say I have a softness for Southern men."

Rand rolled down his shirtsleeves, seeing more challenge in the woman's eyes than softness. "*No* . . . thank you, Patricia. As always."

Her sharp exhale said she'd anticipated his response.

While he struggled with physical desires, only one woman in the town of Timber Ridge had ever made him look twice. Actually, more than twice. But since she'd never indicated the least interest in him—had done quite the opposite, in fact—he'd set his interest aside. Or was trying.

The pounding in the hallway grew closer, as did the muffle of angry voices.

28

Patricia gave a petulant sigh, seemingly unfazed by the altercation on the other side of the door. "Don't you ever long for the pleasure of a woman, Rand? Or wish that instead of listening to my chest through that fancy earpiece of yours, that you could—"

"I'm informing Miss Bailey that I don't want you *entertaining* clients, Patricia, for at least three weeks." Rand delivered a straightforward gaze that silenced any rebuttal. He reached for his suit jacket. "And before you return to work, I want to examine you again. To make sure you're well."

Huffing, she finally dropped the alluring façade. "Miss Battleaxe won't agree to me taking three weeks off and we both know it."

He had to smile at the name the women here had dubbed the proprietress, knowing it wasn't far off the mark. Miss Bailey treated these girls like property, which, to her, they were. "You let me handle Miss Bailey. I don't think I'll have a problem convincing her to—"

"Get your hands *off* of me!" a female voice insisted from the other side of the door.

Rand wasn't personally familiar with the women who worked here, but something in this particular woman's tone told him she wasn't one of Miss Bailey's *girls*. Why would such a woman be—

A pounding on the bedroom door brought him full around.

"Dr. Brookston! Are you in there?"

"He's busy," Patricia called out, laughing and tossing him a playful wink as she struck a seductive pose on the bed.

Throwing her a look of warning, Rand reached for the door. But it opened before he could turn the latch. Stunned, he swallowed. Or tried to. "M-Mrs. Boyd, what are you—"

"We need you! It's Ben Mullins. He just collapsed!" Her expression fierce, Rachel Boyd struggled against a hard-looking blonde on one side and a shirtless miner on the other.

The blonde gave her arm a jerk. "We *told* her she's not supposed to be up here!"

The miner smiled. "Fine by me if she's—"

Rand caught hold of the man's wrist. "Let go of her. *Now.*"

Smirking, the miner complied. The woman did too, daggers in her eyes.

Rachel shrugged them off and gave the blonde a dark look. "I can't be sure about Ben, Doctor, but—" She spoke quickly, breathless. "I think it's his heart."

Rand grabbed his bag. "Where is he?"

"At the store. In the back. Lyda's with him." Her gaze slid past him, and suspicion slipped into her eyes.

Able to guess how Patricia was still positioned on the bed, Rand stepped into Rachel's line of sight, blocking her view. But her conclusions were easily read in her expression. He needed to clarify his purpose in being here, but now wasn't the time. "How long ago did this happen?" He indicated for her to precede him down the hall.

"Fifteen minutes, maybe twenty. Angelo told me where to find you." Unmistakable objection edged her voice. "Did you not hear me calling your name?"

Rand cringed, hearing Patricia's laughter behind him. "I'm sorry, Mrs. Boyd. I didn't." He gestured toward the stairs. "My buckboard is out back."

Miss Bailey stood waiting in the front parlor, arms crossed, expression defiant. She leveled a loathing stare in Rachel's direction, then turned the same on him.

Rand motioned Rachel toward the back door. "I'm right behind you," he said, speaking to Miss Bailey as he followed. "Under no circumstances is Patricia to work for the next three weeks."

The proprietress huffed, trailing him down the hallway. "Three weeks! That's absurd! Out of the question! Do you have any idea how much money I'll lose if she doesn't—"

"Patricia is ill and *highly* contagious to her clients. As you, no doubt, are already aware." Rand turned at the door and watched Miss Bailey's already ruddy complexion turning an even deeper crimson. "Should you choose to ignore my advice, madam, I'll visit every saloon and gaming hall in this town and will let the men know—in detail— what they can expect to get if they visit Patricia

31

before that three weeks is up. Or perhaps you'd prefer a total quarantine?"

Her eyes narrowed. "Get out," she whispered. "This isn't what we agreed to."

Rand obliged her request and strode to the wagon. "This is exactly what we agreed upon, Miss Bailey," he called back, stowing his medical bag beneath the seat. "I'm seeing to the health of these women and to the welfare of Timber Ridge. If you don't like it—take it up with Sheriff McPherson." He couldn't help his thigh brushing against Rachel's when he settled beside her on the narrow bench seat. He also didn't miss how she attempted to put space between them, trying unsuccessfully to remedy that.

A flick of the reins and the mare responded. The buckboard started forward with a jolt. "Was Mr. Mullins conscious when you left him?"

Rachel shook her head. "No."

"How would you classify Mr. Mullins's pulse when you checked it?" Based on their brief interactions prior to today, he was certain she would be able to answer the question.

"Faint, and erratic. All signs of arrhythmia are present. Either that"—she grimaced—"or heart failure."

Feeling precious time slip past, Rand urged the mare to a faster trot.

Reins taut, he took the next corner more sharply than usual, grateful the side street was empty. "Did

you think to tell Mrs. Mullins not to move her husband? In the event of a weakened heart muscle, keeping the patient immobilized is of vital importance due to—"

"The likelihood of increased trauma should the patient be moved." She tossed him a sideways glance. "*Yes,* Dr. Brookston, I gave Lyda Mullins that instruction. It also occurred to me to tell her to keep her husband's head elevated, which aids the body's circulation, especially when the heart is under stress."

Wordless, Rand faced forward again, feeling very much put in his place. "My apologies, Mrs. Boyd, if it sounded as though I were insinuating that you—"

"No offense was taken, Doctor. After all"—her lips curved in a tight smile—"I'm not a trained physician . . . as are you." She spoke the words nicely enough, her Southern accent sweet as honey, but her clenched jawline hinted at her truer feelings.

His male intuition, however deficient and untried when it came to the female gender, told him it was best to leave her statement untouched. Yet—he'd made a misstep somewhere, a serious one, and he wanted to remedy it. "Please let me assure you, Mrs. Boyd, that I regret my presence at the brothel today as much as you do."

She turned and looked up at him, her expression one of surprise. And disappointment.

"Though not for the reason you might think. My being there today was purely of a medical nature, however much it might have appeared otherwise. I regret that you had to come looking for me. And *there,* of all places."

Her features softened. For a brief instant. Then her polite but distant poise returned.

Years of medical instruction and clinical practice had prepared him for the challenges of being a doctor, specifically in the sciences related to the female body and reproduction. But the ability to decipher the workings of a woman's mind . . . He sighed to himself. *That* science remained a mystery.

Yet one thing was indisputable. Any hope he'd entertained of gaining Rachel Boyd's interest— especially after today—was futile.

The Mullinses' store came into view, and he narrowed his thoughts and began praying, as he always did, first for his waiting patient, then for himself. *Lord, give me wisdom and discernment . . . and the courage to act.*

He brought the buckboard to a stop and jumped out, not surprised when Rachel didn't wait for his assistance. He heard her close behind him as he took the stairs leading up to the boardwalk.

Patrons milled about inside the store. A small group of them gathered by the curtain leading to the storerooms in the back, whispering among themselves. They dispersed when they saw him

approaching. Rand paused and turned back to Rachel. "If you could—"

"Take care of things out here, Doctor." She nodded. "Then I'll join you in the back shortly."

"You read my mind, Mrs. Boyd. Thank you." He welcomed her assistance. Last December, she'd aided him in an emergency delivery and surprised him by proving to be a skilled surgical assistant. He was grateful for her medical knowledge. Not missing how intent she seemed on looking anywhere but at him, Rand slipped through the curtained doorway, mindful of prying eyes.

"Mrs. Mullins?"

"We're . . . back here," came a weak voice.

He rounded the corner to see Lyda nestled beside her husband on the floor of a storage closet. Tears streaked her face, and as Rand searched for signs of life in the pallor of Ben's face, his own chest squeezed tight.

He removed his coat and knelt beside them in the cramped quarters, pulling his stethoscope from his bag. "Rest assured, Mrs. Mullins . . ." He unbuttoned Ben's shirt. "I'm going to do everything within my ability to help your husband." He pressed the bell-shaped chest piece over the older gentleman's heart.

Nodding, Lyda sat upright and wiped her cheeks.

"Has he been unconscious since he first collapsed?"

"Yes." She sniffed. "But at least I can feel him

breathing now. For a while there I wondered if he was going to—" A shudder completed her unfinished thought.

Rand adjusted the ivory earpieces and listened, careful to keep his expression smooth and unreadable. Rachel's assessment had been accurate. *Faint* and *erratic* aptly described the storekeeper's pulse.

He moved the stethoscope, listening to the distant thud echoing faintly in his ears before moving the instrument again. With aid of his pocket watch, he timed the intervals between the irregular half beats slipping in and around the already stuttered rhythm, wishing Mrs. Boyd were there to help him. "To your knowledge, has your husband experienced any light-headedness in recent days? Or pain in his chest?"

"No." She stared at Ben, her lips a tremulous line. "At least he never said anything to me about it." She cradled the side of her husband's face. "But Ben has never been a complainer."

Rand gently probed Ben's abdomen, then reached down and pulled up one of his patient's pant legs. "What about any swelling in his legs or ankles?" He saw the answer to his question before Lyda Mullins opened her mouth.

"Ben had me draw him another warm salt bath one night last week." She took an unsteady breath. "His ankles were swelling up again something awful. Another shipment, a big one, came in for the grand opening of the new resort next month. Charlie Daggett was working out at Rachel Boyd's ranch for the afternoon, so Ben unloaded it by himself. I told him to wait for Mr. Daggett to come the next morning, but he wouldn't." She shook her head. "Ben said Mr. Tolliver needed it right away."

Mention of Tolliver and the new Colorado Hot Springs Resort reminded Rand about Brandon Tolliver's "urgent" request to meet with him. Rand had found the note—the second in as many days—nailed to his clinic door when he'd returned home last evening. He had no idea what Tolliver wanted, but since no reference of a medical nature was mentioned, he'd laid the note aside, in no hurry to meet with the man. His general rule of thumb was to remain neutral about folks he didn't know well enough yet, but Brandon Tolliver seemed bent on testing that long-held principle.

With a sigh, Lyda brushed back a lock of her husband's thinning hair. "Later that night Ben said something about how the two of us were getting older, and we laughed." With a weak smile, she looked up, her eyes full of question—and dread.

Rand managed what he hoped was a reassuring look, then leaned down. "Mr. Mullins?" He waited. "Mr. Mullins . . . can you hear me, sir?" Watching for any response, Rand reached for his bag and felt around inside. He'd put a pouch of digitalis in there two days ago, just before he—

Mrs. Willets. He winced.

He'd given the last of the medicine to Loretta Willets yesterday morning when she'd complained of palpitations and shortness of breath. Over a month ago he'd ordered more, but it still hadn't arrived. Ben Mullins would need that medication when he came to.

Rand stifled a groan, angry at himself for not being better prepared and frustrated over how long it took to get supplies freighted up the mountain. The country had a railroad connecting east to west, but it still took an eternity to get medicine delivered to Timber Ridge. As soon as Rachel Boyd joined them—where in heaven's name was she?—he would send her to his office with instructions to check this morning's—

"Dr. Brookston, is something wrong?"

Concern in Lyda's voice drew him back, and Rand saw his own fear and frustration reflected in her expression. With effort, he worked to smooth the tension from his brow and his tone. "No, ma'am," he said softly. "I'm simply . . . ascertaining your husband's condition."

She nodded, not looking convinced.

He inched the stethoscope higher, toward the upper chamber of Ben's heart, resolving to keep his emotions better contained. Not that he desired to appear perfect or as if he had all the answers, but wavering on a decision, showing signs of hesitation or uncertainty, could undermine his relationship with a patient, which could potentially sway them from following his advice. Which could cost lives.

He adjusted the earpieces again to filter out extraneous noise and worked his way downward, listening to Ben's lungs. What he heard settled like a weight inside his own chest.

He'd never seen Ben Mullins as a patient, but he remembered Ben complaining of indigestion in recent weeks. Twice he'd encouraged the man to come see him about it, but Ben had laughed in that easy manner of his and attributed the tightening in his chest to too much fried chicken.

Using his sleeve, Rand wiped the sweat beading his brow. He hadn't said anything further to Mr. Mullins at the time, not wanting to force the issue—or his services, if they weren't desired. But perhaps if he had, he could've diagnosed Ben's heart condition before it reached such an acute stage.

Rand considered the possible diagnoses and swiftly settled on one, his decision made easier, painfully so, by the telling *whoosh* coming through the stethoscope. His responsibility as physician to the people of this town—and to this good man lying on the floor before him—bore down hard.

For two years he'd lived and worked in Timber Ridge, yet he had failed to build what he would term a "respectable practice." Oh, he'd treated scores of people since arriving, had delivered babies. And with the construction of the new resort and with mining operations close by, there was no end to suturing gashes, binding wounds, and setting bones. Thanks to Sheriff McPherson's assistance, he'd even managed to gain the town council's support to conduct fitness examinations on the schoolchildren last fall. But he still felt as if people didn't completely trust him as a doctor, that they didn't see the importance of being under a doctor's care.

They'd accepted him into their town, made him feel welcome enough. But for the most part, they only called on him when they were either bleeding to death or knocking on death's door. Like now. There was so much he wanted to teach these fine people about living a healthier life. So much illness that could be prevented if folks would only listen to—

Rand went absolutely still inside, realizing that the weakened heartbeat thudding faintly in his ears only a second ago had done the same.

His own heart fisted tight.

He repositioned the stethoscope, searching for a pulse, straining to hear something. Anything. A hundred possibilities flew through his mind as he pressed his fingers against the underside of Ben's jaw.

No, God . . . Please don't do this to me. Not again . . .

Knowing what he had to do, yet never having done it himself, Rand felt his insides knot up. Hands trembling, he made a fist and positioned it directly over Ben Mullins's heart, remembering the first time he'd seen a colleague perform this procedure. *Barbaric* was the word that had come to mind then.

He raised his arm.

Lyda gasped. "What are you do—"

Rand brought his fist down directly over Ben's heart.

"No! Dr. Brookston, don't!" Lyda cried.

She tried to block his efforts, but Rand caught hold of her wrists. "Mrs. Mullins, your husband's heart has stopped. If I don't do something, he's going to die!" Saying the words made it even more real, and fear threatened to paralyze his confidence as deeply buried memories clawed their way to the surface.

Suddenly all he could see was Marietta's face.

Her lithe form on the table before him, her crying in soft guttural moans, reaching out to him with one hand while cradling her swollen belly with the other. Remorse stung his eyes as he pictured his sister's sweet face, and that of her child.

He let go of Lyda Mullins, his choices clear. He had no idea whether what he was attempting would save Ben Mullins's life or not. The procedure certainly wasn't without risk, nor was it without its naysayers. But doing nothing would seal Ben's fate without question. Sometimes taking a risk was the best choice.

And sometimes it was the only choice.

41

"Mrs. Mullins, I can restart your husband's heart. I know I can. But you're going to have to let me do this. You're going to have to trust me."

Her face drained of color. "All right," she whispered, voice thin as a reed.

Rand checked again for a heartbeat. Finding none, he rose up on his knees beside Ben. He fit his hands one atop the other over the sternum, straining to recall exactly how he'd seen this demonstrated two years earlier.

Using his own weight for leverage, he pressed down, then let up, pressed down, and let up, silently counting as he did, aware of Lyda's body flinching each time he started a compression.

Stethoscope positioned again, he listened. Still nothing. Perhaps the naysayers were right. . . .

As quickly as the thought came, he banished it, but another nipped its heels. What if he was performing the procedure incorrectly? After all, he'd never done it before.

His nerves worn thin, sweat slicked his body. Rachel had said she'd join him back here *quickly,* but apparently they had different definitions of the word.

With Lyda looking on, her expression fluctuating between agony and disbelief, Rand repeated another compression, praying with each downward thrust, then leaned close again, listening through the earpieces, willing for God to grant his petition.

He knew God could heal with a thought. He also knew, only too well, that sometimes God chose not to. Rand rose up again, clasped hands positioned over Ben's heart. If he had anything to say about it—and he did—he was going to make sure that *this* time, God made the right choice.

3

"Please make your way outside to the boardwalk." Rachel hurried the patrons toward the front doors, frustrated at their lethargic pace. Herding cattle was faster than this. "There's been an emergency and we need to close the store temporarily." She glanced toward the back room, wondering what was happening, when—from the corner of her eye—she saw an older teenage boy loitering in the corner, one hand hidden inside his unbuttoned coat.

Her instincts told her he was up to no good, but she didn't have time to confront whatever he might have done. She ushered him toward the open doors.

At one time, she'd known almost everyone living in Timber Ridge, at least by face. But those days were long past. Every day, it seemed, more people arrived in Timber Ridge, enticed west by the lure of gold.

She'd never seen most of these people before

and didn't know them well enough to trust them alone in the mercantile. Not with what James had told her about the increase in theft. Ben and Lyda had been victims of thieves themselves—boots and clothing gone missing, staple items unaccounted for in the ledger. And though Lyda had never said anything outright, Rachel had gotten the impression that money was tight for them these days too.

She peered through the store's front window, trusting Mitch and Kurt had made it safely to the jail and watching for Angelo, Dr. Brookston's assistant, hoping to see him coming with the medicine. "As soon as possible, Mr. and Mrs. Mullins will reopen the store." Even as she said it, she prayed it would be true. That *both* Ben and Lyda would be opening the doors again.

She trusted Rand Brookston to do all he could for Ben. Having witnessed the doctor's skill firsthand, she knew Timber Ridge was fortunate to have such a gifted physician. Still, something about him grated on her, and she knew she hadn't done a good job of disguising those misgivings. She regretted her curt response moments ago in the buckboard when he asked her if she'd given Lyda the proper instructions. She sensed from his confused expression that he hadn't meant to sound condescending. Even though he had . . .

Maybe it was his self-assurance that she found so off-putting, or the confident manner in which he carried himself. Or the way women watched him when he strode down the boardwalk, or how they fawned over him after church services or at social gatherings. When it came down to it, if someone asked her why she felt the way she did about him, she wouldn't have been able to tell them in definitive terms.

She only knew that he was a physician, as her father had been, which was enough to make her want to keep her personal distance.

"Mama!"

About to latch the front doors, Rachel heard the familiar voice and peered through the glass to spot Mitchell running toward her full force, Kurt fast on his heels.

Mitchell skirted the crowd on the boardwalk and skidded to a stop, his thin chest working hard. "Uncle James had some"—he pushed the words out between heavy breaths—"sheriffin' to do, so he sent us . . . here to stay with Uncle Ben and . . . Aunt Lyda 'til you came."

Rachel brushed the hair from his eyes. "That's fine, that's fine. Catch your breath, the both of you." Mitchell had taken to calling Ben and Lyda "uncle and aunt" some time back, and Kurt had quickly mimicked him, which delighted Ben and Lyda. "Come on inside. Quickly." She waved them through the open door, not missing the perturbed looks from patrons banned to the boardwalk. Pretending not to notice, she closed the door and reached for the lock, then gave an exasperated sigh. It locked by key. A key she didn't have time to look for.

Out on the boardwalk, a kind-looking older gentleman stepped forward. With a quiet nod, he turned his back to the door as though understanding that she needed someone to stand guard. She didn't know him from Adam so wasn't comfortable leaving the store in his hands, but what else could she do?

"Boys, I need to go check on Uncle Ben in the back room. He took sick this afternoon. I want you to keep watch and make sure no one comes inside. Tell them the store is closed for a little while. Is that clear? But if Angelo comes, let him in immediately."

Mitch nodded.

Kurt didn't. "Miss Stafford doesn't like me, Mama. She's always eyein' me funny and tellin' me that I'm a—"

"Kurt, I don't have time for this right now."

"Yeah . . . but she won't let me—"

Rachel held up a finger, an accustomed throb beginning in her left temple. "We'll talk about this tonight. *Tonight!*" she reiterated when Kurt opened his mouth again.

Mitchell pulled something from his coat pocket and Kurt's scowl deepened. "Miss Stafford gave this to me after school, Mama. She said it was her second note this week. She told me to make double sure you got this one."

This one? Miss Stafford hadn't sent her a note this week.

But the frown on Kurt's impish face said differently. Defiance hardened the blue of his eyes, and Rachel felt as though someone had knocked the wind from her. Defeat washed through her, scathing her confidence. Somewhere during the past two and a half years, she'd lost her hand with her younger son. She had no idea why he behaved the way he did now and was at her wits' end to know what to try next.

Mitchell leaned close. "Miss Stafford didn't look happy," he whispered, his expression mirroring maturity beyond his ten years. His brow raised in a way reminiscent of his father. "I told her you were busy with the ranch and with calving, and would come as soon as you could."

Moments slipping past, Rachel nodded, feeling an all-too-familiar burning in her eyes. Mitchell, ever the older brother and peacekeeper, was the "man of the house" now. At least that's what he'd told her not too long ago. Too much to bear for one so young.

"Thank you, son." She took the note and slipped it into her pocket unread. "We'll deal with this tonight, Kurt." And she would. But right now, his misbehavior paled in comparison to what was

47

happening in the back—which was where she needed to be right now!

"Would it be all right if we got something to eat, Mama?" Mitch asked.

Kurt nodded. "You didn't give us enough lunch and we've been starvin' ever since."

They'd eaten the last of the bread at breakfast, so there hadn't been any to include in the boys' lunches, but she'd given them extra ham and cheese. Plenty for lunch. This was simply Kurt's way of punishing her. For what, she didn't know. "You may get a cookie from the jar on the counter. But only one," she said, aiming the warning at Kurt, who let out a whoop and took off for the other side of the store.

Mitch stared up, watching her closely, as he always did. "Is Uncle Ben *bad* sick, Mama?"

She worked to mask her fear. It was so hard to hide things from Mitchell. Just like his father. "Dr. Brookston is with him right now, and I'm sure that—" The words *everything will be fine* wouldn't come. Not when staring into Mitchell's stark blue eyes and knowing that he knew—already, at so young an age—what the death of a loved one felt like, and how permanent it was. At least for this life. "I'm confident Dr. Brookston is taking good care of him, so don't you worry."

Mitch nodded, but his eyes narrowed the slightest bit. He glanced over at his brother. "I'll make sure he doesn't get into anything he

48

shouldn't, and that he only has one cookie so he won't spoil his dinner."

Rachel brushed a swift kiss to his forehead and carried his "little-boy scent" with her as she hurried down the aisle. How much longer would he let her do that? Love on him that way without shying away like Kurt already did. How could two sons born to the same parents, only two years apart, be so different from each other? And how would she ever manage to be both father and mother to them?

Once past the curtain, she heard Lyda's soft weeping and slowed her steps. A hand to her stomach did nothing to ease the sickening quiver.

Neither Dr. Brookston nor Lyda acknowledged her presence when she reached the doorway of the storeroom. She stood, silent, watching as Rand Brookston listened to Ben's chest through his stethoscope. Ben's eyes weren't open, but she thought she heard a sliver of air wheeze past his parted lips, and a trickle of relief passed through her own.

"Keep speaking to him, Mrs. Mullins," Rand Brookston whispered, his voice tense. "Let him hear the sound of your voice."

Perspiration dampened the back of Rand's shirt and the taut set of his shoulders mirrored his anxiety. Rachel wished she'd arrived sooner to help him. Not that she knew anything, medically speaking, that he didn't.

Lyda leaned close to frame Ben's face with her hands. "Ben Everett Mullins, y-you listen to me and you listen good." Her voice held a sternness that might have sounded convincing if not for her tears. "Your heart stopped, Ben, but the good doctor here got it started back up again. You've been given a second chance, my love, but you're going to have to fight."

Started his heart back again? Rachel stared at Ben, at the labored rise and fall of his chest, as Lyda's meaning gradually took hold, then her focus shifted to Rand Brookston.

She'd heard talk of doctors attempting to restart a patient's heart, but that's all it was—talk. Once a person's heart stopped, life was over. Everyone knew that. Some things, once damaged, were beyond mending. Unbidden, the memory of Thomas's shredded, blood-soaked shirt clouded her vision and she blinked hard to clear it away.

Had Rand Brookston really managed to do the impossible? Her respect for the man's abilities deepened even as her personal misgivings about him remained unchanged.

Footsteps sounded down the hallway, and she turned to see Angelo coming through the curtain, envelope in hand. If she read his smile right, he'd found the—

"This is your definition of *shortly,* Mrs. Boyd?"

Rachel turned back, surprised by the curtness in Rand Brookston's tone. And in his expression.

Heat rose to her face. Her mouth moved but no words would come. "I'm . . . sorry. It took longer than I thought to get the patrons to leave."

Rand rose to his full height, stethoscope dangling in his grip. "I could have used your assistance." The intensity in his eyes deepened. "I thought I made that clear."

His manner was polite, yet direct, and Rachel glanced at Ben, then at Lyda, whose attention, thankfully, was focused on her husband. Shame filled her. If her delay had threatened Ben's life in any way . . . after everything Ben and Lyda had done for her. The thought alone made her ill, and the sense of defeat from moments earlier returned with a renewed vengeance.

"I'm sorry, Dr. Brookston," she whispered. "If I can be of help now, I'll—"

"I need medicine." He motioned to Angelo, who had come along beside her. "I'm glad you're here, Angelo. I'd like for you to accompany Mrs. Boyd to my office, please. Check the shipment from this morning first, then the shelves. The medicine will be in an envelope labeled either *digitalis* or *foxglove*. Time is crucial, so—"

"I have it here, sir." Angelo held out an envelope. "It was in the shipment, at the bottom."

Rand stared. "But . . . how did you know I would need this?"

Angelo motioned. "Mrs. Boyd, she told me to look for it, sir . . . when she came looking for you."

The young man pulled a piece of paper from his pocket. "She wrote down the words. See? She asked me to meet you here."

Rachel's face burned. She should have felt vindicated at Angelo's admission, but she couldn't bring herself to look up, even when she sensed Rand Brookston wanting her to. She bit her lower lip and fought back tears.

She was being beyond silly, responding like a cowering child. And to Rand Brookston, of all people. It was foolishness! She was a grown woman. And a mother!

But she felt like a girl again, standing before her father outside one of his patient rooms—scolded and embarrassed—having tried to anticipate his request but without success, and after having tried so hard to please him. Her chest tightened with emotion. How could childhood memories of a parent still hold such sway when adult memories of that same person cast an altogether different light?

And why did she still feel as though she were lacking? She had been right this time! She'd chosen the correct medicine. Yet she felt like a disappointment. As though she'd failed, one more time, to meet not only her own expectations, but someone else's as well.

4

R and wished Rachel would look at him. Her unshed tears barbed his conscience, and rightfully so. He'd been short with her, speaking out of frustration with himself and fear of what could have happened to Ben Mullins. Of what could still happen . . . "Mrs. Boyd, I . . . I didn't mean to—" Her hands, clenched tight at her waist, only encouraged the knot of guilt twisting his stomach. "Believe me when I say that I . . . What I mean to say is that . . ."

What he wanted to say but couldn't was that he'd behaved like a complete and unmitigated—

"Excuse me, I'll get a cup of water for the medicine," she said quietly, then spun on her heel and strode down the hallway.

He started to follow, then decided it might be best if he didn't. Clearly she was hurt. But the swiftness of her stride said she was also riled. And with good reason. He hadn't meant for his remark to come out like it had.

He shot an apologetic look at Angelo, who stood quiet, watchful. "I shouldn't have spoken to Mrs. Boyd in that manner, Angelo," Rand offered quietly. "Or to you either. I'm sorry."

The boy smiled and gave a conciliatory nod. "What you do . . . it is important, Dr. Brookston. Your work is hard. You carry a weight, in here"—he patted his chest—"because of it."

Rand often had to remind himself that Angelo was just a youth. Only fifteen, Angelo had endured more hardship than most boys his age and had the wisdom to prove it. Undaunted admiration filled the boy's eyes, and while Rand appreciated his support, Rand also knew that he owed Rachel Boyd an explanation and an apology. An explanation as to why she'd found him at the local brothel with a woman posed provocatively on a bed, and an apology as to why he'd just behaved like an arrogant jackass.

Angelo glanced past him to Mr. and Mrs. Mullins. His dark brows pulled together. "Is Mr. Mullins going to be all right, sir?" he whispered, leaning closer. "Mrs. Boyd said there might be something wrong with his heart."

Rand nodded, aware that Lyda was probably listening, though she was still speaking to Ben in hushed tones, encouraging him to waken. "Mrs. Boyd was right in her assessment, but I'm doing everything I can to make sure Mr. Mullins recovers." Even as he said it, he knew the journey from this moment to that one would be long, and would depend upon so many factors—most of which were beyond his control.

"Mr. Mullins will be fine, sir. I am sure of this." Angelo's expression turned politely conspiratorial. "He has the finest doctor caring for him. I should know."

Rand felt the compliment reverberating inside him as he watched the boy disappear down the hallway and through the curtained doorway. Angelo's recovery from the beating he'd endured last fall was remarkable, as was his attitude about it. Recalling the event, Rand felt his stomach sour. In the weeks of recuperation following, Angelo had expressed hopes of becoming a doctor one day—a dream Rand thought possible. The boy was sharp minded and learned quickly, and he possessed a compassionate heart that served him well when ministering to people in pain.

Rand planned on writing his colleagues back east about the possibility of Angelo serving as an apprentice in one of their practices. The boy's Italian heritage would be a deterrent to some, but once the doctors witnessed Angelo's aptitude and ability, those possessing more open minds might be willing to consider him. And they wouldn't be disappointed.

Rand took a deep breath and held it, then gave it slow release.

He knew what it was like to be a young man and have no say in your future, to have everything planned out and decided by others before any other options had been explored. And he was determined to give Angelo the chance that he himself had finally been given. Life was too brief to spend it doing something you didn't love. Better to discover what God had created you for, and do that with your whole heart.

A low moan drew him back, and a rush of emotion bolted through him as Ben Mullins struggled to open his eyes. Rand moved closer and knelt. "Mr. Mullins . . . it's nice to have you back with us, sir."

Blinking, Ben stared between him and Lyda, then squeezed his eyes tight, as if trying to make sure that what he was seeing was real. He rubbed his chest and winced, his breath ragged.

Rand gave his shoulder a gentle squeeze. "You're going to be sore for a few days, sir. I'm sorry, that's my fault."

Ben looked confused, but Lyda pressed a kiss to her husband's forehead and narrowed her eyes at Rand, smiling. "Don't you dare apologize, Dr. Brookston. You . . ." Her voice faltered. "You just gave me back my life."

Hurried steps filled the hallway, and Rachel rounded the corner. She scooted into the storeroom behind Lyda and held out a cup of water to Rand, not meeting his gaze.

"Thank you." He mixed the dried foxglove leaves with water and held the cup to Ben's lips, supporting the man's head. "This is digitalis, Mr. Mullins, a medication used to treat arrhythmia—a heartbeat with an irregular or abnormal rhythm, like yours." He tipped the cup as he spoke, taking care not to spill the contents. "Due to Mrs. Boyd's excellent foresight, it was here exactly when we needed it." Along with the proffered olive branch, Rand tried again to snag Rachel's attention, to no avail.

Ben drained the cup, taking in gulps of air between swallows. He let out a sigh. "Thank you, Dr. Brookston. And thank *you,* Rachel."

"Yes." Lyda turned. "Thank you, Rachel, for all you've done. And as for you, Ben Mullins . . ." She fingered the graying hair at his temple. "You frightened years off my life. Years I didn't have to spare."

Ben offered a weak smile. "I've always told you I'm going to be the first to go, woman. Maybe now you'll believe me."

Lyda shook her head and gently swatted his arm, but Rand caught a flicker of dread in her eyes, a hint of the future she was imagining. A future without her husband.

"You ought not say such things to your wife, Ben." Rachel smiled as she said it, but truth permeated her tone. "And for the record, you frightened years off the lives of both of us." She touched his arm. "How are you feeling now?"

He exhaled, his eyes fluttering closed. "Like I almost died."

"You almost did," Lyda whispered.

Ben opened his eyes and stared, frowning.

"Your heart stopped, honey." Lyda's expression softened, her tone revealing she'd told him this before. She indicated Rand with a nod. "Dr. Brookston here got it started again." Her hand trembled against his cheek. "He saved your life."

Ben blinked, and his focus slowly shifted. "Is that so, Doc?"

Rand answered with a steady gaze, grateful that Lyda understood the gravity of the situation. Informing a husband or wife that their spouse had a life-threatening health condition such as Ben's was oftentimes harder than telling the patient himself. People like Ben and Lyda Mullins tended to worry more about those they would leave behind than about themselves.

Ben pursed his lips and a wry smile crept over his face. "Guess this means you'll be wanting all those medical supplies of yours delivered free of charge now, huh, Doc?"

Rand laughed softly. "That thought hadn't crossed my mind, Mr. Mullins. But now that you mention it . . ."

With a soft smirk, Ben gestured. "Speaking of orders, two more cases of lamp oil came in for you this morning. All I can say is you must be doing some mighty lengthy reading at night, Doc."

Rand laughed again but knew, with good reason, that it didn't sound as natural this time. "I like to keep a good supply on hand for surgeries. The lighting in my clinic isn't too good."

Ben nodded and started to push himself up.

"No, sir." Rand urged him back down. "Please

stay where you are. Let's give the medicine a few more minutes to take effect." He positioned the stethoscope over Ben's heart. "I know it's going to hurt, but try to take some deep breaths for me."

Ben complied, grimacing. "Feels like someone slugged me right square in the chest."

Reading skepticism in the older man's gaze, Rand nodded. "Guilty as charged, sir. Once you're feeling better, I'll meet you out on the boardwalk and you can take your best shot at me." A glint of humor lit Ben's expression again, and Rand did his best to keep his own smile from showing. "I'll give you a chance to make things even between us."

Ben cocked his head to one side, as though seriously considering the offer. "You got it, Doc. Soon as I'm up and able, I'm callin' you out."

Appreciating the dry humor and impressed that Ben could manage it in the face of such a serious—and what had to be alarming— discovery for him, Rand leaned closer to listen. Ben's pulse was notably stronger than before, which wasn't saying a great deal compared to a healthy heart. But it was the whooshing echo enveloping the beat that underscored his greatest concern. "Have you experienced any pains or tightness in your chest recently, sir? Any difficulty breathing?"

Ben hesitated, frowning again, and shot a quick look at Lyda, which told Rand plenty.

Lyda's concern gave way to surprise—and

frustration. "Ben Everett Mullins, why didn't you say something?"

Ben took hold of her hand. "I didn't want you worrying. Not with everything that's going on with the store. Besides . . ." He stopped and took a breath. "It's only happened a handful of times, and it wasn't too bad. Once I catch my breath, it goes away. For the most part."

"For the most part," Lyda repeated, her tone indignant but concerned.

Rand's own concern edged up a notch. "How long have you been experiencing the chest pains? And do you recall what you've been doing when they occur . . . ? What brings them on?"

Ben gave a shrug. "They've been coming more often in the past couple of months, maybe a little longer. And it usually happens when I'm unloading a wagon or toting a crate. But it doesn't happen every time."

"So when you're exerting effort?" Rand offered. He glanced around the storeroom. "And what were you doing today?"

Ben glanced at Lyda again, but this time his eyes took on a mischievous sparkle. Lyda looked away, an embarrassed grin lifting the corners of her mouth.

"You might say I was *exerting effort,* Dr. Brookston."

"Ben!" Lyda gave him a scolding glance and her face flushed crimson.

Ben only chuckled and nudged Rand in the arm. "I was kissin' on my wife, Doc. Just making sure she knows how much I still—"

"I think the doctor understands," Lyda said, her gaze averted.

Rand couldn't help but smile, and noticed a ghost of the same in Rachel's flushed expression. "I see. Yes, I believe that would classify as *exerting effort.*"

Ben brought Lyda's hand to his lips. "But I daresay, when it is my time to go, I can't think of a better . . ." He raised his brows, his gaze only for his wife this time. And as if knowing—for the good of his tenuous health—he ought not finish that statement, he winked and closed his mouth.

Touched by the exchange, Rand had a thought. While he knew every biological detail about the physical intimacy God had designed to be shared between a man and a woman, he was the only one among the four present who hadn't personally experienced the pleasure of that relationship. Uninvited, Patricia's earlier question at the brothel returned—*"Don't you ever long for the pleasure of a woman?"*—and despite his effort to block it, Rand felt an unaccustomed blush work its way up his neck and into his face.

He stole a glance at Rachel Boyd. At her dark hair piled atop her head except for a few long curls escaping down her back, at the way the blue cotton dress she wore hugged her figure, which he'd admired more times than was proper—in church, no less—and that he recalled with greater detail than a single man ought to. Her physical beauty contributed to his attraction to her, most certainly, but her intelligence, her knowledge of medicine, her ability to converse with him on topics that other women found unsuitable or unpalatable, those were attributes that drew him. Even though she'd never done anything to encourage his attraction.

He sighed inwardly. Her complete lack of coaxing had been deafening. Still, his gaze took her in, and his mouth went dry at the bold thoughts filling his head—then turned completely to cotton when he realized Rachel was watching him.

5

At the slow arch of Rachel Boyd's dark brow, Rand dropped his gaze, hoping she hadn't read his thoughts as easily as he read her disapproval of his too-close attention. He returned his focus to his patient, chiding himself for behaving like an overeager schoolboy. He could still feel her discerning blue eyes boring into him, and the already-tight quarters of the storeroom shrank by half.

Whatever this lady had against him was "dug in deep and hard, and showed no signs of budging," as an old friend used to say. Remembering that friend now made Rand feel ages beyond his thirty-four years. Like he'd already lived a hundred lifetimes in the space of one.

Clearing his throat, he gathered his frayed thoughts and vowed to clear his mind, once and for all, of any interest pertaining to Mrs. Rachel Boyd.

"Mr. Mullins, if you'll allow me to examine you once more . . ."

Ben lifted a hand. "Only if you'll start calling me Ben. Seems you've earned that familiarity, Doc, at the very least."

In medical school, Rand had been taught to keep a certain distance and formality between himself and his patients. But as with much of what he'd learned in those early days, he'd discovered not all of it worked in every circumstance, and certainly not out west. "Thank you . . . *Ben*." Positioning the stethoscope, he closed his eyes.

The sporadic rhythm of Ben's heart had gradually subsided, and a steadier pattern had taken its place. "Good," Rand whispered, knowing Ben's health would still be classified as tenuous, which portended more serious consequences than he thought either Ben or Lyda realized.

The urgency of the moment had passed, but the dire circumstances hadn't.

He slipped the stethoscope back into his bag. "The digitalis seems to be having the desired effect. Your heart rate has stabilized. I'd like to wait a little longer, though, to be sure, before moving you. I'll enlist some help, and we'll get you home so you can rest more comfortably."

Rachel smiled and whispered something in Lyda's ear, too low for him to hear, and Lyda gave Ben's hand a pat. "We'll be right outside, honey," she whispered, and rose to follow Rachel into the hallway.

Prone on the floor, Ben slowly drew up his legs. "Getting off this hard floor and getting home to bed sounds mighty good, Doc. But I think you and I can manage it alone. Lyda can help us, if we need it."

Having no intention of letting Ben Mullins walk out on his own accord, Rand sat and leaned up against the wall beside him, unwilling to argue the point and confident in his ability to control the outcome.

Ben cradled an arm beneath his head. "I take it by your silence you don't agree with my suggestion."

Rand stretched out his legs, appreciating the chance to do so. "I make it a strict rule, Ben, not to argue with patients who have heart conditions."

Ben chuckled, then coughed and struggled to catch his breath.

"Deep breaths. Slow and steady," Rand urged softly, watching for signs of a recurring episode.

Exhaling, Ben held his chest and made a face. "I'm about as tired . . . and *sore*"—he managed a chastising look that Rand knew better than to take personally—"as I can ever remember. But a good night's rest should remedy that, I think."

A good night's rest? Rand glanced at Lyda and Rachel still huddled together in the hall, their voices hushed, and decided to take advantage of the private moment with his patient.

"Ben," he said softly, "your heart stopped beating a moment ago. Getting a good amount of rest will aid in regaining your strength . . . but rest isn't going to *remedy* this. I'd be doing you a great disservice if I allowed you to believe that the condition of your health is anything other than grave."

Ben's expression grew reflective, and his smile came easily, too easily, and seemed out of place considering the news he'd just been given. Ben opened his mouth as though to say something, then glanced toward the door, where Lyda stood watching them from the threshold.

"Rachel's gone to check on her boys," she said, gesturing. "They've been waiting up front for her all this time, the sweet things." Her look turned tentative. "How are you feeling, honey?"

Ben raised his head a little more. "Good. A mite tired, but a lot better compared to a few minutes ago."

She gave a soft laugh, love for him shining in her eyes. "I'm so glad. And grateful." She directed the latter to Rand. "How does a glass of tea sound to you both? Dr. Brookston, if I remember from Christmas dinner, you're partial to my sweet tea."

"That I am, ma'am. I'd appreciate a glass. Thank you."

Lyda's steps faded down the hall and Ben heaved a sigh, lowering his head back to the floor. Beads of sweat trickled down the side of his temple.

"You're feeling *good?*" Rand asked, eyeing him and knowing better.

Ben's eyes closed. His expression turned sheepish. "All my life, Doc," he whispered, "I've had what you might call a . . . *peculiar* rhythm to my heart. Same as my father, and his father before him." He shrugged. "A little twinge here and there. A pain every now and then. The episodes—that's what the doctor back east labeled them when I was younger . . ." He glanced back at the door. "I've had them all my life. Lyda knows I used to be troubled by them, but I haven't wanted to bother her with it for a while now."

Already guessing the answer, Rand asked the obvious question. "Exactly how long is *a while?*"

Ben's eyes narrowed. "The last eight years or so." He rubbed his forehead, then his eyes.

"Does your head ache?"

"No, it's fine."

Somehow Rand knew he wasn't being completely truthful. "I've got willow bark at the clinic. I'll bring some by as soon as we get you situated at home."

Staring up at the ceiling, Ben sighed. "I'd be much obliged, Doc."

The moment stretched long, its silence hindered only by a clock's steady *ticktock* drifting toward them from somewhere down the corridor. Rand wasn't bothered by the silence. Quite the contrary. He had matters he wanted to discuss, and early on in life he'd learned that remaining quiet often lent the greater advantage. None too surprisingly, he learned so much more that way.

"My wife," Ben finally said, his voice tender, "she worries about things enough as it is. Especially after what happened to our children."

Ben looked over at him, and though he hadn't asked a question, Rand sensed one. He recalled what Esther Calhoun had once told him when he'd stopped by to check on her as she was suffering from a bout of bursitis. Mrs. Calhoun, a widow for eighteen years as she reminded him every time he visited, had a kind nature and knew everything about everybody who attended church in Timber Ridge. She'd shared the heartbreaking story of the Mullinses' children, which happened long before he'd come west.

Rand met Ben's steady gaze and nodded, wishing now that he'd said something to Ben and his wife about their children before today. But the moment had never felt right, and everyone knew it wasn't proper to speak of the dead to loved ones left behind, unless invited. Still, that excuse felt flimsy when faced with the gut-wrenching truth in Ben's eyes.

"I'm so sorry for your loss, Ben," he whispered. "It must have been horrible for you and Lyda."

"I appreciate that, Doc." Ben's voice hovered somewhere above a whisper. "Lyda and me . . . we both still carry a burden inside us over it. Always will, I guess. Some hurts don't heal, even given time. But hers . . ." His jaw muscles corded tight. "Hers is different. It's harder to bear in a way, I think. Which is saying an awful lot, because at first, right after it happened . . . there were days I thought I'd die from the weight of it all. Days when I wanted to."

Ben winced, but Rand sensed the ache he felt wasn't from his heart. Not from his physical heart, anyway.

Rand worked to loosen the tangle of emotion lodged in his throat.

"What I'm trying to say, Doc, is that I'd be obliged if you'd keep the worst of what's going on with me between the two of us. Just for a while. I'll tell my wife, soon, when the time is right." Ben sniffed at unshed tears. "What happened today is due to my own foolishness. I've been overdoing things here at the store. I knew better and I did it anyway. I'm not a young man anymore." He shook his head. "Haven't been for some time. But I know now what all this work is costing me, and I won't push myself like that again."

Rand didn't doubt the sincerity of Ben's request, but what the man was asking went against everything within him. "It's long been my belief, Ben, that when a husband or wife has an illness, especially something as serious as a heart condition, it's best for them to share the prognosis with their spouse. So they can have support, a helpmeet." He measured his next words. "And also . . . so their spouse will be able to prepare for the future."

Ben didn't flinch. Not even a little.

The clock down the hall ticked off the seconds.

"You ever been married, Doc?"

Ben's voice was gentle, but Rand felt the subtle jab. "No . . . I haven't."

"You ever loved a woman so much that you'd gladly give every last ounce of your strength to make sure she's cared for? To make sure she knows without a doubt that her life has made a difference, even if it didn't turn out like she thought it would?"

Feeling less like the physician and more the patient, Rand shook his head. "No, Ben," he whispered. "I haven't."

"You ever held a woman in your arms through the night and knew—" Ben's voice gave way. He took an unsteady breath, his lower lip trembling. "And knew you were holdin' everything you ever wanted? Or ever would want?"

Rand didn't respond this time. He knew Ben already knew the answer.

"I just need some time, Doc. That's all I'm

asking for. I've known this day was coming. Granted, I didn't expect it to come so soon. . . ." He arched his back, no doubt weary of the hard wood floor.

"I'll get someone in here to help us move you." Rand started to rise, but Ben caught his arm.

"I never knew my grandfather, Doc, but I heard the stories. And I watched my father die the same way. A little bit at a time and leaving my mother with too many mouths to feed."

The responsibility pressing on Rand earlier as the sole physician of Timber Ridge took on a viselike grip. He should have insisted Ben come to him sooner. "If I'd known about your condition, Ben, I would've done everything I could to keep this from happening."

Ben's sigh came out in a chuckle. "That's just it, Doc. I'm sure you're a fine physician. One of the best, from what I hear." He nodded toward the hallway. "And that's from Rachel Boyd's own lips, which is praise that doesn't come lightly, in case you haven't figured that out already. But unless you can find a way to put a new heart in this old body of mine, then, as I see it . . . there's not much else to be done."

For the first time the thinnest sheen of fear clouded Ben's eyes, though his steady tone belied it. Yet on closer observation, Rand wondered if he was mistaken. Perhaps it wasn't fear. Perhaps Ben was simply coming face-to-face with his own mortality, something every man or woman did eventually. Rand remembered that sobering moment in his own life, and a reverent shudder stole through him.

He wanted to argue with Ben, try and change his mind. But he'd been caring for people long enough to recognize a mind set on something, and Ben's mind was set firm.

"You've got fluid pooling around your lungs, which is complicating your condition. There's a procedure I can perform, a surgery, to remove some of that fluid," Rand whispered, deciding now wasn't the time to mention that he'd never performed that particular surgery by himself. "It will buy you more time. And as your condition worsens, as it will," he added gently, "I can keep you comfortable. With proper care, that could mean several weeks. Maybe even months. There's no way to know for sure."

"Or it could mean days," Ben said, looking up at him. "Remember, Doc, I've seen this play out before."

Wishing now that he'd studied more about the heart instead of focusing on obstetrics, Rand gave a single nod. "The digitalis will help, but without removing the fluid"—if his prognosis was correct—"the chance for a longer term holds far less hope."

"When would you do it? The surgery, I mean."

"I'd want you to rest up, get some of your strength back. But we'd do it as soon as possible."

Ben's expression went solemn.

Feeling helpless and loathing that feeling, Rand studied the plank floor, combing through years of experience and training in search of other possible remedies, only to have medical science dismiss each as futile.

"Take it easy there, Doc. . . ." Ben reached over and briefly placed a hand on Rand's arm. "I can feel your mind working all the way over here, and it's tuckering me out."

Despite feelings of frustration and inadequacy, Rand smiled. He searched for a response and came up short.

"Buy me however much longer you can, Doc. That's all I'm asking. And don't tell me to go lie down in a bed and wait to die. I won't do it. Not when I stand to lose everything I've worked for all these years. All I've got is tied up in this store. My goal is to make sure my wife is well taken care of when I'm gone, and I aim to see that goal met."

The clamor of footsteps sounded from down the hallway, and Ben cleared his throat. His demeanor noticeably brightened.

Not yet finished with their conversation, Rand realized that his patient apparently was. "I will not lie to your wife," he said quietly.

"And I'm not asking you to," Ben answered. "All I'm asking for is time to get my business in order. And to prepare Lyda for the truth. There's a way to tell a woman something, and a way not to, Doc. I want to do this the right way."

Rand stared ahead, uncomfortable with the way things were being left. Lyda deserved to know the truth about her husband's condition, but Ben needed to be the one to tell her. With reluctance, Rand finally nodded, and Ben's features relaxed in gratitude and relief.

Lyda rounded the corner, glasses of tea balanced on a tray, and with two familiar redheads in tow. The boys' expressions held apprehension, revealing they'd been told about Ben's circumstance, at least as much as they could grasp at their age. Rand stood and readied himself for their mother's return, determined to deliver a flawless apology to her this time.

But Rachel Boyd was nowhere to be seen.

6

The second-story bedroom above the mercantile was tidy enough, even with boxes and crates stacked high on a far wall, but a hint of dust and disuse tainted the air. Rachel deposited the fresh bedding in the rocker by the door and crossed to the window. Bracing her hands on either side, she gave the window a good push. It refused to budge. On her third try the paint-peeled wood finally relented and edged up with creaking complaint.

Brushing the dust from her hands, she looked out

across the town of Timber Ridge and welcomed the chilled breeze.

She breathed deep, willing a calm she didn't feel, despite having time to regain her composure since Rand Brookston's thorough dressing-down. She fingered a crack at the corner of the window. *Dressing-down* was probably too harsh a term for his comment. But still, her body heated again just thinking about the encounter.

Everything she'd suspected about the "good doctor" was true—despite what James had told her. Her brother had a knack for reading people, but he'd read this one wrong. People revealed their true natures under pressure, and Rand Brookston had certainly revealed his. He was short-tempered, demanding, and had an arrogance about him that all but dared a person to contradict him. Just like her father.

She stripped the bed, yanking the rumpled sheets off and shaking the pillows out of their cases.

Rand Brookston was handsome, she guessed, in an aristocratic sort of way, which she'd never personally found appealing. And despite his explanation, she still couldn't erase the image of him opening the bedroom door at the brothel from her mind. The guilty look he wore, the provocative gleam in the eyes of the young woman lying on the bed.

And there was something else. . . .

On certain occasions when she'd been in his

company, she'd caught him staring at her—as he'd been doing today. She could be wrong, but she'd gotten the feeling there might be interest on his part, and *interest* was the last thing she wanted to encourage. When she'd married, she'd done her best to choose a man who was the exact opposite of her father, and that relationship with Thomas had been the sweetest of her life.

But one thing she *was* interested in knowing about Rand Brookston was how he'd restarted Ben Mullins's heart. *If* indeed that's what he'd done. Doctors often overstated their roles in healing, taking credit where little to none was due. One of the less-than-desirable character traits of her father, among other traits she didn't care to dredge from memory.

But if Rand Brookston had indeed accomplished such a thing, he'd saved Ben's life. For that she was most grateful, and eager to know how he'd done it.

After fluffing the mattress ticking, she tucked in the fresh bed sheets and dusted the side tables, knowing it wouldn't be long before Ben occupied the room. She and Lyda had debated the wisdom of taking Ben home to the Mullinses' house a few streets over, versus the two of them living above the store for a while, until Ben regained his health. Lyda had opted for the latter, preferring to keep Ben close so she could check on him throughout the day, and Rachel agreed.

It would also be easier for her to help Lyda with the store and to assist with Ben's care if the couple stayed in the spare upper room. Not that Rachel had an inkling how she would accomplish helping them with every hour of every day spoken for. But Ben and Lyda were like family to her, and she couldn't *not* help them. Plus this room had special meaning to them as a couple, she knew. This was where they'd first lived upon moving to Timber Ridge many years ago, before they'd built their house.

As Rachel moved to wipe off the dresser, a chorus of angry voices drew her attention. She peered out the bay window to see that the crowd waiting on the boardwalk below had multiplied and was pressing forward toward the doors.

"I've got an order to pick up," one man yelled.

"We need to get our supplies!"

"Mullins said they'd be ready today! Why's he closed up so early?"

The chorus of complaints piled one atop the other, and Rachel turned to head downstairs, worried about Mitch and Kurt fending off such an onslaught. Then she caught sight of a gentleman stepping up onto a bench. She looked closer. It was the same man she'd seen on the boardwalk earlier, the one who'd unofficially volunteered to stand guard. Arms outstretched, he addressed the gathering. She couldn't make out his words, but to her surprise, the complaints died down.

She waited, watching, debating whether her assistance was needed. Apparently it wasn't.

She closed the window and hurried to finish dusting, then readied the bed.

"Be careful, please, Mr. Daggett!" Lyda's sharp warning echoed up the twisting stairwell, and Rachel couldn't fault her for it. She'd nearly lost her footing on the stairs herself a moment ago. Lyda's instruction continued. "There's a sharp turn ahead where the stairs grow more narrow."

As Rachel plumped the pillows, Charlie Daggett's heavy footsteps sounded in the hallway, and she turned to see his frame filling the doorway as he cradled Ben in his arms. Ben Mullins was no small man, but he resembled a mere boy when measured against Charlie Daggett. Then again, what man wouldn't?

Rachel motioned. "Here, Mr. Daggett. The bed is all ready."

"Yes, ma'am, Miss Rachel." Charlie moved with surprising agility for so large a man—and with surprising steadiness for being into the bottle so early in the afternoon, if the smell of whiskey wafting toward her held any truth. His drinking wasn't new to her, nor to anyone else in Timber Ridge. But the better she'd gotten to know Charlie over the two months he'd been working at her ranch, the more his drinking puzzled her.

He never showed up for work intoxicated and had never behaved rudely or unseemly toward her or her boys. That wasn't the source of her concern. It was more the question of *why* he often drank to such excess that she found so troubling. A hard worker and a quiet man by nature, Charlie Daggett was stone silent when it came to his past.

Ben grimaced as Charlie lowered him down. "I'm not an invalid, Daggett," Ben grumbled beneath his breath, heaving a sigh when Charlie deposited him on the bed. "At least not yet." He repositioned himself on the mattress, wincing. "I've still got two good legs. I could've climbed those stairs myself."

Charlie's whiskered cheeks pushed up in a customary grin. "I'm just doin' what the doc told me to do, Mr. Mullins."

Looking on, Rachel couldn't tell whether Ben's discomfort stemmed from being carried by Charlie or from the earlier bout with his heart. Knowing Ben, she guessed the former.

"Yes, yes," Ben said. "I know you are. But why don't you try listening to me once in a while? I'm the one who's paying you, after all."

Ben's voice held an edge, but his subtle smile softened his words and hinted at the root of his frustration, which Rachel understood only too well. Being dependent upon others wasn't easy for her either—it never had been. But she'd especially struggled with it following Thomas's death. She didn't know why exactly. Relying on others made her feel as if she were standing too close to a drop-off, on a very slippery slope.

She glanced up at Charlie. Judging from his unhindered grin, she guessed he understood the cause of Ben's annoyance too.

"Mama, Dr. Brookston let me listen to Uncle Ben's heart!" Childish enthusiasm heightened Mitch's voice as he hurried into the room after Lyda and Dr. Brookston.

"Did he, now . . ." Rachel stood near the foot of the bed, not missing how Kurt lagged behind, hanging close to the doorway, looking noticeably less enthused. She glanced in Rand Brookston's direction while intentionally avoiding his gaze. Seeing Mitch in such high spirits did her heart good—he'd been so serious lately. She rumpled his red hair. "This isn't your first time to have done that. You've listened to my heart through your grandfather's stethoscope before, remember?"

"I know, but . . ." Mitch edged closer to Ben. "You can hear a lot better through this one." He pointed to Dr. Brookston's black leather bag.

Dr. Brookston reached inside and withdrew a stethoscope. "Would you mind checking Mr. Mullins's heart again for me, Mitchell?"

Ben huffed. "Why? To make sure it hasn't stopped a second time?"

Rand Brookston's laughter was immediate and full, and in extremely poor taste. Rachel fought to think of something to say to smooth over his lack of tact—until she heard Ben chuckling, and Lyda too. Still not seeing the humor, she noted their smiles and the way they glanced at each other and decided to keep her opinion to herself.

"It's my guess, Mitchell"—Rand Brookston bent closer to her son—"that the reason you can hear better through this stethoscope is that the tubes on your grandfather's stethoscope are likely much shorter than the tubes on this one. Improvements have been made in recent years by lengthening the tubes—" he demonstrated what he meant—"which allows for enhanced auscultation. That's what we call listening to the sounds of the heart or lungs. Do you happen to know how the stethoscope got its name?"

Mitchell's eyes narrowed and his tongue curled between his front teeth, telling signs he was concentrating. He finally shook his head.

"It's from the Greek language. *Stethos* is Greek for chest, and *skopos* means examination." Dr. Brookston gave a self-conscious shrug that Rachel might have considered boyish, perhaps even charming, if she hadn't already glimpsed his true nature. "I picked up that bit of information somewhere."

"Stethos . . . skopos," Mitchell repeated, using the same inflection Dr. Brookston had used, and Rachel knew her older son would remember it. He never forgot anything.

Mitchell fitted the earpieces in his ears and

positioned the bell-shaped amplifier over Ben's chest. "What am I listening for, Dr. Brookston?"

The image of Mitchell bending over Ben Mullins brought future possibilities into clearer focus, and Rachel fought the urge to grab her two sons and run. For years she'd told her boys that they could be anything they wanted to be when they grew up and she would be content, as long as they were happy.

But that wasn't the truth.

Rand went down on one knee. "First, you want to locate the patient's heart, which, depending on their temperament"—he tossed a wink at Ben and Lyda—"is more difficult to do with some patients than with others." Ben and Lyda smiled, which prompted Mitchell to grin. "But you'll know you've located the heart muscle by the particular sound of the . . ."

Rachel looked on, feeling a little like the odd man out. Ben and Lyda seemed to have a more familiar friendship with the doctor than she'd credited them with. And this bedside manner of Rand's . . . this *humor* he used had a way of nurturing the doctor-patient relationship, which was clever, she admitted begrudgingly. She smirked to herself. Apparently he saved "arrogant, abrupt, and rude" for his assistants. *Poor Angelo . . .*

"Miss Rachel?"

Charlie Daggett stood by the door, hat in hand, and Rachel joined him, mindful of Kurt watching

the scene play out on the bed, a faraway look in his eyes. She reached out to give him a reassuring touch, but at the last second he sidestepped her affection.

Aware of Charlie looking on, Rachel pasted on a smile, pretending her son's rejection hadn't hurt. "Yes, Mr. Daggett?"

Charlie turned his hat in his hands, and his gaze briefly dropped to Kurt. His expression grew pensive. "Miss Rachel, I'm glad I ran into you here, ma'am. Fact is, I came into town looking for you."

Rachel waited, a tad unnerved by the seriousness of his voice.

"Mr. Daggett . . ." Lyda walked up beside them and laid a hand on Charlie's coat sleeve. "Excuse me for interrupting, but before you go, let me thank you again for happening by when you did. We couldn't have managed moving Mr. Mullins up here without you."

Charlie ducked his head. "I'm glad I was here to help, ma'am. You and your husband have always treated me kindly. You've been real generous with giving me work too."

Lyda laughed softly. "You're a hard worker, Mr. Daggett. So it's hardly generosity on our part."

Charlie's ruddy complexion deepened. "I'll come by every day, ma'am, and can tote Mr. Mullins up and down the stairs as you need, 'til the doc says he can do it himself."

Lyda nodded. "Thank you. In fact, I was going to ask that very favor of you. I have a feeling it may be several days before Dr. Brookston allows Mr. Mullins to move about on his own."

Lyda returned to the bedside, and Rachel waited, both eager to know what Charlie was going to say and apprehensive at the same time. Charlie let out a sigh, his breath soured with liquor, and she fought the urge to take a backward step.

"I came into town looking for you, ma'am, because I can't find one of the heifers that's due to drop. I went lookin' for her, seein' as more snow's comin' in tonight, but I couldn't find where she's gotten off to."

Rachel relaxed. "I'm sure she'll be fine. Heifers due to calve wander off, but I'll help you look for her as soon as we get home. We'll be leaving here soon."

Charlie's gaze dropped to Kurt again, then slowly slid to Mitchell before moving back. "It's Lady, Miss Rachel," he whispered. "The heifer that's missin'."

Rachel frowned. "But that's not possible. She was in the stall this morning. I checked on her right before breakfast. I don't see how she could've . . ." Sensing more than seeing a shift in Kurt's posture, she peered down, and knew that look on her son's face. A stone sank into the pit of her stomach. "Kurt, did you visit Lady after breakfast this morning? Before we left for school?"

His nod was slow, calculated.

"And did you remember to latch the stall door like I've told you to do?"

"Yes, ma'am, I did," he answered a little too quickly, a note of challenge stiffening his posture.

Kurt had gotten good at lying in recent months, but not so good that she couldn't see through him. Kurt and Mitch loved Lady the way other boys loved their dogs, and while her younger son had no qualms about telling a falsehood, he hadn't yet learned to fully mask his emotions. She saw that he was afraid. Not of her, Rachel knew, but of what might happen to Lady.

She'd disciplined Kurt in every way she knew how. When James, her older brother, lived with them before he'd married Molly last month, he could simply look at Kurt and the boy's defenses would crumble, same as they had with Thomas. When *she* looked at Kurt, it was as if his defenses dug a moat and shored up a five-foot wall of stone.

Anger tightened her throat. Her face burned. For Kurt to misbehave was one thing, but for him to stand there and lie straight-faced to her was another. And in front of Charlie Daggett, no less. "Wait right here for me, young man," she whispered, and turned to Charlie. "Thank you, Mr. Daggett," she managed, "for letting me know. The boys and I will meet you at the ranch as soon as possible."

He slipped his hat on. "I'll take a horse and head

out when I get there, if it's all the same to you."

"Yes, that's fine. I'll meet you up around Crowley's Ridge in about an hour. If you find her, fire two rounds. I'll follow the sound."

"Will do, ma'am. And . . ." Charlie shifted his weight. "I'm sorry, but there's one more thing."

Rachel found his hesitance unnerving. "Yes, Mr. Daggett?"

"I came across another heifer . . . while I was out lookin' for Lady. The one that got tangled in the fencin' last month?"

She nodded.

"I'm sorry, Miss Rachel, but . . ." His voice lowered. "Looks like a cougar got her. Either that, or it might've been a . . ."

He lowered his gaze, and Rachel heard what he didn't, or couldn't, say. *Or it might've been a bear. . . .* Images of what the scene must look like rose in her mind with stinging clarity, and a sick feeling settled in the pit of her stomach. Fighting a shiver, she refused to let her thoughts go toward their natural bent. It was still too early in the season for bear—that's what she told herself. In the end, it didn't really matter what took the heifer down—cougar or bear—but it made a difference to her. And she knew it would matter to the boys. "Please, Mr. Daggett," she whispered where only he could hear. "Don't tell my sons about this. But if they do find out and ask, say you think it was a cougar."

"Yes, ma'am," he said, nodding as he left.

Gaining Kurt's attention again, Rachel gave him a reproving stare as she crossed to the bed. The loss of the other heifer was upsetting, but losing Lady would be devastating. Beyond the emotional attachment she had for the first-time mother-to-be, Rachel silently counted the financial investment Lady represented. Before his passing, Thomas spent the bulk of their savings on a prized bull hailing from superior stock, as did Lady. And their first offspring, due to deliver anytime, promised strong stock for the ranch's future. Which was even more crucial since a snowstorm had cost her the bull last month.

If something happened to Lady and her calf— Rachel cringed inwardly, a barrage of *what ifs* crowded close, tempting her to worry—it would be one more confirmation of her inability to provide for her family.

That was one reminder she didn't need.

Reaching for strength beyond her own, she determined not to borrow trouble that wasn't yet on her doorstep. She cleared her throat. "Mitchell, we need to be leaving, son. Lyda—" She reached for Lyda's hands, aware of the silent protest on Mitch's face. "The boys and I are heading home, but I'll try and come back later this evening."

Lyda shook her head. "There's no need for you to do that. Ben and I will be fine. Dr. Brookston said he'll sit with him while I finish up things with customers downstairs. Then Angelo might come over later if we need more help. Besides"—Lyda glanced toward the window—"more snow's coming, bringing bitter cold, and I . . . I don't want you out on a night like this."

Even if Lyda hadn't squeezed her hand, Rachel would have caught her meaning, and her thoughts turned again to Ben and Lyda's children. As hard as losing Thomas had been, she could not fathom the pain of losing her children.

"Mama?" Mitchell paused by the footboard, his expression both expectant and cautious. "Dr. Brookston said he'd give me a ride home later, if it's all right with you. That way, I could stay and keep checking Uncle Ben's heart to make sure he's okay."

Rachel's throat corded tighter, same as her nerves. She forced herself to look at Dr. Brookston. "That's most kind of you, Doctor. But, Mitchell"—she returned her focus to her son—"I need you to come with me now. Lady has gotten out of the barn, and I could use your help at home."

Mitch's head cocked to one side. "But how did she get . . ." His expression darkened. "It's Kurt's fault, isn't it? I told him not to—"

Rachel held up a hand. "Now's not the time. Please go downstairs with your brother and wait out back for me in the wagon. I'm following right behind you."

"Yes, ma'am. . . ." The firm set of Mitch's mouth

told her he wasn't happy, but as usual, he did as she bade.

Rachel sidestepped Rand Brookston and leaned down to place a kiss on Ben's stubbled cheek. "I'll be back tomorrow to check on you both. Maybe I'll bring some of that potato soup you like."

Ben sighed, looking overtired. "We'll look forward to your visit, but don't you go to any trouble."

"Go to trouble . . . over you?" Rachel shook her head. "I wouldn't dream of it."

Ben covered her hand on his shoulder, and Rachel felt a fresh swell of emotion. She knew enough to know that his condition was serious. What she didn't know was how long he had left. *Don't take him, Lord. Not yet. Please . . . for Lyda and the boys.* And for herself too, but it felt less selfish to ask on behalf of others.

"Mrs. Boyd?"

Hearing Rand Brookston's voice, Rachel straightened and smoothed a hand over her skirt, wondering if her smile looked as brittle as it felt. "Yes, Dr. Brookston?"

"If you have a moment, ma'am, I'd like to speak with you." He motioned toward the hallway.

Eager as she was to get home, she preceded him into the empty hallway. Perhaps he wanted to speak with her about Ben. If that were the case, she wanted to hear what he had to say—and she had a question or two for him as well.

She was surprised when he pulled the door almost closed behind them.

He shifted his weight, suddenly developing an interest in the wooden planks beneath his boots. "Mrs. Boyd, I . . ." He seemed at a loss to know what to do with his hands—odd for one so skilled with the scalpel. "I want to offer an apology for my earlier behavior. The situation with Mr. Mullins was extremely tense, and I . . ." He shook his head. "I took my frustration out on you. I'm sorry. I was out of line. Your assistance in getting the medicine here was nothing short of exemplary. I . . . hope you'll forgive me."

Rachel stared. An apology? She hadn't expected this. The way he stammered and wouldn't look her in the eye—it was almost enough to convince her that she truly *had* misjudged him. What she found equally unexpected was how much she wanted that to be true. "I'm grateful for your apology, Dr. Brookston. And . . . kindly accept it." *I think. . . .*

"Thank you." He exhaled, and a shy smile tipped one side of his mouth. "It wouldn't do to have the sheriff's sister upset at me, now, would it?"

With great effort, Rachel maintained her poise, the tinge of disappointment bitter at the discovery. So that was it. Rand Brookston didn't want to be on her brother's bad side. She should have known. She turned to go, then paused, seizing the opportunity. "Dr. Brookston, would you answer one question for me, please?"

His expression sobered. "Yes, ma'am. Anything."

"Lyda stated that you *restarted* Ben's heart." She lowered her voice. "But we both know that's impossible."

He glanced at the door, then stepped farther down the hall, motioning for her to follow. She did.

"In the past, Mrs. Boyd, when a person's heart had ceased to beat, you're right," he whispered, "it was considered impossible to restart the heart muscle. It's still considered so by many. But, with recent research on external chest compression, we—"

"External chest compression?" she repeated, hearing the wariness in her own voice, as well as the flicker of curiosity.

He nodded. "The procedure involves delivering a series of rhythmic applications of pressure on the lower half of the sternum, like this"—he positioned his hands, one atop the other, demonstrating—"until a heartbeat is achieved again. *If* it can be. I have a paper in my office published not two months ago that I'd be happy to loan to you, if you're interested in reading more about it."

"Yes, I'd appreciate that." While she welcomed knowing more about this new procedure, learning about Ben's current condition was more important. "But tell me . . ." She gestured toward the bedroom door. "What's your prognosis for Ben? And please don't try to spare my feelings. I may not be a physician, but I know from personal experience that when a person suffers from a heart ailment, their future is . . . tenuous." She paused, not wanting to voice her next thought. "I'm thinking he has perhaps a year," she whispered, watching for his reaction. "Maybe a little less?"

Before he said a thing, she read the answer in his eyes.

He looked away. "The amount of time remaining for a patient in this situation is dependent on many factors. It's hard to—"

"That's all right," she whispered, understanding. She already had her answer.

The bedroom door opened and Lyda walked out. "Ben needs a chamber pot," she whispered, her smile tired but laced with relief. "Too much of that tea, I guess." She left the door open, and Rachel caught a glimpse of Ben on the bed, arms resting on his chest, eyes closed. Not a comforting image.

"Mrs. Boyd," Dr. Brookston said softly, "if you'd like to stay longer, you're more than welcome to—"

She shook her head. "It's urgent that I get home. My best heifer is due to drop anytime and she's wandered off." She decided not to share Charlie Daggett's *other* news.

A spark flickered in Rand Brookston's gray eyes. "I'm well versed in animal husbandry, ma'am. Just ask Harvey Conklin. I helped deliver twin foals for him last month. If you need my services, I'd be happy to—"

"No." She held up a hand. "But thank you all the same."

A scuffling noise sounded on the stairs, just beyond the first turn in the staircase, and was followed by a quick staccato of boot steps—*two* sets of boots. She didn't have to guess whom they belonged to. Such behavior from Kurt wasn't surprising, but Mitchell . . . She looked back and saw a slight frown on Rand's face, then realized it mirrored hers. She quickly smoothed it. "Your offer is most kind, but I'm certain I can manage well enough on my own."

"Of that, I have no doubt, Mrs. Boyd," he said, his accent deepening, by his design, without question. "My offer wasn't rooted in my estimation of your inability, ma'am, but rather in a sincere desire to be of assistance."

Surprised at his ability to muster such charm, she weighed his statement, which was, again, so direct. She allowed the hint of a reluctant smile. "Thank you," she whispered, bothered by how much his affirmation meant to her, "but we'll be fine."

She bid him a hasty good-night and took the stairs as quickly as the narrow passage allowed.

A half hour later, Rachel pulled the wagon to a stop in front of their cabin, only to remember she'd never stopped by the bank on her way home. She sighed. Every day she got further and further behind.

Snow-laden clouds veiled the rocky peaks, hanging low in ominous tufts of steel gray and purple. A pale winter sun sought refuge behind them, and for the briefest of seconds, its waning light illuminated the approaching storm. She scanned the horizon, taking it in. She might have thought the scene beautiful if she hadn't experienced firsthand how damaging the snowfall and bitter cold could be to her livelihood.

She sent the boys on inside and guided the wagon and team into the barn. Fifteen minutes later, she strode back to the cabin, not wanting to waste another minute of daylight.

She shrugged into Thomas's old work coat, welcoming its thick layers, and reached for her rifle by the front door, spotting Thomas's rifle beside it, exactly where it had been since James brought it back to her—along with the news of Thomas's death. *Not now . . . Don't do this now.* She didn't have the time, nor the energy, to deal with the flood of memories.

Or to think about the man responsible for Thomas no longer being with her.

"Boys, there's enough ham and beans for your dinner, and milk in the icebox to share. Once you've eaten, do your chores in the barn, then come directly back inside the house. The temperature outside is dropping, so don't dawdle. And wear your coats and gloves. Do you understand me?"

Both boys nodded.

"Then go on to bed. And use your extra blankets. I'll build a fire when I get back." She hated leaving them, but she had no choice. Besides, they were accustomed to being left alone. Owning a ranch meant working whatever hours the ranch demanded, and this ranch was a hard taskmaster. Especially for a woman alone.

Until last spring, she'd managed to employ two ranch hands, and James had helped when he could. But the loss of cattle these last two winters had stripped her budget to the bone. As it was, she owed Charlie Daggett a month's wages and had promised to pay him this week.

She paused at the door and looked back at Mitch and Kurt.

There were moments, like this one, when she wondered if pursuing this dream—Thomas's dream for the ranch—was worth it. Swallowing the mounting doubt, she squared her shoulders. "Take care of each other while I'm gone. I'll be back as soon as I can." She raised a brow. "And no arguing."

She strode to the barn, carrying with her the image of her boys standing there in the hallway. They were so young and innocent, yet already acquainted with loss.

Picturing the scene of a cougar's recent kill, she checked to be sure her rifle was loaded and that extra shells were still tucked in her coat pocket. Then she saddled Chaucer, Thomas's horse, and set out toward Crowley's Ridge just as the first snowflakes fell.

7

A cloth-covered tin, complete with bow, sat wedged against the clinic door alongside a large burlap bag tied tight with string. Both were dusted in snow. Rand bent to pick them up, already guessing who the tin was from—and hoping he was wrong.

Once inside, he shouldered the clinic door shut, but not before the snow and wind burrowed their way in behind him. Cold and tired, back muscles aching, he deposited his satchel in the chair by the door and laid the burlap bag and tin on the examination table.

Glancing again at the burlap bag, he wondered at its contents. It was sure heavy enough. After lighting an oil lamp, he untied the bag to reveal a smoked ham. He read the letter tucked inside and a wave of gratitude overtook him.

With eleven mouths to feed, not counting their own, Mathias and Oleta Tucker could scarcely afford to part with this meat, but for him to refuse it would be considered an insult. Six of their children had been ill with the croup and required medicine, yet all eleven had signed the note thanking him. Oleta had added a line along the bottom explaining, again, that she wished they possessed the money to pay him instead.

Staring again at the Tuckers' form of payment, Rand's gratitude deepened.

A smoked ham wouldn't help toward the down payment on a new clinic—same for live chickens, jars of homemade jams, and varied men's clothing from widows' closets—but he knew what a cost this ham represented to Mathias and Oleta. And he'd known what he was getting into when he came west to such an isolated town . . . for the most part, anyway.

Money certainly wasn't the reason he'd decided to become a doctor. He fingered the frayed edge of the well-worn burlap bag. No matter how much wealth a man acquired, it could always be taken away. What a person was left with after the money was gone—that was what mattered most.

Even so, he wished he could provide the people of Timber Ridge with a proper clinic. This old place was fine enough for him to live in. He didn't need anything fancy. But his patients . . . They deserved better. He intended to stop by and speak with Harold Welch again about the vacant building next to the Mullinses' store. Maybe enough time had passed that Welch would reconsider his offer, low as it was. The building needed a fair amount of work, but it was large, with several rooms, excellent for a clinic. Welch was asking an exorbitant amount, more than Rand could afford, but maybe if he upped his offer a little, and if Welch agreed to let him pay over time . . .

Buying that building was risky with income being so sporadic. But he'd learned long ago that a life lived without risks pretty much wasn't worth living. Life rewarded courage, even when that first step was taken neck-deep in fear.

His gaze slowly shifted to the tin. He hesitated, giving it a long stare before giving the bow a sharp tug.

As he unfolded the checkered cloth, an envelope slipped from its folds and onto the floor. Bending to retrieve it, he glimpsed his name penned in fanciful script on the front. Even in the dim light, he recognized the handwriting and heaved a sigh, feeling more exhausted now than he had seconds earlier.

He lifted the edge of the cloth and a sweet aroma rose to greet him, answering his earlier question. Molasses cookies, his favorite, filled the tin—all perfectly round, identical in size, and sprinkled with sugar. They'd be delicious too, just like before. Only he didn't quite have the appetite for them at the moment.

He turned the envelope in his hand to view the elegant wax seal on the back bearing the initials *J.E.S.*, and then he laid the unopened envelope aside.

Rand lit a fire in the main room, in the only hearth the former cobbler's shop boasted, and knelt to feed the flame, relishing the warmth. Angling his head from side to side, he worked to loosen the tightness, knowing he never should have catnapped in that rocker at the Mullinses' tonight. He'd be paying for that for the next few days.

The clock on the wall read half past one, and outside the wind howled around the north corner of the building, finding every traitorous fissure in the log and chinking.

He stretched, feeling the chill gradually leave his bones, and peered through the window into the darkness beyond. The snow came heavier now, slanting down in sideways sheets. If this kept up, he'd have a four-foot drift against his door come morning.

He hadn't felt comfortable leaving Ben and Lyda earlier in the evening and had opted to stay, insisting that Angelo head home before the storm worsened. Little Italy, the growing community of Italian immigrants just outside of Timber Ridge, was a good half-hour walk from town, and that was in good weather. Angelo's mother and three younger sisters would be waiting on the young man to help care for the animals and make ready for the snowfall.

Rand looked around the clinic, seeing with fresh eyes the blatant lack of homey touches, the absence of anyone waiting for him. A twinge of envy heightened his fatigue.

He would have been hard-pressed to pin a reason on exactly why, but he hadn't wanted to come back to his cabin tonight. Something about being in Ben and Lyda's company was comforting, made him feel as if his presence in Timber Ridge mattered.

That *he* mattered. And not only for his skills as a physician.

For the hundredth time, he debated whether to ride out to Rachel's ranch to see if he could help with the heifer due to calve. If it were anyone else in Timber Ridge, he would have already been there without a second thought. But not with Rachel Boyd. He didn't feel the usual "open door" when it came to her.

Her father had been a physician, as he'd learned from her older brother, which explained where she'd received her medical training, however informal. That initial discovery had given him hope that they might actually share their knowledge with each other and establish some common ground between them. But the only ground they'd shared so far could best be described as painfully polite.

Yet remembering the way she'd looked up at him tonight before she'd taken off down the stairs, that half smile on her face . . . He was almost tempted to hope that there might be a possibility for something more. But in the clarity of the present moment, he knew better.

Changing clothes in the back room, he recalled Mitchell Boyd's interest in the stethoscope. Typically quiet and reserved, from what few times Rand had observed the boy, Mitchell had shown a more inquisitive nature this afternoon. The questions he asked revealed a keen mind.

Watching Mitchell, Rand had gained the impression the boy didn't miss much. He'd also gotten the feeling that Rachel didn't want her older son spending much time around him. He sighed, knowing he could be wrong on that count. But he didn't think so.

In the main room, he stoked the fire in the hearth and banked the flames so they'd burn slow and steady through the night. As he did every evening, he recorded in a ledger the patients he'd seen that day, the diagnosis, medications administered, and plan of treatment. He thumbed back through the pages, reading name after name and recalling many of the faces.

Stacks of medical volumes claimed the majority of his wall space in the tiny back bedroom, and he searched through them until, finally, he found the desired title. Then he crawled between the icy sheets with book in hand.

He read for a while, until he realized he'd skimmed the same paragraph four times over, each with lessening comprehension. Yawning, he laid the thick volume on the floor and turned onto his side, staring at the flame flickering orange within the smoke-browned glass of the oil lamp.

With an air of leisure he did not possess, he reached to turn down the lamp, silently assuring himself, over and over, as he did each night, that this would be the night. A single rotation of the tiny metal knob would extinguish the quivering flame on the end of the oil-soaked wick, and darkness, innocent and powerless, would lie quiet over the room.

It was easy. Any child could do it.

But—Rand stared at his hand, loathing its tremor—he could not.

He closed his eyes, fighting to summon the courage, telling himself the darkness was nothing to be afraid of. Nothing existed in the darkness that wasn't there in the light. He knew that. So why was his heart hammering against his ribs?

Then he smelled it. The cool, musty scent of moist earth.

It filled his nostrils, and in his mind, the tip of his boot touched something hard and immovable. The air became thinner, stealing his breath, pressing closer. He opened his eyes only to have darkness flood them full, complete and utter black. Invisible walls closed in. A stuttered thud, like the sound of a fading heart, filled his ears. He couldn't move. He couldn't breathe—

He bolted upright in bed, trembling, eyes wide, his breath coming hard.

The faint glow from the oil lamp on the bedside table arched in a golden halo across the quilt, and like a parched man gulped water, he drank it in, lungs burning. He stared at the footboard, his vision blurring, then drew up his knees and rested his head in his hands, waiting for his heart to return to a normal rhythm.

A moment passed, followed by another, and another, and finally he lay back down, still shaking. He pulled the quilt over his chest, fending off a familiar and scathing shame. "Maybe tomorrow night," he whispered, drawing his hand back beneath the covers. He reached deep into memory for words God had etched onto his heart years ago, and he repeated the verses of Scripture, over and over, willing their promise to take deeper hold.

He found comfort in the repetition and in knowing he'd filled the oil lamp on his bedside table full that morning, as he always did. But he could still hear the dull thump of Jessup Collum's shovel hitting the lid of the thin pine box.

"Maybe you should've let Dr. Brookston come to help, Mama. Instead of telling him no like you did."

Kneeling beside Mitch in the cramped barn stall, Rachel pushed damp strands of hair from her face, surprised at the tender challenge in her son's voice—and at her lack of a suitable response. Avoiding his appraising stare, she adjusted the lantern and pushed up the sleeves of Thomas's worn leather coat, checking to see if the calf was presenting itself.

She exhaled. No progress yet. And Lady's water sack had ruptured over an hour ago.

First light of dawn fingered its way through timeworn cracks in the barn walls, and pale yellow streaks illuminated swirling specks of dust and dirt that would have otherwise gone unnoticed. Glad to have her older son beside her, Rachel shivered against the cold, grateful the snowfall was finally slacking. Kurt had either fallen back to sleep after she'd awakened him or was still nurturing a grudge about their planned meeting with the schoolteacher. Judging from his attitude before going to bed hours earlier, she guessed the latter.

On the bright side, he was sleeping through the night again. The bad dreams that had plagued him following Thomas's passing, then again briefly a couple of months ago, were something she hoped they would never relive.

Mitch attempted to stroke Lady's neck, but the heifer reared her head and let out a high-pitched bawl. "I heard Dr. Brookston offer to come last night," Mitch continued, his breath puffing white in the chilled air. Ever persistent, he tried again to stroke Lady, and succeeded, but the heifer watched him, her dark eyes bordering on panic. It was a dread Rachel shared. "If you'd said yes to him"— Mitch's gaze met Rachel's and held fast—"then he'd already be here. Now . . . when we need him."

Knowing Mitch was right only added salt to Rachel's already wounded pride, and she struggled not to show how much the truth of his observation stung.

Well into the night, she and Charlie Daggett had searched for Lady in the biting wind and snow until they'd nearly abandoned any hope of finding her. Without Charlie's help, the soon-to-be mother and her calf would have perished in the storm. But thanks to the man's keen eye and familiarity with backwoods trails, the first-time mother and baby stood a chance.

Her fingers numb with cold, Rachel dipped a rag into a bucket of warm, sudsy water. She lingered a few extra seconds, relishing the warmth, then washed the cow's backside as Thomas had taught her to do. She'd assisted him with births before and was familiar with what to expect.

Problem was, this birth wasn't following the normal progression.

She doused the rag in the bucket again and squeezed out the excess water, her attention snagging on the book half hidden in the hay. She frowned. She'd scoured the book earlier in an attempt to find a resolution to Lady's predicament, but the usually helpful *Handy-Book of Husbandry* she'd purchased last year had proven to be not so handy this time.

Still feeling Mitchell's attention, Rachel shot him what she hoped was a confident look. When anticipating this birth in recent weeks, she'd imagined it would be an event she and the boys would share—alone. Something that would draw them closer together. Admitting she needed Rand Brookston's assistance, especially after refusing it so soundly only hours before, left a bitter aftertaste.

Yet not as bitter as the thought of losing Lady, or her calf. Or of not fulfilling her graveside promise to her husband.

"Mr. Daggett should be back anytime with Dr. Brookston, Mitch. I'm certain the doctor has delivered his share of calves. He'll know exactly what to do." Which she feared didn't describe Rand's perspective of Ben's situation. But, in all fairness, what could Rand Brookston do for a failing heart?

"Later this morning," she continued, arranging a smile, "we'll all head into town and check on Uncle Ben. You can tell him and Aunt Lyda all about Lady's—"

The heifer suddenly bellowed and rocked from side to side, her eyes wild. The animal lunged forward, attempting to stand, and Mitch stumbled back, narrowly escaping her sharp hooves. Lady let out a high-pitched whine. Rachel scrambled to hold her down, uncertain of what might happen if the heifer gained her footing at this stage of birth. She couldn't remember this happening the times she'd assisted Thomas.

Leveraging her weight against Lady to keep her down, Rachel took care not to apply too much pressure on her distended belly.

Mitch took a bold step forward, his intent clear.

"No, Mitchell!" She spoke through gritted teeth. "Stay back."

"But why, Mama? I can help!"

"No! It's too dangerous. I don't want you to get hurt." Lady tried again to stand, and Rachel pushed down harder, mindful of the animal's thrashing. From the corner of her eye, she spotted Mitch inching forward yet again. "Mitchell Thomas! I said to—" Lady struggled against the constraint and Rachel fought to maintain hold. "I said stay where you are!"

Her muscles burning from overexertion and fatigue, Rachel didn't let up. And gradually, finally, the heifer calmed. But the expectant mother's pitiful moans indicated her time was drawing close.

Rachel sank to her knees, her legs and arms limp. She couldn't do this alone, and she wouldn't risk the boys getting hurt. As much as she'd wanted to deliver Lady's calf without Rand's help, she couldn't wait for him to arrive.

A rustling behind her drew her attention.

Mitchell stood staring down at her, his spine ramrod straight, his shoulders squared. He appeared much older and taller from her perspective, and Rachel saw so much of Thomas in her son's look and manner.

"You act like I'm still a little boy, Mama." Mitch's voice was quiet and even, like Thomas's. "But I'm not." A hint of unaccustomed defiance glinted in his eyes, but the sheen of unshed tears proved more telling. "I can do more than you think I can."

Rachel stared up, feeling her lungs constrict. Her son's earnestness to prove himself felt achingly familiar, and a pang of regret cut through the layers of woven memories, pulling her back to the last conversation she'd had with her husband. To the last time she'd seen Thomas alive. She closed her eyes against the unwelcome echo of her own voice and tried to shut out the thoughtlessness of what she'd said.

Are you certain you're ready to do this, Thomas? By yourself? Alone? The way he'd looked at her, a mixture of disappointment and hurt. He'd known she hadn't meant it the way it had come out—he'd said as much standing there in the doorway that morning.

Rachel swallowed against the invisible cord tightening around her throat. He had known for certain . . . hadn't he? That she hadn't said it with the intention of hurting him. But it *had* hurt him.

Almost two and a half years had passed, but she could still see the shadow of disappointment in her husband's eyes, even when he'd assured her that he was fine. She made a fist, recalling the chill from the frost-covered windowpane as she'd pressed her hand against it, watching him saddle Chaucer and ride out. A distant pain began to thrum inside her chest. What she wouldn't do to turn back time and relive that moment.

If only she'd known that would be the last time she'd see him alive. . . .

She blinked to dispel the memory and was greeted by her older son's piercing gaze. "Mitchell," she whispered, seeing the unspoken question in his blue eyes. She worked to find her voice. "Son, I . . . I know you're not a little boy anymore. But I need you to understand something. Something very important, something you'll understand as you get older. You're so precious to me. Both you and Kurt are. And if anything ever happened to either of you, I don't know what I'd—"

"*Nothing's* going to happen to us. You worry too much, Mama. Papa said so."

Rachel shook her head, her smile tremulous. "You say that, honey, that nothing's going to happen, but none of us knows what might—"

Lady keened and jerked forward, writhing, and a knifelike stab sank deep and hard into Rachel's thigh. Rachel sucked in a breath and fell backward, knocking over the bucket of water. She rolled onto her side, clutching her thigh, unable to breathe as pain sliced to the bone.

"Mama!" Mitch appeared above her. "Mama, are you all right?"

Resisting the roil of nausea rising inside, Rachel gasped for air as the thick pine beams of the rafters above swam in and out of her vision. "I'm fine, honey," she lied, not wanting to alarm him.

She reached down to where Lady had kicked her. She slipped a hand beneath her coat and ran a shaky hand over her upper thigh. Her skirt was wet, and the once-warm water caused a chill. But she didn't think the injury had broken skin. Grimacing, she gritted her teeth, aware of Lady staggering, struggling to stand again.

The heifer let out a primal cry just before her hind legs buckled. Lady fell back into the straw and rolled onto her side. Rachel barely managed to move in time. Something wasn't right. Maybe the calf wasn't positioned correctly. Or perhaps it was too large for a first-time mother. She'd heard of that happening before.

"Mama, what should we do?"

Rachel took hold of Mitch's arm, wincing. "Help me up, honey. Hurry!"

With his assistance, she struggled to her feet and clutched the side of the stall, her head fuzzy. *So foolish . . .* She hadn't been paying attention. But better Lady kick her than Mitch or Kurt.

The muffled pound of a horse's hooves sounded

outside, followed by the telling crunch of boots on hay. Rachel glanced up, relieved . . . then had to look up a second time, unable to make what she saw match with what she'd expected to see.

8

"Good morning, Mrs. Boyd . . . Mitch. How's our soon-to-be mother faring?"

Rachel could only stare as Rand strode toward them. Dressed in a weathered rawhide duster and matching Stetson, Rand Brookston looked far less like a citified Eastern physician and more like a Colorado-born-and-bred mountain man, dark stubble of a beard and all. Still feeling slightly off-balance, she was tempted to ask him if he was on his way to a gunfight, but refrained. She'd never seen him look so . . . *rustic* before.

Perhaps this was his attempt to fit in better with the locals. Whatever his reasoning, the trans-formation was unexpected—as was its effect on her.

"Mama's hurt, Dr. Brookston!" Mitch pointed. "Lady just kicked her. *Hard!*"

Rand paused beside them in the stall. His gaze moved downward. "You're hurt, Mrs. Boyd?"

Rachel held up a hand, gripping the side of the stall to steady herself. "I'm fine." Though the throbbing in her leg argued otherwise.

He stepped closer. "Is it your ankle? If you'll allow me to—"

"My ankle is fine. I can tend myself later. I'd prefer that you see to my heifer." She gestured. "Her calf is coming, and I . . . I believe something's very wrong." She nodded toward Lady to emphasize her point, hoping Rand would follow her lead.

He didn't.

She had no difficulty deciphering the look he gave her because it was one she gave often to Kurt when he made a suggestion she had absolutely no intention of following.

Rand's attention dropped to where she held her leg. He looked pointedly back up at her. Telling by the faint shadows beneath his eyes, he'd gotten little, if any, sleep since they'd last parted. "Mrs. Boyd, if you're injured, my primary obligation, as you know, is to see to—"

"Dr. Brookston." She tried again, seeing the gray of his eyes darken. He wasn't a man who took kindly to being interrupted. It wasn't something she liked either. "This heifer and her calf are very important to me—to my ranch. My primary obligation, at the moment, is to them."

He looked as if he were about to say something. Then his gaze flickered to Mitch and he closed his mouth.

Rachel could well imagine what his response might have been if they'd been alone. She'd gotten a tiny taste of this man's forthrightness and wasn't eager to repeat the experience, especially in front of her son. "Please, Doctor"—she summoned her most respectful tone—"I'm asking you to see to my heifer and her calf . . . while there's still time." A wave of weakness washed through her, and her fingers tightened on the rough wood. *"Please,"* she added, her voice a whisper.

He stared for a long moment. Then with an almost imperceptible nod, Rand laid aside his medical bag, shed his coat and hat, and rolled up his shirtsleeves. He removed a large brown bottle from his satchel and proceeded to rub a clear ointment over his hands and forearms, then knelt beside Lady. With an ease that bespoke experience in working with animals, he wasted no time in his examination.

Rachel had witnessed countless births in her lifetime—both of babies and livestock—but Mitchell hadn't, and the boy's attention was riveted to the doctor's ministrations. Thomas had allowed the boys to attend a handful of births—after all, they were going to be ranchers like their father. But never had the animal giving birth been so special or loved, and Rachel found herself wondering if she'd made a mistake.

Perhaps letting Mitchell watch this particular birth wasn't such a good idea.

"How long ago did her water break?" Rand asked, his hands moving in slow, arching circles over Lady's distended abdomen. He pressed on her belly and Lady answered with a definitive kick, but his swift reflexes spared him a fate similar to Rachel's.

Seeing his reaction only worsened the ache in Rachel's leg—and in her pride. "At least an hour and a half ago. She tried to stand up, but I managed to keep her down. It wasn't easy."

Rand rose and rinsed his hands and arms in the barrel of icy water outside the stall, then dried them on a rag, saying nothing. Rachel studied his expression, reading no trace of disapproval in his features but sensing it all the same.

Her gaze lowered, and she saw it—

The jagged scar edging a path down the lower left side of his neck and disappearing beneath his open collar. She'd seen it before but never this close up and with his shirt collar unbuttoned. Judging by the length of the scar and the puckered skin, the wound had been deep, and whoever stitched it had not been gifted with the needle. Not like Rand Brookston was.

His expression turned guarded, and realizing he'd caught her staring, she quickly looked away. Much like she'd caught him doing the previous evening. Well, turnabout *was* fair play, wasn't it?

"The calf is in a posterior-facing position, Mrs. Boyd. It needs to be turned."

She didn't respond for a moment, the seriousness of the situation setting in. "But you can do that, can't you? Turn the calf, I mean."

"I can try. But I'm going to need some help." His

attention shifted to Mitch. "Mitchell, are you up to the job?"

Mitch's eyes widened. "Yes, sir!" He took a confident stride forward.

Rachel grabbed at Mitch's shoulder, missed, and nearly lost her balance. "Doctor, if you need help, I'll be happy to assist you." She put weight on her right leg and it gave beneath her. Rand reached out to help but she caught herself in time. She straightened, pain shooting up and down her leg, and she worked to hide how much it hurt. "I'd prefer that Mitch not assist you with this. I-I'll do it instead."

Rand leveled his gaze. "Mrs. Boyd—" He glanced at Lady, then back again. "I can't do this alone. And while I *always* welcome your assistance, ma'am . . . judging by the flush of your face, the fact you can hardly stand, and the way you're favoring that leg . . ." His gaze lifted from her eyes. "Add to that the way you're perspiring . . ."

Rachel reached up to find her forehead damp, despite the morning's chill.

". . . I'm guessing you're in quite a bit of pain right now and in no condition to assist with anything." He retrieved a coiled rope from a peg and fashioned a makeshift harness—in half the time it would have taken her, and with superior results. "So . . . I'll see to your heifer and her calf first, as you've requested me to do. Then I'll be obliged to tend your injury."

Hearing the implied bargain, and none too eager to have Rand Brookston viewing her thigh, Rachel purposefully held back an agreeing nod. She had another idea. "Will Mr. Daggett be joining us soon?"

Rand's tired smile was briefly lived. "That's doubtful." He looped the harness over Lady's head. "The boardwalk in front of the Mullinses' store is piled high with snow. He's helping Lyda dig out so she can open up. Folks are needing supplies."

At the mention of Lyda opening the store, Rachel realized she hadn't yet inquired after Ben.

"I give you my word, Mrs. Boyd." Rand's voice mirrored the confidence in his eyes. "I'll be careful."

Instinctively, she knew he was referring to Mitch and something inside her softened toward him at his reassurance. Knowing she had no alternative, she nodded a hesitant approval and Mitch hurried to take his place beside him.

"I won't get hurt, Mama. I promise."

Rachel couldn't find her voice, so simply nodded again.

"I need you to grip the rope tight, Mitchell. Right here. Hold it firm and steady. I'll tell you when to pull. And stay on your haunches, like this"—Rand demonstrated, sitting in a squatted position—"so you can move quickly when you need to. Not *if* you need to, but when. She's going to kick. They always do. So you have to be ready."

Mitch nodded, stealing a glance in Rachel's direction. Rachel's face went warm.

"Now"—Rand smoothed a hand over Lady's muzzle—"normally after a heifer's been in labor this long, the calf is ready to be born and the mama's lying down. But sometimes, when the calf is large, it'll take more time. I think that's part of Lady's problem. So in situations like this, we need the heifer to stand and move around. Most times they'll try to stand themselves, but if not—"

Rachel cringed, realizing she'd made the wrong decision. Again. To Mitchell's credit, he didn't give her away.

"—then we need to help her. As I said, Lady's calf is posterior-facing, which means—"

"It means it's coming out backwards." Mitch stroked Lady's neck. "I read about it in Mama's book." He indicated the book that lay half buried in the straw.

Her embarrassment now utterly complete, Rachel threw the traitorous *Handy-Book of Husbandry* a glare.

Positioning Mitch at Lady's head, Rand moved to the opposite end. "You and I are going to try and help Lady to turn the calf herself, Mitchell. Most times, the heifer's body will do the work if given the chance. Sometimes it won't. But you don't ever want to force a calf in this position to turn."

"It could hurt it?" Mitch asked, holding on to the rope like a lifeline.

Rand's expression went solemn. "It could hurt them both."

Rand wished he'd followed his instincts and ridden out to the Boyd ranch during the night. He would've seen what was happening early on and could have given the calf more time to rotate before entering the birth canal. As it was, the heifer's birth was progressing rapidly. They still had time. Though not much. "When I count to three, Mitchell, I want you to pull hard on the rope. I'm going to push from this end. You ready?"

Tongue doubled between his front teeth, Mitch nodded. "Yes, sir."

"One . . . two . . . three!" Rand pushed, watchful of Lady's hooves but even more so of Mitchell's footing, and of Rachel standing close beside him.

The heifer didn't budge. She did kick again, however, and Rand narrowly missed a hoof.

"Okay," he panted, pausing to catch a breath. "Let's try again."

They did, and on the fourth try Lady bolted upright—straight toward Mitchell. The boy managed a deft side step to safety and after the initial shock wore off, he began grinning from ear to ear. "We did it, Dr. Brookston! We got her up!"

Rand laughed. "That we did!" The joy in the boy's expression did Rand's heart good. "You've got good reflexes, Mitchell. You're fast too. Remind me never to challenge you to a race."

Mitchell beamed, but it was the smile the boy reserved for his mother that touched Rand most.

"I told you I wouldn't get hurt, Mama. I kept my promise."

Rand heard a soft hiccup beside him and turned to see tears in Rachel's eyes, her gaze centered on her son. He sensed something pass between the two of them and felt a mite intrusive on the moment, yet he wouldn't have chosen to be anywhere else.

Having arrived at Timber Ridge after Thomas Boyd's death, he'd never known Rachel's husband. But he'd heard enough about the man to know he would have been honored to count him as a friend. The handful of times Ben and Lyda Mullins had spoken of Thomas—always in a hushed whisper and with the deepest respect—Rand had sensed their love for him. For this entire family.

Which made him dread, even more, when Rachel learned the truth about Ben's condition, and about how little time he had left. Less than Rachel suspected. Like Lyda, she'd already lost so much.

Rachel touched Mitch's cheek. "I . . ." She took a quick breath, her lips trembling. "I'm s-so . . . very proud of you," she whispered, a tear sliding down her cheek. She looked back at him, and if Rand wasn't mistaken, he read gratitude in her eyes.

Movement from the side drew his attention, and Rand turned to see Kurt standing outside the stall door. For a fraction of a second, the boy's gaze was only for his mother, and his expression registered undeniable hurt. Then Kurt's gaze connected with Rand's and cool defiance rose.

"You found Lady?" Kurt asked, his attention back on his mother, his hair and clothes rumpled, his coat unbuttoned, hands shoved deep into his pockets.

Rand heard more accusation in the boy's tone than question. He hadn't been around Kurt much, or Mitch, for that matter, but one thing was certain—for one so young, Kurt had an edge to him.

Rachel wiped her cheeks and made her way to her younger son, limping and holding on to the wall as she went. Rand indicated for Mitch to follow so they could give Lady run of the stall.

"Yes, honey"—Rachel sniffed—"Mr. Daggett and I found Lady up near the waterfall. She was stuck in the snow." She glanced behind her. "Now she's about to have her calf."

"Why didn't you wake me up? You promised you'd wake me up!"

Surprised at the boy's tone, Rand fought the impulse to look at Rachel. He could feel her tense beside him.

"I *did* awaken you, Kurt." Rachel's tone was a blend of rebuke and embarrassment. She brushed a tuft of hair back from Kurt's forehead—or tried. The boy pulled away, and Rachel slowly withdrew her hand. "You must've fallen back to sleep."

Kurt's scowl clearly said he didn't believe her. "Why is *he* here?"

Rand's brows shot up, realizing Kurt was referring to him.

"Kurtis Ian Boyd!" Rachel said in a harsh whisper. "You will *not* speak to me in that fashion. Do you understand? And you will apologize to Dr. Brookston this instant."

Kurt seemed to weigh his mother's command. "I'm sorry," he finally muttered.

Rachel's attention fluttered to Rand but never settled. Then she briefly bowed her head and massaged her temple. When she looked up again, her carefully arranged smile was back in place, her brow empty of frustration. But Rand found the façade more revealing than convincing.

She exhaled and turned back to Kurt. "I sent for Dr. Brookston because Lady's having difficulty with her labor."

Mitchell stepped forward. "Her calf was going to come out backward, so I got to help Dr. Brookston get Lady to stand up. Now the calf is going to turn itself around. But you don't ever want to force a calf in this position to turn."

Rand had to smile at the authority in Mitch's voice, impressed the boy was quoting him verbatim. "We *hope* the calf is going to turn,"

Rand said, giving Kurt a smile. "I could use another assistant, Kurt . . . if you're interested." He gave Rachel a discreet look to let her know he'd assign Kurt a "safe" job.

But Kurt's lack of enthusiasm at the offer spoke volumes.

Rand turned back to the stall to keep an eye on the heifer's progress. He had no idea what he'd done to get on the boy's bad side. He'd noticed Kurt's standoffishness last evening, the way he'd watched from the doorway.

Lady let out a low bellow and staggered to one side. Her distended belly seemed to grow even more so, and the faint outline of the life within her could be seen shifting and moving as the calf pressed its way into position. Somehow the young mother maintained her footing. But the telling ripple through her abdominal muscles indicated that would soon change.

Rand removed the makeshift harness from Lady's head, untied the rope, and tied a slipknot.

"Should we make her lie down now?" Mitch asked, removing his coat and rolling up his sleeves the way Rand had done.

"No. She'll lie down on her own when she's ready." Rand raised a hand. "And it's best if you all stay out of the way. Let's give her some room."

Aware of his audience waiting at the door of the stall, Rand examined the heifer again to ascertain the calf's position—and his optimism waned.

"What's wrong?" Rachel asked behind him.

He sighed, wondering which bad news to deliver first, and already knowing Rachel well enough to know she'd blame herself.

"The calf didn't turn . . . did it?" she asked.

"No, but that's no fault of yours. Sometimes this just happens. No matter how much time the heifer has."

Lady's hind legs gave way, and her bulk sank into the straw. She rolled onto her side. The calf was beginning to crown—only it wasn't the calf's nose and front hooves that were presenting.

"Mitch, hand me that rope. Kurt, get me the rag on the peg there."

In a blink, Mitch was beside him with the rope. A second later, the rag appeared at his shoulder. Kurt hovered close, eyes wide and watching, apparently having discarded a measure of defiance.

Rand wiped his hands and slipped the looped rope over his wrists.

Mitch leaned closer. "What are you going to do?"

Rand grabbed hold of the calf's hooves, looped the rope over and pulled the slipknot tight. He didn't know why Rachel and her boys had such an affinity for this heifer, but he wished they didn't. "Do you see how Lady's belly is rippling? How the muscles are tightening up?"

The boys nodded.

Too late, he wondered if Rachel minded his teaching the boys about the birthing process. But seeing as their father had been a rancher and their mother was allowing them to witness this in the first place . . . "That's called a contraction. That's how a heifer's body pushes out the calf. But since—"

The calf's legs were slippery from birth fluid, and the rope lost hold. Hurrying, Rand looped the rope around the hooves again and pulled taut, but the contraction had passed.

"If her body's doin' the pushing, why are you havin' to pull?"

"Good question, Kurt. Two reasons . . . First, it's taking a long time for Lady to have this calf and she's getting tired. Second"—now for the other bad news—"the calf is larger than I'd first thought."

The next contraction began.

Body braced, Rand pulled, aware of Rachel coming up beside them, holding on to the wall, watching.

The contraction didn't last long. Lady shuddered and moaned, and the calf made little progress. Rand wiped his hands on the rag, eyeing Lady's belly. When the next contraction started, he put his full weight into it and pulled, and felt Mitch and Kurt behind him, tugging for all they were worth.

The calf's hind legs slid free, followed by its rump.

"Look, Dr. Brookston!" Mitch yelled, his voice high-pitched. "It's coming!"

Rand smiled, but only for a second. "Here comes another contraction, boys. Get ready!"

Following the contraction, a groan issued from the heifer that made Rand hurt for her, and for Rachel and the boys as they watched. "Come on, girl," he whispered, allowing no slack in the rope. His neck and shoulder muscles corded tight. "Just one more good one."

"Come on, Lady," he heard Mitch say behind him.

"Just one more good one," Kurt whispered.

With strength Rand didn't know he had left in him, he pulled, inspired by the tugs on the rope behind him—and the calf's body slid free. He staggered back a step as the boys let out whoops and hollers, seemingly unconcerned by the wash of afterbirth that followed the calf's arrival. He sat back in the straw, watching in wonder at the newness of life as the boys flanked him on either side.

He sneaked a peek at Rachel and found her smiling too, her face radiant.

"Thank you," she whispered, and gave a soft laugh, then looked back at her sons.

Rand stared, knowing he shouldn't allow his thoughts to go where they were going. Not that they were inappropriate, they just weren't wise. But, oh . . . she was one beautiful woman. She had a softness about her now, an openness—as though she'd let down some invisible wall—and he indulged the idea of what it would be like to love this woman, and to be loved by her.

A tug on his shirtsleeve broke the reverie.

Excitement lit Mitchell's face. "I wish we could do that again! That was fun!"

"I helped too." Kurt sat forward and shot a look at his older brother. "I pulled as hard as you did. Even harder!"

Mitch rose up on his knees. "Maybe I could help you again, Dr. Brookston. The next time you deliver a calf."

"I can help too!" Competition thickened Kurt's voice.

Rand nodded, having no desire to encourage the rivalry between the brothers. "You both did well, boys. And I'm impressed with how hard you worked." He rubbed his hands on a fresh patch of straw, noticing Mitch do the same. "I couldn't have done it without you both."

Lady gained her footing and turned to nudge her baby. The calf shook its head, its still-wet ears slapping back and forth as Lady began to lick. Rand untethered the rope from the newborn bull's legs and the bull kicked in response, nearly connecting with his forearm.

Rand laughed. "You're welcome, little one." He never tired of this part of practicing medicine—be it delivering babies or livestock. Watching life come into the world was a gift, one he was grateful to have witnessed many times. "You've got yourself a fine young bull here, Mrs. Boyd. Strong and healthy. He'll serve your ranch well in coming years."

"I hope so," she said softly, and something in her voice brought him around. "I appreciate you coming when I finally sent for you." Her half smile held a trace of chagrin. "And for your offer to come last night."

Rand held her gaze, hearing the subtle apology and savoring this moment of truce between them. He only hoped it would last.

Later in the day, as the boys did their evening chores, Rachel loaded supplies into the wagon and set out the short distance to mend a portion of fencing. The freshly fallen snow and steady ache in her leg made the customary chore more burdensome. Before he'd left, Rand had all but demanded—with the kindest and best of intentions, she knew—to examine her injury. But she'd refused. It was only a bruise. She'd rested awhile, as he'd prescribed, though not for as long as he'd suggested. Life on a ranch wouldn't wait, and neither would mending this fence.

Dressed warmly enough in Thomas's coat and wearing his dungarees beneath her skirt, she managed to get the fallen post uprighted, though lifting the heavy pine crossbeam proved an impossible feat without the full strength in both of her legs.

"That's what you pay me to do, Miss Rachel."

She turned, surprised to see Charlie Daggett coming up behind her. But no wonder she hadn't heard him, not with how hard she was breathing. Overtired and out of breath, she wiped her brow with the back of her gloved hand, careful to keep weight off her injured leg. "I wasn't certain you would be able to return today."

"I'm sorry. The work in town took longer than I thought." Charlie hefted the beam one-handed, nodded to her for the mallet and nails, and pounded the lodgepole pine back into place.

Not for the first time, Rachel admired the man's intuitive gentleness and physical strength, while also noticing the bourbon on his breath. Much stronger than it had been that morning. She worked alongside him, amazed at his steadiness of hand while sensing a quiet, and not unfamiliar, unrest beneath his calm exterior. She wasn't certain, but it seemed that Charlie Daggett was a man who thought none too highly of himself. And she wished there were a way he could see himself through her eyes, as well as the eyes of others in town who knew him well, those who took the time to look beneath the surface.

She waited until they were walking back to the wagon before broaching the subject. "Is everything all right, Mr. Daggett?"

"Everything's fine, ma'am." He glanced down at her. "You're limpin', ma'am. You get yourself hurt today?"

She huffed softly, still frustrated with herself at having let the incident happen in the first place. "I wasn't fast enough around Lady's hooves during the birth. The delivery went well . . . overall," she added, seeing question slip into Charlie's eyes. "She had a bull. Healthy and strong, thanks to Dr. Brookston. And to you, for your help."

"I was glad to do it, ma'am." He assisted her into the wagon and shook his head when she made room for him on the bench seat. "I'll check the herd and the other heifers due to drop, then get the animals fed and tote fresh water from the stream up to the barn. Anything else you need doin'?"

"Would you bring another load of wood to the porch, please?" She massaged her leg, eager to get it elevated again. "I'd be most grateful. And, Mr. Daggett . . ."

He turned back.

"I've been meaning to ask you . . ." She knew she was borderline prying and hoped he wouldn't mind the personal inquiry. "How is Miss Matthews these days? I haven't seen her in town recently." Nor had she seen the two of them together in a while.

Warmth didn't creep into Charlie's face as it usually did when Miss Matthews's name was mentioned. "Miss Lori Beth's in fine health, ma'am.

Real fine. And you're kind to ask after her. She always tells me to give you and your boys her best."

Though Rachel was happy to learn Lori Beth was in good health, Charlie's reaction was telling, and she wondered whether it had anything to do with his heavier drinking. Everyone in town knew about Lori Beth Matthews—Timber Ridge wasn't that large a place—but Rachel had come to like her very much. She deeply respected the woman's courage. "Lori Beth's a very nice person, Mr. Daggett."

He nodded, looking away. "I'm lucky to have her for a friend."

A friend? Rachel smiled and peered at him from the corner of her eye, trying to tease a smile from him. She usually could. "I've gotten the definite impression that you and she were more than just *friends.*"

Charlie looked away, shifting his weight, looking decidedly less comfortable by the second. "It's gonna be dark soon, ma'am. I'd best see to the animals."

Rachel cringed inside. "Forgive me, I'm sorry if I—"

"No harm done, Miss Rachel." Charlie looked up, his eyes more serious—and sadder—than she could remember. "Sometimes it just takes a while for a man to see the truth. But I've seen it . . . And Miss Lori Beth deserves a lot better than the likes of me."

9

W hy don't you let me ride for Doc Brookston? I could be back with him within the hour."

Reining in, Rachel shook her head, doing her best not to wince as she dismounted. "Thank you for your concern, James. But I'm fine." She took deep breaths and held on to the saddle horn until she was certain she had her balance. Pain shot up and down her leg. Perspiration broke out on her forehead. "All he'll advise is to elevate my leg and keep cool compresses on the wound."

"Which you're not doing." James gave her an older-brother look and followed her into the barn.

"Which I *am* doing . . . when time allows, and which I'll have more of this evening, thanks to you for helping me round up the strays." Already looking forward to the cool compresses on the bruise, she led Chaucer to his stall and reached to unstrap the saddle, but James beat her to it.

"Go on inside and get some rest. See to the boys. I'll do this."

Part of her wanted to argue, but the greater part of her didn't. Not with the way her leg was hurting. "Thank you, James. For everything. I appreciate you coming out today."

"My pleasure." He unsaddled Chaucer, a conspiratorial smile stealing across his face. "I have to admit . . ." He paused and took a deep breath. "I've missed this place."

She laughed and settled herself against a stool, enjoying the time with him. She saw him in town often enough, but moments like this when they could talk, just the two of them, were rare these days. "Yes, the smell of manure and sweaty horse holds such appeal. Not to mention the endless work and scant profit."

Laughing softly, he began at Chaucer's neck and moved the curry brush in a circular motion over the horse's hair to loosen the dirt. "I'm serious. I was telling Molly last night that I was looking forward to getting back out here. Then when you and the boys weren't at church this morning, she encouraged me to come on out and check on you." He sighed. "I'm glad I did. I love the feel of this place. Being in the open air, working with the cattle, seeing the new bulls . . ." He gestured toward Gent, the bull that Lady had given birth to, in the opposite stall. A second heifer had given birth earlier that morning—another bull—and, thankfully, it had been an easy birth. The bull remained as yet unnamed by the boys, which suited Rachel fine. Best they not get too attached.

"Well, you're welcome out here anytime. Molly and Jo are too." She glanced back toward the cabin, hoping what she was about to say would come out right. "I miss you, James. Part of me wishes Molly would've moved out here with us after you were married—instead of you moving into town. I mean . . . not permanently." She shrugged, seeing surprise in his expression. "Just for a little while. I would have liked that. But . . ." She sat up straighter and tossed him a wink, not wanting to give the impression that she wasn't managing things well on her own. "You needed your space with your new wife and precious little daughter. And it's good for the boys and me to be on our own again." She purposefully deepened her smile. "We're doing fine, and I couldn't be happier for you."

"Thanks, Rach." James paused from his brushing. "I don't know how you made it through. . . ." He briefly bowed his head. "Already, I can't imagine life without Molly." He looked her way, his expression going tender. "Having Molly in my life, being married now . . . It's given me a better understanding of what you must have gone through in losing Thomas." He shook his head. "I . . . I just can't imagine."

Rachel held his gaze and let the silence between them say what words couldn't. She was reminded again of how much she had relied on her brother's strength and support when Thomas had died. She and James had always been close, but the time he lived with her and the boys had brought them closer.

She wanted to discuss the financial standing of the ranch with him, get his opinion on decisions she faced, but she knew him well enough to know that if she admitted her plight, he would feel obligated to do anything and everything he could to help her. And he had a wife and a daughter now. He was no longer first and foremost her older brother. He was a husband, a father, and a sheriff. His life was his own, and it was crowded enough.

She stood to leave, gritting her teeth against the stiffening pain in her leg. She'd never known a bruise could hurt so much. James had turned back to his task, not noticing. Just as well.

"Rachel?"

Almost to the door of the barn, she looked back to see him standing in the opening of the stall, the expression on his face hard to decipher.

"I'm going to ask Deputy Willis to add his name to the ballot for sheriff."

She stared, not understanding. "Why would you do that?"

"Because Mayor Davenport is buying up votes for his candidate all over town. And also because"—hesitance crept into his tone—"in the past couple of months, people have started to express doubt about whether they want me to continue in the position."

Sensing what James wasn't saying aloud, Rachel's thoughts turned to Molly. There was no question in Rachel's mind that God had directed Molly's path to Timber Ridge last year, even though Molly, by her own admission, hadn't perfectly followed God's path for her life. What person had? Molly had asked everyone's forgiveness for what she'd done and had worked to mend relationships. All of that was in the past now, for Rachel anyway. She just wished people would be as forgiving about Molly's mistakes as they were about their own. But some folks seemed bent on making Molly pay. And, evidently, making James pay too.

"You're the only sheriff Timber Ridge has ever had. Of course people still want you."

He eyed her, his response saying he wasn't so sure. "I'd rather give people another option, just in case. Dean Willis is a good man. He's honest and fair, and I know for a fact that Mayor Davenport doesn't have Willis in his back pocket like he does Bart Shaker—though Davenport tried hard enough. Willis stood up to him. Davenport's also managed to delay the election. He's already received approval from the town council, so the balloting won't take place until this summer. He wants more time to get his man in place, is my guess."

Rachel wouldn't put anything past Mayor Davenport. The man was a snake. James had stood up to the mayor's underhanded ways and backroom dealings and had publicly called him out, more than once. Davenport wanted nothing more than to have James out of his way. Still, she knew this town could have no better sheriff than her brother.

"When it comes down to it, James, I believe people will vote for the best man. And I believe that's you."

His sigh held reservation but also what sounded like a measure of acceptance, maybe even peace. He shifted his weight. "Daniel and Elizabeth were at church this morning," he said a little too casually, watching her a little too closely, and Rachel felt her defenses rise. "Daniel asked about the boys. And about you."

"Please . . ." She shook her head, not wanting their time together today to end on a dissonant note. "I'm too tired for this today, James."

"Rachel, this has gone on long enough between you and Daniel. He wants to make things right. And frankly, he's tried. It's you who can't seem to—"

"Thomas is dead!" she said with more force than intended. Weariness moved through her. Tears rose.

He heaved a sigh. "Despite what you think, Daniel is not responsible for what happened. Thomas decided to go hunting that morning. On his own. He wasn't ready. Daniel had said he'd go with him anytime. But you know as well as I do that once Thomas decided something, nothing could change his mind."

Deep inside, Rachel felt the inexplicable urge to flee—from James, from the conversation, from the accountability he was forcing upon her. But she made herself stay, knowing he would only pursue her if she tried to retreat. She let out a held breath. "How many times must we have this conversation . . . ?"

"As many times as it takes until you see the truth." He stepped closer. "I don't understand why you're so intent on laying the blame at Daniel's feet. It doesn't seem that there's anything to forgive him for, but if there is . . . can't you at least try?" His gaze leveled with hers, and her mouth went dry at the boldness of his stare, at the unwavering love and sense of justice it held.

How could her brother be right about so many things and be so completely off the mark about this? But he was wrong. She knew it. He just couldn't see it because of his love for his childhood friend. She had loved Daniel too, and had tried to forgive him. But whenever she thought of Daniel, when she remembered how Mitch and Kurt used to go on about his hunting escapades in front of Thomas . . .

"Uncle Daniel can track anything in these mountains. He can hunt anything too! He's the best hunter in all the Rockies. I want to grow up to be just like him!" All the keepsakes Daniel brought back hadn't helped either—animal pelts, snakeskins, antlers . . . How was a father supposed to compete with such adulation? And why should he have been made to?

"I know you mean well, James, but . . . I need for you to leave this alone. Please."

"You said something to me, Rachel, one night not long after Thomas died, about how you wished you could go back and live that last morning with him over again. Do you remember saying that? Do you remember what you meant?"

She did remember. Only too well. She also knew that nothing could change the past. What was done was done. James could do nothing to alter it, neither could this conversation, and neither would his trying to mend things with Daniel. "You said something to me too, James, last fall. You told me I was trying to *fix things* between you and Molly. Do you remember saying that?" she said, using the same tone he just had.

A muscle tightened in his jaw.

"You told me, 'This isn't something you can fix.'" She swallowed. "Well . . . this isn't something you can fix either. So, please . . . leave it be."

Not wanting the time with him to be ruined, she forced a brightness to her manner, knowing full well he would see through the pretense. "Thank you again for coming by, and for helping me with the strays. I've missed your company . . . very much."

Disappointment shadowed his features. He fingered the bristles of the brush. "I've missed you too. You sure you're doing all right?"

Somehow she held her smile. "Absolutely," she whispered, not trusting her full voice.

He looked around the barn. His gaze lingered

near the workbench, and she wondered whether he could picture Thomas standing there as easily as she still could. The image of her late husband came, and she cherished it, but time had diminished the pain of his passing.

"What you and Thomas built here together, Rach . . . It's special. Thomas really loved it. He told me so . . . many times. He'd be proud of how you're carrying on, and of how you're doing this for your boys."

Conviction stung, and Rachel summoned fresh courage to bolster her confident façade. "Thank you, that means a lot. This ranch was his dream," she said softly, the next words threatening to stick in her throat. "And mine."

"Ranching can be a challenge, Mrs. Boyd. Especially in this part of the country. But you don't need me to tell you that, now, do you?" Mr. Fossey paused as though searching for his next words, his expression one of compassion. His bushy gray brows knit together as the clock on the mantel behind him sliced off the seconds.

Muted conversation from the bank lobby drifted through the closed office door, and Rachel wondered whether Mr. Fossey's secretary could overhear their exchange. She hoped not. Yet if what Mr. Fossey had told her a moment ago held true—she felt a humorless laugh—it was only a matter of time before everyone in Timber Ridge would know about her predicament. *I'm sorry, Thomas. . . .*

She shifted in the chair, the ache in her leg nearly unbearable.

Since last night, the wound on her thigh had turned purplish black. The poultices she'd applied hadn't eased the swelling or discomfort, and routine chores were next to impossible. Wriggling her toes sent pain shooting up into her back and made walking excruciating. Even seated and still, she could feel the blood pulsing hot through the bruise. She'd finished the last of her willow bark tea yesterday and would have taken laudanum for the pain last night, if she'd had any. She'd honestly thought it was just a bruise.

Now she wondered. . . .

She eyed her grandfather's cane resting against the arm of her chair and felt a subtle stirring inside, a yearning for days past, when she was younger and life was simpler. Or perhaps those days only seemed simpler in the remembering.

"Your late husband, God rest his soul," Mr. Fossey continued, warmth softening the lines wreathing his eyes and mouth, "was a fine man. Thomas managed his accounts with this bank in an exemplary manner, just as you have done." He raised a hand, as though reading her thoughts. "Yes . . . you *have* been late in repaying your loan, but you've also kept me apprised of your circumstances. You informed me your payment

139

would be delayed, which makes my responsibility in answering to the bank's shareholders a much easier task."

Rachel looked down at her gloved hands. "You're kind to offer, Mr. Fossey. With the death of Thomas's prized bull, I've lost the income I would have gained from leasing him to neighboring ranches this spring."

"And I know you were counting on that money." Mr. Fossey's tone reflected regret. "That bull came from fine stock."

Rachel nodded. For the integrity of her own herd's bloodline, she knew she couldn't have bred the bull to her cows again. But losing the potential income from the bull as a herd sire, along with the loss of cattle she'd sustained in the previous two winters, placed her finances in dire straits.

Her gaze slowly lifted to the letter lying faceup on his desk, a letter she'd penned last night after comparing her bills to the ever-decreasing balance in her bankbook. "Regarding my request for more money, and time in which to repay it . . . do you think the board will give it consideration?"

Gilbert Fossey pushed back from his desk, and Rachel tried not to interpret his distancing himself as a bad omen, telling herself it wasn't a deliberate act on his part.

"I assure you the board gives every lender's request serious consideration. They'll be fair in their final rendering. But keep in mind, Mrs. Boyd

. . . these men are not philanthropists. They invest their money in order to receive a return on that investment, as you pledged to them at the outset of your loan."

Rachel nodded, trying to appear confident while feeling as if she were treading water. Perhaps her request wasn't such a good idea after all. Perhaps she was only prolonging the inevitable, getting in over her head. Still, she couldn't simply give up. Not when giving up meant she would be forced to sell half of her land, and not when recalling all she and Thomas had sacrificed through the years. "I understand completely."

Mr. Fossey opened his mouth, then closed it again, giving obvious consideration to whatever thought occupied his mind. "Mrs. Boyd, would you permit me an observation? A most personal one that runs the risk of overstepping the bounds of propriety?"

She stared, completely trusting this man yet not knowing where he was leading.

"Rest assured that my observation issues from the heart of a friend, and *not* as an employee of this bank. And that it comes with the deepest respect for your late husband."

Now Rachel guessed what he was going to say.

As though knowing she'd read his mind, he smiled. "Have you considered the possibility of remarriage? I know . . . for a fact," he said, his tone confident, "that there are successful, wealthy men in this town who would court you on a moment's notice, if you would but give them one look of encouragement. Surely one of them would suit you. If not in a match of the heart, then perhaps one of friendship. Not that you would marry for money, of course, but the fact is, the chances of retaining ownership of your ranch would be greatly improved were you married."

Rachel returned his kind look, not the least offended. She knew of many marriages built on an alliance of wealth or family name. It wasn't uncommon. "I'd be lying to you, Mr. Fossey, if I said I'd never entertained that thought. But Timber Ridge is a small town, and I believe I've already met every man in the county."

He flinched playfully. "You are being most severe on my gender, Mrs. Boyd."

She laughed. "Not at all, sir." Her smile turned inward. "I was simply very much in love with my husband."

He didn't say anything for a moment, but if Rachel wasn't mistaken, a subtle glimmer of admiration shone in his eyes. He stood and she followed suit, wincing at the pain in her leg.

She'd checked with Lyda at the store earlier that morning for willow bark, hoping to find the pain-relieving herb in stock. But Lyda informed her that Rand had purchased all they had. What were the chances she could stop by his clinic for the medicine without him being there? He'd done nothing wrong. Quite the contrary, in fact. While she wasn't ready to relinquish all of her misgivings about the man, he was certainly giving her reason to. She would pay him for the willow bark, of course—she just preferred not to see him so soon, knowing he would inquire about her leg.

But there *was* one thing she would change about the current situation—Rand Brookston was all Mitch talked about. How Rand "rescued" the calf. She sincerely appreciated what he'd done, but she would just as soon undo the impression he—or rather, his profession—had made on her older son.

Mr. Fossey rounded the corner of the desk and glanced down at her cane. Concern crept into his features. "Are you certain your injury isn't more serious, my dear? You look as though you're in a great deal of pain."

Rachel squared her shoulders and stood a little straighter. "I'm fine. I need to work out the soreness—that's all."

He stared as though debating her self-diagnosis, then made his way to the door. "Well . . . as soon as I receive word from the board, I'll let you know." He reached for the knob.

"Mr. Fossey . . ."

He paused.

"I want to thank you again for agreeing to support me in this. I'll do my best not to disappoint you, or the board." Her hand tightened on the curved head of the cane. "You were always fair and generous in your dealings with Thomas, and I realize—" Her throat tightened as she swallowed. She'd promised herself to keep her emotions in check. She was certain the other ranchers in Timber Ridge—all men—never got "choked up" during business meetings with Mr. Fossey. A deep breath helped to dislodge the pebble in her throat. "What I'm trying to say is . . . I realize most men in your position wouldn't have chosen to conduct business with a widow, as you did. I'm grateful for the confidence you've shown in me and for the friendsh—" The words caught. She cleared her throat. "For the friendship our families share."

"Mrs. Boyd . . ." When she didn't look up, Mr. Fossey bent slightly to secure her gaze. "Rachel," he tried again softly. "I assure you, my decision to work with you following Thomas's passing had nothing to do with our families' friendship."

Rachel eyed him, having long suspected otherwise.

"All right . . ." He gave a slight shrug. "Perhaps our friendship did influence my initial decision, but it enabled me to see what a competent and intelligent woman you are. And remember, the board had final say in the matter." He smiled. "You've experienced some recent setbacks—that's all—as has every rancher in the area. The winter's been hard on all of you."

Rachel scoffed softly. "Everyone except Leonard

Rudger. According to what I heard this morning, he made an offer on the Toberlins' ranch." Whose property backed up to hers, though she didn't voice that reminder. "Rumor has it the Toberlins are going to sell and move back to Missouri."

Mr. Fossey's expression revealed nothing. And far too late, Rachel's discretion delivered warning. She blinked. "I'm sorry, sir. Please forgive me. That was imprudent and uncalled for."

A wave of his hand accompanied an understanding look. "No harm done." His hand briefly covered hers on the cane. "I can't begin to imagine what you've endured, losing Thomas the way you did. Add to that the hardship of raising two young boys *and* managing a ranch alone. I admire your strength and courage, Rachel. Sarah and I both do."

His brow furrowed. "Speaking of Sarah, she and I missed you and the boys at church yesterday. She'd like you, Mitchell, and Kurt to come over for Sunday lunch soon. She'd love the visit. I would too."

Rachel adored Gilbert and Sarah Fossey, but she still dreaded social gatherings, even small ones. And this one would be especially awkward if she was still waiting on the board's decision. But more than that, such occasions were a cruel reminder that she was no longer part of a couple, and that Thomas was never coming back. But as her brother had told her countless times, she wouldn't

145

begin to feel "normal" again—whatever that was—until there was normality to her life.

Her practiced "widow's smile" came easily. "I'd love nothing more, Mr. Fossey. Thank you. I'll speak with Sarah about what I can bring."

Giving her elbow a fatherly squeeze, Mr. Fossey opened the door.

Rachel glanced over to say good-bye to his secretary, but the woman wasn't there. Perhaps Miss Graham hadn't overheard their conversation after all. Rachel started for the lobby, mindful of the thick Persian rug, her gait anything but graceful. She was barely aware of the gentleman sitting off to the side, but when he glanced up, it drew her attention.

It took her a moment to place him, but when she did, she stopped mid-limp.

"Edward!" Mr. Fossey said behind her. "I heard you'd arrived in town. It's about time you got over here to see me."

The gentleman stood and accepted Mr. Fossey's outstretched hand. "It's good to see you again, Gilbert. It's been a few years."

"More than I care to count, I'm afraid."

Rachel didn't wish to intrude on the informal reunion, but neither did she want to miss the opportunity to thank the man for the kindness he'd demonstrated at the Mullinses' store days earlier.

Mr. Fossey's grin made him look years younger. "Wherever you're staying, Edward, Sarah's already upset that it's not with us." The men laughed, and then Mr. Fossey's smile faded. "I'm so sorry about Evelyn. I wish Sarah and I could have seen her again, one last time."

The gentleman briefly bowed his head. "I appreciate that, Gilbert," he whispered. "She would have loved to see you both again too." He glanced in Rachel's direction, and Mr. Fossey trailed his gaze.

"Mrs. Boyd! I'm sorry. I didn't realize you were still here. Please allow me to make the introductions." The men lessened the distance. "Edward, may I present Mrs. Rachel Boyd, formerly of Franklin, Tennessee. Mrs. Boyd owns a ranch just outside of town and has two of the cutest redheaded boys you'll ever see. Mrs. Boyd's older brother is currently sheriff of Timber Ridge, has been since the town started up."

Mr. Fossey leaned closer to Rachel and winked. "James has my vote in the upcoming election, by the way. And I predict he'll win it in a landslide. Don't you worry about what the mayor's trying to do with delaying the election. It won't amount to anything."

Hoping he was right, Rachel smiled.

Mr. Fossey straightened and gestured to the gentleman beside him. "Mrs. Boyd, may I present a somewhat ornery but most esteemed former colleague and friend of mine, for over thirty years now, Mr. Edward Westin of New York City."

147

Mr. Westin bowed slightly at the waist, his smile as kind-looking as she remembered. "A pleasure, Mrs. Boyd." His well-trimmed beard, dark but peppered with white, complemented his tailored gray suit. He angled a sideways nod. "I hope you don't believe everything this old geezer says."

Rachel laughed, catching the faintest Northern accent and managing an awkward curtsey. "The pleasure's mine, Mr. Westin. And not to worry, I know when to adhere to Mr. Fossey's counsel and when to dismiss it." She gave Mr. Fossey a knowing look. "I'm glad our paths have crossed for a second time, Mr. Westin, because I wanted to thank you for calming tempers at the Mullinses' store the other day. That was very kind of you."

"You're most welcome, ma'am. I didn't know what was happening at the time. I just sensed something was wrong. I hope Mr. Mullins is faring better after the—" He stopped short. His expression turned sheepish. "After the incident with his heart," he said more softly. "News travels fast in Timber Ridge, or so I've learned in recent days."

Rachel nodded. "That it does." While word had spread about Ben's heart failure, she was certain the details of his prognosis remained private. "Thank you for your concern. When I visited with the Mullinses yesterday, Mr. Mullins was feeling some better."

She'd taken Ben and Lyda dinner yesterday, and

Lyda had seemed in surprisingly good spirits, saying she thought Ben would be up and about in a couple of weeks. Rachel hadn't contradicted her, but she was certain Lyda was being overly optimistic. Either that, or Lyda wasn't aware of the seriousness of Ben's condition. Maybe Dr. Brookston hadn't informed them yet. But that seemed unlikely.

The mantel clock in Mr. Fossey's office chimed three times, and Rachel knew Mitchell and Kurt would be waiting for her at the schoolhouse— along with the young Miss Stafford. Another meeting she'd dreaded all weekend. "If you'll excuse me, gentlemen, I need to be on my way. Thank you again, Mr. Fossey. Pleasure to meet you, Mr. Westin."

Edward Westin tilted his head in acknowledgment. "For the *second* time, Mrs. Boyd."

Rachel arrived at the schoolhouse to find the grounds unusually quiet—and the schoolroom empty. No Mitchell. No Kurt. No Miss Stafford. She pulled Thomas's pocket watch from her reticule. It didn't make sense. Class was supposed to have dismissed only moments ago.

Sighing, she picked a careful path down the icy stairs to the wagon, mindful of her cane slipping on the snow. Perhaps the boys had gone to the jail to wait for her, either there or the store. Taking a deep breath, she gritted her teeth and climbed back into the wagon and up to the buckboard—when her right leg gave way beneath her.

The steady throb in her thigh turned white-hot, and she doubled over, her eyes clenched tight. Her body flushed hot, then cold. A light sweat broke out on her forehead.

Clutching her leg with one hand and the bench seat with the other, Rachel tried to breathe and prayed for the pain to pass.

10

"Have you experienced any more pain? Any tightness in your chest?" Rand eased down on the side of Ben's bed, stethoscope in hand.

Ben shook his head. "Nothing to complain about. Main thing is I just can't seem to catch my breath. Walking from here to there . . ." He pointed to the chamber pot in the corner and gave a frustrated sigh. "You'd think I'd walked a mile."

Nodding, Rand listened to his lungs, mindful of how closely the older man was watching him. "What about urination? You all right in that department?"

"No problem there, Doc." Ben chuckled. "But then, you said I had too much fluid in me."

Rand didn't even attempt to return the humor, and Ben's smile slowly faded. Rand glanced over his shoulder, making certain they were still alone. He kept his voice low. "Have you spoken with her yet?"

For the longest moment, Ben didn't answer. His gaze rested on the bedcovers. Finally, he shook his head. "I'm gettin' worse . . . aren't I?"

Rand fingered the stethoscope in his hand. "Yes . . . I'm sorry. The fluid continues to accumulate around your lungs." He sighed. "We don't know why, but it sometimes happens with people who have heart problems."

Ben took a labored breath, not all that deep, and gave it slow release. "All right, then . . ." Resolve deepened the lines of his face. He pushed himself up in the bed. "Let's do that surgery, Doc. Whatever it is you're wanting to do, as soon as you want to do it. But after that . . ." Finality settled heavy over his body, his shoulders bearing the brunt. "After that, I'm done. It's not that I don't trust you or that I don't respect all the things you learned from that fancy doctors' school back east. But I'm of the mind that a man does what he's able to, and then if God wants to step in and change things, He can. And if He chooses not to, well . . ." His eyes met Rand's. "Then I guess I'll be all right with that too."

Ben's tone was unmistakable. He preferred for God to step in, just as Rand did. What Rand needed Ben to know was that, as his physician, he planned on doing some stepping in himself. "I'll need an assistant for the surgery. If you're agreeable, I'll speak with Mrs. Boyd today about helping me."

"She's as good a nurse as they come."

"Better than most, actually," he said, rising and reaching for his bag. He was already anticipating what Rachel's response would be when she learned about the procedure. If she hadn't heard of external heart compression yet, he doubted she'd heard of the surgery he planned. Nor did he think she'd agree to help him without strong reservations.

Yet this surgery was his only chance of buying Ben a little more time.

He'd looked for her at church yesterday, but she wasn't there. Neither were the boys. He kept picturing her limping around the stall as she had on Friday morning. Remembering how she refused to let him examine her, he silently added *headstrong* to the woman's lengthening list of attributes.

"Before you go, Doc . . ." Wariness flitted across Ben's features. "Exactly how do you plan on gettin' this fluid out of me?"

Rand summoned his most confident and comforting expression. "I'll administer a topical anesthetic, so don't worry—you won't feel a thing."

Ben nailed him with a you-know-better-than-to-try-that-with-me look. "About the only time I ever worry is when a man doesn't give me a straight answer to a straight question."

"I'm sorry. You're right." Rand sat on the edge of the bed again. "For this particular procedure, the patient sits upright and leans on a table with their back exposed."

"You mean I'll be awake? I heard doctors give people bein' operated on something to make them go to sleep."

Rand smiled. "Yes, for some procedures, but not this one. The patient needs to be awake because it's imperative that they hold their breath for short periods of time so the lung isn't pierced. I'll clean the area on your back before inserting the needle."

"Needle?" Ben winced.

"You won't feel a thing, I promise. There will be very little discomfort. After inserting the needle, I'll draw out the—"

"Hang on there, Doc." Ben squeezed his eyes tight. His face lost some of its color. "You can stop right there. If you don't, I might just change my mind."

Rand smiled, and in a gesture that might have felt awkward before the past few days, he reached for Ben's hand. He gently gripped it as if the two of them were shaking on a deal. "I give you my word, Ben, I wouldn't perform this procedure if I didn't believe it will be successful . . . and that it will buy you more time. It'll give you some relief too, help you breathe easier." He held Ben's attention, wanting to reassure him, while also hoping his friend wouldn't ask him how many times he'd performed the surgery. "One more thing . . ."

Ben briefly squeezed his hand before letting go. "I know," he said softly. "I'll tell her."

Hearing his sincerity, Rand didn't press the issue.

"Can you do me a favor, Doc?" Ben pulled out an envelope tucked inside a book by his pillow. "Would you ask Charlie Daggett to run this out to a guest at the resort? It needs to get there this afternoon, if possible."

"I'll ask him on my way out." Rand tucked the envelope in his coat pocket, then checked the pouch of digitalis he'd given to Ben after his first episode. He frowned. Ben had been using it faster than he'd expected.

A ruckus outside the door portended rapid knocking, and before either he or Ben could respond, the door burst open.

Mitchell and Kurt Boyd raced into the room, breathless.

"I'm gettin' to Uncle Ben first!" Kurt yelled.

"But I get to check his heart. 'Cause I know how to do it and you don't!"

Rand jumped up and intercepted the boys at the foot of the bed. "Whoa there, fellas!" Arms outstretched, he secured them—one in each arm—surprised at how much stronger Kurt seemed than his older brother. "Didn't Aunt Lyda warn you to be quiet around Uncle Ben?"

Mitch nodded. "I'm sorry, Dr. Brookston."

Kurt blinked, cookie crumbs clinging to the edges of his mouth.

"Didn't she?" Rand repeated, directing the question solely at Kurt.

Kurt's glare held challenge—and deliberate calculation. "Yes, sir," he said quietly.

His stare steady, Rand waited.

"I'm sorry," the boy murmured, looking away.

Rand released them and gave Kurt's shoulder a quick pat. "You can visit for a few minutes, but do it quietly. And no bouncing on the bed."

He watched the boys approach the bed with fresh caution. Rachel Boyd sure had her hands full. How the woman could run a ranch and raise two sons . . . It tired him out just thinking about it. And yet . . .

He grabbed his bag and his coat, knowing better than to give in to the regret rising inside him. He'd chosen his path in life. His professors in medical school had been married, but it was different back east—civilized, more orderly, doctors had set schedules. He spent most of his days running from home to home, back and forth across Timber Ridge, up and down winding mountain trails caring for the ailing, at the townspeople's beck and call all hours of the day and night. Why he'd ever tried to gain Rachel Boyd's attention, he didn't know. Life was full of choices, and he'd made his long ago.

Still—his grip tightened on the leather handle—moments came when a man was forced to look at his life . . . and wonder.

He checked his pocket watch, needing to be on his way. He had an appointment with a patient this afternoon, and it was an appointment he was eager to keep.

Mitch reached for the older stethoscope Rand had left for him on the bedside table. One of the brass ear tubes was cracked, but with patience, a slight heartbeat could still be detected.

"Go ahead and check my heart, Mitch," Ben said. "See if it's still workin'. "

Mitch tossed Ben a smile but set about fulfilling the request. Kurt looked on, watching carefully. And Rand got the feeling that though Kurt sometimes appeared more detached, aloof, the boy was as attentive and as bright as his older brother.

Rand met Lyda on the way downstairs. "I was just coming down to see you, ma'am."

Lyda paused on a lower step, brushing a strand of hair from her forehead. Charlie Daggett was helping her in the store, but Rand could see the tension behind her smile. And he read the question in her eyes the second before she gave it voice.

"How is my husband doing, Dr. Brookston?" She peered up, eyes wide and trusting.

Rand had delivered painful news to family members before, but something about this situation felt different, and he'd promised Ben he could be the one to tell her. Yet the rugged hope in

Lyda's eyes made this conversation an even greater challenge. Had Ben even mentioned the possibility of surgery to Lyda yet? He doubted it. "He's not as well as I'd like for him to be, Lyda." He chose his words carefully. "There's a . . . *procedure* I can perform that will ease the pain he's experiencing and help him breathe easier." Which was true. It just wasn't the entire truth. "I'd like to proceed as soon as possible."

"A procedure?" She grimaced. "Have you spoken with Ben about it?"

He nodded.

"Did he say yes?"

He nodded a second time.

She looked down at her hand on the stair rail and fingered her wedding band. "Is it dangerous?" she whispered, looking up. The tears in her eyes made them appear even bluer.

"It's not without risk, Lyda. But I believe the benefits to your husband warrant the risks in this instance."

Her lips pressed together, Lyda nodded fragile acceptance. "All right, then. . . . We'll do whatever you think is best, Dr. Brookston."

He gave her hand a squeeze. How alike Ben and Lyda were, in their love and concern for each other, and in their faith and belief in him. Rand promised himself he would do his best not to let them down.

He only hoped God had the same plan.

• • •

After passing along the envelope, with Ben's request, to Charlie Daggett, Rand waited in line at the counter, wanting to see whether another shipment of medicine had arrived for him from Denver. He prayed it had, but chances were slim since he'd just received a shipment last week. His supply of digitalis was low. Dangerously so, with Ben's present condition.

The store was busy for a Monday afternoon. Patrons filled the aisles. Lyda had already arranged for extra help, and Jean Dickey, a woman who assisted them on occasion, caught Rand's eye as she boxed up items for another customer. "Dr. Brookston, what can I do for you, sir?"

"I need to see if another shipment arrived for me. From Denver, I hope. It'll be a box about this size." He gestured with his hands. "And the word *fragile* will be stamped on the side."

Nodding, she deposited the customer's money in the cash drawer, thanked him with a smile, and then searched the shelves beneath, and the ones behind. "It's not up front here, Dr. Brookston, but let me check in the storeroom for you."

"Thank you, Mrs. Dickey." Rand waited, purposefully standing to the side so as not to be in the way of browsing patrons.

"Have you been the doctor here in Timber Ridge for long, sir?"

Rand turned in the direction of the deep-timbered voice, having no trouble determining its owner. A mountain of a black man stood behind him. The man extended his hand, his white teeth brilliant against his dark complexion.

Rand shook his hand, feeling more the size of Mitch or Kurt by comparison. "I've been in Timber Ridge for about two years, but I've been practicing medicine for almost eight."

The man's smile spread wider, as if Rand had said something funny. "A doctor I knew, long time ago now, he used to tell his patients he 'practiced medicine,' and that he'd be practicin' the rest of his life because there was so much to learn."

Rand laughed. "I feel the very same way. No matter how much I learn, there's always more to—"

"I'm sorry, Dr. Brookston." Jean Dickey returned empty-handed. "But we haven't received another shipment yet."

Rand sighed. That meant no more digitalis. "Would you mind sending word the moment it arrives, Mrs. Dickey? It contains medicine I'm needing, and it's crucial I get it as soon as it comes in."

Thanking her, he nodded a brief good-bye to the man behind him and was nearly to the door when he heard someone call his name.

"Dr. Brookston . . ." The black man approached, his expression tentative. "I didn't mean to overhear just now. . . ." He took a step closer. "My name's Isaiah, sir. I don't know if I can be of any help to

159

you, but on the chance I can, I thought it best to say something. You're needing medicine?"

Rand studied him, then nodded, somewhat skeptical.

He followed Isaiah outside to a wagon loaded with furniture. On closer inspection, Rand found the furniture to be of highest quality, carved with painstaking detail and exacting craftsmanship. He admired an especially handsome cabinet, already imagining how well his instruments and supplies would fit inside. But he didn't have the funds. "Did you make all of this, Isaiah?"

"Yes, sir, over the past winter. My wife, Abby, and I"—he pointed to a dress shop across the street where Rand assumed his wife had disappeared into—"we've taken to traveling come spring. We've already sold a few things this trip. I was waiting to meet with Mrs. Mullins inside. Her husband and I exchanged letters some time back. Mr. Mullins, he told me he'd take some pieces for his store here. Said he thought they could sell them."

Rand laughed. "I'll say they could. Most of the furniture in this area is roughhewn from lodgepole pine. But this . . . You certainly have a gift."

"Thank you, sir." Isaiah reached inside the wagon and withdrew a pouch. "What I said inside, about the doctor . . . Doc Lewis was his name. He was a good man. I worked alongside him for years. He taught me about making poultices and remedies, showed me which herbs to pick and what they cured. I don't know what you're needing, but if I have it, it's yours."

Rand didn't know what to say, or whether he could even trust this man's claims. He wasn't very familiar with herbs native to this part of the country, but he knew digitalis when he saw it. "Foxglove is what I need, if you have any. It also goes by the name of—"

"Digitalis." Isaiah's gaze grew thoughtful. "Your patient has a weak heart." It wasn't a question. Isaiah pulled out a small envelope from within the pouch. "I don't have much, Dr. Brookston. But like I said, it's yours if you want it."

Rand peered inside the envelope, then took a tiny pinch and touched the tip of his tongue. He smiled, his skepticism melting away. This man was a godsend. "I'm happy to pay for this, Isaiah. If you'll come with me to my clinic, I'll—"

Isaiah shook his head. "Doc Lewis never charged one penny for all he taught me, so I don't take any money for the herbs." He grinned. "But if you're wantin' some furniture, I'm ready to bargain."

"I wish I could." Rand shook his hand, thanking God for bringing this man to this town, and at just the right time. He knew it was no coincidence. "Perhaps if you're back through here sometime in the future."

Isaiah nodded. "You can count on it, Doc."

• • •

Still smiling, and having replenished Ben's supply of medicine, Rand continued down the boardwalk, filling his lungs with the cold mountain air. Azure blue framed the snow-laden peaks soaring high above the town, while a late afternoon sun bathed them in an iridescent glow. Photographs of these mountains were exquisite but would never replace standing in their shadow. The camera's shades of gray didn't do justice to the brilliant colors of this land.

He pulled the collar of his coat closer about his neck and glanced down at the leather duster he wore. He'd never owned such a coat before, and never thought he would. But he had to admit— even though it was a tad roomy through the middle, he was growing accustomed to it.

He was almost back to his clinic when he spotted Brandon Tolliver rounding the corner at the far end of the street, headed his way. Not wanting to deal with the owner of the new resort and whatever it was he wanted, Rand ducked into the nearby bakery—and immediately wished he hadn't.

11

D r. Brookston! I've been looking for you." Judith Stafford closed the distance between them, gloved hand outstretched. "In fact, I just left your clinic."

"Miss Stafford." Rand took brief hold of her hand while managing a discreet step backward. "What a surprise."

"Indeed! And a pleasant one at that." Her soft laughter bubbled over. "I left word for you with . . ." She frowned as though trying to remember something.

"Angelo?" Rand supplied, guessing the reason for her hesitancy.

"Yes." She smiled. "I left word with Angelo that I needed to see you."

"You're not ill, I trust."

"No, I'm quite well. Thank you for asking." Her eyes lit. "I stopped by your clinic because I'm concerned about two of my students—Benjamin and Paige Foster. They started coughing this morning and only worsened as the day went on. When I checked their foreheads this afternoon, they were both warm to the touch." Her brows arched. "Knowing how swiftly sickness can spread, I thought it wise to dismiss a little early and . . . let you know about it."

Catching the subtle change in her tone, Rand wished he'd made that small step backward a bit larger. As for the Foster siblings being ill, he knew most childhood fevers simply ran their course. But to be safe, he still wanted to examine the children. "Do you know if Benjamin and Paige went straight home?"

"I instructed them to do just that."

"Thank you, Miss Stafford, for being so conscientious. I'll call on the family this evening." With a nod, he turned. But a touch on his arm drew him back.

"Perhaps you'd like for me to accompany you, Dr. Brookston? As the children's teacher, I feel an obligation as well as a responsibility to—"

"That won't be necessary, Miss Stafford. But thank you just the same."

Disappointment clouded her expression. Her gaze lowered.

Realizing he'd come across as abrupt, Rand searched for something to say that would soften the rejection. He didn't want to encourage Miss Stafford's attentiveness, yet he didn't want to be rude.

Mindful of other patrons in the bakery, he kept his voice low. "I appreciate your offer, but I wouldn't want to risk *your* health, Miss Stafford . . . in the event that what the children have is infectious."

Her features sharpened with concern, then smoothed as she exhaled a delicate sigh. "How thoughtful of you, Doctor." She stepped closer. "While at your office earlier, I happened to see you've been enjoying the treat I left for you."

Her voice took on a singsong quality that might have sounded sweet, even delightful, if his feelings for her were of a more tender nature. As it was, he found himself wishing he'd let Brandon Tolliver get ahold of him instead. "Yes . . . the cookies. Thank you, ma'am. They were delicious. As always."

"And they're your favorites."

Nodding, he didn't have the heart to tell her he'd only eaten one. Angelo and his sisters had polished off the rest.

"And . . . did you read my note?"

He swallowed. "Ah . . . yes, I did. Your sentiments were most . . . enlightening." Enlightening hardly described them. What she'd written . . . He grew uncomfortable again just thinking about it.

Since moving to Timber Ridge, Judith Stafford had made no attempt to hide her interest in him, which was flattering in one sense. She was a bright, attractive woman. Intelligent, capable, well thought of in the community, and, from all accounts, a gifted teacher. She possessed many admirable qualities. The problem was, he simply didn't return her . . .

The irony of his next thought stopped him cold.

Was *this* how Rachel Boyd felt about him? The realization stung, and put things into perspective for him with sharp-edged—and deflating—clarity. Eager to leave now more than ever, he made a show of checking his pocket watch. "If you'll excuse me, Miss Stafford, I have an appointment to keep. I appreciate your concern and dedication to your students, and I'll call on the Fosters later this—"

The young teacher glanced past him out the front window, frowning. At the same time, Rand heard someone calling his name. He turned to see a crowd gathering in the street, and when he spotted the man who was yelling for him, he rushed outside to the boardwalk. "Deputy!"

Deputy Willis searched the boardwalk, his focus quickly finding its mark. "Dr. Brookston! Sheriff needs you at the jail right away!"

Rand set out behind the deputy, running to keep up, his thoughts darting to the recent saloon shooting, then to the fatal coal mine explosion a month ago in which three miners were killed when an open flame ignited a pocket of flammable gas. The explosion brought the tunnel down.

Winded from the run, Rand reached the stairs to the sheriff's office two strides behind the deputy and followed him inside.

James McPherson met them at the door that led to the cells in the back. Concern weighted his expression. "It's Rachel," he said, and gestured for him to follow.

Rand rounded the corner and saw her lying on a cot in the first jail cell. She shivered despite the coat she wore, and her eyes were clenched tight. "What happened?" he breathed, then saw how she was clutching her leg.

"She's hurting something awful where the heifer kicked her the other day." McPherson nodded toward the deputy. "Thanks, Willis, for finding him for me." McPherson waited until the young deputy returned to the front office and closed the door behind him. "I told her to come see you, Doc." He bent and caressed the crown of his sister's head. "But she thought it was just a bruise. She showed up here about ten minutes ago, all but passed out in the wagon."

Rachel's eyelids fluttered open. She started to rise. "I need to find the boys. . . ."

Rand gently touched her shoulder. "Your sons are fine, Mrs. Boyd." He deposited his bag on the floor and shrugged off his duster. "They're at the store with Ben and Lyda. I just left them." He draped the long coat over Rachel's body, and her eyes slipped closed.

She shuddered. "Th-thank you. . . ."

Outside the row of empty jail cells, at the far end of the hallway, Rand spotted a potbellied stove. "Can you get a fire going, Sheriff? We could use a little warmth in here."

"Consider it done, Doc."

Rand pressed the palm of his hand against Rachel's forehead—she felt warm.

"Your hand is cold," she whispered.

"I'm sorry."

"No . . ." She shook her head, her chin quivering. "It feels good."

He cupped her face and smiled when the gesture earned him a grateful sigh. "How long has your leg been hurting?"

She swallowed. "Since it happened, but . . . it's gotten worse today."

Rachel Boyd . . . He shook his head to himself, remembering the copy of *The Handy-Book of Husbandry* he'd seen in the barn stall the morning he'd delivered Lady's calf. His estimation of her had only risen over time, especially in the past few days as he'd seen her interact with Ben and Lyda, and had spent more time in her company. But he wondered . . . Had she been this determined and willful before her husband died? Or was this part of how she'd learned to cope? To survive without him?

No question, she was a Southern woman through and through, and like a lot of Southern women, when push came to shove, she had a will of iron that cut straight through the sugar and sweetness. As his mother might have said, and proudly so, "She's a woman to be reckoned with, son." Rand sighed. What he wouldn't do to have Rachel Boyd be open to a little *reckoning* with him.

His next question was absurd, but propriety demanded he ask. "Would you permit me to examine your injury, Mrs. Boyd?"

She looked up at him. "Yes, but . . ." She briefly glanced away. "I'm . . . wearing stockings."

It took him a moment to understand what she was implying. She would need to remove her stockings in order for him to examine her—he glanced around—and a jail cell hardly afforded the privacy they needed.

Sheriff McPherson returned with an armful of wood, and Rand met him in the hallway and explained the situation, knowing Rachel would feel more comfortable with her brother carrying her than him. "So if you could help me move her to the clinic, Sheriff, I'd be obliged."

Fifteen minutes later, James McPherson carried his sister into the clinic, and Rand directed him toward his bedroom as he retrieved a bottle and cup from the medicine shelf. James lowered her to the bed and Rachel sat down on the mattress.

Rand poured and held the cup to her lips. "It's laudanum."

She accepted without hesitance but made a slight face.

Rand commiserated. "Wish I could make it taste better." He raised the cup again, but she turned away. "It will help ease the pain," he encouraged. "I think you'll be glad you took it."

She shook her head, frowning. "I'll be fine."

Believing differently, he placed the bottle and cup aside. "Do you need help removing your undergarments?"

"No." She glanced back at the bed. "May I lie down here?"

He'd planned on moving her to the examination table in the front room, where it was warmer, but this would do. "Yes, that'll be fine. Whatever is easiest for you."

She started unbuttoning her coat.

He motioned James toward the door and followed, pausing before he pulled it closed. "Would you like your brother to be present during the examination? He's welcome to stay."

"No, that's all right," she whispered, then looked at James. "But if you could get Mitch and Kurt from the store, and get my wagon from your office, I'd appreciate it."

Her brother gave a mock salute. "Molly will take care of the boys. Don't you worry about a thing."

After James left, Rand stoked the fire in the hearth before retrieving the instruments he anticipated needing. He spotted the note Angelo had left him about Miss Stafford on the desk, which jarred another recollection loose—his appointment. He glanced at the clock on the—

A knock sounded on the door.

What timing. . . . He balanced the syringe, bandages, and fresh towels in the crook of his arm, mindful of the scalpel in his grip, and answered the door.

"Dr. Brookston, I'm sorry I'm late." Elizabeth Ranslett attempted to cover an anxious expression with a smile, as did her husband behind her, but Rand knew them well enough to recognize the look of contrived hope. She glanced back at

Daniel. "I hope you don't mind me bringing a friend this time."

Rand smiled. "Not at all, Elizabeth." He nodded to Daniel. "Ranslett, it's good to see you again. Come on in. That goes for Beau too."

"Thanks, Doc." Daniel snapped his fingers at the dog by his side, and the aging beagle trotted through the door and over to the hearth, where he sank down on the rug, eyes doleful but obedient.

Rand noticed Elizabeth eying the scalpel in his hand and hastened to reassure her. "These aren't for your visit today, Elizabeth." He indicated the bedroom door with a nod, fairly confident about the idea just now forming. "I have another patient here, and I'm—"

"Do we need to come back later?" she asked.

"Not at all. In fact . . . your timing is impeccable."

12

Rachel eased back onto the bed and positioned her skirt over her legs and bare feet, then drew the blanket up to her waist. Her petticoats, woolen stockings, and drawers lay draped over a chair, tucked from sight beneath her coat. She turned onto her side, gritting her teeth to stifle a groan. While the bruise still ached, what was more worrisome was the patch of darker skin that had formed toward the center. It tingled in a painful way, like when her foot fell asleep.

With no hearth in this room, the air was chilled. Grimacing, she scooted over on the bed to take advantage of a sliver of sunshine falling across the covers. She yawned, feeling the effects of the laudanum, grateful to know Mitch and Kurt were with James and Molly.

She stared at the bottle of laudanum turning a tawny gold in the yellow light. The medicine Rand had given her had taken the edge off the pain. A second dose would have caused her to sleep, which she didn't want. She intended to be awake for the examination.

Stacks of books, sitting floor to waist high, lined one of the walls of the bedroom. All medical volumes from what she could see, and all well tabbed with notes sticking out here and there. She had no doubt Rand had read them all. At least twice. He'd graduated from the College of Physicians in Philadelphia with highest honors. She'd done some checking on him when he'd first moved to town. It helped having a sheriff for a brother. The college was prestigious, and according to what she'd read, its graduates went on to occupy top positions in hospitals back east. Yet Rand had left all that to come west.

A rap on the door. "Rachel?"

Surprised at the feminine voice, Rachel lifted her head as the door creaked open. "Elizabeth! What are you doing here?"

Her friend stepped inside and closed the door.

"I've got an appointment with Dr. Brookston this afternoon." She reached for Rachel's hand, her tentative smile thinning. "He just told us about what happened with the heifer. I'm so sorry."

Rachel's focus moved past her. Told *us?*

Elizabeth nodded, her gaze discerning. "Daniel's here. He insisted on coming with me today." A series of emotions flitted across her face—longing, anticipation . . . fear. "We're hoping Dr. Brookston gives us good news this time."

Rachel squeezed her friend's hand tight, ashamed for dreading the possibility of seeing Daniel when Elizabeth was struggling with such disappointment. And it was a disappointment she understood. After marrying Thomas, it had taken her two years to conceive the first time, and another two years until the second. "I've been thinking of you, Lizzie . . . and praying. I hope it *is* good news today."

Tears rose in Elizabeth's eyes. "Daniel says it doesn't matter to him." She gave a fragile laugh. "He says that Beau and I are enough."

Rachel smiled when thinking of Daniel's dog, remembering when Daniel had gotten Beau as a pup, many years ago, back in Tennessee. They'd kidded then that the beagle would never grow into his ears. She couldn't recall how old the dog was now, but those days seemed like another lifetime.

Elizabeth's smile faded. "Daniel's concerned

about you too, Rachel. He asked if there was anything he could do. Anything at all."

Seeing the tender plea in Elizabeth's face, hearing it in her voice, Rachel felt an unexpected rush of emotion. Though she could hardly admit it to herself, a part of her *did* miss Daniel. Most of her life, he'd been like a brother to her. Thomas had loved him from the start too, despite Daniel giving him such a hard time when Thomas sought to court her. But how could she forgive Daniel's negligence? The events he'd set into motion—however unknowingly, if what James had said to her recently was true. Maybe one day in the future she would be able to look at him and not see Thomas lying there in the woods, his body bloodied and—

Rachel took a steadying breath. "Don't you worry about me. I'll be fine. Tell me about you . . . and your situation."

The gentle rise of Elizabeth's brow said she wasn't fooled in the slightest by Rachel's all-too-obvious attempt to change the subject, but her sigh said she wouldn't press the issue. For the moment, at least.

"Daniel wants a child, Rachel. I know he does. He wants one as much as I do. And Dr. Brookston has been wonderful. He gave me some herbs, and I've been taking them for the past few months." She lifted a shoulder and let it fall. "Maybe those have helped. I hope so, because—" she blew out a breath—"I'm not getting any younger."

Rachel shifted to look intently into Elizabeth's tear-filled eyes. "Don't you worry one minute about age. You're still plenty young. It will happen, in time. It *will*." But even as she said it, Rachel knew in her heart that, however well intentioned, her words might not be true. She saw in Lizzie's eyes that she was thinking the very same thing. It wasn't that God lacked the power to bless her friend's womb. The question was whether it was His will to do so. That was one of the risky things about faith—laying your heart's desires before the Lord while also surrendering your will to His. Wanting what you wanted, yet wanting what He wanted for you . . . even more.

"Mrs. Boyd?"

Hearing Rand's voice from the other side of the door, Rachel gave Elizabeth's hand one last squeeze. "Will you stay with me? While he examines my leg?"

"Of course." Elizabeth smiled. "He already asked me if I would."

Rand entered and closed the door behind him, and the first thing Rachel spotted was the scalpel in his hand. She pointed. "What's *that* for?"

His expression was the epitome of trustworthiness—and placation. "It's simply precautionary. I like to anticipate what we may need before we need it."

Her trust level slipped a notch. How many times had her father used a similar explanation as she'd stood beside him assisting a trusting—but soon to be unpleasantly surprised—patient? Yet she could feel Elizabeth watching her and didn't want to appear nervous or frightened, which she was.

Lying on her side, facing Elizabeth, Rachel heard Rand arranging instruments on a table behind her and tried not to imagine what the rest of those items might be, or how he planned on using them. While she had a deep appreciation for the field of medicine, being on the receiving end of a doctor's services had never been her preference.

Rand touched her ankle and her entire body tensed. His grip was warm and confident.

"Mrs. Boyd," he said, his voice reassuring, "where exactly is the injury located?"

"On my . . ." Rachel swallowed, keenly aware of his hand on her leg, and of the discomfort tightening her throat. "On my thigh. Here . . ." She touched the spot on the blanket that covered her bruise.

He pulled aside the blanket and eased her skirt up, barely touching her, taking obvious care not to reveal more than necessary, yet her anxiety escalated as the fabric rose. She closed her eyes, trying to reason her way through the haze of emotions. Rand Brookston was a physician. He was examining her. That was all. She'd been to doctors before. For heaven's sake, her father had been a doctor! There was no reason for the disquiet she felt. It was unreasonable, unwarranted. Yet the tightness in her throat said otherwise.

And she gradually realized why.

Thomas was the only man who had ever touched her in an intimate way, and it was *his* touch she remembered, that she wanted to remember. The tenderness in his hands, the safety of his arms, the closeness they'd shared after twelve years of marriage, the familiarity after having known him for the better half of her life. Rand Brookston was a doctor who was examining a wound. He was doing his job. That was all. She knew that. But, however unknowingly, however little sense it made, even to her, he was encroaching upon a memory, upon a precious part of her life that she preferred to keep—

Pressure on her upper thigh sent stabbing pain into her hip and down through her leg, piercing hot. Gasping, she instinctively shielded the place on her leg, her vision swimming.

A hand cradled the top of her head, much like James might have done if he were there. She looked up and Rand's face came into view.

"I'm so sorry, Mrs. Boyd." Compassion weighed his gaze. "I know this is painful, but the bruising on your leg is extensive. Can you move your toes for me?" He reached down to gently squeeze her right foot.

She tried and winced. "I can't." She took a quick breath. "It hurts too much."

"Do you feel any tingling or numbness? In your foot or your leg?"

"Yes," she whispered, both comforted—and not—that he knew the right questions to ask.

His expression held a depth of empathy. "I need to be certain the femur isn't broken, and then determine whether blood is still flowing to all areas of the wound. If it's not, I'll need to remedy that."

She closed her eyes, dreading the pain. She was certain the bone wasn't broken. At least she thought she was. But his other comment gave her pause. Her gaze moved to the instruments on the table. "The scalpel?" she guessed, catching Lizzie's pained expression as her friend stared, wide-eyed, at her leg.

He nodded. "I'll work as quickly, and as gently, as I can."

He straightened, and Rachel took a deep breath, wishing now that she'd accepted more laudanum when he'd offered. She could request another dose and had no doubt he would give it to her. But the thought of doing that made her feel indecisive and weak, and she was beyond weary of feeling that way. And especially didn't want to appear that way to him.

She slid a hand under the pillow beneath her head, gripping it tightly and bracing herself for what was coming. The pillow was soft against her cheek, and she caught a whiff of bayberry and spice. For weeks following Thomas's passing, she'd slept with his pillow, relishing his scent, imagining he was still there beside her in the darkness.

And then one night, she'd reached for his pillow and the scent was gone. She'd cried herself to sleep. Again.

The distinctive *tink* of glass on metal brought her eyes open.

Rand knelt before her, cup in hand. Searching his face, she rose up on one elbow, not seeing the slightest trace of "I told you so" in his discerning gray eyes. He held the cup to her lips and she briefly covered his hand with hers, drinking every last drop.

She awakened some time later in her own bed, surprised to see the light of a fully risen sun filtering through the bedroom curtains. Her back muscles sore, Rachel slowly shifted positions, preparing herself for the pain. But to her surprise, her thigh, while achy and sore, didn't hurt nearly as much as before.

The hot, pulsing sensation was gone.

Pillows cushioned her right calf, elevating the leg. Bracing herself—just in case—she wiggled her toes . . . without wanting to scream in pain! She sighed. Rand Brookston was a gifted physician and surgeon.

Though memories following the second dose of

laudanum were sketchy, she recalled snippets of the freezing ride home from the clinic. The merciless bumps and jolts over rutted trails in the back of the wagon, and the jagged outline of mountain peaks against a star-studded sky. She swallowed, her mouth like cotton, and experienced yet another vivid recollection.

The bitter, blissful aftertaste of laudanum.

She fingered the bulk of bandages enwrapping her thigh, thankful to have been spared the memory of the procedure Rand had performed. She vaguely remembered awakening to see him standing over her in the clinic, his face shifting in and out of focus, as had most of what he'd said to her.

Her leg wasn't in a splint, so it wasn't broken. And she did remember the word *incision,* so she knew he'd used the scalpel, which meant sutures. But this wasn't the first time she'd been sutured. She knew what to expect.

He'd also mentioned something about bed rest—which sounded good to her, at least for the morning, once she checked on the boys. She looked around the room for her cane but didn't see it. She'd been blessed with a high threshold for pain. She knew her limits and wouldn't risk overtaxing herself, but time to rest was a luxury she didn't have. Not with the ranch in its current state and young boys to raise.

With deliberate, measured movements, she

scooted to the side of the bed and gently eased her legs over the edge, careful of the bandage. A slow, steady throb began in her thigh, reminiscent of yesterday's pain. The more she moved, the harder the pounding became. Light-headed, she gripped the headboard for support.

Walking could be more challenging than she'd thought. . . .

Footsteps came from the hallway, and she peered past the partially open bedroom door, expecting Mitch or Kurt to come running in.

"I know, I feel that way too," a voice whispered, followed by soft, stuttered sobs. "I'd just spent so much time h-hoping—"

Elizabeth.

Unable to make out the remainder of what she said, Rachel felt her chest clench tight. Rand must have given her and Daniel more disappointing news. She ran a hand over her abdomen, hurting for her friend and remembering what it felt like to carry a life inside her, to feel that child growing and moving. She and Thomas had hoped for more children, but two healthy sons . . . That was a lot to be thankful for. Especially now.

The door edged open with a squeak, and Elizabeth paused at the threshold. Her eyes went wide. "Rachel Boyd! What do you think you're doing? Dr. Brookston gave express orders for you to rest! He said you shouldn't be out of bed."

Rachel gave her a weak smile, touched by her

protective nature. Even from several feet away, she saw Lizzie's red-rimmed eyes and knew she'd guessed correctly about the discouraging news. "I'm so sorry, Lizzie," she whispered, nodding toward the hallway. "I couldn't help but overhear just now."

Lizzie's features clouded.

Rachel motioned for her to come in and reached for her hand, eager to reassure her. "I don't know what Dr. Brookston told you, but contrary to what some people think, doctors aren't infallible. And they don't know everything. The body has ways of healing itself . . . I know. It took two years for me to conceive the first time with Mitch. Though, granted, it seemed like an eternity at the time, praying and waiting."

Lizzie seated herself on the bed and looked down at the quilt, fingering the patchwork pieces Rachel had sewn from Thomas's shirts following his death. "It *has* felt like we've been waiting for a long time, I admit. I'm sorry if I sounded like I was complaining yesterday."

"You've never sounded that way to me. Ever."

"I'm glad, because . . . according to Dr. Brookston"—a smile blossomed on Lizzie's pretty face—"we've been patient long enough. Come December or January, Daniel and I will be having a child."

Rachel stared. Her gaze flitted to where Lizzie rested her hand on her stomach, and she let out a squeal. Rachel hugged her tight, imagining all that lay in store, and so grateful this woman had come into her life. The first time she'd seen Lizzie, almost two years ago—Elizabeth *Westbrook,* at the time—standing in the general store, looking so confident and businesslike, she'd been drawn to her. Yet she'd doubted whether such an educated, successful woman would view friendship with her as something worthy of pursuit.

But despite being opposites in many ways—and holding such differing opinions of Daniel—she and Elizabeth had fast become friends.

Rachel gave her arm a squeeze. "You're going to make a wonderful mother."

Elizabeth rolled her eyes. "I'm afraid that remains to be seen. I can't even get children to sit still for a photograph."

Rachel waved off the comment. "You'll do just fine. You'll see."

Smiling, Elizabeth rose. "Thank you. Now, we need to get you back to bed and get that leg elevated. Doctor's orders!"

Ignoring the gentle admonishment, Rachel glanced toward the hallway. "Speaking of children, I guess mine are in school?"

Elizabeth's expression turned questioning. "You don't remember our conversation earlier this morning?"

Rachel cast a playful glance at the bottle of laudanum on the bedside table, and Lizzie cocked

183

her head as though to say she understood. Then her humor faded.

"Mitch and Kurt didn't go to school today, Rachel. None of the children did. Yesterday, Benjamin and Paige Foster came down with fever, so Miss Stafford dismissed classes early. Late last night, after seeing you home and settled, Dr. Brookston rode out to check on them."

Rand was here? That was another detail Rachel didn't recall. "How are the Fosters' children? Have you heard anything?"

Lizzie hesitated, as though reluctant to voice her thoughts. "Charlie Daggett came from town a few minutes ago. And, mind you, this is just a rumor. He hasn't seen Dr. Brookston yet to confirm it. But . . . Charlie told me that folks are saying it's influenza."

13

Rand smoothed the hair from Paige Foster's forehead, feeling heat radiate from her skin. Severe headache, muscle pain, malaise. Similar symptoms to influenza but with two major differences in this case—the intestinal ravages on the body and the rose-colored spots dotting the upper abdomen.

Fairly confident in his diagnosis, Rand knew there was only one way to be certain.

Ten-year-old Paige was in worse condition than

her older brother, who lay sleeping on a pallet in the corner of the bedroom. She was lithe and fragile, and had a sweet disposition to match.

She drew in labored breaths through parched lips. Her eyes fluttered open. It took a moment for her to focus. "Thank you . . . Dr. Brookston," she whispered, her fingers tightening around the piece of stick candy.

"You're welcome, sweetie. There's more where that came from as soon as you're feeling better." He checked her pulse. Slightly elevated, but that was to be expected with the high fever.

He heard Mrs. Foster in the next room, preparing soup her daughter hadn't requested, nor that she would likely eat. Not in her current condition.

The hour had to be approaching noon. His jacket lay across the room with his pocket watch tucked inside, but he was too tired to retrieve it.

Rand sank down in a chair by the bed and rested his head in his hands. He'd been up most of the night and needed to get back to town to check on Ben and Rachel, and whoever—and whatever—else might be waiting for him at the clinic.

He stared at the little girl in the bed before him, considering the labored rise and fall of her chest, and wishing he had better facilities in which to care for his patients, more reliable methods for receiving medications. And—the greatest luxury of all—more opportunity to educate the people of Timber Ridge about proper hygiene and nutrition.

The weight of responsibility he'd felt when crouching over Ben Mullins, trying to get Ben's heart restarted, returned with a force that sucked his breath away and pulled him back to a moment years past.

"You care too much about your patients, Dr. Brookston," the head of medicine at a New York City hospital had admonished. "You must learn to keep a proper distance, emotionally. You must view patients through the framework of science, learning all you can during the course of treatment and then building on that knowledge for future patients. We want to encourage when needed, comfort as we can. But you'll never grow to be the physician I know you can be—that I already see in you—if you persist in caring about them in such a personal manner."

Rand exhaled, knowing that if Dr. Bellingham could see him now, he would not approve—just as the venerated physician hadn't approved of the choices Rand had made following medical school, or of his decision to come to Timber Ridge.

He ran a hand through his hair, hoping Rachel would follow his orders of complete bed rest. His conveniently "forgetting" to send her cane home with her would greatly increase those odds. It was imperative she stay off that leg for three to four days, at a minimum, in order to give the incision time to heal, as he'd explained to her last night.

Her wound was more serious than she'd let on, and the sutures more invasive than he'd originally thought they would be.

But there was another reason she needed to heal quickly, one she didn't even know about yet—he needed her assistance with Ben's surgery.

Pulling his thoughts back, Rand probed the slender column of Paige's throat. "Tell me if I press on a place that hurts worse than the others, all right?"

She nodded.

He palpated the back of her neck and shoulders, then checked her arms and legs. The rash hadn't spread, not yet, at least. Hoping to coax a smile, he gave her cute little button nose a tweak. "How about there?"

She sighed a tired giggle.

Anticipating her next reaction and already regretting it, Rand pressed on her belly, under her rib cage, and literally felt the confirmation to his diagnosis.

Paige let out a gasp and drew up her legs. "That hurts bad," she whimpered, tears edging from the corners of her eyes.

"I'm sorry, honey." Rand cradled the side of her face, so small and warm against his palm. "I won't do it again." He didn't need to. He'd seen the symptoms before, and seeing them again dredged up memories he preferred remain buried.

Unsummoned, haunting images of Confederate

camps returned, one after another. The rows of filthy tents, tattered and beaten down, like their occupants. All these years later, the memory of the stench was still thick—the grounds littered with refuse and rubbish, heaps of manure and offal only steps away from where the men slept. For every grave he'd dug for a fellow soldier struck down by bullets, he'd dug three more for one struck by disease.

Typhoid being among the most devastating.

The bedroom door opened behind him, and heavy boot steps rang hollow on the wood floor. They stopped abruptly at his back.

"I need a word with you, Brookston."

Rand turned and adjusted his gaze slightly upward to meet the solemn stare of Graham Foster, Paige's father.

"Look, Papa . . ." Paige held out her hand, the candy sticky in her palm. "See what Dr. Brookston gave me?"

Graham Foster's gruff demeanor softened ever so slightly. "That's real good, darlin'. " He patted his daughter's arm as though he feared she might break. "I'll be right back. I just need to talk with the doctor for a minute, all right?"

She looked from him to Rand, her uncertainty clear.

Foster inclined his head toward the hallway and Rand followed, surprised when Foster strode through the kitchen and toward the front porch.

Helen Foster stood by the stove, watching as they passed.

Once outside, Foster stopped short. "Just so we're clear, Brookston"—he stood close—"my wife believes in doctors . . . I don't. If it weren't for her, you wouldn't be here." A bead of sweat trailed down Foster's forehead and into his eye. He didn't blink. "All doctors are good for is promisin' things they can't deliver. They feed you full of their concoctions with one hand, while robbin' your pockets with the other." He moved closer. Rand felt the heat of his anger. And fear. "I won't have you fillin' my wife's head with notions that aren't true. I've seen this sickness before." He swallowed, his eyes hardening. "I know what it does."

Rand stood his ground, sharing the man's fear, though unable to show it. "I've seen it too, Mr. Foster. I know how to treat it and I know how it spreads. And I'm not going to give you false hope. I believe your son will be fine, but your . . ." Rand saw the glisten of emotion rise in Foster's eyes. "But Paige," he continued, voice soft, "is very ill. Still, I'll do everything I can for her, and you don't need to pay me a thing."

An hour later, Rand guided his mare down the mountain trail leading from the Fosters' cabin into town, feeling the weight of Graham Foster's love for his family, and also of his distrust. Rand intended to do everything he could to earn the man's confidence but feared that might not be possible in this case.

He rode on, intending to check on Ben first and then stop by the sheriff's office to see McPherson—to let him know about the typhoid fever. But as he neared the main thoroughfare, he heard a low thrum, like the sound of water rushing over rocks. And when he rounded the corner, he reined in sharp.

A horde of people surged in and out of the Mullinses' store, pushing and shoving their way across the crowded boardwalk. Guiding his horse through the fray, Rand spotted Lyda standing in the doorway of the store, her back to the street, arms outstretched.

People rushed past her, their arms loaded with goods.

A burly, unkempt-looking man—a miner, judging by his coat and dungarees—exited the store, holding as much as he could carry. Lyda attempted to stop him, and Rand watched in disbelief as the man shoved her back, nearly knocking her off her feet.

Rand leapt from his horse, keeping Lyda in his focus. She somehow gained her balance and pursued the man, grabbing hold of his shirtsleeve. "You need to pay for those!"

The man shrugged her off again, and Lyda would have fallen if a gentleman hadn't come to her aid.

Rand headed straight for the miner, cutting a path through the human maze.

Rifle shots shattered the chaos, and Rand came to a skidding halt. As did everyone else. The blasts thundered off the mountain range and echoed back across town. People turned in all directions, searching the street, clinging to what they held.

"Everybody stay right where you are!" James McPherson stepped to the boardwalk, rifle in one hand, the other resting on the pistol holstered at his hip. His gaze moved to the miner who'd strode past Lyda, and the aim of his rifle followed suit.

Rand felt the heat of McPherson's indignation from where he stood.

Apparently the miner did too, because the man shifted the items in his arms, looking decidedly less belligerent than moments before. "I told that woman there"—the miner nodded toward Lyda— "to put this on my credit."

McPherson looked at Lyda, who shook her head.

McPherson cocked the rifle. "The lady says that's not the way of it, friend. So why don't you head on back in there and settle up with her. Then you and I can settle our account over at the jail."

"But, Sheriff," another man said, "we heard about the influenza. We need these supplies!"

A young woman moved closer, baby on one hip, a sack of flour on the other. "Once people start gettin' sick, Sheriff, the stages won't come through. How are we supposed to feed our—"

Rand stepped forward. "It's *not* influenza!"

James's attention shot to him, and his eyes narrowed as if he wished he knew what Rand was about to say. Then he gave a subtle nod.

Rand stepped to the boardwalk alongside James. "It's not influenza," he repeated, "and there's no need to panic. There *is* need for precaution, however—"

A restless murmur rose from the crowd.

Seeing the opportunity, Rand raised an arm. "How many of you are sick right now? Right this minute. Raise your hand." People scanned those gathered, then gradually traced a visual path back to him. No one lifted their hand. "The truth is"— he lowered his arm—"none of you are sick. And the odds are *great* that none of you will get sick. *If* we'll all take some simple precautions."

The man who'd spoken earlier scoffed. "I heard the Fosters' two kids came down with fever and chills. If it's not influenza, then what is it?"

Rand thought fast. How to admit the truth without inciting panic? Everyone knew the devastation typhoid fever could bring, but few understood what caused it. Even Paige Foster's mother had taken a step back when Rand told her, her expression defensive, as if he'd accused her of giving the disease to her children herself. Having learned from his experience with Mrs. Foster, he hoped a more subtle approach would work better. "How many of you wash your hands each time before you eat?" The comment was met with blank stares. "What about washing your food before you cook it? And the water you drink . . . Would you be willing to boil it to make sure it's clean?"

"I been gettin' my water from the stream for years," an older woman said. "Never had to boil it before."

"And you won't have to always boil it in the future. But for now, I'm asking you to do these things. It will help prevent you and your families from becoming ill." He read confusion in some faces, skepticism in others, and still borderline panic in a few, and chose his words carefully. "I've seen typhoid before—"

A collective gasp rose from the crowd.

"Listen to me." Rand raised his voice. "I've seen typhoid firsthand, many times, just like you have. We know what can happen. But it doesn't *have* to happen here in Timber Ridge. Once you know what causes typhoid, it's easier to stop it from spreading." He felt a ripple through the crowd and willed a calm to his manner that would somehow ease the air of uncertainty. "The most common way in which people contract typhoid fever is by eating food and drinking water that's been contaminated with human feces."

As he expected, looks of disgust replaced those of fear and worry.

He turned his attention to the man responsible for most of the instigating. "I just came from the

Fosters' home. Their son, Benjamin, is already showing improvement. He contracted a much milder case. But the Fosters' daughter, Paige . . ." His throat tightened remembering how small and weak Paige looked, and how brave a girl she was. "She's very sick. She's fighting hard and needs our prayers, but those are the only two cases that have been reported. And hopefully, if we all work together, there won't be any more."

The woman with the baby on her hip raised her hand. "What about the milk we give our children? Do we need to boil that too?"

Another woman spoke up. "And what about the meat we get from the butcher? Has that been washed?"

More questions followed, one atop the other, and Rand raised his hand, feeling a gratitude for the people of Timber Ridge that he hadn't before. He also sensed the sheriff wanting to say something. "I'll answer any and all questions that you have . . . after Sheriff McPherson is done."

Gratitude shone in James McPherson's expression. "The sheriff's office will work alongside Dr. Brookston to get the information out to everyone. We'll ask Mrs. Ranslett at the newspaper to print a special edition first thing tomorrow morning with the doctor's instructions on what to do." He briefly looked at Rand, who nodded his agreement.

"But for now . . ." McPherson's focus shifted

back to the miner still in his aim. "To those of you who haven't paid for what you took from Ben and Lyda's store . . . and we all know who you are." He leveled his gaze. "Either pay up, or my deputies and I will be paying you a visit."

Being a student of human nature as well as science, Rand found it easy to distinguish the guilty parties. Patrons who were innocent looked directly at Lyda. Those who weren't either studied the ground or the items they'd stolen.

Rand stayed after and answered everyone's questions, feeling a renewed sense of why God had directed him to Timber Ridge. As he was leaving, he saw Mathias Tucker pull up in a wagon. Concern on the man's face portended ill news, and Rand met him in the street.

Tucker motioned. "I got two of my girls in the back of the wagon. They got fever real bad."

Rand took one look, and knew.

14

Later that night, after checking on Ben, Rand climbed the stairs to Rachel's unlit cabin, bone cold and weary, feeling every hour of lost sleep. He rapped on the door, and made himself wait a full ten seconds before knocking a second time. The moonless night draped the covered porch in shadows, and though his heart didn't race the way it usually did when he was alone in bed and the memory returned, he breathed easier when blessed lamplight illuminated the darkened window.

Molly McPherson peered through the curtain before lifting the latch. "Dr. Brookston." She motioned him inside.

"Dr. McPherson." He returned the professional courtesy to the former college professor, glad to be out of the cold and wind. "How's Mrs. Boyd?"

Molly's smile, along with the shake of her head, told him much. "She's in bed, for now, asleep. One thing I've learned today . . . those with the most knowledge about medicine make the least cooperative patients."

He frowned. "She didn't get out of bed, did she?"

"She tried, the stubborn thing. Once with Elizabeth this morning, and another time with me this afternoon. She said she needed to get to her chores. I told her Charlie Daggett was seeing to things." Molly sighed. "She hardly got as far as the bedroom door. It must have hurt pretty badly, though, because she asked for laudanum afterward."

Rand rubbed the knotted muscles in his neck. If Rachel had torn those sutures . . . He'd warned her not to get out of bed, and of the dangers of putting weight on her leg before it had time to heal properly. Perhaps he needed to warn her again, in more graphic detail this time.

"Looks like it's been a long day." Molly's expression held both understanding and concern.

"From what James tells me, it's been a busy one for you. Come on back. I've got coffee on the stove."

He followed her to the kitchen, where her daughter, Jo, lay nestled in a basket on the table. He brushed a finger against Jo's cheek, pleased when the baby gurgled and reached for his hand— and made contact on her first try. Good hand-eye coordination. She'd been born prematurely but was progressing well, and was a beautiful child.

"Thank you." He accepted the steaming cup and took a sip. "*Mmmm . . . that's good.*"

Molly claimed the chair closest to the baby. "One of the most important things I've learned since becoming the sheriff's wife is to always have a pot of coffee on the stove in case company drops by, no matter how late in the evening."

Rand returned her smile, admiring Molly's gracious spirit. He knew only too well that Molly and James didn't have much "company" dropping by. Molly McPherson had gotten a rocky start to life in Timber Ridge, and people in town were still reluctant to fully accept her, especially since she and James had married. In truth, she hadn't made the best choices upon her arrival, but in his estimation, she'd more than paid for those mistakes and was working to bring good from them—if people would let her.

He updated her on Ben Mullins's unchanged condition, the Tuckers' two children, and the three miners who had shown up at the clinic with similar symptoms—thankfully, none of them as serious as Paige Foster's. He'd left word with James about where he'd be and had also tacked a note to the clinic door. He'd needed to check on Rachel—or that's what he told himself. Truth to right, he *wanted* to check on her.

He stood and reached for his bag. "The boys are here, I take it?"

She nodded. "Asleep in their room. I'm staying the night, and Elizabeth will be back in the morning." She reached for his empty cup. "I left a lamp burning on the hallway table."

Knowing the layout of the house, Rand made his way toward Rachel's bedroom, oil lamp in hand. He stopped outside Mitchell and Kurt's bedroom and peered inside the dark room, a familiar sense of shame creeping up on him. No light had to be left burning on a bedside table for these boys.

"Dr. Brookston?" a whisper came. "Is that you?"

Rand smiled. "Yes, Mitchell," he whispered back. "It's me."

The rumple of sheets, followed by the soft pitter-pat of feet on a wooden floor, and Mitchell appeared. "You're here to check on Mama?"

"I am."

"You want me to help you? I will, if you want."

"I think your mama would prefer for you to get a good night's rest instead. But I'll come and get you if I need any help, how's that?"

Mitchell's chest puffed out.

"You and your brother feeling all right tonight?" Not knowing whether anyone had told them about the typhoid, Rand chose not to say anything specific, but he wanted to make sure they weren't getting sick.

Mitchell nodded matter-of-factly, and his countenance took on a more mature depth. "Mama's going to get better . . . right?"

Rand knew he might be imagining it, but he sensed Kurt was awake too, and listening. "Yes, your mother's going to be fine. Her leg will be sore for a few days and she needs to rest, but she should heal completely." As long as she stayed off that leg, which he intended on making perfectly clear to the woman. "You get on back to bed now."

Mitchell turned, then did a direct about-face. "I'm glad you're her doctor. If I ever get sick, I want you to be my doctor too."

Rand gave the boy's hair a good tousle. "You've got yourself a deal, buddy."

Mitchell stuck out his hand, and Rand gripped it tight enough to let the boy know he meant every word.

The door to Rachel's room announced his arrival with a creak. The soft glow of lamplight illumined the dark, and Rand winced when he saw Rachel stir. She awakened, blinking, her eyelids heavy.

"I'm sorry," he whispered from where he stood, not wanting to frighten her. "I didn't mean to awaken you."

She lifted her head and squinted, then yawned and lay back down. "That's all right. Come on in. . . ."

He set his satchel on the floor by the dresser. "How are you feeling?"

She took a moment to answer, shifting in the bed as though taking inventory. "Sleepy. My back hurts, and my leg feels like you tried to saw it off. Other than that, I'm just dandy."

He laughed, not having expected that response. "I think laudanum's improving your sense of humor. I should have prescribed it months ago."

She smiled again, groggy.

He motioned to the pitcher on the dresser. "Would you like a drink of water?"

"Yes, please."

"With or without laudanum?" he asked in all seriousness.

"Without . . . but ask me again later."

Enjoying this more relaxed side of her, he slipped a hand beneath her neck as she drank. Her skin was warm, and he hoped his hand wasn't too chilled. If it was, she didn't say anything.

He needed two commitments from her before he left, and before administering another dose of medicine—he needed her agreement to assist him with Ben's surgery, and her promise to follow his medical advice without question.

He knew which would be the more difficult to obtain.

"Thank you." She wiped the edges of her mouth. "What time is it?"

"A little after midnight. I meant to come by earlier, but I had other patients to see." As soon as the words were out, he wished he could take them back. The way he'd said it made it sound as if she was one of many, instead of the one he'd been wanting most to see. "What I meant was—"

"I know what you meant." She took a deep breath and gave it slow release, her eyes closing. "My father was a doctor too. Remember?"

Rand stared, welcoming the muted flicker of the oil lamp and the fact that Rachel wasn't looking at him. *My father was a doctor too.* So much said in so few words, and her tone . . .

Bitter best described it.

He'd known her father was a doctor. What he found so disturbing was what else her seemingly innocent statement told him, far more than she'd likely intended to reveal. Sorting through the tangle of emotions she'd just laid at his feet, Rand got the feeling that the seed of who this woman was, or at least a determining factor in who she had become, lay rooted in that statement about her father.

Something else became clear. His being a physician—something he'd hoped might eventually enable him and Rachel to find common ground—would likely wind up having the exact opposite effect.

• • •

Rachel wished she could take back her last statement.

Not that what she'd insinuated about her father wasn't true, but it was inappropriate to speak ill of the dead. And that she would do so—of her father, no less—spoke volumes about her. By no means had her father been perfect, but neither had he been all bad. He had possessed a *few* redeeming qualities, among the others that stood out most vividly in her memory. But having those memories, those opinions, was one thing. Speaking them aloud was another.

And voicing them in front of the well-mannered, proper, and always dignified Dr. Rand Brookston—she sighed inwardly—that constituted an even greater offense.

Not caring for the silence in the room or the way Rand was staring at her, Rachel gave the buttons on her nightgown a discreet check, then pushed herself up in the bed. She needed to use the chamber pot but wasn't about to ask him for assistance with that.

"Here, let me help you." He came behind her and arranged the pillows to better support her back.

Seeing him up close, Rachel noticed the dark circles beneath his eyes. He looked as if he hadn't slept in days. The dark stubble on his jawline was becoming the norm, it would seem, as were his rumpled clothes and the way his bow tie hung loosely about his neck. Yet something about him made her look twice. And something about the way he looked back at her, lingering close a second or two longer before he straightened, made her look away.

"Thank you," she said softly, smoothing the bedcovers, the ache in her back already lessening. "You look tired."

He ran a hand across his face and sighed. "I could use some shut-eye about now, as my grandpappy used to say."

Hearing the endearment in his tone, she started to ask him about his grandfather, wanting to know more, and then caught herself. It was one thing to discuss medical issues with him. It was another to invite conversation on more personal topics. Best stick to the medical.

He knelt and studied the framed photograph on her bedside table. "Elizabeth took this?"

"Yes. Last year." She loved that picture of her boys.

"How did she manage to keep them still for that long?"

"Bribery," she answered, surprised at how much she enjoyed his spontaneous laughter.

"I use a similar tactic." He stood and glanced toward his bag. "I've got a sugar stick with me. You want one?"

She did but shook her head no. She didn't really know why.

He walked to his bag and pulled one out. "Sometimes it's all right to simply say yes and accept the gift." He handed it to her.

Surprised at being so easily read, she took it and smiled.

He studied her for a moment. "My spies tell me you tried to get out of bed today."

The comment caught her off guard. She bristled slightly at the mild reprimand, and at the fact that either Molly or Elizabeth had tattled on her. Yet remembering her indebtedness to this man, she summoned patience, and pulled the candy from her mouth. "I appreciate all you've done for me, Doctor. Truly, I do. But . . . I have a ranch to operate and a family to raise. I'm afraid I don't have the luxury of lying abed right now."

A muscle twitched in his jaw, and oddly enough, seeing it enabled her to further sweeten her disposition. "But don't worry, I've had sutures before. I won't push past my limits, I assure you."

The steadiness of his stare became unnerving, and she looked away first.

He walked to the corner, where she thought he was going to take a seat in the straight-back chair. Instead, he picked it up and plunked it down backward on the floor beside her, and straddled it.

15

Rachel could count on one hand, with fingers left over, the times that Thomas had been truly exasperated with her. She remembered the look in his eyes as clearly as if he were standing in front of her now. Rand wore a similar expression.

"Did Mrs. Ranslett fail to pass along my instruction that you stay in bed with your leg elevated?"

Feeling like a child and resenting his attempt—no, his *ability*—to make her feel like one, Rachel laid aside her candy. "Yes, she told me you'd *left orders* for me to stay in bed. But I'm familiar with incisions and am aware of the possible complications." She lifted her chin. "That's what I'm trying to tell you. I'm not your *usual* patient." Grateful as she was, she also found his behavior to be absurd—his preoccupation with always being right, being obeyed. So like her father, in that respect. "If it will relieve you of unnecessary concern, I'll take full responsibility for my healing. You needn't worry."

He gave a humorless laugh. "I needn't worry," he repeated, rubbing his eyes. Hands clasped, forearms resting on the back of the chair, he pinned her with his gaze. "You're familiar, *Mrs. Boyd,* with the femoral artery."

It wasn't a question, but still she nodded.

"Are you also familiar with the complications stemming from an occluded femoral artery?"

Wanting to say yes with everything in her, she couldn't lie, not with his being so close and watching her the way he was. She shook her head.

"A severe blow to the body—let's say . . . being kicked by a heifer, for instance—renders a contusion, which, in turn, causes the tissue in the affected area—for example . . . your *thigh*—to swell." He leaned forward, his shirt pulling taut against broad shoulders, his focus intent. "Imagine the muscles, ligaments, nerves, and blood vessels in that affected area forming a kind of . . . compartment. The swelling in that particular compartment"—he made a fist—"cuts off the circulation of blood, and you know what happens to the body when the circulation is obstructed."

She knew, only too well.

"The symptoms are"—he counted on his left hand—"pain, swelling, weakness, warmth of the bruised area, tenderness of skin"—then moved to his right—"tingling and numbness of the leg or foot, and the inability to lift the toes, so that a person must limp to keep the foot from dragging. Sometimes," he said, his voice lowering, "one so afflicted might even resort to using a cane."

Rachel stared, wordless, feeling as if she'd wandered into a house that wasn't hers. A house that should have been locked, for her safety, as well as that of the owner. Instinctively, she reached down and covered the bandage on her leg.

"Would you like to know what happens when these symptoms remain untreated?" Rand stared back. "Or if, following the surgery, the artery isn't given proper time to heal?"

The same muscle in his jaw corded tight, and she knew his question was rhetorical.

"Gangrene, leading to permanent dysfunction of the limb"—his gaze moved down over her body—"or as I witnessed during the war more times than I care to remember . . . amputation."

Still struggling to absorb the words *gangrene* and *permanent dysfunction of the limb,* Rachel went cold inside. She confined her focus to her lap, unable to look at him. Here she'd thought he'd made a simple incision, and that it was his arrogance that was causing him to be so . . . "I'm sorry," she heard herself whisper, seeing Mitch's and Kurt's faces in her mind. "I . . . I didn't realize h-how serious it was. I just assumed . . ."

Seconds passed, strained and silent.

He finally exhaled, and his sigh seemed to drain the tension from the room.

He rose and returned the chair to the corner. "May I check your incision?" he asked, hand on the footboard.

"Yes," she whispered, turning onto her side.

"Would you like for me to ask Molly to come in?"

Face half hidden in the pillow, Rachel shook her head. "No. I'm fine."

She glimpsed his profile in the mirror above the dresser. He looked as if an invisible weight were strapped to his shoulders, and she felt responsible, at least in part, for putting it there.

Gently, he removed the bandages, examined the incision, and applied a fresh dressing.

Aware of his warm hands on her skin and the cool air on her bare thigh, Rachel felt a continued unease with his closeness, regardless of his being her doctor. But her discomfort seemed minuscule in comparison to what he'd just told her. She saw blood on the soiled cloths, and thought again of Mitchell and Kurt, and about what would become of them if something happened to her. "Did I tear the sutures?"

"Only one. But I've been stitching up patients long enough to know to add an extra knot or two." She couldn't see his face, but his voice sounded like he was smiling, at least a little. When he finished, he arranged her nightgown over her legs, pulled the covers up to her chest, and paused, his hand on her shoulder. "You didn't do any damage that I can see."

That I can see . . ." The words reverberated inside her. She'd seen the blood on her father's surgical apron after he'd removed someone's limb due to gangrene. No matter how many times the apron was washed, the stains never left. She felt Rand looking at her in the mirror.

"Mrs. Boyd," he said softly.

She couldn't look back.

He gently squeezed her arm. "Rachel . . . look at me."

Slowly she did as he asked, watching him in the mirror's reflection, glad for the distance between them, even if he was standing right behind her.

"There's no evidence on the skin of internal bleeding, which there would be if you'd damaged the artery again. You know that."

She nodded, needing for him to leave before the knot in her throat made it impossible to breathe.

He repacked his instruments in his bag, then turned to her. "Ben Mullins needs surgery. And I need for you to assist me."

That brought her attention back. She rose on one elbow. "What kind of surgery?"

"He has fluid on his lungs. I can remove it, and that will buy him more time."

She eased back down on the bed, hand resting on her forehead, the truth sinking in. "How *much* time?"

"A few weeks, at best. Perhaps less."

She sank back onto the pillow. Tears pricked the corners of her eyes. "Does Lyda know?"

"I don't think so. Ben said he wanted to be the one to tell her. But if he doesn't tell her soon, I will. She needs to know the truth."

Rachel nodded. A wife deserved to be told if her

husband was about to die, just as children deserved to be raised by both their father and their mother. But it didn't always turn out that way. "I'll help you in whatever way I can with Ben's surgery, and . . . I'll do whatever you advise to get well."

Rand stared at the man, unable to mask his disappointment. "I understand the reasoning behind your decision, Mr. Welch." And he did. He just didn't like it.

"I'm sorry, Dr. Brookston, but that building's been sittin' empty for months now. I needed to get it sold." Harold Welch's attention swept over the street teeming with Saturday shoppers to a building on the opposite side, adjacent to the Mullinses' store. "I know what you'd planned on doing with it, and that's real noble of you. But I needed money in my pocket now, not the promise of money in the future. And no offense, Doc, but"—Welch glanced back, his laughter abrupt— "I've seen the way folks around here pay you for your services. Smoked hams and jars of jam don't pay a mortgage."

Rand swallowed a bitter sigh. How well he knew. . . . With effort, he extended his hand. "Thank you for seeking me out to tell me, Mr. Welch." Knowing he shouldn't inquire further, his curiosity got the best of him. "If it's not too far out of line, may I ask if the selling price was much beyond what I'd proposed?"

Welch's satisfied look gave answer before he did. "The buyer met my asking price, plus he gave me an extra hundred dollars to get the place cleaned up and ready by the end of the month."

Rand whistled low, knowing he'd been beat—and *good*. "I'd say that's a mite better than my offer. What's he going to do with the building?"

"Don't know and don't care. He gave me cash on the table. Every last penny." Welch adjusted his hat and gave Rand an odd sideways glance. "I hope you're not the type to hold a grudge, Doc."

Rand eyed him, not certain what he meant.

"You know . . ." Welch shrugged. "In case me or my family comes down with the typhoid."

Rand exhaled, allowing the hint of a smile. But only just. "You know me better than that, Welch. Although"—he shook his head—"I can tell you right now I won't be giving you any candy."

Welch laughed and clapped him on the shoulder. Rand continued down the boardwalk, trying to shake the feeling of having failed. He'd had such vision for that building, but apparently God didn't think Timber Ridge needed a real clinic. At least not yet.

No new cases of typhoid had been reported in the past two days, so the number of patients held at seven, which wasn't many, considering how swiftly typhoid could spread. It wasn't enough to mandate a quarantine of the town—yet—and Paige's condition continued to be the most serious by far. With every evaluation, she'd grown weaker.

Rand reached the buckboard and tossed his bag up on the seat. He could still see the girl clutching the half-melted stick candy in her sweaty little hand.

"I'm saving this one . . . for later," she'd whispered to him late last night between coughing spells. "Mama says . . . I need to . . . eat my soup first." After sharing with the Fosters about their daughter's worsened condition, he'd encouraged Helen Foster to let Paige have anything she wanted to eat, to make all of Paige's favorite foods, whether it be cookies or meatloaf. Mrs. Foster's expression had sobered, and Rand had spoken to them more plainly about their daughter's prognosis.

It was a fine line to walk, deciding how forthcoming to be with patients—or in this case, the patient's parents—about the prognosis. He wanted to give them hope, wanted to leave room for God to intervene if He chose to, yet he also wanted them to know the truth so they could have time to be better prepared. If there was such a thing. Knowing death was coming, or not knowing . . . Both ways held blessings, he guessed.

He climbed into the wagon and gathered the reins. He'd seen God work in miraculous ways. He'd also seen God remain silent. Well, not exactly silent, he reckoned. God always spoke. Sometimes His answer just wasn't the one a man wanted.

Rand guided the buckboard down the crowded street toward Miss Clara's cafe, trying to dislodge the melancholy that settled over him. Miss Clara would have his usual breakfast waiting for him, and he'd sit at his usual table by the window and watch the townspeople as he ate. He knew how to cook. A man didn't live thirty-four years, nearly half of those without a woman in his life, or in his kitchen, without picking up a thing or two about cooking.

His specialty? Hot-boiled peanuts.

He smiled, his stomach growling. Knowing how to make boiled peanuts was hardly something to brag about, but those peanuts helped him earn his keep through medical school in Philadelphia, then during his training in New York City. For all the boast and swagger with which Yankees regarded the South, Northerners loved boiled peanuts.

Miss Clara must have been watching for him, because when Rand pulled the buckboard up to her restaurant and walked inside, the older woman was bustling down a side aisle, covered plate in hand.

"Morning, Dr. Brookston! I got your biscuits slathered in gravy, scrambled eggs, and sausage right here. Hot, wrapped, and ready to go!"

Ready to go? Rand frowned, seeing his usual table open by the window. "You eager to be rid of me this morning, Miss Clara?" He summoned his best hurt-puppy look, not having to work at it too hard.

She squeezed his arm tight and gave him a grandmotherly hug. "Don't you go tryin' to make an old woman feel bad. I'm just thinkin' you don't have the time. A boy was in here a few minutes ago. Cute little dark-headed thing, came in yellin' your name. Bless him, he couldn't say much of anything else, leastwise that I understood. I just nodded and told him you'd be coming by anytime. He gave me this."

Rand took the envelope dusted with flour and read his name on the front. He opened it. The thickness of the stationery should have been a clue as to its sender, but when he read *Colorado Hot Springs Resort* in fancy type across the top of the paper, he guessed no further.

Dr. Brookston,

A guest at my resort is in immediate need of your attention. Please come at the earliest possible moment.

With kindest regards,
Brandon H. Tolliver

Rand slid the note and envelope in his side pocket, praying it wasn't another case of typhoid. The resort's grand opening was only three weeks away—as if anyone in Timber Ridge could forget with the banners Tolliver had strung up all over town—and an outbreak of typhoid in town already didn't bode well. But at the resort . . . That raised another level of concern.

"Thank you, Miss Clara." He brushed a kiss to her papery cheek. "You're an angel."

"If I was thirty years younger, you wouldn't dare be kissin' me like that."

He smiled at her reproving look.

Then she smiled too and winked. "Which sure makes me glad I'm not. Run on, now." She patted his arm. "You've got some doctoring to do. I'll have fried chicken and mashed sweet potatoes tonight, so come on back and see me."

"It's a date," he said, and gave her another quick peck on the cheek.

His mood slightly more hopeful, Rand maneuvered the buckboard past farm wagons lined up by the feed store. Past the congestion, he urged the mare onto the road leading from town to the resort and ate his breakfast on the way, his patients occupying his thoughts.

One patient in particular, at the moment.

He'd seen Rachel yesterday afternoon and was pleased with how her incision was healing. What pleased him almost as much was the friendship, for lack of a better term, that seemed to have been forged between them. He wasn't fool enough to think she'd changed her opinion about him personally—Rachel Boyd was not a fickle woman. Her mind, once stayed on something, wouldn't be easily swayed. He knew that well enough.

But her opinion about him as a doctor had changed.

He found it hard to put into words, yet he felt it when she looked at him, when she asked questions about the procedure he'd performed on her leg, and about the surgery they would perform together on Ben Mullins. As best he could define it, Rachel had respected his abilities before.

Now she respected *him* . . . as a doctor.

She'd asked for information on Ben's upcoming procedure, and he'd given her a paper a colleague had written detailing the steps and the possible complications, as well as what to watch for during recovery.

Ben's breathing had worsened in recent days. A wheeze had set in, signaling more fluid on his lungs, but his strength wasn't what it needed to be to undergo the procedure. As of yesterday, Ben still hadn't told Lyda the truth of his situation. Ben insisted that he was waiting for the right moment. Rand sighed. He'd told Ben that, come Monday, if Ben hadn't told Lyda the truth, *he* would.

Rand rounded a curve and spotted a man on foot up ahead. Recognizing Charlie Daggett and his lumbering gait, Rand slowed the wagon alongside him. "Morning there, Charlie. Headed out to the resort?"

"Morning, Doc." Nodding, Charlie patted his

coat pocket. "I got me some—" he paused, squinting until his eyes almost closed— "*documents of great import* for Mr. Tolliver." He sighed, his whiskered face relaxing in a grin. "Least that's what he called them."

Rand smiled at Charlie's astute assessment. "Would you and your . . . *important documents* like a ride?"

Charlie lifted a muddy boot. "You sure you're offerin'?"

Rand waved him up to the bench seat, knowing it would be a tight fit. "Come on up."

The buckboard creaked beneath Charlie's weight, and even before Charlie settled in beside him, Rand smelled liquor thick on the man. He gave the reins a flick.

Charlie belched, and the taint of soured bourbon pressed closer. It wasn't even nine o'clock yet. Either Charlie had started early this morning or he'd gotten a late start last night.

"So tell me, Charlie, how are things going for you?"

"Good, I guess. Got more work than I know what to do with and a body that can do the work. That's a good pairin' in my book."

"Indeed. I'd have to agree." Rand glanced down at Charlie's hands. Huge hardly described them. Work-worn and thick-fingered, Charlie's hands looked as if they could snap a piece of lumber clean in two. He remembered Charlie doing something similar to a man's wrist last fall. But according to Sheriff McPherson, the fella had deserved it. "You've been in Timber Ridge for, what . . . seven years?"

"Eight. Come August." Charlie fidgeted with one of the remaining buttons on his coat.

"How long have you been helping out Ben Mullins?"

"Ever since I came. I walked into his store that first day, asked if he needed help unloading the wagon out back. Mr. Mullins . . . he looked at me"—Charlie mimicked the actions—"looked back at the wagon, then looked back at me again, and hired me right where I stood."

Rand smiled, able to imagine that scene quite well, from both sides. "How's Miss Lori Beth Matthews these days?"

Charlie went quiet. "She's good, I guess. Last I saw her."

For a time, Rand had seen Charlie and Lori Beth together on occasion and could tell Charlie had it bad for the woman. And Lori Beth looked equally enamored. But he hadn't seen them together in a long time and had begun to wonder. "From where I sit, she sure seemed to enjoy your company, Charlie. And you, hers."

Charlie's expression remained carefully guarded. "Sometimes a person can't see everything from where they're sittin', Doc."

Surprised at his response, Rand toyed with how

218

to phrase his next question, having waited a long time for the right setting in which to ask it. He could be subtle when needed, but being a doctor gave him license to dispense with that subtlety on occasion. Especially when it involved the welfare of a friend and patient, whether or not that patient knew yet that they were sick. "How long have you been drinking, Charlie?"

Charlie's hand stilled on his coat button. He looked off over the fields covered with snow. "A long time, Doc."

The creak of wagon wheels and the steady thud of the horse's hooves marked off the silence, lengthening the moments. Most people couldn't abide the quiet when they were with someone else, but Rand welcomed it. With the right person, even the quiet became a kind of conversation.

Charlie kept his head turned, still gripping the button on his coat. Clearly, he was done talking.

Rand had spoken with Charlie on many occasions in the past two years, but this was the first time he could remember Charlie Daggett shutting down the conversation, which told him Charlie was hiding something. Not surprising. Every person he'd known who was dependent on liquor or morphine or some other substance had a secret hurt. It provided a way to dull the pain, be it from a physical ailment or an emotional one.

One look at the emptiness in Charlie's face and hearing the way his breath came quick, Rand grew even more certain—Charlie's wound was emotional.

He left Charlie to his silence, and as they rounded the final curve leading to the resort, Rand found his gaze being drawn upward. *Impressive* was the first word that came to mind. *Money* was the second.

From a stately stand of spruce and aspen, the main hotel of the Colorado Hot Springs Resort rose in four-storied splendor. An expansive porch, braced with thick honey-colored pine beams, encompassed the front and sides of the structure and appeared to extend all the way around the building. Shuttered floor-to-ceiling windows, trimmed in black and burgundy, sat evenly spaced on each level, row after perfect row, accentuating the stunning white-painted timber. No expense spared.

It looked more like a painting than real life. As if this little pocketed valley hidden deep in the Rockies had been waiting, carved out specially for this occasion, since the mountains were formed.

Rand pulled the buckboard to a stop in front of an ornately carved hitching post.

A young boy dressed in finery worthy of a Southern cotillion ran to meet them. He grasped the mare's bridle. "Welcome, *Signore* Brookston. *Signore* Daggett." He had a special smile for Charlie, and no wonder, with the animated wink Charlie gave him.

Rand set the brake and climbed down. He dug into his pocket for a coin and pressed it into the boy's hand. *"Grazie,"* he said softly, silently thanking Angelo again for teaching him a few phrases in Italian.

Triple pairs of French doors, decorated with fragrant evergreen boughs, stood like sentinels on the front porch, waiting to welcome guests. He gave a low whistle. How had Brandon Tolliver managed to build such a place? Much less fund it?

"You ain't never been out here, Doc?" Charlie joined him at the edge of the flagstone walkway.

"Not in a few months. It looked impressive then, but . . . *this.*"

"It's fancy, all right." Charlie nudged him in the arm. "Wait 'til you see the innards."

Smiling at Charlie's phrasing, Rand watched a man and woman exit the hotel through one of the French doors. Dressed as if they were headed to an evening at the opera in New York City, the couple continued down one of the many strolling paths that meandered around the trees and boulders. "I didn't think the resort was open yet."

"It's not," Charlie answered. "We're having what Mr. Tolliver calls a dry run. He invited in all the *higher-ups* who gave money to help build this place, them and their families. They're staying here for free. Tryin' things out and makin' sure everything works before the payin' folks arrive."

221

Rand nodded. A good idea, and what a way to be thanked.

The door opened again, and two more couples, equally opulent and graceful, shadowed the previous couple's steps, then took a path leading down to one of several smaller buildings dotting the grounds—the hot springhouses where patrons could partake of the area's famous mineral pools.

Rand took it all in, unable to deny the fact that he was impressed with Tolliver's accomplishment, while knowing full well that the contagious nature of typhoid fever would not be.

16

Brandon Tolliver greeted them on the porch stairs, looking every bit the exclusive resort host. "Welcome, Dr. Brookston." He offered his hand, and Rand shook it. "I'm honored you've come for a visit. Perhaps you'll let me give you a tour of our facilities this morning."

Tour of the facilities? Rand stared, thinking again of what Tolliver had written in his note. "I'm sorry, but I thought I was requested because one of your—"

Tolliver's grip tightened around his hand, and Rand caught his host's subtle glance at nearby patrons. A woman standing poised by the marble fountain in the front courtyard smiled invitingly, inclining her head in Rand's direction, as did two other women with her. Rand smiled in return, finally understanding what Tolliver was doing. He valued discretion as well, up to a point.

"Mr. Daggett." Tolliver's gaze shifted to Charlie's mud-clad boots, then trailed the large tracks marring the flagstone walkway. The smile that already wasn't reaching his eyes dimmed further. "Do you have the papers I requested?"

Charlie shifted his weight. "Yes, sir, Mr. Tolliver. I've got 'em right here." He looked down. "Sorry about the mess, sir. I'll get it cleaned right up."

"That would be appreciated." With a curt nod, Tolliver gestured for Rand to follow him.

Rand did so, grudgingly, feeling for Charlie and disliking Tolliver more by the second.

Inside the lobby, Rand was tempted to stare at his surroundings—which rivaled, if not surpassed, the exterior of the hotel—but he didn't want to give Tolliver the satisfaction.

Without exception, every employee was Italian. Though Rand was thankful the newly arrived immigrants had secured employment, something not everyone in Timber Ridge could say, he already knew Tolliver wasn't the most generous, nor the fairest, employer.

He transferred his medical bag from one hand to the other, eager to examine his patient and praying he, or she, wasn't sick with typhoid. While he didn't care much for Tolliver, he did care about the guests in this hotel. One person contracting typhoid in this setting would be even more serious than in town because the guests here ate from the same kitchen and drank from the same water source. Not to mention the close confines the guests shared in the hot springs.

If even one guest or employee became ill with the fever, or was already sick . . .

Tolliver paused in the lobby. "Perhaps you truly *would* enjoy a tour of the resort, Doctor. I believe it would render you even more impressed than you currently are."

"While I'm grateful for your hospitality"—Rand lowered his voice—"perhaps it would be most prudent if you'd take me to see the guest you wrote me about."

Tolliver's eyes narrowed. Then he smiled. "You're right, of course. Let's begin in the Health Suite, shall we?"

The Health Suite . . . That had an interesting ring to it.

Rand followed Tolliver down a spacious hallway. Polished hardwood floors gleamed beneath his dusty boots. He sidestepped a Persian rug and thought of his precious mother, God rest her soul. How many times, in younger years, had he tromped all over her nice rugs without a second thought. And how often in recent years had he wished he could go back and relive moments with her. His father too, despite the differences they'd had.

Tolliver paused by a door bearing a placard with the name *Health Suite*. Beneath it was a second placard. *Dr. Newton Rochester.* Tolliver's hand rested on the door latch. "Thank you for filling in at the last minute, Dr. Brookston. The resort's private physician, the distinguished Dr. Newton Rochester, is scheduled to arrive before the grand opening. You're familiar with Boston General, I presume?"

Rand nodded, aware of Tolliver's tone. "Of course." Boston General was the most prestigious teaching hospital in the country. But then, that was Tolliver's point.

"I can see you're a man dedicated to his profession, Dr. Brookston. I appreciate that. I also appreciate your responding so quickly after you received my note this morning. . . ."

Rand couldn't be certain, but he didn't think he was imagining Tolliver's hint of displeasure. Most likely the man was frustrated at his lack of response to earlier requests for a meeting. Under the circumstances, and seeing how Tolliver had treated Charlie Daggett, Rand felt no obligation to apologize. He glanced down the hallway to make sure they were alone. "What symptoms has your guest been experiencing, Mr. Tolliver? And when did they first appear?"

Tolliver turned the polished latch. "I believe those questions would be best answered by the guest, Doctor. But perhaps when you're done, we could meet to discuss your findings. My office is down the hallway." He opened the door and motioned for Rand to precede him.

Rand walked into the room feeling as if he'd traveled sixteen hundred miles in three small steps. If he didn't know better, he could have been standing in the hospital in Philadelphia, in the private wing where distinguished patients were treated. Spacious shelves lined with medicine bottles and supplies covered one wall. Two doors opened to his right. One led to a small room with an examination table—a surgical room and a fine one. Narrow horizontal windows had been placed at regular intervals, inches below the ceiling line to allow for daylight while still maintaining privacy. The next room looked similar to the first, but with a hospital bed, for recovery, he presumed. Tolliver had thought of everything.

He heard the door close behind him. At the same time, he spotted an older gentleman sitting off to his left before a fireplace in a cozy nook.

The gentleman rose from a wingback chair, laying his book aside. "Dr. Brookston?"

Rand nodded, closing the distance. "Yes, that's right." They exchanged a handshake, Rand already examining the man—who didn't show the slightest appearance of being sick, much less of having typhoid fever.

"I'm indebted to you for agreeing to see me, Doctor, and so quickly. Sometimes I wait for hours to see my personal physician in New York. Guess a man has to come west to find a doctor who considers his patient's time equal to his own." A sheepish look crossed his face. "Forgive me. I'm Edward Westin, newly arrived to your wonderful community and currently a guest in Mr. Tolliver's hotel."

Rand nodded a second greeting, still at odds with Tolliver and wondering why this man needed a doctor. He searched his memory for why his name sounded so familiar, and came up blank. "Pleasure to meet you, Mr. Westin. I'll help you in whatever way I can. Though, I must say"—Rand softened his observation with a raised brow—"for being in need of a physician, you appear quite fit to me."

Westin's demeanor was friendly and not at all assuming. "I appreciate that diagnosis, Doctor. I guess I'll have to blame it on the fresh mountain air or maybe the change in altitude." He glanced away, his smile fading by a degree. "To be honest, I feel better than I have in a long time. Except for this pain in my shoulder." Grimacing, he angled his neck and massaged his right trapezius. "I was climbing yesterday and must have pulled something. It's been hurting ever since. I mentioned it to Mr. Tolliver last night at dinner, and he insisted on sending for you this morning."

"Did he?" Rand nodded, smiling, careful to keep his tone even. "Well, why don't we move on in there"—he gestured to the examination room—"and see what the problem might be."

For the moment, he would tend his new patient, then take care of Brandon Tolliver.

As Rand finished the examination, it struck him where he'd seen the man's name. *Edward Westin* was the name on the envelope Ben Mullins had given him, and that he'd passed on to Charlie to deliver to the hotel. Riddle finally solved—but another niggled into place. Why was Ben Mullins writing to Edward Westin? Not that it was any of Rand's business.

"You can put your shirt back on, Mr. Westin."

"Please, call me Edward."

Rand nodded and reached for a sheet of paper and fountain pen on a nearby desk. "You said that yesterday was your first time climbing. Are you customarily this active?"

"I used to be, but . . . I haven't been in the last couple of years."

Rand sketched a rudimentary drawing of the shoulder and back muscles and how they connected. "Muscle pain can be attributed to several different things: simple muscle pain from overstress, muscle tears, bruising, or a more significant injury." Rachel suddenly came to mind, an image of her lying on the bed in her room, her bruised but shapely thigh exposed in the soft lamplight, and Rand lost all train of thought.

He blinked to clear his mind of the image. Without success.

All he could see was her giving those tiny little buttons on her nightgown a subtle check when she'd caught him staring overlong, and then the way she'd looked at him in the mirror when he'd called her by her given name.

He felt Edward Westin staring. *What* had he been saying to the man? Thankfully, the picture he'd drawn provided a point of reference. "Most of the time," Rand continued, clearing his throat, "in cases such as this, you've simply overextended the muscle. You've pushed your body beyond what it was prepared for. Time and rest should heal it. Although the tendons surrounding the shoulder *are* susceptible to deterioration, and do weaken with age."

Westin finished buttoning his shirt, a ghost of a smile appearing. "So what you're saying, Doc, is that I'm getting old."

Rand laughed. "What I'm saying is that these bodies of ours weren't designed to last forever. You're in excellent health, Edward, especially for a man of fifty-six." He'd been surprised to learn Westin's age at the outset of the examination. He would have guessed younger. As a precautionary measure, he alerted Westin to the typhoid outbreak.

"Thank you for the warning, Doctor. And I'll take it to heart. I contracted typhoid as a younger man, so I know what you're up against. If my understanding is correct, that makes me less susceptible to getting it again."

Rand nodded. "That's true. Still, it's good to be mindful." He returned the pen to the desk. "There's no reason why you can't be out climbing again in a couple of weeks. Just take it easy until then. Ask a hotel clerk to bring you a warm towel tonight— that should help with the discomfort. And be sure to stretch your muscles like I showed you before you set out again."

Before they left the room, Rand looked around a final time, knowing Dr. Newton Rochester of Boston General would not be disappointed. Only then did he see a detailed framed drawing of the human body on the wall, all organs and muscles labeled. He sighed to himself. And he couldn't even afford to give Timber Ridge a proper clinic.

He followed Edward into the hallway.

"Dr. Brookston, thank you again. I appreciate your coming all the way out here."

Rand accepted Edward's handshake and came away with a five-dollar bill. He shook his head. "This is too—"

"You spent nearly an hour in there with me. You took time to explain things my doctor in New York never did. I want to show my gratitude."

Thanking him, Rand reluctantly pocketed the bill, which would help provide more medicine. They walked together toward the lobby. "Do you plan on being in Timber Ridge long, sir?"

"I do indeed. In fact . . ." Edward paused. "This may sound premature, but I hope to live the rest of my days in these mountains, in this town." He lowered his gaze. When he raised his head again, his eyes were misty. "My wife, Evelyn, saw a painting of Colorado a few years back. . . . She wanted to see it for herself, so badly. But I was busy traveling around the country at the time, building railroads. Almost three years ago, Evelyn became ill. Out of the blue. All her life she was healthy." He clenched his jaw. "We were married for thirty-six years, and she was gone in six months."

Rand briefly gripped his arm. "I'm so sorry, Edward." He shook his head at a hotel clerk, indicating they were fine, as she passed them in the hallway.

After a moment, Edward sniffed. "Are you married, Doctor?"

"No . . . I'm not."

"I highly recommend it, if you find the right woman," Edward said, regaining his composure. "I think you'd be good at it."

"Is that so?" Rand laughed, wishing he shared that confidence. "Did you and Evelyn have children?"

"Two. A boy and a girl. They both have children and lives of their own now. I didn't want to leave them at first, and on the way out here I wondered if I'd done the right thing in coming. But they insisted, knowing how much their mother wanted it. And I'm glad I did." He glanced out the floor-to-ceiling windows surrounding the lobby. "The paintings and photographs don't do this land justice."

They talked for a few more minutes, until Rand spotted Brandon Tolliver's office. "Edward, it was a pleasure to meet you, sir. Take care of that shoulder. And your next two doctor visits are on me."

Waiting until Westin was out of earshot, Rand knocked on Brandon Tolliver's door.

No answer.

He knocked again, his frustration returning when he thought about how Tolliver had manipulated him into coming out here.

"I'm sorry, Dr. Brookston, but Mr. Tolliver isn't in his office."

Rand turned to see the same hotel clerk who had passed them in the hallway earlier. Immaculately dressed, she was young and pretty, and of course, Italian. "Do you know when he'll be back? It's urgent that I speak with him."

"He had to leave the premises, but he asked me to extend an invitation to you to stay for lunch as his guest. I'll show you the way to the dining room."

Rand shook his head. "That's very kind of you, but I'm afraid I can't spare the time."

"Mr. Tolliver anticipated as much." She smiled.

"So I had a plate prepared. If you'll come with me, I'll get it for you."

If it were Tolliver voicing the offer, Rand would have flatly refused. However, this young woman seemed eager to help, and he didn't want her to bear the repercussions of his refusal, should there be any.

Waiting inside the kitchen doorway, Rand stared at the rows of brand-spanking-new cast-iron stoves and thought of how much Miss Clara would enjoy cooking in a place like this.

"Here you are, sir."

He accepted the covered plate from the clerk with thanks and was nearly to his wagon when he glimpsed an older man weaving an unsteady path toward him. A gardener at the resort, if Rand wasn't mistaken. Rand paused. The man's eyes were glassy, his shirt damp with sweat.

"Medico," the older man whispered, his face flushed and glistening. *"Medico, per favore,"* he pleaded, just before he collapsed.

17

I appreciate you and Kurt meeting me here, Mrs. Boyd. And I apologize for the wait. Monday afternoons are always hectic." With an abbreviated sigh, Judith Stafford settled into her desk chair.

Rachel offered an understanding smile, hoping to mask her nervousness. "I was in town anyway, so it was no bother. I'm grateful for the time you set aside to meet with us."

Miss Stafford straightened the stack of books on her desk, then the row of pencils. "With so many students under my tutelage, my schedule is demanding. But I'm finding that, on the whole, working with the students here in Timber Ridge is very rewarding." She cut a narrow look at Kurt. "With students who actually have a desire to learn."

Rachel felt a pinch in the comment but knew that, with Kurt's recent misbehavior—and what they were here to talk about today—it was deserved. She so wanted this meeting to go well and was willing to do anything to help the situation improve. That included getting her relationship with this young woman on surer footing. "I hope you're enjoying living here, Miss Stafford. It's quite different from Dallas, I suppose."

"Oh yes, very different. But I'm feeling at home here now, despite some rough patches along the way." She sneaked another look at Kurt.

Rachel sensed all wasn't forgiven and forgotten, and she couldn't blame Miss Stafford for still being upset about the outhouse incident. Kurt must be presenting quite a challenge for the first-time teacher. She quelled a sigh. He was a challenge for *her,* and she was his mother!

Miss Stafford leaned forward, pencil in hand, and looked down at an open file on her desk.

Rachel made a discreet attempt to read it as well, but couldn't.

"Are you aware, Mrs. Boyd"—Miss Stafford lifted her head—"of your son's most recent breach of conduct?"

Rachel's gaze went involuntarily to the wood-burning stove in the corner, and her face went warm. "Yes, ma'am, I am. He told me he . . . placed a book inside the stove, and that it was burned."

Miss Stafford's gaze slid to Kurt, then back. "Did he tell you *which* book it was that he placed into the stove?"

Rachel blinked. When she'd finally wrangled the truth out of Kurt, she'd been so angry she hadn't stopped to clarify details. Mitch hadn't seen Kurt put the book into the stove, and apparently none of the other students had either. Or if so, no one was talking. She cleared her throat. "I'd assumed it was his textbook. The one assigned to him."

Miss Stafford slowly shook her head. With a less-than-friendly smile, she pulled open a side drawer and withdrew a charred object. She held it between her thumb and forefinger, as if it were a dead rat. "Your son put my grade book into the fire . . . *after* he earned a failing mark on an assignment."

Rachel swallowed, staring at what once might have been a book. She wanted to look at Kurt to see his reaction, but Miss Stafford was watching her so closely she felt as though she were the guilty party, as if *she* were the one being disciplined. And something didn't make sense. After Kurt had earned a "failing mark"?

When Molly taught this classroom last fall, Rachel clearly recalled her sister-in-law say that Kurt had finished strong in his studies, despite having given Molly some tense moments during class. Remembering the incidents with the mouse and the snake, Rachel cringed.

But burning Miss Stafford's grade book . . . That had more serious ramifications than anything he'd done before.

Her thigh began to ache. Every muscle in her body was taut. A thousand thoughts flitted through her mind, foremost of which was that none of this would be happening—with the ranch, with Kurt— if Thomas were still alive.

Kurt had been barely six years old when Thomas died, and Thomas had merely to give Kurt a stern look and the boy toed the line. But her stern looks went ignored, her threats unheeded. Even the paddlings she'd given him—that hurt her far more than they hurt him—yielded no noticeable change.

"Mrs. Boyd . . ."

Rachel lifted her gaze to see Miss Stafford wearing a surprisingly thoughtful look, her hands clasped before her on the desk. It occurred to her then how very young a woman Judith was. And how pretty, with her brunette hair swept back in a stylish lace chignon. And how snug she wore her shirtwaists.

"Be assured, Mrs. Boyd, I'll continue to be as patient as I can be with your son. But his behavior must show improvement." A brief glance included Kurt in the warning. "Molasses on the drawer pulls of my desk and making faces at the other children in class is disruptive. Making inappropriate noises that boys often make in order to draw attention to themselves is disturbing. But burning something . . ." Miss Stafford frowned. "That's another issue entirely. I've spoken with a member of the town council, and we feel that—"

"Pardon me?" Rachel said before she could stop herself. Surely she hadn't heard correctly. "You spoke with a member of the town council, about my son, before speaking with me?"

Judith Stafford sat taller, traces of thoughtfulness now gone. "As the teacher in Timber Ridge, I report to the town council. If I'm experiencing problems with a child—"

"Then you should speak with the child's parent first," Rachel said with a calmness she didn't feel.

"Which I did." Miss Stafford's mouth curved in a tight smile. "As you will recall, I'm sure."

Rachel pressed her lips together—embarrassed, ashamed . . . and furious. Both with Miss Stafford for the liberties she'd taken, with Kurt for his antics, and with herself for not having better control of her son. She could well imagine which member of the town council Miss Stafford had spoken with. Mayor David Davenport, a close personal friend of Judith's aunt and uncle who lived in town. She felt sick inside.

If LuEllen Spivey, Judith's aunt and the biggest gossip in town, got wind of what Kurt had done with Miss Stafford's grade book . . .

"Kurt, wait for me outside in the wagon, please. And close the door on your way out."

Still shaking, Rachel guided the wagon into town, aware of Kurt's furtive glances but not trusting herself to say anything to him. Perhaps it was her imagination, but she felt people watching her as she drove by. Mayor Davenport knew about Kurt burning Miss Stafford's grade book. . . .

She squeezed her eyes tight. She needed to tell James. Mayor Davenport had caused her brother such trouble, what with James moving in with her and the boys after Thomas died, and Kurt's misbehavior in school last fall, which had endangered Molly and led to her being injured, which then filtered back to the town council and led straight back to James.

Just as it would again.

She took a deep breath. Davenport would attempt to use this situation against James too, in the upcoming sheriff's election.

She brought the team to a stop in front of the store, and Kurt immediately jumped from the bench seat. As she carefully climbed down, the sharp pain in her leg reminded her of Rand's restrictions. He'd declared her well enough to walk, with limitations she intended to heed. Another week of healing, he'd said, and she should be strong enough to walk without assistance. But still needing some support, she retrieved the cane from beneath the bench seat, and when she looked up, she saw Kurt waiting for her by the team. Odd, he usually ran on ahead. Of course he wanted to know what had happened with Miss Stafford, but she had no intention of discussing it right now.

She picked a path toward the boardwalk, mindful of the mud and muck. The warmer temperatures in recent days were welcome, especially with May still a week away, but the melting snow combined with deposits from animals was not.

"Mama?"

She managed the two steps up to the boardwalk, wishing for a handrail. "Yes, Kurt?"

"Do I . . ." Hands in his pockets, he stared at his feet. "Do I still go to school?"

She couldn't see his face, so couldn't tell whether he hoped her answer would be yes or no. "Yes, of course you still go to school. Why?"

He licked his lips. His little shoulders rose and fell. "I just wondered."

Wishing she could bend down to be eye level with him, she gently urged his chin upward. To her surprise, he didn't pull away. "Miss Stafford is giving you another chance. But, Kurt, you must respect your teacher." She glanced at a woman passing by and pasted on a "How do you do?" smile that lasted all of three seconds.

She thought of a question Miss Stafford had asked her, for which she had no answer. "Can you tell me, son . . . why are you doing these things? You never got into this kind of trouble before . . ." She caught herself before saying "your papa died" and decided to leave the question hanging, wondering if he hadn't already finished the sentence in his mind, as she had.

Kurt stared up, eyes wide and blue, shining with beguiling innocence. He gave a slow shrug, as if he too wished he knew the answer.

Rachel sighed and nodded for him to go on. She watched him walk into the store, loving him, hurting for him, praying for him, while still wanting to shake him senseless.

Mitch was waiting for them inside, but she needed a moment to gather her composure. She shuffled to an out-of-the-way bench and eased down, welcoming a moment to rest. Sitting provided immediate relief to her leg. She looked back in the direction of the school and felt her stomach knot tight again. She hadn't been this angry in a long time.

She took a deep breath, held it for as long as she could, then slowly gave it release.

Miss Stafford wasn't the most patient teacher,

nor had she demonstrated the best judgment in contacting the town council, but Kurt was to blame too, Rachel knew. As was she . . .

From her sequestered bench, she watched the townspeople pass, glad to be the one doing the watching. She considered walking the short distance to the sheriff's office to talk to James, but her promise to Rand that she would take it easy kept her where she was.

A boy passed by on the street below. A tiny puppy followed him, working hard to keep up. The dog nipped at the boy's heels and the boy tripped and nearly fell. Rachel giggled to herself. For as long as she could remember, Mitch and Kurt had wanted a dog. But that was one more responsibility—and one more mouth to feed—that she didn't need right now.

She shifted on the bench and felt the layer of bandages protecting her incision. She was fortunate her wound was healing so well, and that Rand was so skilled a surgeon. She arched her back, stretching her shoulder muscles.

Rand Brookston . . .

There was definitely more to the man than she'd originally believed. He was a doctor, yes, but each time they were together she saw less of her father's traits in him and more of . . . well, more of a very kind, generous, and selfless man. An odd combination for so gifted a physician.

The surgery he planned to perform on Ben

sounded fraught with risk, and she had a list of questions for him. She'd known Ben's condition was serious but not that his remaining time was so short. A pang tightened her chest. Rand had shared that if Ben hadn't told Lyda about his prognosis by today, he would. Devastating as that would be for Lyda, she agreed with him. Lyda deserved to know while there was still time to say the things that needed to be said.

She'd read Rand's article in the special edition of the *Timber Ridge Reporter* over the weekend. Well written and informative, the article cited facts about typhoid fever, how a person could lessen their likelihood of contracting the disease, and what to do if symptoms presented themselves. She'd heard of no other reported cases.

Recalling something Rand said to her when he'd examined her a few nights ago, and how he'd said it, she felt the start of a smile.

"A severe blow to the body—let's say . . . being kicked by a heifer . . ."

She'd been on the receiving end of his sarcasm before, but something about his attitude that night had been different. And when he'd used her given name, making her look at him . . . She leaned back on the bench, relishing the sunshine. And surprisingly, the memory.

Moments passed, and finally, with the aid of her cane, she rose.

She spotted Mitch and Kurt as she entered the

store, seated off to the side, each eating a cookie. She held up two fingers as she passed, indicating their cookie limit, and the boys nodded.

Jean Dickey was behind the counter, helping a customer. "Lyda's upstairs," she whispered, her customary smile at the ready, and returned to her task.

Rachel continued through the curtained doorway and up the stairs, looking forward to seeing Lyda and Ben, yet dreading it as well. Life could change so quickly. As she reached the second-floor landing, she heard muffled cries, and rounding the corner saw Lyda in Rand's arms.

Lyda sobbed against his chest, covering her face with her hands. Rand held her close and stroked her back, whispering something in her ear. A floorboard creaked beneath Rachel's boot, and Rand looked up. He didn't say a word. He didn't have to.

Lyda knew.

18

R and stood by the window in the bedroom, feeling for Ben as the silence lengthened. Ben seemed hesitant to meet his wife's gaze, much less answer the question she'd just asked him. Rachel sat in the rocker a few feet away, her head bowed. Rand was grateful she'd stopped by when she did. She'd comforted Lyda in a way he never could.

And once again he found himself in awe of the *weaker* sex, of their quiet, formidable strength.

Rachel looked up and their eyes met. What was she thinking about? Her husband, Thomas, perhaps? Was she putting herself in Lyda's place and remembering what it had felt like when she'd learned of his death?

Propped up in bed, Ben was situated with pillows behind his back, and his breath came heavy. "I didn't tell you before now, Lyda, because . . . I didn't want to add to your worry. You've been"—the wheeze in his lungs worsened—"worrying enough about the store in recent months."

Lyda shook her head. "I don't care about this store, Ben. I care about *you*." Lyda's struggle to accept the truth about Ben's condition was etched in the lines on her face. And her desire to be brave, in the firm set of her shoulders. But her eyes . . . Despite her questioning Ben, her eyes were filled with only love for her husband, and that love spilled down her cheeks. "You said . . ." The words caught in her throat. "You said the benefits of this surgery are worth the risks."

Realizing she was addressing him, Rand stepped closer. He shot Ben a look, having discussed this with him earlier, along with deciding the date for the surgery. "That's right—I believe they are." The quiet of the room encouraged a softer voice. "I wish I could give you guarantees, but I can't. I can tell you that if we don't do the surgery, the fluid will continue to gather around Ben's lungs, increasing the stress to his heart at a more rapid rate." He pulled a chair to the bedside and sat down. "The biggest risk involved is surgical fever. It's a fever that can set in any-where from three to five days following the operation. We don't know the cause, and not everyone develops it." He leaned forward. "I don't want to mislead you. Anytime the body is opened by an incision, no matter how small, it's serious. But I wouldn't recommend this proce-dure if I didn't believe it would be successful. And that it will give Ben more time.

"And there's something else you need to know." He hesitated, not second-guessing what he was going to say next—what he'd already told Ben this afternoon—but wishing someone with more experience could perform the operation instead of him. Time didn't allow for a colleague to travel from back east, if he could even find one willing to make the journey. Most had tried to talk him out of coming to such a place as Timber Ridge. From his peripheral vision, he saw Rachel's head come up. "I haven't performed this procedure before. Not by myself."

Lyda blinked, then looked at Ben.

"I've assisted," Rand said. "Once."

"And what was the outcome?" Rachel asked, her voice stronger than he had expected.

"As I told Ben earlier today, the patient's health was critical, like his. But the gentleman was five years younger." Rand saw the question in Lyda's eyes common to anyone who'd just been told their spouse was terminally ill. "The gentleman lived for four months following the surgery," he answered softly.

Lyda swayed slightly on the bed, and summoned a brave expression as truth peeled back another layer of her future.

With a laugh, Ben shook his head. "But I'm bettin' he wasn't as ornery an old cuss as I am." Even if his humor hadn't fallen flat, the misty look in his eyes would have betrayed him.

Rand smiled for Ben's benefit, noting that the women weren't. He saw Ben's coughing fit coming on and held Ben's shoulders as Lyda assisted him with sips of water. After a moment, Ben regained his breath.

"I'd like to perform the procedure this week," Rand said quietly, anticipating Rachel's surprise. To her credit, she nodded and gave him a look that promised further discussion.

He'd thought the scenario through many times and had discussed it with Ben this afternoon. He intended to ask Brandon Tolliver if he could perform the operation in the surgical room at the resort. Ben's health was stable enough to make the three-mile trip out there, then following a brief recovery period, to make the trip back home.

The resort's facilities were far superior to his makeshift clinic and greatly increased the likelihood of the surgery's success and of Ben's recovery. Other than the gardener who had shown symptoms of typhoid last Friday, no one else at the resort had reported having fever. But numerous patients had been in and out of his clinic in town. He could scrub the place for a month and it still wouldn't be as clean—or as well-equipped—as Tolliver's medical suite.

For the past year, Ben Mullins had bent over backward to accommodate Brandon Tolliver's special "rush" shipments. If Tolliver had a scrap of decency in him, which was debatable, the man would grant the request.

Sensing Ben and Lyda needed time alone, Rand stood. Rachel did likewise.

"Before you go," Ben said, glancing up, then quickly down again. "There's one more thing I need to get said." He looked as if he might take hold of Lyda's hand, and then pulled his hand back, apparently deciding against it. "What I need to say is that I've . . ." He swallowed, looking more apprehensive by the second.

Lyda scooted closer. "Honey, what is it? Are you feeling worse?" She touched his forehead.

Ben pulled away. "No, I . . ." Worrying the edge of the quilt, he sighed. "I've sold the store."

It took Rand a moment to decide whether Ben was serious or not. When he realized he was, he looked at Lyda to see her reaction. The shock on her face mirrored his own. Rachel's too.

Lyda stammered. "I . . . I don't understand. What do you mean you've *sold* the store?"

"Not all of it. Only a part." Ben sat up straighter. "You still own fifty-one percent, so you have what Gilbert Fossey calls *controlling interest*." He formed the semblance of a grin. "Not that you haven't already had that for years."

Lyda squeezed her eyes tight, as though not wanting to hear, and Rand couldn't fault her reaction, not on top of everything else she'd learned today. Yet he couldn't fault Ben either, understanding the man's underlying motivation.

Ben's smile faded. "I promised to take care of you, Lyda. I pledged to . . ." Ben's chin trembled. "I knew you'd tell me not to do it, honey. But . . . I won't leave you lacking. Not like my father left my mother." He shook his head, his jaw clenching tight. "I won't do it."

Lyda opened her eyes. "Who did you sell to?"

"He bought the building next to us, Lyda. He's going to expand the store, just like you always talked about wantin' to do. Remember?"

"*Who,* Ben? Who did you sell to?" she repeated.

Rand leaned forward, eager to hear the answer to that question himself—who had purchased the building that he had dreamed would one day house his expanded clinic?

"You met him the other night. The man who I

said wanted to talk to us about carrying some newfangled stovetop ovens, like the stores do back east. He and I did talk about that," he added quickly. "But then we moved on to other things . . . once you left. He just moved to Timber Ridge. His name is Edward Westin."

Rachel felt a tweak of guilt over her eagerness to leave the confines of the store and the weight of emotion in the upstairs bedroom, if only for a while. She limped to the edge of the boardwalk, welcoming the crisp, cool air. Her leg ached, but only a little, and a late afternoon sun warmed her face.

Drinking in the routine rhythms of life around her, she closed her eyes, one hand on the stair rail, and prayed for Ben and Lyda and what lay ahead for them. The horse-drawn carts and wagons plodded their way up and down the street, snippets of indistinct conversation drifting toward her from passersby. The aroma of baking bread, coming from either the Boldens' bakery or Miss Clara's cafe, made her mouth water with hunger.

Ben had sold a portion of the store . . . and to Edward Westin! Mr. Westin's arrival in Timber Ridge made more sense now, as did his business with Mr. Fossey. Rachel opened her eyes and looked up at the sign hanging above her head— *Mullins General Store*—and still couldn't believe Ben had made that decision without Lyda.

And yet, she could.

How often had she wished that Thomas would have left her and the boys in better financial standing? The very thought felt dishonoring to his memory, yet that wasn't her intent in the slightest. If Thomas had known he was going to die, he would have prepared better. She knew that about him. Ben *did* have time to prepare, and his decision was an act of love.

She'd told Lyda as much a moment ago when they'd spoken in the hallway, alone. But Lyda couldn't see that right now, she was too close to the grief and shock, and Rachel didn't blame her.

"Rachel."

Hearing her name, she turned.

Rand strode toward her in that weathered duster of his, Stetson in hand, looking more like a gunfighter than a physician, and she wondered . . . was he as good with a rifle as he was with a scalpel? Intrigued by that question, she glimpsed Mitchell hot on his trail, toting Rand's medical bag, and Kurt behind him, hurrying to keep up.

Rand came alongside her. "How's your leg?"

"It's fine."

He eyed her. "That means it hurts, but you're not going to admit it."

She smiled, aware of the way his eyes lit when she did. She looked away, trying to remember exactly when he'd lost his annoying, arrogant edge. She could still recall it, though, and pledged to remind herself of it each time she entertained the thought she was entertaining right now—of how handsome a man he really was.

He slipped his hat on. "I'm grateful you came along when you did, with Lyda and Ben. I appreciate your being there. They did too. Ben told me as much when you and Lyda were in the hallway. And I'm sorry, I hadn't seen you to tell you about setting the date for the procedure."

She waved a hand. "Whenever it's scheduled, I'll be there. Just let me know when you settle on the day, so I can arrange for Molly to keep the boys." She touched her leg. "I'm not sure I'll be able to stand the whole time, though."

"I'll have a stool for you. I'm going to ask Brandon Tolliver if he'll let us use the medical facilities at the resort."

She frowned. "You think it would be better to do it out there?"

He gave her an odd look. "Have you seen the resort yet?"

She gave a short laugh. "No, but I know that man has caused more problems for this town than he's worth. As well as problems for my brother."

His expression was a mixture of humor and concern. "Granted, Tolliver's not the most—"

"Dr. Brookston?"

They turned.

"Mrs. Calhoun!" Rand greeted the elderly widow walking toward them and slipped an arm around her thin shoulders. "Good to see you, ma'am."

The woman snuggled into his embrace, then drew back and looked him up and down—twice—tears pooling in her eyes. "You're wearing it," she whispered, running a hand along the sleeve of his coat. "And you look so handsome in it too. My Edgar would be so proud. A doctor, wearing his coat and hat." She sniffed. "It was just like looking at him again, coming down the boardwalk and seeing you standing there."

Rachel looked at Rand, then at Mrs. Calhoun, the pieces coming together. Mrs. Calhoun winked in her direction and rubbed the boys' heads.

Rand fingered the lapel of the duster. "I appreciate your giving them to me, ma'am. They've kept me a lot warmer than that old dress coat and hat I brought from Tennessee."

Mrs. Calhoun beamed. "You would've frozen for sure." She patted his chest. "I'm beholden to you for coming by every week to check on me, and for bringing my medicine. I already have another of Edgar's shirts washed and ironed for you." She winked again. "A token of my thanks."

"Token of my thanks . . ." Touched by Mrs. Calhoun's generosity, Rachel also cringed, barely hearing the rest of the conversation. How could she have forgotten? She hadn't paid Rand anything, much less even offered. Not for delivering the calf, not for what he'd done for her

leg, not for the numerous times he'd stopped by the house to check on her since. And she'd considered *him* rude!

After a few moments, Mrs. Calhoun bid them good afternoon. Rachel did likewise, watching the woman walk away while silently rehearsing, over and over in her mind, an apology to Rand. No matter what she came up with, it all sounded trite and—

"Can we, Mama? Can we?"

"*Please,* Mama?"

Feeling the tugs on her skirt and seeing the wide-eyed hope in both her boys' eyes, Rachel knew she'd missed something.

Rand peered at her from beneath the brim of his hat. His expression held mischief. "Should I take that as a yes or a no?" His eyes narrowed. "For dinner," he added, his mouth tipping in a wry grin.

"Dinner?" she repeated.

He nodded. "If my memory holds right, Miss Clara serves pork chops and mashed potatoes with gravy on Mondays."

"With biscuits," Kurt added. "And not cold ones either."

Rachel frowned, a little hurt by that comment. She used to make fresh biscuits every morning. Now she baked a batch on Sunday and hoped the biscuits would last through the week. Which, with two boys, they never did.

"Please, Mama." Mitch took hold of her hand.

"We haven't been to Miss Clara's in a long time."

Torn, Rachel focused on a point down the street. A hot dinner at Miss Clara's sounded heavenly, but she couldn't justify spending the money with her finances so lean and with the cupboards stocked at home. She looked at Rand, thinking of yet another reason that this dinner might not be the best idea. She told herself again that she could be imagining it, but there were moments, like this one—when he looked at her the way he was looking at her now— when she wondered if he wished there was something more to their friendship than . . . well, friendship.

But that "something more" was not something she welcomed.

19

Rand was certain he'd won Rachel over to his dinner invitation and could already taste Miss Clara's buttery mashed potatoes, which would taste even better with these three joining him. Each time he was with Rachel, he grew fonder of her. And though it hadn't been easy, he thought he'd done a good job of keeping those feelings under wraps—which was best, considering she'd yet to give him any real encouragement on that front.

"I'm sorry," she said with a dip of her chin, "but the boys and I should really be heading back to the ranch." Mitch and Kurt groaned. A quick arch of

Rachel's brow quieted Mitch, but Kurt's scowl took deep root. "We have chores to do, boys, and there's plenty to eat at home. But we thank you, Dr. Brookston, for—"

"But he said he'd pay," Kurt insisted, taking hold of Rand's sleeve. "Didn't you?"

Knowing better than to encourage a disagreement, Rand motioned down the boardwalk, more disappointed than Mitch and Kurt combined. "Boys, before you head home, would you mind running down there and seeing if the newspaper office is still open? Your mother and I will meet you there in a minute."

With a long face, Mitch held out Rand's medical bag.

But Rand shook his head. "If you don't mind carrying it on down there for me, I'd appreciate it." He rubbed his shoulder, feigning a grimace. "Gets heavy lugging that thing around all the time."

Mitch pumped the bag up and down as if it were a barbell. "I don't think it's heavy at all."

Smiling, Rand dug into his pocket for a nickel, already seeing the dark glare Kurt aimed at his brother. "Kurt, would you mind picking me up a copy of the paper, if Mrs. Ranslett has any left?" He dropped the coin in Kurt's outstretched palm and would've sworn the boy grew an inch, though traces of his scowl lingered.

Mitchell and Kurt raced down the boardwalk, Kurt's shorter legs pumping to keep up.

Rand started to speak, then noticed Rachel's thoughtful focus following her sons. Not wanting to interrupt, he watched the boys and wondered, not for the first time, what it would have been like if he'd had a brother. If his parents had given birth to another son. A son who wouldn't have "forsaken his birthright," as his father had referred to Rand's decision to become a doctor. A son who would have wanted to stay and inherit the family business.

The family business . . .

That made him think of Ben selling a share of the store. Rand sighed. So Westin was the man responsible for purchasing Timber Ridge's future clinic out from under him. Still frustrated over what had happened, Rand couldn't fault the man, not when he really thought about it. Because that meant Edward Westin was also responsible for providing a more secure future for Lyda Mullins, which was what Ben was living for. Quite literally.

With a wave of his hand, Rand drew Rachel's attention back. "I hope you're not upset that I sent the boys down there," he said quietly. "I wanted the chance to speak with you. Privately."

"On the contrary." She blinked. "I thank you for respecting my wishes. And . . ." Her voice grew softer. "I have something I'd like to say to you too."

Rand got the feeling this conversation might not turn out the way he'd hoped. "Ladies first, then."

A blush crept into her cheeks. "Offering to treat us to dinner was very kind of you, *Rand*," she said quietly, and he liked the sound of his name on her lips. "But I'm the one who owes *you*. I'm ashamed to admit"—she winced—"that I hadn't given a single thought to paying you for all you've done for us, until . . ." Her gaze dropped to his coat and she briefly touched the front of it. "But I will. I give you my word I'll pay you for your services. For delivering the calf, for taking care of my injury. I just need some time to . . . get the funds together."

If this woman was trying to endear herself to him, which Rand was sure she wasn't, she could not have done a better job. "You don't owe me a thing, Rachel. It was my pleasure to do those things."

Her polite smile said she didn't believe him. Then her pretense faded. Genuine enthusiasm took its place. "I know what I can give you. Beef!" She hesitated. "You do like beef, don't you?"

He couldn't keep from laughing. "Yes, I like beef. Very much."

"I need to slaughter another cow for me and the boys, and as soon as I do that, I'll give you a side of beef."

This woman . . . "I truly appreciate the offer, but I'm afraid I have no place to store a side of beef." Seeing her excitement wane, he got an idea. "But I love *roast* beef, with those little potatoes on the side." He leaned in as though they were in cahoots together. "How about I trade you one side of beef for one roast, cooked by you, and eaten at your table?"

Watching her weigh the proposition, he hoped Rachel Boyd would never try to play poker. He could read her like a copy of the *Timber Ridge Reporter*. And he could see that he'd scared the woman to death. Grappling with how to salvage the moment, he watched her take a tiny step backward. She arranged a refined, ladylike smile on her pretty face.

"All right," she said, nodding once.

Shocked, he smiled. "Are you serious?"

"I am. One roast, cooked by me. Eaten at my table."

"*With* those little potatoes," he added, hoping to coax that dry look she sometimes gave him. He wasn't disappointed.

Next morning, Rand set out for the resort before seven o'clock, eager to speak with Tolliver about Ben's surgery. He made a detour by the Fosters' cabin on the way, wanting to check on Paige. The young girl's fever had finally subsided, but as was often the case with typhoid, ravages from the disease had left her fatigued and malnourished. Cautiously hopeful and wishing he had a better prognosis, he gently told Mr. and Mrs. Foster that things could still go either way. He hadn't missed the look of "I told you so" in Mr. Foster's somber expression.

He'd stayed up late into the night grinding herbs for Paige and his other typhoid patients—one batch to be mixed with hot tea, the other to be combined with milk to make poultices for those with fever. He'd filled pouches for each of his eight patients, including Tolliver's employee. It was remarkable more people hadn't gotten sick. Folks who had never spoken to him before about medical issues were stopping him in the street now, asking questions about simple health issues. And he couldn't have been more pleased to answer.

He dismounted in front of the main hotel, already tired. He tugged off his gloves and handed the reins, along with a coin, to the stableboy. A different lad than before. Grinning, the boy led the mare toward the stalls.

Rand took the flagstone walkway to the wraparound porch, taking in the beauty of the Maroon Bells in the distance.

The hotel lobby was quiet. The employee behind the elaborate reception desk was assisting a patron, so Rand skirted quietly around the side, not wanting to take the chance of being stopped.

Down the hallway in the restaurant, silverware clattered against china and a low buzz of conversation seeped into the corridor. As he passed the open double doors, he glanced inside, then slowed his steps. He marveled again at the extravagance of the resort and of its patrons. White linen tablecloths and fine china and crystal, even at breakfast.

But he wouldn't have traded any of this for the deal he'd made with Rachel. One roast, made by her, eaten at her table. Glad he'd thought of the compromise, he still couldn't believe she'd said yes!

He continued down the empty hallway to Tolliver's office, praying the man was in a generous mood this morning. He raised his fist to knock—

"I don't care what *you* think is best, Miss Valente!"

Rand paused at the harsh voice coming from Tolliver's office.

"I don't pay you to think! I pay you to do what I tell you to do!" A loud crash sounded, like glass shattering. "Is it so difficult to remember to pick up the telegrams each day and bring them to me? Because if it is, I'll find someone else capable of doing it."

"I'm sorry, Mr. Tolliver," a feminine voice answered. "I just—"

"This telegram arrived last Wednesday, Maria. *Five* days ago! And I have to hear about its contents from some yokel in town."

"I'm very sorry, sir. It won't happen again."

A harsh laugh. "You're right—it won't! Or

you'll be back in that kitchen with the rest of your sisters."

Tense seconds ticked past. Rand felt his own chest burning. The audacity of that pompous—The door latch turned, and he stepped to one side.

"Will there be anything else, Mr. Tolliver?" the woman asked.

"No. Not unless you care to enlighten me on your other areas of incompetence."

The door opened and out stepped the young woman who had assisted him last time. Head bowed, obviously flustered, she closed the office door and hurried down the hallway, never looking his way.

Watching her, Rand felt a pang of remorse remembering how he'd snapped at Rachel that day in the storeroom. He hadn't been as condescending as Tolliver just now, but his actions had been just as wrong. He wasn't catching Tolliver in a good mood, if there was such a thing, but his request couldn't wait. He knocked on the door.

A not-so-muted curse filtered from the office. "What is it *now,* Maria?"

Rand entered and was halfway into the room before Tolliver looked up from his desk.

Tolliver groaned. "I told you, Doctor, I'm not delaying the grand opening of this hotel. None of my other workers have come down sick, and I've spent too much—"

"I'm not here about the typhoid, Mr. Tolliver."

Though I'm touched, as would be your employees—or guests, for that matter—at your concern, he wanted to add but didn't, considering his purpose in coming.

Exhaling, Tolliver pushed back from his desk. "Then you must be here to gloat, Dr. Brookston. Is that it? If so, go ahead and get it over with." He retrieved a file from a cabinet behind his desk. "I have a resort to run."

Rand gave a humorless laugh. "I have no idea what you're talking about. I'm here on a professional matter."

Tolliver stilled, suspicion hardening his stare. "So . . . you haven't heard that Dr. Rochester recently declined the position he accepted with the resort over a year ago."

Rand's gaze went to the telegram now in Tolliver's grip, and the situation came into clearer focus. "You mean the *distinguished* Dr. Newton Rochester from Boston General?" he asked, trying to capture a hint of the tone Tolliver had used when introducing Rand to the resort's Health Suite.

Tolliver responded with a glare.

"Sorry." Rand raised a hand in mock truce. "No, I hadn't heard. I realize that must put you in a very difficult position. I hope you're able to fill the position soon."

While he couldn't bring himself to feel sympathy for Tolliver, he *was* aware that the resort, with its hot mineral springs, was touted in advertisements as being a place of healing. Handbills described guests as "partaking of the waters under a physician's care" to help rejuvenate achy joints and ligaments and relieve back and neck pain. But Dr. Rochester's failure to keep his word wasn't Rand's problem. He shifted his weight, sensing the timing was as right as it would ever be.

"If you have a moment, Mr. Tolliver, I'd like to discuss a matter of great—"

"Would you consider accepting the position, Dr. Brookston?"

Rand blinked, then heard himself laugh, expecting Tolliver to do the same. But he didn't. Was the man serious? Rand slowly shook his head. "Ah . . . no. But thank you, Mr. Tolliver," he said, amused. He perused the well-furnished office and spotted the shattered remains of a wine decanter on the floor in the corner. Evidence of Tolliver's temper, no doubt. "I appreciate the offer, but I already have a practice."

This time it was Tolliver who looked amused. "Yes, I'm aware of your . . . *practice* in town, Doctor."

Reminding himself again of why he was here, Rand said nothing.

"You do fine work, Dr. Brookston. I mean that in all seriousness. And I should know." He smirked. "You've sutured more of my employees than I care to count."

"I've sutured forty-seven of your employees, to

be exact. And I *did* care enough to count." Rand savored Tolliver's look of surprise, but even more, the subtle hint of respect in the man's unwavering stare.

"Are you certain I can't interest you in the position here, Doctor? There's nothing that will change your mind?"

Rand shook his head. "I'm doing exactly what I want to be doing." Well, that wasn't completely true. He wanted to do so much more as the doctor of Timber Ridge, and it seemed as if the door might finally be opening for that to happen. Folks were becoming more receptive to his medical advice. Now if he could just find a way to provide a proper clinic in which to care for them. But working at a place like the resort wasn't an aspiration, and certainly not for a man like Brandon Tolliver.

Merely nodding, Tolliver crossed the room to the three-tiered paned window that framed a breathtaking view of the Rocky Mountains. His gaze fixed on some unknown point, his eyes narrowed. "Graduated first in your class, with the highest honors the College of Physicians in Philadelphia could bestow. You were offered a prestigious fellowship to practice at St. Mary's Hospital in New York, which you declined."

Rand stared, wordless.

"You were offered the head of obstetrics at Mercy Hospital in Philadelphia. . . ." Tolliver turned and looked back. "But again, you said no. And forgive me, Dr. Brookston, but a man like myself has to wonder why such a talented physician with so many opportunities open to him would choose to come to a place like Timber Ridge."

20

Rand had no idea how Tolliver knew so much about him. Not that it mattered. "The real question here, Tolliver, is why you would go to such great lengths to learn so much about me."

Tolliver walked to his desk and sat down. "Don't flatter yourself, Brookston. I hardly went to great lengths. A telegram or two and the information was at my fingertips. Nevertheless, I pride myself on knowing my counterparts."

Rand raised a brow.

"Oh yes, I consider you a peer, Doctor. One of the very few here in Timber Ridge, in fact."

Rand laughed inwardly, knowing Tolliver meant that as a compliment in his own twisted way. Could the man be more arrogant? Checking the clock on the mantel, Rand saw the morning slipping past. He had medicine to deliver to patients and a question yet to be posed. "I know you're a busy man, *Mr.* Tolliver, so may I come straight to the point about why I came to see you this morning?"

Tolliver tilted his head in acknowledgment.

Rand considered how to best frame his request and decided the direct approach would be most effective. "Ben Mullins needs an operation. He recently experienced heart failure, but he's beginning to regain his strength. However, he's suffering from pleural effusion." He tried to gauge Tolliver's reaction so far but couldn't get a good reading. "Fluid is collecting on his lungs, and it needs to be removed. I'm asking for your permission to use your facilities to conduct the procedure. I need to do it as soon as possible, within the week is my preference. Following the operation, Ben will need to recuperate here for a couple of days, maybe more depending on how the procedure goes and how he progresses. Then I'll arrange to have him moved back home."

Rand waited as Tolliver continued to stare. The man's expression never changed.

Finally, the slightest frown appeared. "So am I to understand that Ben Mullins's heart actually stopped beating? And that you started it again?"

That was all Tolliver had gotten out of everything he'd said? "I only did what I was trained to do."

Tolliver scoffed. "Your modesty is a blemish on your profession." He rose and walked around his desk. "I built this resort with one thing in mind, Doctor. Excellence," he said quietly. "Everything at Colorado Hot Springs Resort is of the finest quality and of the latest invention. You were impressed with the Health Suite, I take it?"

Rand nodded, not liking that Tolliver wasn't answering his question.

"How could you not be? I fashioned it after a surgical wing at Boston General."

Growing impatient, Rand sought to steer the conversation back to his request. "Ben's chances for a successful surgery and full recovery are greatly increased if I conduct the procedure here. My clinic in town is—"

"Antiquated? Grossly inadequate?" Tolliver asked.

"Not as well equipped or as clean was what I was going to say."

Tolliver smiled. "One and the same."

The irony of the moment wasn't lost on Rand. Brandon Tolliver was the exact kind of man who had eventually influenced him to decline all of the positions offered in those hospitals back east. Self-seeking, manipulative, and controlling, men like Tolliver relished keeping others under their thumb, and that was one place Rand would never be again. Not when it came to his patients, their health and their lives.

Tolliver moved back behind his desk, sat down, and picked up the fountain pen. "I appreciate you coming all the way out here to talk to me this morning, Dr. Brookston. And after carefully considering your request"—he began writing—"my answer . . . is no."

Rand stepped forward. "You can't be serious. After all that Ben Mullins has done for you in recent months?" He thought of what Lyda had told him. "Ben has personally loaded and unloaded your shipments, no telling how many times. He's arranged for countless special orders on your behalf. I've seen him in the—"

"I know this is important to you, Dr. Brookston." Tolliver looked up. "The only thing we have to determine now is *how* important."

Rachel couldn't stop staring. No matter how many evenings she stood in this very spot and watched, it felt like her first time. Leaving her cane by the door, she crossed the porch and eased down to sit on the top step, her attention fixed on the snow-covered steeples of the Rockies. She drew her shawl closer about her shoulders, certain in this moment that heaven must exist just beyond the golden orb sinking steadily behind the lofty spires.

A longing took hold deep inside, one both fresh and ancient, familiar yet unfathomable. Regardless of all that had happened in the past two and a half years, she had so much to be thankful for.

She'd received word from Mr. Fossey that the board had approved her request for more time, *and* for more money. But the advance was only half the amount she'd requested, and the note carried a higher rate of interest. She'd signed the agreement, knowing she had little choice. Now to make good on that promise on paper, just like the promise she'd made to Thomas in her heart.

Her gaze was drawn to the thinnest line of purple-gray sky that separated the edge of day from approaching night, and for a brief moment she almost believed that, if she sat still enough, if she looked closely enough, she might just catch a fleeting glimpse of eternity.

The scene reminded her of a photograph Elizabeth had taken not long ago. And while part of her was grateful people who had never visited these mountains were given the opportunity to share in this land's beauty, she also knew that no photograph would ever capture it completely. She hoped Elizabeth's pregnancy was progressing well and wished she could share that journey with her friend. But the distance Elizabeth and Daniel lived from town made that impossible. Rachel felt a prick inside her—as did her relationship with Daniel.

"Dr. Brookston hasn't come yet?" Door slamming behind him, Mitch dropped down beside her on the porch step, already in his nightshirt.

Welcoming the company, Rachel cuddled Mitch close, sharing his warmth and anticipating his disappointment. "Not yet. And remember what I said at dinner. . . . He may not be able to come after all." And likely wouldn't, if her past experience with doctors proved correct. Not that Rand would intentionally go back on his word, but she knew how overcrowded a doctor's schedule could get.

"He'll come." Mitch nodded. "He said he would."

"I know that's what he said, Mitch, but doctors get very busy, and their patients always come bef—" She caught herself, realizing she was speaking of Rand . . . while picturing her father. Rand said he would stop by that afternoon to discuss the procedure for Ben's surgery scheduled two days hence, and she'd made the mistake of mentioning his visit to the boys. A tad disappointed that Rand hadn't come, she was more put out with herself for having said anything. "If Dr. Brookston doesn't come tonight, we'll see him tomorrow."

When Rand told her about Brandon Tolliver saying yes to his request, she'd hardly believed him. From her brief dealings with Mr. Tolliver— and knowing how he'd given James such a difficult time during the resort's construction—she wouldn't have figured the man to have a compassionate side.

Rand had seemed pleased with Tolliver's decision, but something else weighed on him—she could tell. She'd also sensed he hadn't wanted to talk about it. So she hadn't pushed.

"Mama, kids at school are saying Paige Foster's gonna die."

Rachel winced. Children had so few boundaries when it came to speaking about such things. "Paige is still very sick. Dr. Brookston says she got the worst case of it. Her fever is gone, and though she's still weak, that doesn't mean she's going to die. We just need to continue to pray and ask God to make her well."

Mitch nodded, staring out across the mountain peaks as she'd done moments earlier. "But that doesn't mean He will. Right?"

Rachel felt a stab near her heart and ran a hand through her son's hair, the sunset giving the strands a fiery glow. "I'm choosing to believe, with all my heart, Mitchell, that God *is* going to heal Paige. But . . . if she doesn't get well, it won't be because God *can't* heal her. It will be because"—oh, how she wished she could give him a different answer—"for some reason we won't understand, and that will be most difficult for her parents, and us, to accept . . . God will have decided, in His wisdom, to take her home instead."

Her boys knew what she meant when she used the word *home*. That was how she'd described where Thomas had been since the day of his passing.

The front door creaked open behind them, and without turning, Rachel indicated for Mitch to scoot over. At the same time, she extended an arm to Kurt. "Come join us!"

Kurt claimed the empty space beside her without getting too close. Rachel gave his knee a quick squeeze and tried to be satisfied with the fact that he didn't pull away.

"Why does the sky do that?" Kurt pointed.

"Do what?" she asked.

"Turn all red and orange. 'Cause some nights it doesn't."

Digging deep in her memory, she came up woefully short of any scientific explanation, though her father would have had one. "I tend to think it's because God likes to remind us of how creative and powerful He is. And of how beautiful heaven must be." The colors on the horizon seemed to change by the second, red fading to orange, and orange to a dusky gold.

Mitch looped his arm through hers. "Do you think Papa can see us?"

How often she'd wondered that herself, at times praying he could. Then at other times . . . "I'm not sure. . . . I think he knows we miss him very, very much. And I think he also knows we're doing all right."

Mitch seemed to soak up that answer, while his brother still wore a perplexed look.

Mitch fingered one of the buttons on the sleeve of her shirtwaist. "Do you remember that one time when he took us up to the waterfall and we had that picnic? And the chipmunks got into the cookies?"

"Yes, I do." Rachel laughed along with him, remembering several of those picnics they'd taken with the boys. And some more intimate ones, without. Noticing Kurt wasn't smiling, she gently nudged him. "Papa carried you on his shoulders, all the way up there and then back down, remember? He offered to carry you too"—she looked at Mitch—"but you said you were big enough to walk on your own."

"I coulda walked on my own if I'd wanted," Kurt murmured, sending Mitch a challenging look.

Not wanting to start the "back and forth" between them again—she'd already arbitrated a heated round over dinner—she hurried to think of something to say, but was spared the task when the romp of horse's hooves signaled an approaching rider.

She recognized him, even in the fading light, sitting tall and easy in the saddle.

According to James, for three generations Rand's family had owned a cotton plantation some miles north of Nashville. Yet here was Rand Brookston, in the wilds of Colorado, a doctor, and not a boll of cotton in sight. She wondered how his family had felt about that, his father specifically.

Rand reined in by the porch, and the boys hopped down to the bottom step, eager to meet him. He greeted them each by rumpling their hair while sneaking quick tickles to their ribs. Mitch laughed, halfheartedly dodging Rand's efforts, while Kurt only smiled, staring up at him, his expression more hopeful than exuberant.

Hand on the porch rail, Rachel stood, treasuring the moment, yet not completely.

She couldn't explain why, especially after Rand

had been so kind to her and the boys, but—seeing the scene now—a part of her almost wished he hadn't shown up. As she watched him walk up the stairs, his gaze steady on hers while he still kidded with her sons, the reason became uncomfortably clear.

And the problem was with *her*, not him.

The tiniest spark lit inside her, the slightest flicker, and it dawned on her what it was— anticipation at seeing him again, followed by a flood of questions she wanted to ask. Had he eaten dinner yet or not? She half hoped he hadn't so she could fix him a plate. What about the patients he'd seen that day, and his diagnosis for each, and how he planned on treating them? What about the shipment of medicine he'd been waiting on for days now? Had it arrived? Not to mention the—

A cool wind of warning blew through her that had nothing to do with the breeze coming off the mountains. Chilled, she turned and reached for her cane, aware of Rand's attention.

One step shy of the porch, he paused and removed his hat. "I'm sorry I'm late." A smile hovered at the edges of his mouth, almost there, yet not quite, his expression one of sincere regret. "Patients," he said softly, near eye level with her. "But I guess you already knew that."

She remembered what she'd said to him about her father having been a physician, and read assumption in his face. He thought she was comparing his lateness as a doctor with the many nights her father had been late. He was right, of course—at least that was part of all that had been going through her mind. She just wished he wasn't so discerning a man. She looked away.

Maybe she could tell him the hour had grown too late and that the boys needed to get to bed for school in the morning, which they did. She could suggest they meet tomorrow at his clinic to discuss Ben's—

Mitch grabbed his medical bag. "I'll carry this inside."

"I've got your hat." Kurt didn't wait to be asked but snatched the hat from Rand's fingers, fast on Mitch's heels.

Rand laughed, looking at his empty hands. "Quite the little hosts you've got there."

"Yes . . ." She smiled. "They can be."

His smile faded. He watched her in a way that made her wonder if he knew all she was feeling. "Is something wrong? Other than my being woefully late."

"Not at all." She glanced at her boys waiting inside the open doorway, Rand's hat and bag in their grips, expectation on their faces, and common courtesy forced her hand. "Come inside, please."

She led him to the front room and gestured to the couch. "Won't you have a seat?" Aware of the forced brightness in her voice, she tried to sound normal, but couldn't. She also noticed Rand wasn't sitting. "I need to get the boys to bed. Then we can get straight to business."

"But, Mama . . ." Kurt dropped Rand's hat in the chair. "You said I could have some more chicken. You promised!"

Mitch nodded. "You did, Mama. I heard it." He pivoted to Rand. "Mama made fried chicken tonight. There's lots left. Do you want some?"

Before Rand could respond, Mitch retrieved the covered plate from the kitchen and plunked it down on the table beside the sofa. "It's good and crispy."

"We got half a potato left too," Kurt said. "And biscuits! You can have some milk with them. You want some milk?"

Rachel's face went warm. Her boys were better hosts than she was. "I'm sorry, Dr. Brookston, forgive me. I should have asked if you'd—"

Rand held up a hand. "I'm fine, really. It's late, and I'm sure you and the boys need to be getting to bed. I figure it'll only take about an hour to go over the details of Ben's surgery." He glanced at his bag on the couch. "I've got some diagrams in my satchel that I've drawn to help illustrate what I hope we can accomplish."

What *we* can accomplish. He made it sound as though she was actually going to take part in the procedure, instead of simply handing him instruments and administering chloroform. A weariness she hadn't noticed before edged his eyes, along with a sincerity that put her to shame. Whatever kind of relationship Rand might, or might not, be seeking with her—he was her friend. Plain and simple. But she wasn't treating him much like one. "Have you had dinner yet?" she asked softly.

"I'm fine . . . really."

Hearing the truth in his noncommittal response, she smiled, remembering word for word what he'd said to her the other night. "Sometimes, Dr. Brookston, it's all right to simply say yes and accept the gift."

The slow smile he gave her threatened to fan that tiny, dangerous spark into flame. But she guarded her heart closely, ever mindful of the cost if she didn't.

In the kitchen, Rachel fixed Rand a plate of dinner and set it inside the oven to warm. She peered into the main room. "Your dinner will be ready in—"

Rand wasn't there.

Hearing voices coming from the boys' bedroom, she tiptoed down the darkened hallway, feeling more than a little silly. She paused outside the open door.

"So you have a microscope too?" Mitch asked.

"Yes. It's an older one, but it still works well. I'll show it to you both the next time you're in town. Each of you can choose a leaf, and we'll look at them under the lens."

"What will they look like under there?" Kurt's voice sounded different somehow, but Rachel couldn't pinpoint why.

Rand laughed softly. "Very different than they look on the tree. The microscope lets you see all the details the human eye can't detect."

"Details like what?" Mitch asked.

"The veins of the leaf, and the tiny little bugs that you can't see just by looking."

"Bugs?" Kurt's voice rose with excitement. "I like bugs!"

More soft laughter. "I like bugs too, Kurt. Wait until you see them under the microscope. It's amazing how many intricate parts they have."

"Kurt's good at catching bugs." Mitch's tone held quiet pride. "And snakes and mice and frogs and lizards and . . ."

Rachel smiled at the list Mitch rattled off, her heart warming at his affirmation for his brother.

"You guys better get on to sleep now. I don't want to get in trouble with your mother."

"You're smart, aren't you, Dr. Brookston?"

Rachel smiled at Kurt's comment, knowing how rarely the boy praised anything or anyone, and wondering if Rand knew how big a compliment he'd just been paid.

"I've studied a lot, that's all. I like to read too. I learn a lot by reading."

Rachel rolled her eyes, remembering the stacks and stacks of books piled high in the man's bedroom.

"I like to read too." Mitch sighed. "But I've already read all the books we have here. And Miss Stafford won't let us take books outside the schoolhouse. She says they're too important and might get ruined. But she let Amanda Spivey take some home."

Rachel gritted her teeth. *That's not fair!* Miss Stafford allowing her niece to take home books while the other children couldn't. Talk about playing favorites. Of course, Kurt *had* ruined a book, thereby forfeiting his—

She heard Rand's boot steps, and panicked. She turned, not wanting to be caught eavesdropping.

"About those books, Mitch—"

Rand paused, and Rachel did too, her heart pounding.

"I've got some books at the clinic. A lot of them probably wouldn't be of interest to you, but I've got some from when I was about your age, and I'd be happy to let you borrow them. Kurt too, if he wants."

"You mean . . . we could bring them home with us?"

"Of course you can. Books are meant to be read. I think that's why writers write them."

Rachel could picture the smile on Mitch's face. Rand's too.

"Can I ask you one more thing, Dr. Brookston?" Kurt's quiet tone hinted at the question's importance, and Rachel leaned closer to the door.

"Sure thing, buddy."

"Do you know why the sky turns all red and orange at night?"

Closing her eyes, Rachel leaned back against the wall, loving her younger son more than words could capture. Rand's quiet footsteps sounded, only they weren't moving toward her. She heard the creak of a bed and felt the sting of tears.

"You mean when the sun goes down?" A short pause. "Well, it's really all about light. You already know that light comes from the sun, and as the sun begins to set, the light has to travel farther through the atmosphere before it gets to us. More of that light is scattered and reflected and as less of it reaches you directly, the sun appears less bright. When it's really red, like it was tonight, that's because the air contains dust or water particles that reflect the light in all directions, making the sunset . . ."

Wiping her eyes, Rachel scooted back down the hallway into the kitchen. She had Rand's dinner waiting on the table minutes later when he walked in.

He took the chair opposite hers, where she'd set his plate. "Your boys ask a lot of questions."

"Especially the closer bedtime gets," she answered with a wry smile. Looking at him again, she noticed how tired he seemed.

"Thank you for dinner. I don't want you to think I expected this, because I didn't."

"I know. And it's no trouble. I'm glad to do it."
And she was.

"But just so we're clear . . ." He leaned forward,
a gleam in his eyes. "Don't think this counts for
that roast beef dinner you owe me. I'm not lettin'
you off that easy."

She grinned.

He reached across the table, and it took her a
second to realize he was reaching for her hand. She
slipped hers into his and bowed her head as he
offered thanks. God forgive her, but she couldn't
think of anything but the warmth of his hand
around hers. Keeping her head still, she risked a
glance up at him. His head was bowed, his eyes
closed, and though his lips moved, she could only
stare at their hands. Whereas Thomas's hands had
been thick and rough from farm work, Rand's were
long and graceful, made to hold a scalpel.

"Amen," she whispered, echoing him, aware
he'd let go of her hand. She drew it back into her
lap.

"Excuse me." He rose. "Let me get those
sketches and we can go ahead and cover some of
this while I eat. I'm designing an instrument for
the procedure and am eager to see what you think."
He returned with several pages in hand. He ate a
few bites, obviously hungry, before beginning. "I
know from working with you before that you're
already familiar with surgical procedures, but—"
he took a drink of water—"for both our sakes, I've

made a list of everything we'll do . . . before, during, and after."

Rachel listened and studied the diagrams across the table, impressed at the detail with which he'd drawn them, and the time he'd taken to prepare for Ben's surgery. She brewed a pot of coffee, and they moved into the main room. The room was cooler than the kitchen, but not enough to light a fire in the hearth.

He took a seat on the sofa and gestured to her cane across the room. "I see you're using that less frequently."

She nodded. "I still need it on occasion. But I'm feeling stronger every day."

"And the incision?"

"Still healing very well, thanks to you."

Rand welcomed her queries and answered each one with an enthusiasm that made her feel as though her questions were important. As though *she* was important.

When she next happened to look at the clock on the mantel, she was shocked at the time. After midnight. She couldn't believe how quickly the hours had passed.

Seated on the sofa, Rand arched his back and stretched. "I can't thank you enough for assisting me like this, Rachel." His voice went soft. "As I said, there's no way to reverse the damage to Ben's heart, but I do think we can buy him more time. I'd like to start the procedure at eight o'clock on

Saturday morning, so if you could be at the resort by seven thirty, that would work best."

She nodded.

"I'm transporting Ben out there tomorrow afternoon. Lyda's coming too. She's arranged to have some women help her in the store for a few days."

"Do you need help moving Ben?"

He shook his head. "Angelo and Mr. Daggett are helping me. We'll be fine. We'll take it nice and slow. The main thing is to keep Ben comfortable, keep his pulse from elevating. Or dropping too low." He began gathering his papers.

She helped him, then straightened the lace doily. "I still can't believe Brandon Tolliver agreed to let you use the resort's facilities. All I'll say is watch out for the man. He may offer you something, but his price is always higher than you bargained for."

Rand paused. "Have you had dealings with him?"

"Not personally. But his reputation precedes him. Lyda's told me, more than once, that he's had Ben order something special for him, only to cancel the order once it's already shipped from Denver. Ben's been stuck paying for shipping costs several times." She shook her head. "I told Lyda to stop placing orders for him unless he pays ahead of time, including the shipping." She softly scoffed. "Only a fool would get involved with that man."

Rand's smile came slowly, and had a sheepish look about it. "Well . . . then, I guess that makes m—"

"Mama?"

Rachel glanced down the hallway. "That's Mitchell." She rose. "It's probably his legs again. He wakes up some during the night with leg cramps."

"Do you need me to help?" Rand started to rise.

"No, that's all right." She gestured for him to stay. "I'll be right back."

Sure enough, Mitchell was sitting up in bed, holding one knee against his chest. "It's hurting again, Mama."

"Let me rub it for you. You just lie down."

Rachel gently massaged the calf muscle, feeling Mitch relax, while also feeling the effects of the past few hours of conversation. Once Mitchell was asleep again, she covered him back up and checked Kurt in the bed beside him. She tucked his little hand back beneath the blanket and left the bedroom door ajar.

"I'm sorry that took so long, Rand. I—"

She stopped midstep and smiled at the scene. Leaned back on the couch, Rand was fast asleep, papers in his grip. "Rand," she whispered.

He didn't move.

She started to try again, then looked at the clock. Almost twelve twenty. If he left now, it would be nearly one o'clock by the time he got his horse saddled and reached home. Knowing morning would arrive all too soon, she pulled the blanket from the chair and draped it across his legs. That would keep him warm enough, even without a fire in the hearth.

She took the opportunity to look at him, unhurried and without the risk of being caught. His head tilted slightly to one side, his pulse beat solidly in the strong curve of his throat. Dark hair fell across his forehead, begging to be brushed away, but she didn't dare. Had there really been a time when she hadn't considered this man attractive? She sighed, unexpected emotion tightening her chest.

She'd missed evenings like tonight. Evenings spent talking with someone . . . No, not just someone. She missed a *man's* presence in her life—the companionship, the laughter, the comfort of familiarity and of being known. It made her feel like a woman again.

And she hadn't felt like a woman in a very long time.

Eager to get to bed, and knowing better than to give the notions inside her further encouragement, Rachel made sure the front door was locked. She paused in the hallway and admired the man on her sofa, one last time, before extinguishing the flame in the oil lamp.

21

Rachel awakened with a start. She bolted upright in bed, blinking in the darkness, wondering if she'd dreamed the noise or if she'd actually heard something. Still so tired and her eyelids heavy, she knew she couldn't have been asleep too long.

She sat perfectly still, listening for what seemed like a long time, then she exhaled. *Nothing.* Relaxing, she lay back down again and yawned, unable to remember the last time she'd had that vivid of a drea—

There it was again. She sat up. A definite thud this time, then the shuffle of footsteps. Perhaps one of the boys was up. Or maybe it was Rand. What she heard next propelled her from bed. The sound of something—or someone—falling.

Reliving one of many nights following Thomas's passing, she grabbed her robe and hurried down the hallway, not bothering to light a lamp. She'd awakened before to the same sound—of Kurt having a nightmare. And more than once, he'd fallen from bed. She'd thought he'd grown beyond having these awful dreams. Or at least she'd prayed he had.

After Thomas died, Kurt would awaken screaming, terrified something was outside the cabin trying to break in and get him. At times he'd been so frightened, so convinced he'd heard something, she'd hardly been able to go back to sleep herself.

The boys' bedroom door was ajar, as she'd left it. Shadows draped the room in darkness, but she could just make out the contours of their sleeping forms. "Kurt?" she whispered, waiting for the telling rustle of sheets or those deep, choking breaths. He didn't stir. Neither did Mitch.

A loud *thunk* came from the front room, followed by the sharp fracture of breaking glass, and she turned back to the hallway.

"Mama? Is something wrong?" Mitch stirred and sat up.

She crossed to his bed and brushed a kiss to his forehead. "No, everything's fine, sweetie." She glanced behind her, hoping that was true. "I was just checking on you and your brother. Go back to sleep."

Not needing to be told twice, Mitch nestled his face back into the pillow.

Rachel closed the boys' door behind her and only then realized how cold the floor was on her bare feet. A draft of air whooshed down the corridor and up her robe. She pulled it tighter, shivering as she picked her way down the darkened hall.

Peering around the corner into the parlor, she tried to see if Rand was still on the sofa, but the room was pitch black, the curtains drawn. "Rand?" she whispered. She took another step and tripped over something. Nearly landing on all fours, she regained her balance, her shin throbbing. She bent and groped in the darkness before her. One of the rail-back chairs lay on its side. "Rand?" she said louder, righting the chair with more force than necessary.

Still no answer, and her concern mounted.

She made her way to the bureau by the hearth, located the oil lamp kept there, and struck a match. Pale yellow light stretched out across the room, and her concern escalated.

The sofa was shoved back from its place, the cushions disheveled, some on the floor. A crystal vase, a family heirloom and gift from her mother on her wedding day, lay shattered. And the front door stood wide open. No wonder it was so cold.

She peered into the kitchen. Rand wasn't there. Maybe he'd gone to the outhouse. But why would he leave the door open? Or maybe he'd decided to return to town . . . and failed to check the latch? That didn't seem like something he would—

Labored breathing came from just beyond the front door.

"Rand?" Her voice tight, it barely broke a whisper. She raised the oil lamp, but the darkened porch lay beyond the light's reach. "Rand, is that you?"

Noiselessly as she could, heart pounding, she retraced her steps to the bureau, her attention never leaving the doorway. What was she doing living so far from town with two young boys? Unable to deal with that question right now, she shoved the thought aside and opened the top drawer, wincing at the scrape of wood on wood.

She rummaged beneath the embroidered tablecloths and linen napkins until her fingers brushed the cold steel of Thomas's Smith & Wesson. Revolver in her grip, she flipped the safety lever, wishing she could take the lamp too. But she'd fired this gun before. She would need both hands.

She inched forward. Her right hand trembled and she steadied it with her left, correcting her aim and targeting the area she imagined would be chest level on most men. James had taught her at a young age how to shoot and defend herself, and what he'd said most often was that the decision to shoot couldn't be an afterthought. Once she made the decision to pull the trigger, she needed to be committed to it.

Thinking of her sons lying asleep in the bedroom down the hall, she thought she could pull the trigger. But what if Rand was out there? She couldn't risk shooting him.

Almost to the door, she heard footsteps on the porch and a bolt of fear sliced through her. Senses sharpened, she gathered her courage and peered outside. A shadow moved to her right at the edge of the porch. She leveled the gun and took aim.

• • •

"Rachel! It's me!" Rand dared not move for fear the woman's aim was as accurate as her stance promised it would be.

"Rand?" she said, her tone incredulous. "What are you *doing* out here!"

Hoping to avoid that explanation, he held up a hand, his breathing still unsteady. When he'd awakened to absolute darkness, full panic had set in and was taking its time to abate. "I'll explain, but would you mind not aiming that at me, please?"

She hesitated, as though only now realizing she still held the gun on him. She lowered her arm. "Why didn't you answer me! I've been calling you!"

"I'm sorry. I didn't hear you." Though he had no problem hearing her now.

"You didn't hear me?" Her sharp exhale communicated doubt. "You about scared me to death, Rand Brookston!" She took a step closer, pointing back to the house. "What happened? Are you all right?"

The pressure in his temples made his head feel like it was about to split open, and the shrillness in her voice didn't help. The last thing he wanted to do was tell her why he was standing on her porch in the middle of the night, much less have her see him this way—shaky, unable to catch his breath. She was already going to brand him a fool for agreeing to work with Brandon Tolliver—though he hadn't had much of a choice in the matter. Once she discovered he was afraid of the dark . . .

He shook his head. He'd be quite the man in her eyes.

He worked to keep the edge from his voice. "I said I'm *fine,* Rachel. If you'll just go back inside and—"

"You don't *sound* fine to me. And my parlor doesn't *look* fine. What on earth happened in there?"

He glanced past her to the open door, where a faint but precious hint of light glowed warm. He hoped he hadn't done any damage. He remembered awakening, groping in the darkness, determined to find a way out. He'd tripped over something—he did remember that. Maybe a chair . . . "I'm sorry about the mess. I-I'll clean it up before I go." He pressed the heels of his hands against his temples, willing the ache to subside. "Just . . . give me a minute, *please.*"

"Rand, I don't care so much about the room—just tell me what's going on. Why are you out here in the middle of the night? And why is my front door standing wide open?" She took a step closer. "You're shivering. . . ." Her voice softened. "Are you ill? Is that it?" She tried to touch his forehead, but he brushed her hand away.

"Rachel, please . . . go back inside."

"I want to know if you're ill."

"I'm not ill!" He dodged her hand again, his

291

nerves—and pride—stretched thin. "You are the most stubborn woman I've—"

"*I'm* stubborn?" She gave a disbelieving laugh. "I walk into my parlor in the middle of the night to find it in shambles, then come out here to find you *lurking* on the—"

"Lurking?" he repeated.

"Yes, lurking! And you won't even tell me why. *And* you won't let me check to see if you have fever when you're obviously sick!" She shook her head. "And *I'm* the one who's stubborn?"

"I'm a doctor, Rachel." He gave a dry laugh. "I think I'd know if I had fever." He saw her stiffen and knew he'd said exactly the wrong thing.

"Do you have any idea, Rand, how arrogant that makes you sound?"

He stared, unable to see her expression, but easily imagining the fire in her eyes. This lady could get downright riled when she put her mind to it—and when she had good reason, which he'd just given to her in spades.

She walked back into the house, leaving the door open.

He dragged a hand across his face and sighed. The evening had gone so well until this. . . .

He followed her inside and found her stowing the gun in the top bureau drawer. He walked up beside her. She didn't look at him. "I'm sorry, Rachel. I shouldn't have said that. And you're right. It was arrogant and uncalled for."

She closed the drawer harder than he imagined was needed. "It scared me . . . finding the room this way, and you gone."

Instinctively, he touched her arm. She moved away, and he didn't blame her. "I'm not sick, Rachel. I just—" He didn't want to lie, but he also couldn't tell her the truth. Men were supposed to be the brave ones, the protectors, the ones brandishing guns.

He looked at her standing by the fireplace, her back to him, her bare heels peeking out from beneath her robe. *Beautiful* hardly described Rachel Boyd. Her dark hair fell about her shoulders in disarray, and the way she'd cinched her robe about her waist—modesty her intent, no doubt—only drew more attention to the soft curves of her hips and thighs he remembered so well. . . .

He thought of her late husband and a sense of trespass resonated within him. Somehow it felt wrong, him standing here in the home Thomas Boyd had built, desiring the woman Thomas Boyd had loved. But what he felt for Rachel was so much more than desire alone.

He needed to give her an explanation for his behavior and knew by her demeanor that she was waiting for one. He only hoped a portion of the truth would suffice. He crossed to where she stood, mindful to keep distance between them.

"Sometimes, at night," he started, finally giving up on gaining her attention, "I wake up and . . . I can't remember where I am. And I get to feeling a little . . ." He shrugged, hoping to make it sound more casual, less terrifying than it actually was. "A little closed in, I guess. That's what happened tonight." He swallowed, the half truth bitter on his tongue and pricking his conscience. Only then did he realize she was watching him.

A keenness sharpened her gaze, one he might have considered engaging if he weren't trying to hide something.

"A little closed in," she repeated. Her eyes narrowed the slightest bit. Not so much with suspicion, he thought, as with curiosity. "Does it ever hurt, still?" she asked softly.

He frowned, not following what she was saying. She lowered her gaze, and he became aware that he was fingering the scar at his throat. He lowered his hand. His face heated. "No . . . not anymore."

"Would it be rude if I ask what happened?"

Her tentative tone encouraged his equally tentative smile. "It's from the war."

She didn't say anything for a moment. "Where did it happen?"

"The last night of the battle in Nashville," he said quietly. "December sev—"

"Seventeenth," she said along with him, her expression awash in memory. "James fought there. Thomas too," she whispered, looking openly at his scar now. "It's a wonder a wound like that didn't cost you your life."

"It did . . . in a sense." The lingering question in her expression touched something inside him, and reminded him that events from that night twelve years ago were not all horrific. At least not the final outcome. "I would never have become a doctor had it not been for this." He briefly touched the scar again.

He vividly remembered the searing hot lead of a minié ball ripping through his neck, then the metallic taste of blood. He lay on the battlefield, for how long he didn't know, his mind telling his lungs to fill only to have them respond with sluggish, hindered obedience. He must have lost consciousness, because the next time he awakened was on a cot in a surgeon's tent, and the next . . . to the darkest night he could ever remember. And would never forget. The memory was still horrifying.

And yet, looking back, the field surgeon pronouncing him dead had given him new life.

"So you became a doctor because of your wound. . . ." Her voice was quiet yet held singular interest. "But why one specializing in obstetrics?"

Rand eyed the rustic hand-hewn mantel before them, taken aback by how much the heart could remember, even when the mind couldn't. He couldn't recall the exact nuances of his sister's face, nor that of her infant daughter, but he recalled with painful accuracy the rending feeling of separation at their passing. His feelings had mirrored those Marietta had described to him after she'd knelt by his graveside the evening following the Battle of Nashville.

Aware of Rachel's stare, he pulled his thoughts back. "My younger sister . . . Marietta," he whispered, a lifetime of memories accompanying the name. "She died while giving birth to her first child . . . a daughter, who died not long after."

A soft gasp. "I'm so sorry, Rand."

He ran his thumb along the smoothed edge of the mantel, where wood had given way to a knife's sharp edge, and imagined Thomas Boyd doing much the same as he'd fashioned it for his home. "I was already a year into my medical training at the time and hadn't yet decided which area of study interested me most. When Marietta and her baby died, my decision became clear." He winced, recalling the events leading up to his sister's and niece's deaths. "Marietta's baby came early and her body wasn't prepared to deliver the child." He stared down at the cold hearth. "The doctor didn't know how to perform a—"

"Cesarean delivery . . ." Rachel nodded, her voice falling away.

He nodded.

A moment passed before she spoke again. "Last fall . . . when I helped you deliver little Jo . . ." She shook her head. "That must have been so painful, so frightening. Yet you didn't look it in the least."

He gave a soft laugh. "I was scared to death . . . on

the inside." Oh, how he wished he could tell her the truth about his reaction tonight. He felt as if God himself were opening a door for him to do just that, and yet Rand couldn't bring himself to walk through.

Aware of the lengthening silence and of the condition of Rachel's parlor, he gestured to the sofa and pillows. "I'll straighten things up before I leave." He took a step and something crunched beneath his boot. Looking down, he felt a fresh wave of regret. He held out an arm to make sure Rachel didn't step in the shards of glass. "Did I do this?"

"Don't worry," she said softly. "I'll clean it up."

He knelt and picked up one of the larger pieces of broken glass. Or *crystal,* he decided on closer inspection. "I'm sorry, Rachel." He hoped it wasn't something Thomas had given her.

"It's all right." She bent down.

"No . . . it's not." Renewed shame cut through him. Somehow, he had to learn to conquer his fear. He'd lived too long within its grip. "Was this special to you?"

"No," she answered, a second too late for it to have been the truth. "It was just a vase."

"I'll replace it."

She briefly touched his arm. "You don't need to, Rand."

"I want to," he said softly, seeing the trust in her eyes and wishing he'd had the courage to tell her the whole truth.

22

Saturday morning came early and Rand awakened well before sunrise. He'd slept hard, exhausted from the events of the day before. Even with the oil lamp burning on the table in the corner, it took a few seconds for his surroundings to register. He was at the resort, in the physician's quarters in the Health Suite, and Ben's surgery was scheduled in four hours.

The fog of sleep gradually cleared, and his lingering embarrassment over what had happened at Rachel's home resurfaced. She'd been more than understanding, but he still cringed when he thought of how foolish he must have appeared to her.

Both dreading and eager to see her again, he rose and dressed. The headache that accompanied his panic attacks had subsided yesterday afternoon, which was good. He needed to be clearheaded and sharp for Ben's procedure.

After checking on Ben and Lyda, who were still asleep in the patient-convalescing room, he slipped down to the kitchen to see if he could scrounge up some breakfast. He wasn't hungry but knew it might be his last chance to eat for several hours.

The kitchen was already bustling with cooks and servers, the clank of pots and pans an orchestra all its own. Within minutes of his request for black coffee and plain toast, one of the cooks presented him with a plate piled high with scrambled eggs, sausage, and fried potatoes, with a couple of griddle cakes placed artfully to one side.

Rand's eyes widened. *"Grazie, signora."*

The older woman smiled. "I am the one to thank *you,* Dr. Brookston. You helped my brother, Fernando."

He nodded. He'd visited Fernando, the resort gardener who had contracted typhoid, several times in Little Italy. "He's still improving, I hope?"

The woman smirked. "Too much, his wife says. She say he is bossing everyone around at home again. And eating everything he can." She shrugged in that carefree manner of Italian women. "I tell her it is better him bothering her there than bothering me"—she spread her arms and gestured proudly—"in my kitchen."

Rand grinned, seeing the twinkle in the woman's eyes. He held up the plate. "Thank you again."

She patted his arm, leaning close. "I fix Signore and Signora Mullins something to eat, *sí?*"

Rand matched her conspiratorial tone. "I'm sure Signora Mullins would appreciate something. But nothing for Signore Mullins this morning. Maybe later tonight."

She nodded. "You do the surgery today? On his lungs?"

Word sure got around in this little town. "Yes, that's today."

"You will do good job. I know it already." She threw a stern glare at one of the servers standing watching them until the young girl moved out of earshot. "I hear you are working for Signore Tolliver now." Her knit brow said she hoped it wasn't true. "You will no longer be doctor for Timber Ridge . . . and for us?"

Rand wanted to throttle Brandon Tolliver. Tolliver had given his word he wouldn't tell anyone about their agreement for at least a week, and it had barely been four days since they'd shaken hands on the deal—however reluctantly on Rand's part. It was only temporary, until Tolliver found someone to take the position full time, and Rand still needed time to tell some people about it. Namely, Rachel. "I'm still the doctor for Timber Ridge. My working with the resort is part-time, and it's only temporary."

She looked up at him with those dark eyes and nodded. *"Si,"* she said softly. "I hope that is true."

"It is. So don't worry. If you or your family get sick, you still send for me." He winked as he left the kitchen, not blind to the question in her eyes, but he knew what he was doing. Being allowed to perform Ben's surgery at the resort was worth whatever inconvenience it caused him personally.

The surgical instruments alone made his agreement with Tolliver worthwhile, but the facilities . . . highest quality all around. And there was a bonus reason he'd said yes to the agreement.

With what Tolliver agreed to pay him, even if it was just for a few weeks, he could purchase new supplies, replenish dwindling pharmaceutical items, and still have a small amount left over that he could put toward renovating another building in town—once one became available.

No sooner did he think of the building he'd lost than he saw Edward Westin speaking with Rachel in the lobby. Westin casually touched her arm, the briefest gesture, in no sense inappropriate, but still . . .

Rand paused, watching, and experiencing an unwelcome twinge of jealousy. He hadn't known they were acquainted.

"Dr. Brookston!" Edward spotted him and waved him over. "Good to see you again."

Sneaking a look at Rachel, who acknowledged him with a smile, Rand shook his hand. "Same to you, Edward. How's that shoulder feeling these days?"

Westin made a show of working the joint back and forth. "It hasn't felt this good in ages." Westin leaned in toward Rachel with a familiarity that confirmed this wasn't their first meeting. "As I was telling you last evening, Mrs. Boyd, I highly recommend Dr. Brookston's services. If you have any ailments, he's your man."

Rachel's smile deepened, though it lacked its usual warmth. "Yes, I'm aware of Dr. Brookston's expertise. Timber Ridge is lucky to have him. Or was . . . before he began working for the resort."

Rand nearly dropped his plate. A scalpel to the gut would have been more subtle. Rachel's expression invited him to correct her, and he wished he could. "I was going to tell you. . . ." He caught himself, and included Westin in his nod. "I was going to tell everyone. I just made the decision this week," he added quickly. "It's only part-time. And short-term. Until Mr. Tolliver can find a replacement."

Rachel nodded, her disappointment palpable. "News travels fast in Timber Ridge, Dr. Brookston."

Westin nodded. "I learned that the day I arrived. Speaking of . . ." He turned to Rand. "I read in this morning's paper that you're operating on Ben Mullins today. Removing fluid from his lungs?" His features reflected wonder. "It's amazing what you fellas can do these days."

Rand gulped. "You . . . read about the surgery in the newspaper?"

Westin withdrew a copy from the inside of his suit coat. "You can have mine. I'm finished with it."

To Rand's marginal relief, he realized it was a copy of the *Colorado Hot Springs Resort Weekly*, not the *Timber Ridge Reporter*. Then he glimpsed the bolded oversized print on the front page, right under the *Special Edition* banner—NEW RESORT HOSTS REVOLUTIONARY SURGERY—and he felt the pressure building in his temples.

Westin motioned to the front desk. "More copies

302

are available from the concierge, in case you need them. Tolliver told me over breakfast that, starting today, he's making the paper available in town too. He's mighty proud of what you're doing, Doctor."

Rand felt ill.

"Miss Rachel?" Charlie Daggett appeared beside them, looking rather sheepish holding a woman's reticule. "You forgot this in the wagon, ma'am."

Rachel checked her arm, then shook her head. "Thank you, Mr. Daggett. I was in such a rush to get here this morning. . . ."

Tipping his hat, Charlie turned to leave, but Rand caught the quizzical look he gave Westin. "Mr. Daggett—" He touched Charlie's coat sleeve, knowing that if these two men hadn't yet met, they needed to, considering their future connection at the store. He made the introductions, welcoming the shift of attention. "Mr. Daggett is the hardest working man in Timber Ridge, Westin. There's nothing he doesn't know how to do."

Westin nodded. "So I've heard from Mr. and Mrs. Mullins. It's a pleasure to meet you, Mr. Daggett. The Mullinses speak very highly of you. They tell me you're their most valuable worker."

Charlie ducked his head. "I think right highly of them too, sir."

Westin eyed him. "Charlie Daggett . . . Your name sounds familiar to me for some reason. Any chance our paths have crossed before?"

Charlie gave an affable grin. "I've worked all over

Colorado and Wyoming, sir. I ran freight wagons in Cheyenne, then worked at the stockyards in Denver. Then at a hog farm over in . . ."

Still listening to Charlie, Rand chanced a look at Rachel, eager for a moment alone with her. She wasn't looking at him, but he sensed she knew he was looking at her.

"I'm afraid, Mr. Daggett, that this is my first venture west." Westin smiled. "I spent the bulk of my years cooped up back east, building the iron road."

"You . . . you worked on the railroad, sir?" Charlie's jovial manner faded a shade.

Wanting to avoid any misunderstanding for Charlie about Westin's position with the railroad, Rand jumped in. "Mr. Westin was an executive with Union Pacific for . . ." Rand looked to Westin.

"Sixteen years," Westin supplied. "But I've been in railroading all my life." He took a peek at his pocket watch, then gripped Charlie's hand again. "It was a pleasure, Mr. Daggett. It might take a while, but I'll remember where I've heard that name." He gave a confirming wink. "I hate to take my leave of you fine people, but I need to get to my next appointment.'"

"So do I," Charlie added, doffing his hat and leaving as quickly as he'd come. A bit paler too, Rand noticed.

Rand gauged Charlie's abrupt departure, curious, then felt a touch on his arm.

"One last thing, Doctor," Westin said. "I want you to know just how much I appreciate all you're doing for Ben Mullins, and I'm not the only one. You don't have to be in Timber Ridge long to realize what fine folks Ben and Lyda Mullins are and what they mean to this town. You have a lot of people praying for the operation this morning. Count me among them."

He turned to Rachel. "And, Mrs. Boyd, thank you again for the pleasure of your company at Miss Clara's last evening. And that of your boys. Kurt's as cute as he can be, and that Mitch . . . sharp as a whip."

Rand caught the brief discomfort in Rachel's expression before she smoothed it away.

Westin's departure left an awkward silence, and Rand chanced another glance at Rachel, who wasn't looking at him. So she'd accepted a dinner invitation from Edward Westin while refusing the same from him? His morning kept getting better and better.

"Should we prepare for the procedure, Doctor?"

Looking at her, Rand frowned. "Rachel, please don't call me—"

"Not here," she whispered, and smiled at two older couples sitting nearby looking their way, obviously eavesdropping. "Why don't you take me to see Mr. and Mrs. Mullins? I'd love to visit with them both before we begin."

Rand nodded, struggling to conceal his frustration. "It's this way."

As they passed the restaurant, he handed his untouched plate to a server. Once they reached the door to the Health Suite, he stopped Rachel with a touch, taking advantage of the moment alone. "Rachel, I was going to tell you the other night—about my taking the position here. The only reason I—"

"You don't owe me an explanation, Rand." Her laugh was airy. "I'm not your mother, after all. I was simply surprised to learn the news. I'd gathered your goals as a physician ran along . . . *other* lines."

"They *do* run along other lines. That's what I'm trying to tell—"

"Excuse me, Dr. Brookston?"

Rand looked up to see Brandon Tolliver's personal assistant walking toward them, portfolio in hand. Summoning patience long depleted, he turned to her. "Yes, Miss Valente?"

Smiling, she handed him a sheet of paper. "Here's your patient roster for the day, sir."

Rand scanned the sheet. "I don't understand. What is this?"

"It's your schedule for the day. I have listed the guests who have requested to see you, along with each of their ailments."

Rand quickly counted. Eleven guests, and eleven different "concerns," ranging from an ingrown toenail to a slight ache in the left forefinger to excessive freckling across the bridge of the nose. These were their *ailments?* He looked up again, half expecting to see Miss Valente smiling, as though this were some sort of joke. And she *was* smiling, but apparently this was no joke.

Rachel smiled too, but in an "I told you so" kind of way.

He blew out a breath. Per his agreement with Tolliver, he would see guests about health issues on a part-time basis, and he aimed to keep his word. But he had a sinking feeling it wasn't going to be the kind of arrangement he'd anticipated.

"Thank you, Miss Valente." He pulled his pocket watch from his suit coat. "It will be two o'clock before I'll be able to start seeing these guests. I'll be with Ben Mullins until that time."

She nodded. "That's fine, Doctor. I'll see to it that the appointments are arranged at thirty-minute intervals."

Rand quickly did the math, taking into account the severity of the guests' concerns. *Excessive freckling* . . . "Why don't we make that fifteen-minute intervals. I believe that will be more than sufficient."

With a bounce in her step, Miss Valente retraced her path down the hall.

Rachel reached for the door latch to the Health Suite, but Rand covered her hand on the knob.

"Rachel, as I was saying . . . the reason I took this job—"

"I told you, Rand—"

He pressed two fingers against her lips, exasperated. "If you'd be quiet for two seconds straight and let me get this out . . ."

He expected the raised brow, but not the sly smile that accompanied it. Her lips were incredibly soft against his fingertips and enticed his imagination, which needed no encouragement when it came to this woman. And her blue eyes— he had to smile—her blue eyes held a no-nonsense look that told him her indulgence had its limits. Though tempted to see what those limits were, he resolved to save that for a more appropriate time.

He removed his hand. "The reason I agreed to this arrangement with Tolliver was because he gave me no choice. He wasn't going to let us perform the surgery here if I didn't agree to help out in the short term. And we both know how much greater Ben's chances are for a successful surgery and recuperation here at the resort rather than at my clinic, and certainly rather than in the bedroom above the store."

Satisfied he'd at least told his side of the story, he reached for the doorknob, wondering if she'd still consider him a fool for making the agreement with Tolliver.

As the door opened, she brushed her hand

against his on the brass latch. "Thank you, Rand," she whispered, "for letting me know that. And for using the word *us* when referring to performing the surgery, even though we both know it's you."

23

Rachel held the cannula between her fingers, careful not to touch the sharp tip of the hollow needle. Despite Rand's instructions on this procedure and her poring over his notes and illustrations, she still felt some anxiety over what they—or rather *he*—were about to do. Rand had been generous to include her in the "us" reference earlier, but she was under no delusion about who was performing the intricate procedure. Nor did she take lightly the risks involved, however much the benefits of this surgery might outweigh the alternative of doing nothing.

At the table in the corner, Rand prepared the topical anesthetic—his measurements exact, his movements deft and certain. Gratitude wafted through her again. Not only was she witnessing this surgery, a slice of history for Timber Ridge, she was privileged to assist with it and to help Ben and Lyda in some small way.

She scooted the stool Rand had obtained for her closer to the examination table and sat down, glad to rest her leg. She couldn't believe Edward Westin had mentioned having dinner with her and the boys at Miss Clara's last night. The look on Rand's face had been enough to make her want to dig a hole and crawl inside. Yet the circumstances of the dinner hadn't been what she could clearly see Rand was thinking, and she intended on telling him exactly that as soon as they had another moment alone.

Ben was seated on the side of an examination table that could be raised and lowered by turning a crank, and he leaned forward on a tall padded table, shirtless. Rachel had been surprised when Rand told her he would perform this procedure with Ben in a seated position. "The pressure in the lungs when fully inflated," Rand had explained, demonstrating as he'd sat on her sofa in the parlor, "combined with the pull of gravity will force the fluid to gather at the base of the pleural space, thereby making it easier to extract when the patient is in an upright position."

After studying Rand's drawings of the lungs and discussing the surgical steps, it made perfect sense.

Ben wore a pair of loose-fitting drawstring trousers that Rand had found in one of the many well-stocked cabinets in the main room. No wonder Rand had been determined to have the surgery at the resort. This facility was beyond her imaginings. And though she still didn't like the idea of Rand working for Brandon Tolliver, even temporarily, she understood why he'd said yes. She would have done the same thing.

Standing before Ben, Lyda touched his face with tenderness born only of a well-aged love. "You know what I've told you every single day of our marriage," she whispered, her voice fragile.

Ben looked at her, his eyes mirroring the love in hers, his expression a mixture of apprehension and nervous hope. "And you know what I've told you right back."

Lyda leaned down and kissed his cheek, then whispered something into his ear. She drew back and looked at Rand. "Please come and get me as soon as you're through." Her eyes glistened. "To tell me that everything went well."

Only then did Rachel see it—the yellow flowered hair ribbon in Lyda's grip. Once bright, the fabric was now faded and frayed around the edges. It had been years since she'd seen it, though she'd never once doubted that Lyda still carried it with her, and always would. Just as she was certain Ben still carried the suede pouch with a wooden ball and twelve metal jacks.

Rand put an arm around Lyda's shoulders. "Ben will be fine." His voice was confident, reassuring. "I'm hoping this procedure will lessen his orneriness, but I can't guarantee it."

Lyda smiled, a smidgen of relief showing. "That's all right." She squeezed Ben's hand. "I don't mind a little orneriness. Not when it comes with the rest of him."

Rand accompanied Lyda outside and returned,

closing the door behind him. "Shall we begin?"

Ben shifted on the table. "I don't think you want me answering that, Doc."

Rachel noticed the slight tremor in his hands and rose to briefly cover them with hers. "You're in good hands," she whispered, thinking both of God's hands and also of Rand's. The trusting smile Ben gave her was one she would carry with her forever.

Rand leaned down and looked Ben squarely in the eyes. "I appreciate your trust, Ben, and I won't let you down. The only thing you need to concentrate on, as we talked about before, is breathing when I tell you to breathe, and holding your breath when I tell you to hold it. We'll be done in no time."

Ben nodded and focused at the door through which Lyda had exited, and Rachel felt his love for his wife. And she wondered . . . what it must be like for him, knowing he was close to the end of his life? At least his life on earth. Everyone died. That was a given. But not everyone was warned of death's approach. And she wondered whether knowing was better, or worse. She decided the former, based on the regrets she had with Thomas, wishing she'd had the chance to talk to him one last time.

Rand placed Ben's arms on the chest-high table positioned in front of him so that Ben was leaning forward, his back slightly arched. "Is that comfortable for you?" At Ben's nod, Rand moved around behind him and gave Rachel a thoughtful look, his shoulders lifting as he took a breath through his nose and exhaled through his mouth.

The poultice mixture he'd applied on two small areas of Ben's back a half hour earlier were still moist. With a fresh cloth, he wiped one of the spots clean. He lightly pressed the tip of the hollow needle against Ben's skin. "Tell me when you feel something."

Seconds ticked past.

Ben turned his head to one side. "Well, go ahead, Doc. I'm not gettin' any younger just sittin' here."

Rachel smiled at the playful sarcasm in Ben's voice. She mentally reviewed the details of the surgery and the illustrations Rand had drawn depicting the various steps. He would insert the needle into the outer sac that encased each lung, the place where the fluid gathered, being careful not to puncture the lungs. To do so would cause the lungs to collapse—the greatest risk involved in the surgery itself, besides the possibility of developing a fever.

With expert focus, Rand inserted the tip of the needle just below the skin, then paused. "All right, Ben, no sudden movements. I want you to take some normal breaths, like we discussed a few minutes ago. Yes, good, just like that. After I start counting, you're going to feel a slight sense of *pulling* or pressure in your chest. Tell me if you start to feel faint or if you have any shortness of breath, or if you need to cough. Because I *must* remove the needle from the pleural cavity before you do. That's imperative. Do you understand?"

"I gotcha, Doc." Ben kept breathing as he'd been instructed.

Rand gave Rachel a nod, and she readied the apparatus in her hands, the instrument Rand told her he'd designed for this procedure. "I'll count to ten," he said. "On the count of two, Ben, hold your breath. On the count of ten, exhale. It's that simple."

"You sure you can count that high, Doc?"

A tiny smile eased the tension in Rand's expression. "Mrs. Boyd is here. She'll keep me on track. Here we go. . . ." He briefly closed his eyes, squeezing them tight, then opened them again. Needle positioned, he slid it in farther. "One . . . two, hold your breath"—Rand leaned in as though every sense available to him was honed on that needle's progress—"three . . . four . . ."

He held the needle still and signaled to Rachel. She began pulling back on the plunger portion of the syringe, which was attached to a small bottle, which was affixed via a narrow tube to the hollow needle. The science behind the apparatus was simple yet amazingly clever. As she pulled back on the plunger, the suction created a vacuum effect inside the bottle and pulled the fluid from the outer sac encompassing the lung.

"Steady," Rand whispered to her, nodding his approval. "Six . . . seven—"

Fluid filtered through the tube and into the bottle at a surprising rate, faster than Rachel had expected. Which, according to what Rand told her during their discussion the other night, indicated a greater amount of fluid present. Which wasn't good.

"Nine"—he signaled for her to stop and then pulled the needle back—"Ten, and exhale now, Ben."

Ben did and coughed hard. He took some rattled breaths.

"You all right?" Rand leaned around to look at him, hand on Ben's shoulder.

"Sitting still like that was a mite harder than I thought it would be." He coughed again. "But I'm fine. Did you get anything, Doc?"

"We sure did." Rand held up the bottle for him to see.

Ben's eyes widened. "Well . . . what do you know. No wonder I'm having such trouble breathing."

"Mrs. Boyd performed the extraction herself." Rand looked over at her. "And she couldn't have done a better job."

Rachel beamed, despite knowing his praise was overly generous. "I had the easy part. And, Ben, you did wonderfully," she added, grateful for the chance to be a part of the process, to be helping.

She couldn't quite define what it was she was feeling in that moment, but whatever it was, it felt *wonderful*. A kind of wonderful she hadn't felt in a long time. If ever.

"As soon as you've gained your breath, Ben, we need to do that again on the same side. Did you feel any discomfort?"

Ben shook his head. "Just felt like something was tugging on me from the inside a little. Didn't hurt, though."

They withdrew two more syringes full of fluid from the left lung, then moved to the right and proceeded to do the same. Rachel glanced at the clock. Twenty-five minutes had passed. Lyda must be worrying something awful. She started to ask Rand if she could step out and give Lyda an update when he straightened, stretching his back muscles.

"Twice more on this side, Ben, and we'll be done." Perspiration beaded Rand's brow, and Rachel dabbed it dry, remembering having done the same for her father. Rand thanked her for the simple gesture—something she couldn't remember her father ever doing.

Ben took a deep breath. "I think I can already feel the difference, Doc. You're pretty good at this."

The three of them laughed. They had this procedure down to a routine now, and as Rand counted to ten again, Rachel pulled back on the syringe, slow and steady.

"Five . . . six, almost done." Rand nodded to her, indicating all was well. "Seven . . . eig—"

Ben's upper body jerked hard as he tried to stifle a cough, and couldn't. Rand gripped Ben's shoulder and pulled the needle from his back, but judging by the dread in Rand's eyes, Rachel knew something had gone wrong. She grabbed the needle from him as he reached for Ben.

Rand held him as Ben gripped his left arm. "Rachel! The digitalis!"

She knew right where it was. Rand had insisted they have everything at the ready, so the digitalis was already mixed. She held the cup to Ben's mouth. Ben drank in noisy gulps, sounding as though he might choke on it.

"Is it his lung?" she asked, thinking the needle had punctured it.

"I don't think so," Rand said. "I think it's his heart."

Ben grimaced, his face twisted in pain, then he suddenly went limp. Rachel went cold inside. *Oh, God, no. Not yet.*

Rand pressed two fingers against the underside of Ben's throat. "Help me lay him back."

She slipped an arm about Ben's waist, her leg already aching from the added pressure, and helped reposition Ben on the examination table. "What can I do?"

"Talk to him," Rand said, reaching for his stethoscope.

She leaned close to his ear. "Ben, stay with us, *please*. It's not time for you to go yet." She felt Rand watching her as he listened to Ben's chest. She grabbed Ben's hand and squeezed it tight. "You did so well during the surgery. You were so brave." She swallowed the emotion rising in her throat. "This procedure is going to give you more time . . . just like you wanted." She looked up at Rand, praying to God she wasn't lying.

"His heartbeat is weak but steady."

Ben's eyes suddenly shot open. He sucked in a noisy breath.

"Ben!" Rachel drew closer. "Can you hear me?"

He blinked, his eyes glassy, as though he wasn't sure where he was. "How could I not hear you . . . with you screamin' in my ear."

Laughing, she kissed his stubbled cheek, unable to speak.

Rand checked Ben's eyes, pulling down on each lower lid. "So much for the procedure helping your orneriness, Ben Mullins."

Ben smiled, then winced. "Don't make me laugh, Doc. . . . It hurts too much." He looked around, as though just remembering where he was. "What happened?"

Rand removed the stethoscope from his ears. "From what I can tell, you had another heart episode, less serious than last time, thank God. But still . . ." He looked at Rachel, concern lining his features. "Administering the digitalis so quickly helped, I'm sure. Thank you for being here . . . Mrs. Boyd."

Rachel glimpsed far more than gratitude in his eyes. "My pleasure," she whispered, feeling braver in the moment than she would have if they'd been alone.

Ben reached up and gently patted the side of her face. "Thomas would be so proud of you, Rachel. He always said you had a gift for doctoring."

Silently questioning, she knew Ben wasn't a man given to exaggeration. "You mean . . . ?" She firmed her lips to keep them from trembling. "You're saying that Thomas . . . *he* said that to you?"

"He sure did, honey. More than once. You didn't know?"

She closed her eyes and tasted the salt of tears on her tongue. Thomas had paid her countless compliments in their marriage, but never that one, and she didn't have to think long to come up with the reason why. She sniffed and chanced a look up, and felt her breath steal away.

In the space of a blink, she read every unguarded emotion in Rand's face. Gratitude, pride, relief, humility—and a depth of desire so intense it reached inside her and set to flame that tiny flicker of a spark she'd worked so hard to shelter.

That afternoon, as Rand saw guests from the resort in the first patient room, Rachel tended to Ben and Lyda in the other and tidied up the surgical area. It had been years since she'd worked in a setting resembling this one. And in an odd but good way, it felt like coming home. Even if this "home" was only temporary.

Rand had made the decision not to continue the procedure on Ben's right lung, and she agreed wholeheartedly in light of what had happened. That meant Ben would be staying at the resort longer than planned and that they would complete the procedure in a few days, which Ben wasn't thrilled about. Lyda, on the other hand, seemed relieved that Rand insisted on keeping him there.

Rand's voice carried as he met with patients, and Rachel noted the conversational tone he used when speaking with them. Almost as if they were sitting across a table, sharing a cup of coffee. No wonder people opened up to him like they did. More than once, she laughed to herself at the ailments the guests were seeing him about. A woman complaining about the wrinkles on her neck, a man concerned about his thinning hair . . .

No arguing the fact—the Colorado Hot Springs Resort catered to the rich and privileged. She looked around the pristine clinic, all crisp and white, the shelves of bottles and tins bearing familiar names, the medical instruments with recognizable, but also slightly different, updated looks. And she couldn't help but compare it all to the muck and mire of the ranch. She ran a finger over the work-worn calluses lining her palms.

Running a ranch wasn't the life she would have chosen on her own, but it *was* the life she and Thomas had chosen together, and she was still determined to make a success of it. She just needed help figuring out how to do that, especially since she'd guaranteed Mr. Fossey that, come fall, she'd be caught up on her loan payments.

James and Molly, who were at the cabin with Mitch and Kurt today, had invited her and the boys over for lunch soon. James had inquired again about the ranch and she'd decided to run some ideas by him, see what he thought.

It seemed her cattle simply weren't strong enough to make it through the bitter months of freezing temperatures. Sickness and cold were picking them off one by one, same as those on other ranches. Except the other ranches were larger, more profitable, and employed numerous ranch hands. They could absorb the losses far better than she could. Maybe James would have some ideas, but if he attempted to come to her rescue, she would simply be firm about wanting to handle things herself.

Rand checked on Ben several times throughout the afternoon, and each time she sensed concern in his guarded manner. Throughout the day, Lyda never left Ben's side. She seemed to anticipate his needs before he could voice them.

A server from the restaurant delivered dinner at six o'clock sharp, and Rachel dined with Lyda and

Ben in the patient recovery room, where the couple would stay for however long it took Ben to recuperate. She kept Rand's plate covered as his appointments ran long. When Ben and Lyda decided to retire early, she checked Ben's temperature again, watchful for the least sign of fever that often set in following surgery. But his temperature remained normal and the places on his back where Rand had inserted the needle showed no irritation.

Bidding them good night, Rachel closed the door to their room, then limped across the suite to the physician's quarters. Exhausted, her leg aching, she sank into a chair and leaned her head back, watching through the window as the sun bathed the mountains in hues of gold and red. She smiled, knowing now why the sky turned those colors. She wondered if the boys were staring at the sunset too. She was eager to get home to them.

She yawned, closing her eyes. Charlie Daggett had agreed to escort her home but had indicated it could be after nine o'clock before his work at the resort was done. A few minutes rest would do her good, but only a few. . . .

24

Rachel awakened to lamplight and the soft scratch of fountain pen on paper. She stirred, seeing the world beyond the window now bathed in darkness, and not one but *four* oil lamps illuminating the physician's quarters. The fountain pen went silent.

"Good evening," Rand whispered, looking at her from the chair opposite hers, pen in hand. A journal of some sort rested on his thigh. "You looked so peaceful, I hated to wake you."

Rachel smiled and sat up straighter, stretching. Napping was heavenly, and something unaccustomed. It gave her peace of mind to know the boys were with James and Molly until she returned home. Mitch and Kurt were loving the company, no doubt. She glanced at the number of lamps adorning the room again, remembering the night Rand had fallen asleep in her parlor, and how shaken he'd seemed when she found him outside on the porch. *"I wake up,"* he'd said, *"and can't remember where I am. I get to feeling a little closed in sometimes."* She guessed the extra lamps made sense. By nature, Rand was a man who liked to be prepared. But still, *four?* She yawned, deciding not to comment. "How long have I been asleep?"

"Not long enough, I'd daresay."

She laughed and smoothed the sides of her hair. "Is it that bad?"

His expression turned decidedly intimate. "Not at all. But I know you, Rachel Boyd. You never rest when there's work to be done. You scrubbed the surgery room clean and put it to right, along with all the instruments and medicine. You wiped down every counter and table in sight. You made files for the patients I saw today." He shook his head. "You even penned a list of the supplies we used for Ben's surgery"—he pulled a loose sheet of paper from the journal—"so that I'd know what needs to be replaced." He held her gaze. "You're very thorough, which is a trait I admire. Very much."

She probably should have been uncomfortable at his close attention. But strangely, she wasn't. He'd noticed everything she'd done, down to the last detail, and it made her feel . . . *special.* Appreciated.

"Thank you," she said, sensing their conversation was at a crossroad. Coaxing a carefree smile, she chose the less serious path. "Remind me never to try and sneak something by you, Dr. Brookston."

"On the contrary, I wish you *would.*" A mischievous gleam lit his eyes. "You must know by now . . . I enjoy a challenge."

Outwardly, she laughed off his playfulness. But inwardly, she felt herself softening toward him even more, despite knowing it would be safer if she didn't. The look in his eyes, the subtle flirtation, made her pulse beat a little faster. He reached to the side, and only then did she notice the silver tea service on the table adjacent to them.

He poured a cup and handed it to her with a wink. "I have connections in the kitchen."

She sipped, the fragrant steam wafting from the cup. Orange and cinnamon spice. Delicious. "Very *good* connections, I'd say."

He stared at her for a moment, and she knew something was on his mind. She also knew it was late, they were both tired, and she needed to get home to the boys. Apparently Charlie Daggett hadn't come by for her yet, so she had time. And something in Rand's expression invited her to stay, which was exactly what she wanted to do.

She grew warmer by the second and blamed it on the tea. But glancing over the rim of her cup at the man seated across from her, she knew that wasn't true. "The amount of fluid you extracted from Ben's lungs," she said, not so artfully steering the conversation away from the more personal. "I sensed that wasn't what you were expecting. From that one side, anyway." It remained to be seen if the right lung held as much.

The faint narrowing of his eyes hinted at Rand's acknowledgment of what she was doing. He took a drink of tea. "It wasn't what I'd hoped for, but it was what I suspected. The more fluid that collects in the pleural cavity, the graver the patient's prognosis. We don't know why the fluid collects." He sighed as though the not knowing frustrated him. "But excessive fluid always portends the latter stages of a disease. Be it heart failure, or tuberculosis, or one of a hundred other illnesses for which the cause remains elusive." He set down his cup, his gaze confined to the floor, his shoulders bearing that invisible weight she'd witnessed before. "There's still so much we don't understand. So much we still can't do."

She leaned forward in her chair in an effort to regain his attention. "But doctors are learning more every day, Rand. You said so yourself when we were preparing for Ben's surgery."

He didn't respond.

"Take the typhoid outbreak, for example," she said.

His gaze lifted.

"Eight people have come down with typhoid since the outbreak. Only *eight!* And no deaths so far. That's unheard of. Shortly before you came to Timber Ridge, thirty-seven people died from typhoid in a town not far from Denver. But that kind of tragedy isn't going to happen here . . . because of you. It's the truth," she said quickly, seeing him shake his head in disagreement. "The article you wrote for the newspaper, the instructions about what causes typhoid and what precautions to take to prevent contracting it . . ." She arched a brow, trying to draw a smile from him. "As Sir Francis Bacon once wrote, 'Knowledge *is* power.'"

That earned her a laugh. Rand's gaze moved over her face and turned serious. "Thank you," he said quietly.

She shrugged, feigning nonchalance. "For what?"

"For being here now. With me."

His bluntness caught her off guard. She knew full well what he was referring to, but she wasn't ready for her heart to go there. Not yet. Maybe not ever. She took another sip of tea and sat straighter in her chair. "I'm glad I was here too. I'm grateful you asked me to assist you."

His slow-coming smile said he saw through her ploy. "You know that's not what I meant."

She bit her lower lip, resisting the overpowering urge to look away. "I know," she whispered, her heart beating double time now. "But it's what I need for you to mean."

Understanding moved in behind his eyes, only managing to draw her closer to him, while also confusing her further. She suddenly empathized with how he sometimes felt closed in, and the openness of the room, the warm glow of lamplight, did nothing to calm her. On the contrary, it felt as if everything she was thinking and feeling—and fearing—lay fully exposed. "It's getting late. I need to get home." Yet she couldn't move.

"Isn't Charlie supposed to come by for you?"

She nodded, slowly coming undone inside. The vulnerability in his eyes wasn't helping.

Rand stood, his movements measured and thoughtful, as if she were a doe that might bolt at any second. He knelt beside her chair. "Rachel . . ."

She shook her head, hearing the tenderness in his voice. She cared for him more than she should, more than she'd allowed herself to admit before this moment. But the thought of opening more of her life to him, of opening her heart, set something trembling deep inside her. She feared, once it started, she wouldn't be able to stop it.

"Look at me," he whispered. "Please . . ."

She shook her head again. "I . . . I can't."

"Sure you can." His hand covered hers clasped tightly in her lap, and gently, patiently, he wove his fingers, so warm and sure and purposeful, between hers. "You were looking at me easily enough just a minute ago." His hand tightened around hers. "You're shaking." He brought her hand to his lips and kissed it.

Rachel drew in a breath.

He turned her hand over and kissed her open palm—once, twice—and she forgot how to breathe. Didn't he know what he was doing to her? Couldn't he tell?

Gathering her wounded resolve, she finally did as he asked and looked at him—then wished she hadn't. His unguarded desire roused her own, and the woman inside her ached for him. Not for a man, any man, but for *him*. And not only in the way of a woman with a man, but in the way that two halves made a whole, as God intended.

A shiver stole through her. She couldn't do this again—risk giving herself to someone else only to lose them. She wouldn't survive another—

He leaned forward, slowly enough that she could

have turned her head away if she'd wanted to. But, God help her, she didn't want to. He kissed her temple, her cheek, then the corner of her mouth, his breath warm and spicy like the tea, and Rachel felt the wall she'd carefully built to protect her heart melt in a puddle at her feet.

He stilled, his face so close to hers, his unspoken question filling the silence.

Measuring the cost of her answer, she drew back slightly. Disappointment shone in his eyes. But when she touched his face, and traced his lips, her hand still trembling, his disappointment faded and eager longing took its place.

He kissed her, feather soft at first, his lips a whisper of a promise against hers. He awakened desires she'd known were still there, but she had forgotten their raw strength. His stubbled jaw was rough against her skin, but she welcomed the maleness of his touch. A hunger dawned inside her and she drew him closer. His kiss tasted like cinnamon, his lips eager against hers, and when he deepened the kiss, their—

He suddenly pulled back.

She opened her eyes. It took her a second to focus, and when she saw his look of surprise, it struck her. *She'd* been the one to deepen the kiss, to pull him closer. She, the grieving widow who had worked so hard to keep him at arm's length, and had made certain he knew it. Her face went hot. "I'm sorry," she gasped.

He exhaled, smiling. "Please don't say that, because I'm certainly not." He cradled the side of her face. "It's just that—"

She held up a hand, praying he wouldn't say anything else. "I understand." She stood, and he did likewise. "I should go."

He reached out. "Rachel, please, let's just talk for a—"

Out in the main room of the Health Suite, she grabbed her coat, careful not to make a noise that would awaken Ben and Lyda in the next room. Rand helped her with her coat, and she fumbled with the buttons in the dim light of an oil lamp on the far wall. Finally giving up, she grabbed her scarf and reticule.

Rand beat her to the door and placed his palm firmly against it. "Rachel," he whispered, leaning close behind her. "Don't run away like this."

Hand on the latch, she bowed her head, tears coming fast.

He stroked her hair. "I've wanted that to happen for so long. I've dreamed about kissing you like that." His laughter was soft. "I was just a little surpris—"

"I loved my husband." She looked up at him. "I loved Thomas with all my heart."

He didn't say anything for a moment, then drew her against his chest. She clung to him, holding on to him the way she used to hold on to Thomas.

Rand kissed the crown of her head. "I know you

loved him. No one will ever question that, Rachel. *I* will never question that."

"When he died," she whispered, "I thought I would die with him."

His arms tightened around her. "And if I'd been here, I would have done everything I could to save him."

Eyes closed, she felt the hard lines of his body against hers. He felt so different from Thomas, yet she fit him perfectly, just as she had her husband.

A knock sounded on the door. She stiffened and Rand let go of her.

Guessing who it was, Rachel wiped her cheeks and gave the latch a turn. "Good evening, Mr. Daggett." Her voice sounded almost normal.

Charlie tipped his hat. "I'm ready to go when you are, ma'am. I've got the wagon out front."

She smiled. "Thank you. I'll be right out." Waiting until he'd walked on, she pushed the door almost closed again, then looked up. The right words wouldn't come, and she had no time to search for them. She reached for Rand's hand and held it in hers. "Thank you . . . for understanding. And for today. It meant more to me than you know."

He stepped closer, their bodies almost touching again. "Ben was right," he whispered. "As was Thomas. You have a gift, Rachel. And I'm honored to work alongside you, which we'll need to do again as soon as Ben's able. The remaining fluid needs to be extracted, but I'm thinking it'll be at least two or three days before we can attempt that again. I'll let you know."

Riding home beside Charlie, who was unusually quiet, Rachel revisited the events of the day, prayed for Ben and Lyda, and considered what had happened with Rand. They'd crossed a line from friendship to something much more, and it would be hard—if not next to impossible—to go back again. Some lines, once crossed, were forever erased.

By the time she slipped into her gown and into bed, cradling the extra pillow against her chest, she knew going back wasn't an option. Nor did she want to. Yet a part of her resisted and told her to shore up her heart, to keep it safe and protected.

She lay in the darkness, in the bed she'd shared with one man, and tried to imagine sharing it with another. Rand Brookston was so different from Thomas. And he was a doctor—gifted and intelligent, yet not at all like her father, as she'd first thought. It wasn't a question anymore of whether she cared for Rand. Or whether she could someday grow to love him. The question wasn't *could* she. But rather, would she allow herself to?

She closed her eyes, wondering if she already had. . . .

She drew the covers up tighter about her chin, staving off a shiver that came from somewhere deep inside. From nowhere, Mr. Fossey's counsel returned. *"Have you considered the possibility of remarriage? . . . If not in a match of the heart, then perhaps one of friendship?"*

She snuggled deeper beneath the covers, the well-intentioned counsel playing over and over in her mind. Remembering how Rand had held her, kissed her, how moved she'd been by him, she knew she could never again look upon him as simply a friend. And he'd made it quite clear he desired much more. Oh, how much safer and simpler a path this would be if it wasn't a match of the heart. If she chose to say yes to him, then what of the ranch? What of her pledge to give the boys the life Thomas had wanted for them?

She willed sleep to come and silence the questions, yet they came. Why would she choose to risk her heart again knowing only too well the cost such a choice could demand from her?

For a second time.

25

How long has your throat been hurting, Miss Stafford?" Rand retrieved a tongue depressor from a tin on his overcrowded medicine shelf, then a dentistry mirror from a nearby drawer.

"It started this morning. . . ." Situating herself on the patient table, the young teacher winced. "And it's only gotten worse as the day's gone on."

"I'm sorry to hear that." He bent slightly. "If you'll open your mouth for me, please, I'll take a look."

"I didn't see you at church yesterday, Doctor. I hope you weren't ill?"

Rand straightened. "No, not at all. I was about to leave for services, in fact, when a patient stopped by. By the time we were through, church was already over." He stole a glance at the clock on the wall.

He hadn't seen Rachel since Saturday night at the resort, following Ben's surgery. He'd planned on catching a few moments with her yesterday afternoon following church, but since that hadn't happened, he'd hoped to see her in town today. Yet chances for that were growing slim as the day wore on. He wanted to speak with her about assisting him with the remainder of Ben's procedure, tentatively set for the end of this week, given Ben was strong enough. Though Rand doubted that would be the case. The heart episode had weakened him considerably. Brandon Tolliver wasn't pleased with the extension of Ben's stay in the Health Suite, but that was the least of Rand's concerns.

Rand motioned with the tongue depressor. "If you'll open your mouth, Miss Stafford, I'll take a quick look."

She smiled. "It wasn't anything serious, I hope."

He blinked. "Beg your pardon?"

"The patient yesterday . . . I hope it wasn't anything serious."

"Oh no. Just routine. Now"—he indicated with a nod—"if you'll open your mouth, please."

She licked her lips, tipped back her head, and did as he requested.

He slid the wooden depressor onto her tongue, then with the aid of the long-handled mirror, examined the back of her throat. "There doesn't seem to be any redness or irritation." He angled the mirror toward her tonsils. No irritation there either. He stepped back, instruments in hand. "Does it hurt when you swallow?"

She nodded. "Yes, on occasion." As though to prove her point, she swallowed, grimacing as she did. Then she smoothed a hand over her bodice. "Are you planning on attending the spring festival?"

Rand looked back, beginning to doubt the veracity of the woman's complaint of a sore throat. "Honestly, I hadn't given it much thought. I couldn't even tell you when it is."

"June sixteenth," she said quickly. "It was just announced in the paper this morning. It will be my first time to attend." Her laugh sounded more like that of a schoolgirl than a teacher. "I'm going to bake the molasses cookies you like so much and enter them into the baking contest."

Rand forced a smile. Already aware of Miss Stafford's interest in him, he grew decidedly more skeptical of her motivation for stopping by the clinic. He would check for one more symptom, then would chalk this office visit up to a social call.

He glanced at the clock again, making sure she saw him this time. "I've got another appointment in town, but I'd like to check for swollen lymph nodes, just to be sure. If you'd unfasten just the top two buttons of your dress, please . . ." He tossed the tongue depressor into the trash pail and put the mirror aside to be washed, then rinsed his hands in the washbasin and turned back. "Sometimes, when there's soreness in the—"

Miss Stafford's shirtwaist lay open, far more than the requested two buttons, exposing a corset cinched so tightly it was a wonder the woman could breathe. A lace chemise stretched taut over her bosom, and the rise and fall of her chest was sharply exaggerated.

With effort, Rand kept his focus on her eyes, and nothing else. Yet her gaze told him little, her expression neither overly demure nor excessively bold. Debating, he quickly decided to err in favor of a misunderstanding, however much he doubted that probability.

He palpated the sides of her neck, then the underside of her throat, feeling for the least sign of swelling. But the only swelling he could find afflicting Miss Judith Stafford at the moment would be remedied if she would simply cut the ties on that corset.

"I'm sorry you're not feeling well, Miss

Stafford, but I'm not finding any symptoms that cause concern. Since this just started this morning, let's give it a week or so to clear up. In the meantime, I do have something that might help." He turned away. "While you situate your clothing, I'll get some tea leaves you can brew when the soreness is bothersome."

Without waiting for her response, he walked to the bookshelf on the far wall, briefly glimpsing her profile in a mirror. With a petulant pout, she frowned and began buttoning her shirtwaist, removing all doubt from his mind as to her intentions.

Busying himself with *searching* for the tea, he waited an appropriate time before returning. "Here we are." He placed the colored tin beside her on the table. "Brew two teaspoons with hot water. And you may take it as often as needed." He offered his hand as she negotiated the footstool to the floor, then noticed her fingers.

She tugged her hand away.

He frowned. "I'm sorry, Miss Stafford, but did you—"

"It's nothing." She gathered her reticule and reached for the tea.

He'd only caught a glimpse, but her fingers looked discolored. Bruised perhaps? "Did you catch your hand in a door? If you'd like for me to look at—"

"It's nothing like that." Her cheeks flushed.

"It's . . ." Her lips firmed. "One of my students thought it amusing to paint my desk drawer pulls with ink this afternoon." She yanked her sleeve farther down. "I *failed* to see the humor."

Rand didn't doubt that for a minute, seeing her annoyance. He worked at curbing a grin. "Rubbing alcohol does wonders in removing ink. But be sure and use lotion afterwards. The alcohol is very drying."

A smile warmed her frustration. "Why, thank you, Dr. Brookston. That's so kind of you to—"

A knock at the door interrupted them, and Rand couldn't reach for the latch fast enough.

"Mr. Daggett!" Rand shook Charlie's hand, discreetly pulling the man inside—no easy task. "What can I do for you?"

Charlie eyed him, then Miss Stafford. "I'm just makin' deliveries." He handed Rand an envelope. "I got somethin' out in the wagon. It's from Miss Rachel."

"From *Rachel?*" Rand followed Charlie to the door. What would she be sending him?

Charlie spoke over his shoulder. "She said it's her way of sayin' thanks. Somethin' about you lettin' her help with the surgery and her thankin' you for it. I'm guessin' it's all in the note there."

Rand spotted something large and rectangular in the wagon bed, wrapped in a blanket. He smiled, thinking again of the moment he and Rachel had shared in the—

Then he felt it—the heat of Miss Stafford's attention. He hadn't forgotten she was there. Not exactly, anyway. He'd simply been distracted. Hurt lined Judith Stafford's face, her focus on the envelope in his hand.

Stepping back inside, he slipped the envelope into his jacket pocket. "My apologies, Miss Stafford." He sensed she was awaiting further explanation but felt no compulsion to offer such. "I do hope you get to feeling better very soon."

The hurt in her eyes slowly melted away. A cool, flat stare took its place. She walked past him to the door, looked out at the wagon, then back at him. "How fortunate that Mrs. Boyd, or *Rachel* . . . has such a love for medicine, and that you hold her in such high regard." A smile tipped her mouth but didn't alter the displeasure in her eyes. "However, I can't help but wonder"—she stepped past him onto the boardwalk—"if perhaps her time might be more wisely spent at home, disciplining her younger son."

Miss Stafford cut a path across the street and disappeared around the corner, leaving Rand staring.

He thought of Kurt, then of Miss Stafford's desk drawer pulls, and saw the prank playing out all too clearly in his mind. *That boy* . . . Remembering what it was like to be Kurt's age and how tempting it was to do anything that might draw a laugh, he almost smiled. Yet he couldn't. Not while knowing that Rachel would see nothing amusing about her son's latest antic, and not while he himself had a growing concern over Kurt's misbehavior.

"Hey, Doc, could you grab the other end of this?"

Rand blinked and glanced back at the wagon, and couldn't believe his eyes. *Rachel Boyd . . . you sweet woman.*

Rand dismounted, already hearing the laughter and conversation coming through an open window. He checked his pocket watch again and winced. He was more than an hour late, and he knew how Rachel felt about his not showing up on time. They'd probably finished lunch by now—and he was famished. He looped the mare's reins over the rail and took the stairs by twos up to James and Molly McPherson's front porch.

The first week of May had delivered on its promise of spring, and he loosened his tie a little at the collar before knocking. When James had invited him for Sunday lunch a few days ago, he'd added, with a telling grin, that Rachel and the boys would be present. Rand appreciated being included in the family gathering, but more than anything, he was eager to be in Rachel's company again and to thank her for her gift.

Their paths still hadn't crossed in town, and it had been over a week now. He'd delayed the reprisal of Ben's surgery until the coming week, pleased with Ben's progress but not wanting to push things. He'd kept expecting—hoping—to see Rachel in town or when she'd visited Ben and Lyda at the resort, but they always seemed to have just missed each other.

He wondered now whether coincidence had dictated that, or if perhaps Rachel had helped it along.

She'd been uncomfortable after they'd kissed—that was evident. *"I loved my husband."* That was an admission he would never doubt, and always cherish. It told him so much about her, about the woman she was. For so long, he'd admired her from afar, and now to think that she cared for him . . .

If she *was* avoiding him, for whatever reason, he planned on putting an end to that today.

He peered through the window and knocked again, harder this time, recalling the way she'd responded to his kiss. . . . He blew out a breath, wishing he'd reacted with more tact. But when she'd—

The front door opened, and Rand's vivid thoughts screeched to a halt. Staring up at Rachel's older brother, he was grateful James McPherson couldn't read his mind. "McPherson . . ." They shook hands. "Sorry I'm late."

"Not a problem, Doc. Come on in." James motioned him through the doorway. "The women had about given up on you, but I still held out hope. However waning . . ."

Catching McPherson's sarcasm, Rand smiled.

"How's Ben doin' this morning? And Lyda . . . Is she still holding up all right?"

Rand nodded. "He's improved a little, though not as much as I'd like. It'll help if we can get the rest of that fluid off his lungs. Lyda's strong, but this is weighing on her."

With a thoughtful look, McPherson clapped him on the back. "I'm glad God brought you to Timber Ridge, Doc."

"I am too, Sheriff." Rand followed him down the hall. "Sorry again to be late, but there was a situation at the resort this morning, and I had to—" Rounding the corner, Rand saw Edward Westin seated next to Rachel at the kitchen table. His thoughts derailed. Making matters worse, it looked as though they'd already finished eating. And he saw no empty place setting at the table. "I, ah . . ." He forced a pleasant countenance. "I had to see to the situation before I could leave."

The prettiest smile lit Rachel's face, which did his heart—and flagging enthusiasm—some good. Until he questioned whether that smile was for him, or whether it had been there before he arrived, for Westin.

"Dr. Brookston." Molly jumped up from her seat. "I'm so glad you're able to join us. We waited lunch for a while, then assumed you'd been called away by a patient. Here—" She moved a platter containing the half-eaten carcass of a hen from the table to the stove, revealing a fifth place setting, between Molly and Westin.

His appetite somewhat diminished, Rand accepted the chair James passed to him and squeezed in. "Thank you," he said, taking his seat, wondering if he could possibly feel more awkward and ill at ease. "Again, my apologies for being late." He tried to catch Rachel's attention, wanting her to know he truly did regret his late arrival, but she was laughing at something Westin had apparently said. He glanced around, seeing little Josephine, the McPhersons' daughter, asleep in a crib, yet saw no sign of Mitch or Kurt. He waited for a break in the conversation. "Where are the boys?"

Rachel motioned, her gaze skittish. "They're on the back porch . . . playing with a train Mr. Westin so kindly gave to them."

Westin waved off the inferred thanks. "It's just something from my days at the railroad. I've got grandchildren about their age. I figured the boys would enjoy it."

Rand nodded, struggling with a sense of possessiveness he told himself was unwarranted, yet becoming more certain by the second that Rachel *was* avoiding him. Endless appointments with patients—both those at the resort and in town—had kept him busy the past week, and he'd found it nearly impossible to keep up.

But if he'd known this was the reception he would get, especially after what they'd shared, he would've been on her doorstep that very first night. Still, what reason did she have to be acting so evasive? His attention slid to Westin. Could it be that . . . *No.* He immediately dismissed the idea. Westin was nearly old enough to be her father. And yet, the man *had* taken her and the boys to dinner. . . .

"You weren't at church this morning."

Rachel's comment brought him back, and the faint concern in her voice lent him hope.

"A guest at the resort, an elderly gentleman, was experiencing chest pains." He smiled his thanks to Molly, who spooned mashed potatoes onto his plate. "Turns out his heart is completely fine," he added quickly, noting their looks of concern. "It was indigestion. Courtesy of all the rich food he's been eating at the resort's restaurant."

Everyone smiled, nodding.

Molly doled out generous portions of baked chicken, green beans, and corn bread slathered with butter alongside the potatoes. "I'm afraid everything's gotten cold, Rand. Would you like for me to warm your plate? It won't take but fifteen or twenty minutes."

Rand held on to his plate when she reached for it. "No, no, this is fine. It looks delicious. Thank you." He loaded his fork with mashed potatoes and took a bite, determined to eat quickly. Maybe then he could find an excuse to get Rachel alone to ask her what was going on.

Edward leaned forward, reaching for his glass of tea. "From what Mrs. Boyd tells me, Dr. Brookston, and from what I've personally witnessed, you're single-handedly responsible for avoiding an all-out epidemic in Timber Ridge."

Rachel averted her gaze, looking as though she'd been caught doing something she would have preferred to have kept secret.

Rand shook his head. "Not at all. The sheriff here"—he nodded toward McPherson—"along with the editor of the paper, worked hard to get the critical information out to everyone. After all . . . as Sir Francis Bacon once wrote, 'Knowledge is power.'"

The surprising twinkle in Rachel's eyes, coupled with the brief intimacy in her expression, bolstered Rand's determination to get to the bottom of whatever was going on.

"How're your patients doing?" McPherson asked. "The ones with typhoid?"

Rand felt a sobering. "One of the miners who contracted the disease died a couple of days ago—an older gentleman. As for everyone else, they're all on the mend . . . except for Paige Foster." He paused, knowing this news would affect them more because everyone knew the Fosters. "Paige is over the typhoid and isn't contagious any longer, but she's not regaining her strength. As of two days ago, she's still not eating much." And if she didn't start eating soon, he knew she likely wouldn't recover.

"I'm going to ride out to check on her again this afternoon." He hoped for a chance to ask Rachel and the boys to accompany him. Maybe seeing a couple of schoolmates would do Paige some good.

He was relieved when the conversation continued without him. The food tasted good, even cold, and he took the chance to pray for Paige and her parents again—especially her father, Graham—knowing that Graham would hold him personally responsible if Paige didn't make it. But he knew he'd done everything he could for the little girl. She was in God's hands now. . . .

Like the stinging end of a whip, his last thought burned inside him. *She is in God's hands* now.

He stared, unseeing, at his plate, reminded of something Rachel had said to him. *"Do you have any idea, Rand, how arrogant that makes you sound?"* Though he heard the conversation and laughter being parried back and forth around him, he felt a profound stillness inside him. And though he sat firm in his chair, inwardly he went to his knees. *Paige has always been in your hands, Lord. Whether you choose to heal her or not. I know that is true. And you are always the one to heal—I'm merely an instrument in your hands.* He'd known that too. He swallowed.

But he knew it even better now.

Over the next hour, Westin entertained them with lively tales from his career with the railroad, and

Rand actually enjoyed it. He got the impression the man had lived an interesting life. Amid the laughter and comments, Rand watched Rachel and caught her sneaking looks at him. Each time their eyes met, he grew less bothered by Westin's unexpected presence. Rachel's dress, a delicate shade of violet, brought out the intensity of her blue eyes, and he welcomed the chance to admire her. And didn't mind her seeing him do it.

"I wish I hadn't waited so long to retire from the railroad. I should've come west years ago . . . when Evelyn first wanted to. While she was still alive."

Westin's somber acknowledgment drew Rand's renewed sympathies. The faces around the table revealed understanding, and he gathered everyone knew about Westin's late wife.

"I had a chance to retire a few years back," Westin continued, smoothing a nonexistent wrinkle from the tablecloth. "But I didn't. I thought we had plenty of years ahead of us, my wife and me." His soft sigh revealed regret. "But I've learned in these latter years that life passes all too quickly. If you have something you want to do, and God opens a door for you to do it, then you need to walk through that door. Don't hesitate. Don't wait. Because you may not get another chance. It's like what you talked about in your sermon this morning, Sheriff."

Rand glanced across the table. *McPherson* had preached today? He regretted having missed church even more now. And he fully agreed with Westin's advice. He thought about what Ben—and Thomas Boyd—had said about Rachel's gift for doctoring. Seeing the contemplative look on her face, he guessed she was weighing Westin's counsel too. What he wouldn't have given to know her thoughts.

He wouldn't dare admit it to anyone, but he'd be lying if he said he'd never imagined her taking up medicine alongside him, their being partners, in every way. She had the ranch to run, he knew, but he'd gotten the impression it wasn't her first love, by any means. Not compared to medicine. And judging from vague comments Charlie Daggett had made, he guessed the ranch was proving to be none too profitable.

"Evelyn would have loved Timber Ridge." Westin's tone, and countenance, had brightened. "She would have loved all of you too."

"And I'm sure we would have loved her as well." Rachel briefly patted Westin's arm. "Very much."

The silence lengthened. The boys' laughter drifted in from the back porch and helped mellow the moment.

Molly stood and started gathering plates. "I've got cherry pie staying warm in the oven. Who'd like some coffee?"

Hands went up around the table.

Later, with the pie devoured and the afternoon stretching on, everyone pushed back from the table and stood. After thanking James and Molly for the meal, Rand followed Rachel outside—right behind Edward Westin.

"Dr. Brookston, do you need help delivering any more calves?" Mitch asked, coming alongside him.

Rand laughed. "I'm sure I will soon enough. I'll send for you and your brother, I promise." He winked at Kurt, who wasn't far behind them, and was rewarded with a mischievous grin. Tempted to ask the boy how school had gone that week, Rand refrained, not about to bring up the incident with the ink. He turned to see Rachel shaking hands with Westin.

"I'd be most appreciative of that, Mr. Westin," she said with enthusiasm. "Any evening this week would be fine."

Any evening this week? Rand didn't care for the spark of jealousy inside him, yet he couldn't help it either. Grateful when Westin took his leave, he waited for James and Molly to go back inside, then accompanied Rachel to her wagon. James and Molly's home, a modest rented clapboard house— as old as the Rockies and about as cold in the winter, according to James—was centered in town, not two blocks off Main Street, and with the warmer weather, townspeople were out walking in droves.

Rachel nodded a greeting to a couple passing by, then turned back to him, a carefully arranged smile on her face. "It really was nice to see you again, Rand. I'm glad you were able to join us."

He stared, knowing he was doing a poor job of hiding his frustration. Sincerity marked her voice, yet her manner was so formal. Aware of the boys in the back of the wagon, arms propped on the side, watching and listening, he chose his words carefully, knowing he wasn't exactly playing fair. "Thank you, Rachel. It was nice to see you all too. Maybe we could do this again. Say, dinner one night this week . . . any evening would be fine."

Color rose in her cheeks. The boys cheered.

She looked down for a moment, then back up. Gone was the façade. A pleading quality had replaced her smile. "I'm . . . not sure I can do this," she whispered, pressing her lips together. "I'm sorry."

Her transparency swept aside every trace of frustration. Rand didn't have to ask what she meant. He knew, and he felt responsible. She was scared to death of what was happening between them. He'd moved too quickly. He shouldn't have kissed her.

In the same breath, what she'd said took on new meaning. She was scared of what was happening between them. Meaning . . . something *was* happening, not just for him, but for her too. Curiosity about Westin and her association with him tangled with his thoughts, but he decided the moment was crowded enough.

Slowly, he reached out and took hold of her hand, remembering the frightened-doe look in her eyes from the other night, similar to what he saw in their depths now. "I'm a patient man, Rachel." Especially when it came to her.

She took a breath and slowly let it out, noticeably relaxing.

"Thank you for the cabinet," he said softly, seizing the opportunity and enjoying the pleasure lighting her eyes.

"I thought you could use it. It was my father's."

He'd figured as much. "It's beautiful."

"He stored medicine in it, along with his surgical instruments. I . . . I wasn't really using it, and . . ." She motioned behind her. "I asked James if he minded my giving it to you, and he said he thought you should have it."

"I've already been using it. In fact, I stayed up that night and transferred every bottle and tin over. It all fit perfectly." Just like she did with him. "Thank you," he said again, unable to keep his gaze from lowering to her mouth. "Now, about that dinner. You and the boys . . ." He glanced at Mitch and Kurt, unable to remember them ever being so quiet. "You still need to eat, right?" He didn't wait for her response. "It's only dinner, Rachel." For now, anyway.

"Yeah, Mama, it's only dinner," Mitch said behind her.

"And we gotta eat," Kurt piped in.

351

Curbing his smile, Rand planned on doing something really special for those boys.

"All right," she said after a moment, giving a firm nod, as though dinner with him was something she was going to have to work herself up for. "How does Thursday sound? We'll meet you at Miss Clar—" She stopped, looking past him. "Rand," she whispered, her brow knitting.

He turned to follow her gaze, and saw Paige Foster's father walking straight toward him, emotion straining the lines of his face.

26

Rand steeled himself as Graham Foster strode toward him, fists clenched tight. He pictured Foster's sweet daughter and knew he'd done everything he could for Paige. Yet in moments like this, *everything* still felt like not enough. Without shifting his focus, Rand reached beside him and urged Rachel back a few steps.

"Dr. Brookston—" Breathing heavily, Foster moved in close, staring hard.

Rand's gut twisted tight. No matter how many times he'd faced this situation, it never got easier. Especially when it involved children, and parents who felt about doctors the way Graham Foster did. Rand wished Rachel and the boys didn't have to see this. "Foster . . . I'm—"

The man grabbed him by the shoulders. "Thank

you, Doc"—his voice broke with a sob—"for savin' my daughter." Foster embraced him hard, then just as quickly, stepped back.

It took Rand a minute to react, the news sinking in, his body still braced for a blow. "She's eating? She's getting better?"

Foster smiled, his chin quivering. "The girl's about to strip our cupboards bare. Her momma can't seem to keep her full."

Rand let out a quick breath, emotion burning his eyes. He gripped Foster's forearm and squeezed it tight, a shudder of relief and gratitude moving through him. As did the whisper of a profound stillness. *Thank you, Lord . . . for healing her.*

Foster's laughter drew him back, as did Rachel's presence beside him.

Foster removed his hat, nodding Rachel's way. "Paige woke up yesterday afternoon late, and asked her momma for some biscuits and gravy. We weren't sure what to think of it at the time, but she ate that and has been eatin' ever since. Gettin' better by the hour. She even got up from bed this morning and sat at the table with us for a little while."

Rachel beamed. "We're so happy for the news, Mr. Foster. Please give Paige and your entire family our love."

"Thank you, ma'am. I'll do that." Foster briefly looked away, his expression sobering. "Dr. Brookston . . . as you know, I've never put much stock in doctors and what they had to say. I guess I was pretty clear on that from the outset."

Rand let his grin answer for him.

"I just want you to know . . . I'm grateful to you, sir, for healing my daughter."

Rand smiled. "I didn't heal your daughter, Foster. God did that. All I did was help a little. And it was an honor to work alongside Him."

Foster considered him for a long moment, then nodded. "Mel Lester, that crusty old cuss . . . He's been after me for over two years to sell him my prize hog. But I wouldn't do it." He stuck out his hand. "Until now."

Rand saw the envelope but didn't take it.

"I heard you've been tryin' to find a place in town, Doc. A place where you can have a proper clinic. Where you can take folks in and care for them when they're sick."

Rand eyed him.

The man smiled. "Harold Welch is worse than an ol' banty hen when it comes to gossip. He told me about that building of his next to the Mullinses' store. Said you'd been after him to sell it to you, but some fella new to town came in and snapped it up at top price."

Rand felt Rachel's attention shift to him and wondered what she was thinking.

Foster glanced downward. "What I'm giving you won't buy no clinic, Doc. But it's a step closer to one." Earnestness sharpened his features. "Take it, please . . . as thanks for what you've done for me and my family."

Rand finally accepted the envelope, feeling unworthy of its contents, whatever the amount. He cleared his throat. "Thank you, Mr. Foster. I appreciate this more than you know. And I give you my word, it'll go toward a new clinic."

Still staring at the envelope after Foster left, Rand felt a touch on his arm and turned. If ever he'd seen loving pride in someone's eyes, he saw it in Rachel's now.

"You're making such a difference in people's lives, Rand. And in this town."

He covered her hand on his arm, reliving what it had felt like to work alongside her during Ben's surgery. "And so could you, Rachel." Even before the furrow in her brow, he wanted to kick himself. He winced. "What I meant is that you could make a difference in the same way. In relation to medicine. You're already making such a difference, Rachel. But it's evident how much you enjoy—"

She held up a hand, her expression surprisingly smooth, absent of anger. "I know what you meant," she said softly. "I *do*. And I'm grateful for the sentiment, but . . . I've got my own responsibilities. I've got the ranch to run and the boys to think of." It almost sounded as if she were trying to convince herself. "And I've got plans." She lifted her chin. A trace of defensiveness—or maybe it was protectiveness—crept into her tone. "Mr. Westin and I are meeting this week to discuss a business undertaking."

Rand didn't like the sound of that one bit. "A business undertaking?"

She nodded.

"Just what kind of *undertaking* did Westin propose?"

She gave him an indulgent look, one he imagined Kurt saw often. "He suggested I look into purchasing a new breed of cattle. From Scotland."

His first instinct was to smile. The second was to track down Westin and demand an explanation. Instead, he tried for a pensive look. "Cattle from Scotland?"

She nodded again, but her eyes narrowed as though she doubted his sincerity. "He said they're bred for the highlands, for bitter winters. They'll be able to withstand the cold here better than the herd I have now." She huffed. "I can't take another winter like the last two. I'll have no cattle and no ranch left."

Rand weighed his options. He wasn't privy to Rachel's personal finances, but Timber Ridge was a small town, and just as news about him traveled, so did news about her. In addition to Charlie Daggett's subtle comments now and then, he'd heard rumor that her ranch might be in trouble. He had a hard time believing she wanted to spend the rest of her life working cattle. It didn't fit with the woman he knew.

"This new breed," he said, knowing to tread carefully. "Is that what this dinner with Westin is about?"

She smiled in a way that made him want to shield her from anything, or anyone, that would ever try to do her harm.

"Yes, that's what our dinner this week is about. And the dinner before . . ." She tilted her head. "That was simply a coincidence. The boys and I decided to go to Miss Clara's, and Mr. Westin arrived at the same time and invited us to join him." She gave a gentle shrug. "That's all."

Enjoying a measure of relief, he still had a hundred other questions he wanted to pose. But he didn't feel at liberty—first, because it was none of his business, and second, because he was fairly certain Rachel would interpret those questions as insinuations that she wasn't capable of making a decision for herself. And purposefully alienating this woman was the last thing he wanted to do.

He seemed to do that easily enough without trying.

Rand repositioned the stethoscope on Ben's chest. "May I check your abdomen?"

"No need to ask, Doc. You've already seen everything I got. More than once." Though Ben's

357

expression held no trace of humor, his tone hinted at a little.

Smiling more on the outside than in, Rand lifted up Ben's shirt. Lyda had gone into town after lunch to check on things at the store again, and he was glad she'd gotten away for a while. She rarely left her husband's side, and the stress of recent weeks was beginning to show.

Two days ago, with Rachel's assistance, he'd completed draining Ben's lungs. The procedure had gone without complication this time, and Rachel hadn't seemed nearly as nervous. With patients in town needing tending, he'd had to leave for a while, so she'd stayed with Ben for the afternoon. Two resort guests had stopped by the clinic, one needing a powder for a headache, the other a curative for an upset stomach. In his absence, Rachel had taken care of both. And if her recounting of the events was any proof, she'd enjoyed every minute.

He gently probed Ben's abdomen, watching for the least sign of discomfort.

Ben winced.

"Does it hurt there?" Rand asked.

"No, your hands are just cold."

Rand shook his head. "Lyda's right, you know—you're an ornery old coot."

Ben laughed softly. "I'm gonna miss you too, Doc." His smile faded. "If missin' is somethin' we're allowed to do in the hereafter."

The raw truth of Ben's statement caused a knot to twist tight at the base of Rand's throat, and he thought about the warning a mentor had given him years ago, about getting too close to his patients. "I'm going to miss you too, Ben." Rand waited to speak until certain his voice would hold. "You're a good man. One of the finest I've ever known."

Ben's lower lip quivered. "Well . . . that's kind of you to say, Doc." He sniffed. "But that just goes to show you haven't gotten out much."

They both laughed and Rand claimed the chair beside the bed. A parcel of time passed between them, quiet and unhindered. Rand had grown to enjoy these times with Ben. Sitting together and talking, or sometimes just sitting. Somehow, during the course of recent days, his prayers for Ben had changed. He found himself asking God to give Ben and Lyda a peace, a comfort, in the unseen bends of the road ahead. It wasn't that he didn't pray for healing anymore. He did. But it sure seemed that healing—on this side of eternity, anyway—wasn't part of the Great Physician's plan.

Still, Rand couldn't ignore the physician within himself and the obligation he felt to do everything he could for his patient. "In another three or four days, Ben, maybe sooner if your strength improves, Rachel and I can do the procedure again and draw that fluid off your lungs."

Ben shook his head. "I'm grateful for what you

did, but I'm not doing that again. I told you that early on, remember?"

Rand had expected this response. "Yes, I remember. I've just been hoping you would change your mind. We know this procedure will work for you, that it gives you relief, and that it *will* buy you some more time. I know Lyda's in favor of it."

Ben's lack of response sounded overloud in the silence.

Rand leaned forward in his chair, further softening his voice. "I understand your decision, Ben, and I'd never seek to encourage you to do something against your will. But as your physician, I feel an obligation to advise you of every option available."

Ben looked toward the mountains, and Rand did too, praying for wisdom and discernment. For them both.

Eventually, Ben turned back. "Time is somethin' I've had a lot of in recent days, Doc. Time to think, time to look at life. And I think that, in the end, no matter what we do, God decides."

Rand waited, not sure what he meant.

Ben shifted on the bed. "Seems to me that God keeps us each here until we've finished whatever it is He has for us to do. Then He calls us home." Peace settled over Ben's features, even as his eyes grew misty. "And seein' as the Almighty hasn't let me down yet, I guess I'm all right with that."

Hasn't let me down yet . . . Rand bowed his head, in awe that Ben could still say that in light of losing his children as he had. But still, he struggled. The doctor in him had a hard time accepting Ben's decision not to take advantage of every possible medical intervention. A creak brought his head up.

Rand saw Lyda standing in the doorway, just out of Ben's sight. Tears traced her cheeks, so much love in her eyes that he felt an ache in his gut. An ache that only made Ben's choice that much tougher to accept.

27

Aren't you ready yet?" Kurt sighed and slumped across the foot of the bed.

"In a minute. Be patient, please." Rachel coerced a wayward curl into place, securing it with a silver comb. She'd rushed through her chores and already had the wagon hitched and ready out front, wanting to have that done before she got dressed. She stepped back from the mirror and studied her reflection, wondering where the vivacious young woman who once stared back at her had gone.

She frowned at the dark stain encircling the hem of her skirt, same as all her others. No matter how much she brushed or washed, the remnants of dirt and mud remained. All part of living in such a rugged place, she knew. Still, there were times she longed for paved streets and indoor plumbing, and a hem unstained by six inches of muck.

She pictured the women she'd seen at the resort, refined and elegant, hair arranged in stylish fashion, their dresses trimmed in expensive lace, and—she smirked—not a smudge of manure anywhere on them.

"You don't think Miss Clara will run out of biscuits before we get there, do you?"

Reaching for her shawl, she smiled at Mitch's question. His tone was less whiny than Kurt's, but both communicated the same thing—they were impatient to leave. And so was she. For the most part.

Rand had said this was only dinner. But it felt like something more. Maybe if she wasn't so eager to see him again. . . .

With the boys behind her in the wagon bed, Rachel guided the rig down the mountain toward town. Her teeth jarred together as the wheels bumped and jolted over deep winter ruts. Repeated days of thawing and refreezing left clawlike ribbons in the road, and she kept one eye on the boulders situated high above them as she navigated the narrow pass. Occasionally, during the spring melt, rocks would lose their grip on the mountain and come tumbling down.

Thomas used to keep the path clean, cleared of debris. She knew Charlie Daggett would keep it the same way if she asked. But she hated to ask, what with him working as hard as he did and her paying him so little. The additional funds from the bank had allowed her to cover his salary to date, but she didn't know how much longer she'd be able to do that.

However, if what Mr. Westin had said during their dinner held true, the new breed of cattle might be the answer to her problems. As well as her prayers.

She guided the wagon into town, feeling a swell of pride remembering Rand's conversation with Graham Foster. What a miracle it was that Paige had recovered, and even more, that Rand—she smiled to herself—had taken none of the credit. She felt slightly wicked at the teasing thought, but the Rand she'd come to know in recent weeks wasn't the man she'd kept at arm's length for the past two years.

Still, he wasn't without his moments. Like when he'd told her that she *too* could make a difference. She'd known what he meant, but the comment had stung a little. Still did.

She turned down the street toward Miss Clara's and brought the horses to a stop in front of the restaurant, tugging hard on the reins. She was committed to making the ranch a success and believed she was closer to that happening now than ever before. *If* she didn't lose it all in the process.

She set the brake and started to climb down.

"Hold on there, ma'am. Not so fast."

She looked up to see Rand walking from the restaurant, and Elijah Birch following him with a covered plate in hand. A definite twinkle lit the young man's eyes.

"Mrs. Boyd," Elijah said, nodding in his mannerly way, just like his father, Josiah. "How are you this evenin', ma'am?"

"I'm very well, Elijah. Thank you." She sneaked a look at Rand, seeing Elijah do the same. Rand Brookston was up to something, and Elijah was his willing accomplice. "Are you helping Miss Clara in the restaurant this evening?"

The boy nodded, grinning, his green eyes a striking contrast against his light mahogany complexion. "Yes, ma'am, I am. We'll be movin' the cafe back outdoors soon as the weather's nice enough." He handed Rand the plate.

"I look forward to that. Please give your parents my best regards."

"I will, ma'am." Elijah slid another look Rand's way. "Y'all have yourselves a good evenin' now."

Rachel thought she heard Elijah chuckle as he walked back inside. She started to climb down, but Rand held up his hand.

"Just stay in the wagon, if you would."

Stay in the wagon? She frowned. "I thought we were going to eat."

"We are." Rand winked, his smile secretive. "We'll start with the appetizer now and work our

364

way to the entreé." He handed the plate to Kurt, who scrunched his nose.

"What's an ap-pe-tizer?"

Listening as Mitch explained to his younger brother, Rachel was surprised when Rand climbed up beside her. She made room on the bench seat, noticing how nice he looked, his suit pressed and cleaned, and how he smelled—she breathed in. *Mmmm* . . . bay rum and spice. She'd take that as her appetizer any day.

He gestured to the reins in her hands. "Would you mind if I drove?"

"Would you mind telling me where we're going first?"

He narrowed his eyes as though seriously considering her request, all the while moving a hand closer to the reins. "Would you mind if I didn't?"

She held them just out of his reach, determined to keep the sparkle from her eyes, but apparently failing miserably judging by the one in his. She would've sworn he'd said they were going to Miss Clara's, but thinking back on it now, she wasn't sure.

"Biscuits!" Mitch leaned over the bench seat, crowding between them and holding out the tin plate. "Miss Clara made us biscuits. And they're still warm."

"They got butter on 'em too." Kurt wriggled in beside his brother, draping an arm over Rand's shoulder. "Can we eat 'em now, Dr. Brookston? Since they're supposed to come first?"

Rand glanced her way, question in his eyes.

Rachel studied the three boyish expressions staring back at her and grinned. "Only if I can have one too!" She grabbed a biscuit and, with a look of playful warning, handed Rand the reins. Whatever he had planned for this evening, she strongly suspected it wasn't going to be "just dinner."

She was certain she'd figured out Rand's surprise—until he drove on past his clinic, then past the street where James and Molly lived. When he guided the team onto the road leading out of town, her concern notched up considerably. She attempted a casual tone. "Where are we going?"

Focused ahead, Rand smiled. "You don't like surprises?"

"Of course I like surprises. As long as I know what they are beforehand."

He grinned. "Only problem is . . . then they wouldn't be surprises."

The wagon bounced and jostled over the washboard road, and she gripped the side of the seat. She glanced down at her simple shirtwaist and skirt, then at the stains darkening her hem. She was dressed well enough for Miss Clara's, so were the boys, but . . . "Rand . . ."

He looked over at her, traces of boyish enthusiasm in his features.

She hesitated, not wanting to hurt his feelings, especially if he planned on taking them where she feared he was taking them. The expense alone made her uncomfortable, but add to that their lack of proper attire. "The boys and I . . ." She leaned closer, not wanting Mitch and Kurt to hear. "We're not dressed appropriately for the restaurant at the resort."

"Good," he said succinctly. "Because that's not where we're eating."

"Oh . . . well . . . fine, then." She sat back, feeling presumptuous and vain.

"But just so you know . . ." His gaze moved from her eyes to her mouth, then slowly took in the rest of her. "No matter what you're wearing, Rachel, you'll be the most beautiful woman in the room." With a satisfied look, he faced forward.

Not knowing how to respond, she didn't even try. How did he *do* that? How did he look at her that way without making her feel uneasy, or as if he were having thoughts he shouldn't? She didn't know. But one thing was certain—she definitely didn't need her shawl. Fanning herself discreetly, she let it slip from her shoulders.

The boys chattered behind them, but she heard only snatches of their conversation over the wagon's rumble—something about how far they could jump, and from how high a perch. She knew by Kurt's tone that he was trying to best Mitch's estimate, whatever it had been. Would there forever be this competition between them?

"How was your dinner earlier this week?"

Knowing exactly what he meant, she gave him a sideways glance, surprised at the question and recognizing his attempt at a casual air. "It was nice. We ate at Miss Clara's and had pork chops and new potatoes. I thought about ordering pie, but decided against it."

Purposefully sighing, she stared out across the fields, relishing the dry look he was no doubt giving her. After a moment, she grinned. "My *meeting* with Mr. Westin went very well, thank you. He's already sent a telegram on my behalf requesting information and pricing on the cattle. He said we might hear something back as early as next week."

In the silence that followed, she discovered she really would have liked to have known his opinion—but not enough to ask for it. Especially when she had a fairly good idea what his suggestion would be.

On either side of the road, the brown-clad landscape still wore its winter coat, and the surrounding mountains, flocked in snow to the highest peaks, spoke a similar refrain. The sky yawned a cloudless blue overhead, and she leaned back enough to watch Rand without him knowing. "I'm sorry the building beside the store didn't work out. It would have been perfect for a clinic."

"Yes, it would have." He shrugged. "But the way I see it, things have worked out the way they were supposed to."

"How's that?"

"If Westin hadn't bought that building, then Ben wouldn't be able to provide for Lyda's future the way he wants to. Ben and I talked for a while yesterday while Lyda was in town. He and Westin are moving forward with the plans to expand the store. Westin's making good progress too. Have you been by there recently?"

"Not since last week."

"They've already got doorways cut through to the other building and shelving going up. According to Ben, he and Westin are broadening their stock to carry almost twice the items they do now."

Hearing that news was bittersweet. "Lyda's been after Ben to do that for years, but they didn't have the space." Or the money, she knew. They rode in silence until she spotted the resort in the distance. "I thought you said we weren't going to the resort."

He smiled. "Don't you trust me?"

Ignoring his hurt look, she leveled her gaze, insinuating she'd rather not answer that question.

"I never said we weren't going there. What I indicated was that we weren't eating at the resort's *restaurant*." His attention remained on the road. "You really don't like surprises, do you?"

Hearing a hint of disappointment in his voice, she sighed. "Saying it that way makes it sound as if I don't know how to enjoy myself—which I do." She picked a piece of grass from her skirt. "I simply like to know what's coming, so I can be prepared."

He cut his gaze her way, his laughter rich. "I enjoy your company, Mrs. Boyd. Very much." He looked toward the mountains, and a moment passed before he spoke again. "I'd hoped we might be able to bring Ben home tomorrow, but he's developed a cough deep in his chest, and I don't want to risk it. After discussing it with him and Lyda, they agreed. The rest and nutrition they're getting at the resort is good, for both of them. And all the construction going on at the store right now—the sawdust and nails pounding—wouldn't be conducive to Ben getting the rest he needs."

She agreed and was grateful Ben and Lyda had too. "Do you think the cough's related to his heart?"

"More than likely it's the fluid on his lungs."

"So you think it's already gathering that quickly again?"

"I'm sure of it, just like it did before."

She looked up at him. "But you can perform the procedure again. Right?"

"After he regains his strength—*if* we can get Ben to agree to it."

The way he said it made her think he'd already tried to convince Ben, and failed.

The wagon jolted hard to the right, dropping into a deep rut, and Rachel grabbed hold of the seat. Rand put his arm out, securing her beside him. He glanced back. "You boys okay back there?"

Boyish laughter erupted. "Do that again, Dr. Brookston! That was fun!"

Smiling, Rand looked over at her. "You've got yourself a couple of pistols back there."

"Don't I know." She rolled her eyes, realizing he didn't know the half of it. Not in regard to Kurt, anyway. Not at all bothered by Rand's closeness, she found herself a tiny bit disappointed when he moved back to his side of the bench seat.

She glanced back at the boys, remembering the ink-on-Miss-Stafford's-drawer-pulls stunt. She'd written yet another note of apology to Miss Stafford, as had Kurt, and she'd hand-delivered them both. But Miss Stafford's reaction proved to be especially cool this time, her behavior bordering on rude. Yet when Rachel put herself in the young teacher's place, she couldn't say she blamed her. For Kurt's punishment, Rachel had assigned him a month of extra chores in the barn, but she honestly didn't feel as if that was addressing the issue. But what was the issue? Only God knew, and she prayed constantly that He would show her.

The closer they got to the resort, the more conspicuous Rachel began to feel.

Three large carriages, two of them covered and

all of them far nicer than a farm wagon, were parked in front of the resort entrance. Rand guided the wagon to a stop beside them, and a boy who looked no older than Kurt, dressed in a crisp white shirt and black trousers, raced to meet them.

"Good evening, Signore Brookston." Holding the bridle of the lead mare, the boy offered a half bow to Rachel.

Once down, Rand slipped the boy a coin. "Thank you, Gino."

Mitch and Kurt catapulted out of the wagon, staring up at the resort, eyes wide.

"This is where we're eatin'?" Kurt said none too quietly.

Rachel put a finger to her lips, glancing at Rand, who was still speaking to the young Italian boy. "I'm not exactly sure. But please, you must both be on your best behavior. Do you understand?"

They both agreed, jaws hanging slightly open.

The vistas were stunning from this vantage point, the Rocky Mountains breathtaking in their splendor and height. And she could well imagine how they would look draped in a crimson sunset.

Rand came up behind her, briefly touching the small of her back. "Shall we go inside?"

Holding her gently by the elbow, he led the way.

28

G ood evening, Dr. Brookston." With a stately bow, a handsome Italian man greeted them on the porch and held open the wide ornate doors. "Mrs. Boyd, how nice of you and your sons to join us. I hope you very much enjoy your evening here, ma'am."

If she wasn't mistaken, Rachel caught a glint of amusement in the man's eyes when he glanced at Rand. And how did he know her name? She couldn't recall having met him before. "Thank you, sir." Smiling, she gave a brief curtsey. "I'm certain we will."

She ushered Mitch and Kurt on ahead of her, wanting to keep an eye on them. Guests crowded the lobby for the dinner hour, and Rachel's earlier recollection of their elegance was confirmed in the hand-beaded gowns of silk and taffeta, accentuated by the sparkle of bejeweled necklines and wrists glistening in the lamplight. Everywhere she looked there were flowers. Brandon Tolliver must have ordered them by the hundreds from the hothouses in Denver. No telling how much that cost him. Then it dawned on her.

The coming weekend was the grand opening. In the blur of recent life, she'd forgotten.

Rand appeared at her side. "I hope you don't mind, but we're going to escape all this."

"With pleasure," she whispered and indicated for the boys to follow, pleased at how well they were behaving. For the time being, at least.

Again Rand surprised her when they passed the Health Suite. She tugged on his sleeve, slowing her steps. "Do you think we could stop in and see Ben and Lyda for a moment? The boys would like to say hello, and I'd like to show them where you performed Ben's surgery."

He glanced down the hall, then stepped closer. "I promise, we'll do both of those things before the evening's over. But for now, we have reservations we need to keep."

She glanced at the boys, then back at the Health Suite, a little disappointed Rand had not been more sensitive to her request. Then again, she had the impression he'd gone to a great deal of trouble to plan the evening.

"Shall we?" he said softly, offering his arm.

She tucked her hand into the crook of his arm and they continued down the hallway, the boys beside them, gawking and whispering to each other.

When they rounded the corner, a young woman standing by a door at the far end straightened in recognition. Rachel remembered her. Brandon Tolliver's assistant.

"Dr. Brookston, I'm so glad you arrived." Warm welcome shone in Miss Valente's face. "Mrs. Boyd, how are you this evening?"

"Very well, thank you," Rachel answered, and made quick introductions between Miss Valente and the boys. Rachel couldn't remember a more polite staff, which was befuddling considering Brandon Tolliver's demanding, ill-tempered disposition. Rand had shared with her that Mr. Tolliver was not at all pleased with Ben and Lyda's continued presence at the resort, but apparently Rand had managed to reach some sort of agreement with him.

A glimmer similar to that in the doorman's smile shone in Miss Valente's as well. "Everything is prepared as you requested, Dr. Brookston. If there's anything else you require"—she directed the statement to all of them—"*please* ask for me."

"Thank you, Miss Valente." Rand briefly took her hand. "For everything."

"It is very little, Doctor, compared to what you have done for us." Miss Valente's retreating footsteps barely made a sound on the plush carpet.

Rand winked at the boys. "Are you ready to eat?"

At their simultaneous nod, he opened the door.

For a moment, Rachel could only stare. She heard a gasp, then quickly realized it had come from her. She stepped into the private dining room, her focus drawn to the sweeping view that lay beyond the panoramic window—the vista she had admired just moments ago. Only now a sunset of crimson and gold blazed over the white-capped peaks. Her gaze went to the table set with china and crystal, and with flickering candles spiraling high, and to where Ben and Lyda sat waiting.

Ben peered around the candelabra and waved. Lyda grinned and scrunched her shoulders as though the excitement of the experience was too much to hold inside. Rachel couldn't have agreed more.

She heard Rand whispering beside her and turned to see him on his knees, eye level with Mitch and Kurt. The boys hung on his every word. She couldn't hear what he was saying, but her sons each shook his hand as if sealing a deal. They walked to the table, looking more like little men than boys at the moment. They hugged their uncle Ben and aunt Lyda, then slipped into their seats.

Emotion welling in her throat, Rachel tried to etch the details and nuances of the moment into her memory, wanting to be able to take it out and relive this feeling again. She'd forgotten what it had felt like to be cherished, to be treated with such forethought and tender concern. There had been moments like this with Thomas, but he'd been gone for so long it seemed. . . .

And until recent days, until *Rand*—her throat tightened to an ache—she'd not allowed herself to imagine what it would be like to have that kind of love in her life again.

"May I escort you to your chair, madam?"

Blinking back tears, she nodded, warming

beneath Rand's attention. He showed her to her seat and lingered for a second, tenderly caressing her shoulder before taking his chair.

Servers promptly appeared with delicate crystal bowls of chilled fruit—bits of apples, oranges, and pears—all covered with a tangy sauce that tasted of summer and of warmer climes. Next came an entrée that Rachel didn't recognize, but that Francesca, the woman serving them, explained was the specialty of the resort.

"It is called lasagna, madam," she said, her accent thick and her enunciation flawless. "The recipe belonged to my great-grandmother—God rest her soul."

Rachel's mouth watered at the layers of melted cheese, meat, and noodles. "It looks delicious." And the aroma . . . heavenly.

Servers replenished baskets of hot crusty bread and butter before they were even emptied, and Rachel knew her boys would be talking about this meal, and this evening, for weeks to come.

Ben grinned from across the table, raising his wineglass. "It's good eatin' here, isn't it?"

Rachel laughed and lifted hers in suit. "It most certainly is."

In the midst of her laugh she caught Lyda's gaze, and they stared at one another for a moment, the conversation and laughter swirling about them. Instinctively she knew what Lyda was thinking and could almost feel the solid *tick-tick-tick* of the clock, and of the passing of their time remaining with Ben.

Then Lyda blinked. Focused joy returned to her eyes. And again Rachel understood. Lyda didn't want to think about any of that tonight, about life without Ben. And neither did she.

Somewhere between dessert and coffee, when listening ears and watching eyes were occupied, Rachel leaned close to Rand. "Thank you," she whispered so only he could hear. "And to answer your earlier question . . . yes, Rand, I trust you."

Later, seated by the hearth in the Health Suite, Rachel giggled as she watched Rand and the boys huddled together over a microscope.

"Dr. Brookston, I can see his legs!" Kurt peered down through the lens at the bug. "And they're *hairy!*"

"And look at his eyes," Mitch added, jostling his brother out of the way for another quick peek. "His eyes are huge!"

Enjoying their banter, Rachel glanced at the patient room where Ben and Lyda had stayed for almost two weeks. The absence of light beneath the door told her they were already in bed. They'd enjoyed the evening as much as she had and appreciated what Rand had done, but Ben was ready to go home. He'd said as much to her following dinner. Lyda was ready too, in a way, but Lyda also wanted Ben to be where he could receive the best care, which was at the resort, with Rand, for the time being. A cough had started deep in Ben's chest, and Rachel feared his being up and about had taxed his strength more than he'd let on. Still, she was grateful Rand had included her dear friends. It couldn't have been a more perfect evening.

Dinner had been as delectable as it was exquisitely presented, and then there was the "viewing of the stars." From a private fourth-floor balcony, Rand had set up a telescope and shown them constellations she'd never heard of, much less known how to find in the night sky. The boys were mesmerized and asked a hundred different questions, for which Rand had known the answers or promised to read until he discovered them.

She yawned as she sat by the hearth, the sumptuous meal and enjoyable evening bringing contentment she hadn't felt in a long time.

She hated to admit it, knowing what type of man Brandon Tolliver was, but Tolliver was sitting on a gold mine. He'd built a magnificent property in one of the most beautiful places in the country, with amenities that rivaled any she'd heard of or read about. She'd underestimated the boon the resort would bring to Timber Ridge—to the businesses and trades, to the community as a whole. And perhaps, if all went as planned, for her ranch as well.

As Mr. Westin had pointed out, more people meant an increased demand for beef, which she would be able to provide. She hoped.

The main door to the suite opened and she turned, expecting to see Miss Valente. But—as if her thoughts had summoned him—Brandon Tolliver strode toward her instead. She rose from her chair, glancing to see if Rand had noticed. He wasn't looking her way.

"Mr. Tolliver. How are you this evening?"

"Extremely busy, Mrs. Boyd." He glanced around. His focus snagged on Rand and the boys. "Having a little family gathering, are we?"

In that instant, Rachel wondered whether Rand had told Tolliver about their activities at the resort that evening. On the chance he hadn't, she didn't want to be the one to alert him. Yet she didn't want to lie. . . .

"I asked Dr. Brookston to show the boys where he and I conducted the surgery on Mr. Mullins, and he was kind enough—"

"He and I?" he repeated, a sardonic grin tipping his mouth. "I didn't realize you were trained in the medicines, Mrs. Boyd."

Her face heated. "That's not what I—"

"No doubt there are a great many things you fail to realize, Tolliver," Rand said, appearing at her side. His smile—cool, detached—was not one Rachel recognized. "Mrs. Boyd did a great service to Ben Mullins, and to me. I couldn't have conducted the surgery on my own, as I've told you before."

Tolliver stared, his expression changing from cynical to amused. "I trust you enjoyed—or *are* enjoying—your private little soirée?"

Rand tensed beside her. "Yes, we are. Very much."

Rubbing his jaw, Tolliver slowly looked between them, as though trying to ascertain the nature of their relationship. Rachel grew uncomfortable beneath his attention.

Rand shifted his weight. "Is there something I can do for you, Tolliver? Or is this one of your rare social calls."

Rachel blinked, surprised to hear Rand speak so bluntly to the man who was, in effect, his employer. But Tolliver didn't seem to mind. In fact, his grin said he was enjoying the exchange.

"My purpose in stopping by is twofold, Doctor. I want to confirm that you're going to be here Saturday. I've got a group of men coming in for the grand opening who are eager to meet you. I'd like for you to tell them about the surgery you performed and provide a tour of the facility. Give them a good show, so to speak."

Looking slightly ill, Rand nodded.

"And secondly, I want to make sure that the understanding we reached regarding Mr. Mullins's recuperation—which is stretching my patience, mind you—is still intact."

Rand nodded. "It is. I'm planning on moving Mr. Mullins back to his home as soon as he's able. By Monday at the latest."

"Monday?" Tolliver shook his head. "I said through tomorrow, Brookston."

"I agreed to Friday *if* Ben's condition warranted him being moved, which it doesn't. I made it clear to you that—"

"Come Saturday morning, I need this medical facility cleaned and in order, ready to be toured."

A muscle tensed in Rand's jaw. "Mr. Mullins has experienced some minor setbacks. He's not as strong as I expected him to be at this stage, and it's inadvisable for him to be moved right now."

"Take my carriage." Tolliver gestured as if the matter were settled. "Just be sure and have it back here by Saturday morning at six o'clock."

Rand didn't answer immediately. "I don't think you understand what I'm saying to you. If I try to transport Ben now, especially with the roads the way they are—"

"I understand your predicament, Brookston. But you need to understand mine. I'm running a resort here. Not a hospital. And certainly not some two-bit, bleeding-heart—pardon the pun in this instance—clinic that exists to serve the masses."

Rand fisted his hands, and Rachel moved closer to him, hoping he wouldn't do anything rash. Especially with the boys watching.

"Look around you, Doctor," Tolliver continued,

his arm sweeping the space. "All of this was built with money belonging to some very powerful men. And those men arrive Saturday morning to see what I've done with that money. And—I'll leave it up to you as to how you get it done—Mr. Mullins is not to be here when they arrive."

Silence stretched the seconds.

Rachel saw movement from the corner of her eye. Mitch and Kurt stood by the microscope, confusion on their faces. Kurt took a step forward, but Rachel shook her head ever so slightly. He stopped.

Rand took a deep breath. "Are there any rooms available at the resort this weekend? I'll pay for Ben and Lyda to stay here, if that's what it takes."

Tolliver laughed, then shook his head. "Don't forget, Doctor, I know how much you make. And believe me, you can't afford it." He turned and was almost to the door when Rand called his name. He looked back.

"I know this weekend is important to you, Tolliver." Rand's voice was surprisingly even and controlled. *Too* controlled, considering Tolliver's blatant disregard for Ben. "The only thing we have to determine now is *how* important."

Tolliver's eyes narrowed. "Exactly what does that mean?"

Rachel watched Rand, eager to know the answer to that question herself.

"It means that I'm assuming you'd be

disappointed if these visitors were unable to meet the physician who performed the *revolutionary* surgery conducted right here in your very own resort. I'm guessing they've already received copies of that special edition of your newspaper."

Rachel cringed at the sarcasm in Rand's tone, and even more at the hardening in Tolliver's expression. She got the distinct feeling there was an entirely different conversation going on than the one she was listening to.

Tolliver retraced his steps. "I suggest you tread carefully, Dr. Brookston. I have a long memory, and I'm a very influential man in this town."

A smile crept over Rand's expression, calm and unfazed. "And may I suggest you do the same, Tolliver. I'm the only physician within a fifty-seven-mile radius."

29

Rachel couldn't believe the transformation in Ben and Lyda's store, and in such a short period of time. Beside her, Lyda scooted closer and tucked her hand through the crook of Rachel's arm.

"What do you think?" Lyda whispered, a watery smile in her eyes, and in her voice.

"I think you and Ben and Mr. Westin have done an extraordinary job, Lyda." She squeezed her friend's hand. "And that Ben's going to be very pleased when he comes home and sees it."

Lyda's eyes brightened, though not enough to erase the veil of concern clouding her features. While Ben hadn't suffered another heart episode or other setback in recent days, he also wasn't gaining strength as they'd hoped. Prior to the resort's grand opening last Saturday, Brandon Tolliver had demanded, for a second time, that Ben be removed from the Health Suite. Rand had flatly refused, according to Lyda, and had taken pride in introducing Ben to the important hotel investors as they toured the medical facilities. Ben felt honored beyond words at the attention, answering questions posed to him about the surgery and the resort's medical accommodations. But mostly, he appreciated Rand standing up to the likes of Brandon Tolliver on his behalf.

"Every afternoon for the past week," Lyda said, "Mr. Westin has stopped by the Health Suite to give Ben an update on the store. He describes the progress the workers have made. He even drew a sketch of the new counter over there so Ben could picture it exactly as it is." She shook her head. "This is what I've been after Ben to do for years." She let out a breath, her expression giving way to the grief she tried hard to hide. "But I'd give every bit of it up—this store, everything we own, today, right this minute—if Ben could be made whole again. If I could keep him with me."

Rachel slipped her arm around Lyda's waist. "I know you would, and Ben knows it too. But let him do this for you, Lyda." She leaned closer. "And try to take pleasure in it . . . for his sake. The happiness he's getting in doing this for you is giving him such joy."

The next day, Rachel saw the boys to school, then spent the morning feeding the animals, milking the cow, and mucking out the stalls. Charlie arrived midmorning and helped her lay fresh straw and tote water from the stream. Quiet and somewhat sullen, he rode to check on the cattle as she gathered eggs and set two loaves of bread to rising.

That afternoon, back aching and with her fingernails still stained from barn work despite repeated washings, Rachel met the boys after school and walked them the short distance to James and Molly's house. Molly had agreed to watch them while she met with Mr. Westin.

Important decisions awaited, ones Rachel wasn't sure she was ready to make.

She made a brief stop by the general store to check the basket she'd left beside the front doors on the boardwalk. With Rand's help, she'd fashioned a rustic wooden sign with the inscription *Notes of Encouragement for Ben and Lyda Mullins* and they'd hung it above. Without fail, each day the basket held a collection of letters and notes.

Today was no exception. Rachel tucked them into her reticule to deliver later.

True to young Elijah's word, the warmer weather once again found Miss Clara's cafe situated beneath the canopy of the ancient ponderosa pine. Miss Clara's cast-iron stove skulked black and smoky beside the familiar array of mismatched tables, most of them already occupied, their blue-and-white-checkered cloths fluttering in the breeze. How comforting the simple routines of life often were, and how sweet.

Rachel spotted Edward Westin seated and waiting. He rose as she approached and held out her chair.

"You're early, Mr. Westin."

He glanced at his pocket watch. "As are you, Mrs. Boyd."

She smiled. "I'm always early when I'm nervous."

His expression held playful reproof. "No need to be nervous. As we discussed, I'm simply going to lay out the options available to you and let you decide. I have no financial stake whatsoever in the matter. I'm merely a liaison between a very intelligent and capable rancher"—he nodded in her direction—"and a former business partner of mine back east. Your decision is completely and utterly your own."

Rachel felt a jitter. "I'm not sure if that makes me feel better or only contributes to my nerves."

He laughed and nodded when Miss Clara came by with a pot of hot coffee.

"It's still a mite early, so dinner's not ready," Miss Clara said, "but I'll bring hot corn bread as soon as it's done."

Nodding his thanks, Mr. Westin withdrew a stack of papers from his satchel beside his chair. "I've worked the figures on your behalf, Mrs. Boyd, as you requested, based on the information you provided and . . ."

Listening, Rachel spotted James seated at a table on the opposite side of the cafe, near the stove. She discreetly tilted her head to the side, wanting to see who he was—

Rand. He was with Rand. *Odd* . . . She'd seen Rand last evening, and he hadn't said a word about getting together with James today. Not that he had to tell her his schedule, but James *was* her brother, and it only seemed—

"So you can see from the figures here, Mrs. Boyd . . ."

Rachel quickly readjusted her focus.

". . . that you do indeed have enough capital for this venture *if* you're willing to sell your current herd and take out a manageable loan for the remainder of the investment. My former partner's willing to personally underwrite your loan, in fact."

That got her attention, as did Mr. Westin's detailed financial analysis. "And, by chance, does this former partner realize to whom he's making the loan?"

"I don't quite know what you mean, ma'am."

Recalling what Mr. Fossey had said about how the bank's investors would feel more secure if she were married, she felt she had to ask. "Does he understand that I'm a widow? *Un*married?"

Westin's head tilted in acknowledgment. "He understands your situation, yes. And his willingness to make the loan is based in part on the market value of your land—the section not currently being held as collateral by the bank here, of course. As well as on the personal reference Mr. Fossey penned himself on your behalf. It was a stellar reference, Mrs. Boyd."

Rachel stared, letting that sink in. "That was very kind of him."

"I assure you, while Gilbert Fossey *is* kind, he's also an excellent judge of character in relation to evaluating potential risks. You qualified for the loan on your own merit, though I feel sure your dealings with the bank here, as well as those of your late husband, influenced the final outcome. Gilbert has spoken most highly of your late husband to me, Mrs. Boyd. Of you both," he said softly.

He said nothing for a moment, seeming slightly uncomfortable, then returned his attention to the papers on the table. "Now . . . in the event you decide not to purchase the Scottish Highlanders and choose to continue with your current operation, I've taken the liberty of working those figures as well. As you can see . . ."

Touched by what Mr. Westin had said about Thomas, and still mulling over Mr. Fossey's generous reference, Rachel picked James's laughter out of the crowd and was tempted to look over again. But instead, she made herself follow the column of figures down the page as Mr. Westin pointed to and explained each one.

Miss Clara brought dinner, and they continued to discuss business as they ate. Rachel chanced another look across the cafe, glad to find James and Rand still there, though neither gave any indication of seeing her. Whatever the two were discussing now, they seemed deep in conversation. Rand's expression was especially serious. Her imagination led her down a very short path in regard to the reason behind their meeting, and the singular conclusion she reached might've tempted her to smile if it hadn't nearly scared her to death.

The more time she spent with Rand, the more she wanted to spend. They were compatible in so many ways, and Mitchell adored him. Kurt did too, although Kurt was still a touch reserved around him. Rand was so different from Thomas, and she couldn't keep from comparing them. She was the same woman. And yet, at times, she felt like someone completely different when she was with Rand.

And odd as it sounded, even to her, she liked that woman.

Rand hadn't tried to kiss her again since that night at the clinic, which was probably for the best . . . she guessed. Still, she hadn't gone out of her way to discourage him.

A boisterous party of miners arrived and claimed two tables near the center of the outdoor cafe, which blocked her view of James and Rand. Taking the obstruction as a reminder of why she was here, Rachel pulled her focus back and concentrated on giving Mr. Westin her full and undivided attention, certain he hadn't noticed.

Enjoying Miss Clara's signature fried chicken and creamed potatoes, she reviewed the different scenarios Mr. Westin had so thoroughly researched on her behalf, and one thing became clear. She had to make a change. Either risk making the investment and buy the Scottish Highlanders, or decide to sell. Doing nothing wasn't an option. And neither was purchasing more of the same cattle—not with how the harsh Colorado winters were picking them off one by one.

If Mr. Westin's calculations were right—and she had no reason to believe they weren't—if she made no changes, then within two years, and perhaps sooner if faced with another winter like the past one, the ranch would be bankrupt.

"Are there any questions I haven't answered, Mrs. Boyd?"

Rachel sighed, her mind swirling. "I'm sure I'll think of some after I leave, but none for now. You've been very thorough. All I need is time to think things through . . . to *pray* things through."

"I understand completely." He leaned a little closer. "And frankly, I would've been disappointed if you'd answered any other way."

She stood, gathering her reticule, and glanced back across the cafe. James and Rand's table was empty. She scanned the surrounding area for them. Gone. Disappointment trickled through her, though she told herself it was foolish. Still, they might have at least said hello.

She reached inside her reticule for her change purse.

"Please, allow me," Westin said, tucking the bills beside his empty plate. "Which way are you headed, Mrs. Boyd?"

Thanking him, she motioned in the direction of James and Molly's house, and he fell into step beside her.

"The question you asked me before, ma'am . . . about whether my colleague knew that you're an unmarried woman." He eyed her with some humor. "I presume you've been encouraged by someone to enter into marriage again before seeking another loan?"

Rachel looked over at him, matching his smile. "They didn't exactly *encourage* it, but yes, the suggestion was made that I would stand a better chance of being approved if I had a husband."

Nodding, he looked ahead. "I'll take a shot in the dark here, but I'm guessing that suggestion didn't go over very well with you. Nor would I expect it to. After having been married to the love of your life, I can't begin to fathom marrying again only for the sake of a business partnership."

"Yes!" She nodded, liking this man more and more. "Those were my sentiments exactly!"

They walked in companionable silence for another block.

"May I ask you something else, Mrs. Boyd? Something of a far more personal nature?"

The tone of his question roused her curiosity. "Of course." She took the stairs to the boardwalk, glad there were few pedestrians.

"Let me preface my question by saying that under normal circumstances I would never inquire about this. But understanding how closely I'm working with Mr. and Mrs. Mullins, and that we're partners in the store now . . ." He sighed, looking down. "I'm making a mess of this."

Rachel smiled, hoping to ease his discomfort. "Why not simply ask the question outright? That's often best."

He nodded. "I showed Ben a picture of my grandchildren the other day, one my daughter sent me last week, and then I asked him whether he and Lyda had any children."

Rachel winced and saw him do the same.

"It was a thoughtless question on my part, I realized immediately. But Ben was gracious, as seems his nature. He told me they'd had a boy and a girl, twins, but that their children were gone now. That's all he said. And, of course, I didn't press for more. But I was wondering if . . ."

"You'd like to know what happened," Rachel said softly, understanding.

Eyes remorseful, yet hopeful, he nodded.

"I'm sure they wouldn't mind me telling you, Mr. Westin. Most everyone in town knows, at least those who've lived here long enough." Rachel confined her gaze to the weathered planks passing beneath her boots, but her eyes briefly closed as an image of the children returned. She slowed her steps. "It's been eight years ago now. The twins were four years old. It was winter, and it had been snowing throughout the day." She felt a shiver, not from the memory of the bitter cold as much as the anguish in Lyda's face when she and Thomas had arrived at the house.

"Ben and Lyda had taken the children sledding. Up on a hill near the edge of town. It wasn't until they'd gotten home that their daughter realized she'd left her doll behind. A storm had moved in, and it was snowing hard by then." Rachel stopped at the end of the boardwalk and looked out across the street, remembering. Mr. Westin stood beside her, quiet. "When they put the children to bed, little Ellie Grace was still crying for her doll. Their son, Andrew, said he'd go back and look for it. But, of course, Ben and Lyda said no, that they'd go look for it the next day." Just as she and Thomas would have done.

Rachel clenched her jaw, still unable to fathom what Ben and Lyda had gone through, the regret they still carried. "Next morning, they found the children's beds empty, and the front door ajar."

Edward Westin slowly bowed his head.

"Search parties combed the hill where they'd been sledding, then all around town and up into the foothills. But the snow covered whatever tracks there'd been. Come nightfall, the men lit fires up there along the ridge"—she pointed—"near our home, hoping the children would see them and find their way." She shook her head, remembering how she and Lyda stood in the biting wind and snow, waiting, praying, feeling hope slip away like a whisper on the wind. "They found Andrew and Ellie Grace the next morning. . . . They'd fallen through the ice on a creek near where they'd been sledding."

A deep sigh sounded beside her, but Rachel didn't look over.

"Thank you for telling me, Mrs. Boyd." A moment passed before he spoke again. "It's one thing to lose your spouse, as you and I well know. But I can't begin to imagine the pain Evelyn and I would have experienced if we'd had to bury our children."

The warm breeze was cool on her cheeks, and Rachel wiped away the moisture, recalling details she hadn't shared with Edward Westin. Ben had accompanied one of the search parties. Lyda wanted to go too, but they urged her to stay near home, in case the children returned. Everyone knew how searches went in the mountains. Two shots were fired when the person was found alive. Only one shot was fired when the body was recovered. Ben had told Lyda to listen for two shots. But only one shot came.

They walked on, until Westin paused at the next street. "I think I'll head over to the store, see how things are going."

"Thank you again, Mr. Westin, for dinner and for your excellent counsel. I'll let you know my decision as soon as it's made." She hesitated, wanting to word her observation the right way. "It sounds like your Evelyn was an extraordinary woman. I wish I could have known her. Thomas and I were only married for twelve years. I can't comprehend the loss you must be feeling after thirty-six years with someone."

"Thirty-six wonderful years that I would relive again in a heartbeat, if I could. You're a beautiful young woman, Mrs. Boyd. I pray you have the opportunity to share your life with someone for that long. There's incredible joy in knowing your partner so well."

Not knowing quite how to respond to that, she

decided some humor was needed to offset the seriousness. "I don't know whether or not I'll ever marry again. But if I do, it will be for love. Not for a loan!"

He smiled, rubbing his jawline. "And if *I* ever marry again, Mrs. Boyd"—he gave her a wink—"it'll be when a woman looks at me the way you look at Rand Brookston . . . when you think no one else is looking."

He chuckled as he walked away.

30

By the time Rand got to Rachel's house it was nearly dark. He'd been looking forward to this night all week, and despite being dog tired, he wouldn't have chosen to be anywhere else. True to her word, Rachel served a delicious roast dinner, complete with tiny potatoes and all the trimmings, and he enjoyed every bite and every minute with her and the boys.

After dinner, Kurt disappeared from the table only to return a minute later with a box in his hands. "Can you stay to play dominoes?"

Rachel shook her head. "Dr. Brookston's had a long day, son. We need to let him—"

Rand touched her arm. "Sure I can. But only if we can play more than one game. I hear you and your brother are mean domino players, so you need to give me a fair chance to win."

Later, the boys in bed, he readied to leave, and Rachel walked him to the door.

She pulled her shawl tight around her shoulders, quieter than she'd been all evening. "I'm glad you came tonight, Rand."

"I am too, Rachel." He loved it when her mouth tipped up on one side like that. Sort of a half smile. "Thank you for the invitation."

She stared, her expression all but lost to him in the shadows. "And thank you again for the wonderful evening at the resort. Even though it's been a week, the boys are still talking about it, as you saw at dinner. It really made an impression on them."

He wanted to kiss her so badly but held back, not wanting to move too quickly, having promised himself he'd be patient. But that was easier said than done. He'd seen her the other afternoon with Edward Westin at Miss Clara's cafe. She'd told him beforehand about the meeting so he wasn't surprised to see them there together. He'd gone out of his way not to intrude, to give her space. More than once in recent days, he'd asked her about the ranch, and she always told him, "I'm managing just fine."

He knew she wasn't, and he wished she would confide in him about it. But again, he was determined not to push. He thought of his meeting with James that same afternoon and knew Rachel had to have seen them. He'd been more nervous than he'd thought he would be and was glad that particular task was behind him.

Slowly, Rachel rose on tiptoe, and for one brief, hopeful second he thought she might be issuing an invitation. But just as quickly, she pressed her lips against his cheek and then retreated into the cabin, giving him one last smile before closing the door.

Carrying that smile with him, along with her kiss, he stopped by the clinic to make sure no one had left a note requesting his assistance, then headed back out to the resort.

After checking on Ben, he fell into bed, exhausted, only to awaken in the wee hours of the morning, unable to sleep. He heard Ben coughing and went to check on him, taking one of several lamps he kept lit.

On the off chance Lyda was still asleep on the cot across the room, he kept the light low so as not to awaken her. "You all right, Ben?" he whispered.

"Yeah," Ben finally whispered back. "I'm fine, Doc." But he didn't sound it.

Rand moved closer, lamplight illuminating his steps. "Is there anything I can get you? Are you experiencing any pain?"

"No. I'm fine. Just can't sleep for some reason." His laugh held no humor. "Maybe 'cause that's all I've been doing lately."

Rand got him a drink of water, and they spoke softly in the dark. When Ben's cough persisted, Rand gave him a dose of laudanum. Lyda stirred on the cot, and Rand was almost certain she was awake. Yet she said nothing.

Ben took a breath and exhaled. "This time of night's got to be the loneliest of all, Doc. Feels like everybody else in the world is asleep." Reminiscence thickened his voice. "Makes a man take inventory of his life and wish he'd done better with the time God gave him."

Hollow regret filled the silence.

Rand knew the root of Ben's feelings. This kind of reflection, and regret, was common when people were facing their own mortality. "I'd wager most men haven't done half as well as you have, Ben, with the way they've lived their lives. I know your wife would agree. And I think the people in town would too."

Ben didn't say anything, but his quiet sniff a minute later was answer enough.

Rand took hold of his hand. "Could I pray for you, Ben?"

Ben's feeble grip tightened, and Rand bowed his head.

"I'm tired of this place, Doc. I want to go home."

Rand situated the pillows behind Ben's head and warmed the bell-shaped end of the stethoscope in his palm, hearing the weariness in Ben's voice. And no wonder, with how Ben had slept during the night. "I know you do. But you're not strong enough to make the trip just yet. Especially not with what happened this morning." The heart episode he'd experienced following breakfast hadn't been severe, but Rand knew that keeping him at the resort for another few days would be best. "The swelling in your legs and feet tells me you're retaining a substantial amount of fluid. The medicine I gave you earlier should help that, but we need to give it a couple of days." He paused, waiting until Ben looked at him. "I promise, Ben. . . . As soon as you're able, we'll get you home."

Ben stared up for several long seconds, then closed his eyes.

Rand positioned the stethoscope on his chest, not unsympathetic to Ben's request, nor having forgotten his and Ben's conversation during the early-morning hours. "Take some deep breaths for me, if you would. Hold . . . then exhale."

Eyes closed, Ben cooperated and Rand heard what he did not want to hear. Fluid was thick and tight around Ben's lungs. Again.

The low howl of wind drew Rand's attention outside, and he watched a cluster of stalwart pines—some seventy feet tall and two feet around—sway to and fro, yielding to nature's will.

Since noon, the temperature had dropped at least twenty degrees. Typical for a late Colorado spring, winter was returning to the mountains for one final, bitter stand.

"Doc?"

Rand looked up.

"I'm grateful to you for everything you've done for me. For everything you've helped me do for Lyda. The extra time you bought me . . ." He smiled his easy smile and drew in a breath. "But I don't want to spend my last days here in this place. I want to be back in my own bed . . . in the room above the store . . . where Lyda and I first lived when we moved to Timber Ridge." His exhale carried a weight of fatigue and memories. "Where we used to lie in bed at night . . . dream of all we'd do with the store. Where she gave birth to our children. And where—" His voice caught. "Where we held them for the last time." He stared ahead, not bothering to wipe away the tears. "I don't mean any disrespect by this, but . . . it only seems right that the person dyin' should get to choose."

The words resonated within Rand. And not for the first time with this man, he felt less like the doctor and more like the patient. Part of him wanted to argue, wanted to try and persuade Ben to keep on fighting, to hold on to this life. Then he looked at Ben, and as if looking into a mirror, he saw himself—in this situation, in these circumstances—and a certainty settled deep inside him, silencing every remaining argument.

Head bowed, he covered Ben's hand with his. "You're right," he said softly. "The person dying should get to choose." He rose from his chair. "I'll make the arrangements, and we'll have you home tonight."

He prayed Ben would survive the ride back into town, through the bitter cold, over the washboard roads. Yet he feared the odds of that happening were slim. But if that was what Ben wanted, that is what he would do. Slipping the stethoscope back into his bag, he glanced out the window, the gray of late day gradually giving way to approaching evening—and he paused. Then he squinted to make sure what he was seeing was real.

He'd seen God work in many ways, but this . . . He felt the touch of a smile inside, sensing those less-than-favorable odds shift in their favor.

31

R and checked the clock over the mantel again. A quarter past eight and it was already dark. When he'd spotted the first snowflake, he'd thought it was an answer to prayer.

Now he wondered. . . .

In the past hour, the storm had intensified. The wind gusted, churning the snow sideways and pelting the windows with bits of ice. Where was Charlie? And why was he taking so long? All he had to do was go to Rachel's house, then come back. Rand rubbed the back of his neck. He'd told Charlie to wait until enough snow had fallen to smooth the roads, not bury the Rockies.

He looked at Ben lying in the bed, and at Lyda beside him in the chair. The room was quiet, still—

yet he felt a tension. A weariness. The moments crept by with each *ticktock* of the clock on the wall. Perhaps Charlie's not showing up was a sign that they weren't supposed to try and make this trip today after all. He'd made Ben a promise, but surely Ben would understand if the weather—

The door to the Health Suite burst open. Mitch and Kurt came barreling in, Rachel a few steps behind.

Mitch's hair was plastered to his head, wet with snow. "Mama says to tell you we're here!"

Kurt skidded to a halt by Ben's bed. "We're supposed to make sure you're bundled up, Uncle Ben. But that's all we're supposed to say."

Rand didn't miss the exaggerated look of warning the older brother gave the younger, nor the playful look Rachel gave them both. She smiled up at him, and instantly, Rand felt his spirits brighten. As did the mood in the room.

Rachel leaned down and kissed Ben's cheek. "Your carriage awaits, kind sir. Are you ready to take a ride?"

Grinning like he hadn't done in days, Ben waggled his brows. "That depends on who's drivin'!"

She chuckled. "Let's get you out of that bed and bundled up, and we'll take you to see!"

With everyone helping, they got Ben ready and situated in the wheelchair. Rand administered a dose of laudanum and digitalis, both preventative measures for the trip. As Lyda tucked a second blanket around Ben, Rand pulled Rachel aside.

"You are an absolute answer to prayer," he whispered, meaning it in so many ways.

She looked into his eyes, and only then did he glimpse how difficult this was for her, how much she was hurting, despite her cheery demeanor. They weren't just "taking Ben home," and she knew it.

She pressed a hand to his chest. "Please . . . don't make me cry, Rand," she whispered, her smile tremulous. "Not now." Taking a deep breath, she turned. "Mitch, Kurt, grab those bags, and we'll be on our way!"

Rand watched her, admiring her strength and courage, and her love for Ben and Lyda.

With Ben in the wheelchair, dressed warmly and with extra blankets tucked around him, they headed for the lobby. Guests of the resort mingled in small clusters, drinks in hand. Some looked their way and smiled. But every employee they saw paused from their work to come and hug Ben and Lyda and say their good-byes.

The bellman held open the doors, and Rand pushed Ben's wheelchair through, readying himself for a chilling blast of wind. But none came.

The night was absolute stillness. Not a breath of wind stirred. Snow continued to fall, but the flakes drifted lazily downward, unhurried and unhindered, cushioning every footfall and muffling their voices.

"Well, I'll be," Ben said softly.

Rand wasn't sure whether Ben was referring to the night's quiet, or to the huge sleigh wagon Charlie Daggett stood beside, but he shared the reaction.

Lyda turned to Rachel. "Where on earth did you find that wagon?"

"I didn't." Rachel gestured. "Charlie did. It belongs to a family in Little Italy. They were kind enough to let us borrow it. That's what took us a little longer."

Charlie stepped forward. "We got you a nice, warm spot back here, Mr. Mullins. You too, Miss Lyda. We warmed up some bricks and stuffed them down beneath so it'd be nice and cozy for you." Charlie ran a hand along the oversized wagon bed layered with hay and blankets. "It's gonna be nice havin' you back in the store, sir."

Once Ben and Lyda were comfortable, covered up and toasty, the boys burrowed in with them. Rand assisted Rachel and claimed a spot beside her. He leaned closer. "Why do I have a feeling this isn't everything you and Charlie have planned?"

She laughed softly but said nothing.

After a jerky start, the sleigh glided across the fresh-fallen snow like warm butter over homemade bread. A myriad of stars twinkled above, and the blanketed ground reflected the moonlight, making it easy to see the path ahead.

Rand kept an eye on Ben, recognizing the sedating effects of the laudanum and watching for anything unusual that might indicate a problem.

"Hey!" Mitch rose up on his knees, pointing skyward. "There's Orion!"

Rand felt a nudge in his ribs and caught Rachel's smile. His attention immediately swung to Kurt. He knew the boy would be frantically searching the night sky, not wanting to be outdone by his older brother. And sure enough, Kurt stared up, tongue doubled between his teeth, eyes darting this way and that. Feeling for him, Rand began to pray. Not just that Kurt would find a constellation he knew, but that he would discover that certain *something* within himself that all boys needed to find before they could begin to realize who they were, as well as the man they would grow to be.

Kurt's face lit. "I see it! I see the Big Dipper!"

Rand nodded his approval, wishing God answered all his prayers so quickly.

They reached town and Charlie slowed the horses' pace. It soon became apparent why.

Bordering Main Street and leading all the way to the Mullinses' store were oil lamps, spaced at regular intervals, burning bright in the night, casting a warm glow across the snow. It looked like a scene from a painting.

"What on earth?" Lyda said, rising up to look. She nudged Ben, who did the same.

"Oh . . ." Ben sighed, blinking. "Would you look at that. . . ."

Rachel leaned forward. "People heard you were coming home tonight, Ben, and they wanted to do something special for you. It's their way of welcoming you back."

The closer they got to the store, the more people were gathered on the boardwalk, James and Molly among them, little Josephine in James's arms. Josiah and Belle Birch and their son, Elijah, waved and called out greetings as the wagon passed, as did countless others.

"Good to see you back, Mr. Mullins! We've been missin' you!"

"Hurry up and get back behind that counter, Ben!"

"We love you, Ben! You too, Lyda!"

Lips pinched tight, chin quivering, Ben raised his hand and waved. Lyda leaned into him and slipped her arms around his waist.

With Charlie's help, they got Ben inside and upstairs, taking time to let Ben see the renovation the store had undergone. "Wonderful," he whispered, taking everything in. "Just like I pictured it."

Ben groaned as Charlie laid him into bed. He held his chest as Rand checked his pulse. Shallow. Erratic. Rand administered more digitalis and supported Ben's head as he drank, telling himself again that he'd made the right choice in bringing

Ben home. *"The person dying gets to choose."* Seeing the silent affirmation in Rachel's pained expression helped.

Lyda took the empty cup and set it aside, staying ever close by her husband.

"I know"—Ben struggled for breath—"what you're thinkin', Doc. And . . ." He shook his head. "You stop it . . . right now. If you'd said no to bringin' me home, I . . ." He grimaced. "I woulda had to call you out, son. Like I said I would. Remember?"

Rand gripped Ben's hand, willing the digitalis to act quickly. "Of course I remember. Why do you think I said yes?"

Eyes closed, Ben smiled.

Moments passed and his breathing evened, though his inhalation still sounded congested and moist. At least his pain had eased. For now.

Rand leaned closer, wanting Ben to hear. "That scene outside a few minutes ago, when we drove up . . . I'd think that would make a man look back on his life and realize what a *fine* job he's done with the time God gave him."

Eyes still closed, Ben gripped Rand's hand tighter, a tear slipping from the corner of his eye.

Later, with Ben resting comfortably, Rand made a trip to the clinic for more medicine. His latest shipment had finally arrived from Denver, but several of the bottles had broken in transit, and the vendor sent smaller quantities than he'd ordered. So his supplies were running low—again.

When he returned to the store, it was nearing eleven o'clock. He found Lyda reading a story to the boys, one nestled on either side of her. The boys yawned, their eyelids heavy.

Lyda paused from reading. "Rachel's upstairs with Ben," she said softly. "She insists that she and the boys are going to stay the night, but . . ." She shook her head. "I've encouraged her to take them on home and get some rest." She patted each of the boys on the leg, smiling as they stared up at her. "These sweet boys have already said good night to their uncle Ben." She looked back at Rand, her weary smile fading.

She didn't have to voice the question. Rand understood without her saying a thing, and wished he had the answer. "I don't know," he whispered, then reached down and pinched the toe of Mitch's boot, then Kurt's. "Did you boys give your uncle Ben a good hug tonight?"

"Yes, sir," they answered.

"But not too hard, like you said," Kurt added.

Nodding, he rose, seeing Lyda's tears, feeling his own. As much as he loved Ben, he hoped for Ben's sake that it wouldn't be long, and knew that Lyda would begin to hope the same, as it soon became more and more difficult for Ben to breathe.

He climbed the stairs, each boot step heavier than the last. He placed the pouch of medicine on the hallway table and took a moment to gather his emotions, knowing he needed to be strong. For Ben, for Lyda. For everyone.

The door to Ben and Lyda's bedroom was slightly ajar, and as he reached to open it farther, he saw Rachel seated on the edge of the bed, her back to him, speaking to Ben in a halting whisper. He couldn't hear what she said, but judging by the fatherly way Ben lifted a hand to her cheek, he gathered it was a private moment and stepped back into the hall.

"I'll tell him, honey." Ben's voice was gentle, yet held unwavering certainty. "He already knows, I'm sure. But I'll tell him."

Rachel whispered something else Rand couldn't quite make out, and then he heard the soft tap of her boots. He stepped farther back into the hall, not wanting her to think he'd been standing there listening, even though he had. Or had tried.

The door opened. Her face was wet with tears. Seeing him, she quickly wiped them away. "I think the boys and I are going to stay. We'll make pallets downstairs in the—"

"Rachel . . ." he whispered, shaking his head.

Her face crumpled, and he pulled her to him. Her arms came around his waist.

"There's nothing else you can do tonight." He stroked her back, kissed the top of her head. "Go on home and get some rest. I'll be here."

She took a hiccuped breath, then finally nodded. "We'll be back in the morning. First thing."

He tipped her chin up and kissed her forehead, lingering, praying, wondering what message she'd given to Ben. And if it was meant for him.

32

Her shoulders burning from exertion, Rachel thrust the pitchfork into the hay, hefted the load, and lugged it to the last stall. The first hint of morning shone through cracks in the plank wood as she heaved the feed over the stall with more force than necessary. The horse whinnied and stamped, but Rachel paid the animal no mind. She shoved the pitchfork back on the nail and grabbed the mallet from the workbench as irretrievable moments ticked past.

She should have been with Ben and Lyda at that moment instead of taking care of her *confounded* animals—she hammered the layer of ice on the water barrel—on her *blasted* ranch—shards went flying—that she'd never really wanted Thomas to—

The mallet slipped from her grip and sailed into the air behind her, hitting the barn wall with a crash. Rachel bit back harsh words as angry tears rose.

She sucked in a breath and dragged her fingers through her hair, slowly exhaling, her breath fogging white. What was she doing? She looked around the barn. Was this what she wanted to do with the rest of her life? She clenched her jaw, remembering what Ben had said last night. *"Don't be afraid of being happy again, Rachel."* She brushed away a tear, sick of the conflict inside her, wanting to be true to Thomas while also being honest with herself.

During the night, she'd awakened and decided that she would ask Ben what he thought about her selling the ranch—right now, as it was, before she bought the cattle from Mr. Westin's colleague. Ben had known Thomas, and Thomas had confided in him, apparently more than she'd realized at the time. Ben would give her an honest answer and good counsel. He always had. But she needed to hurry. If there was one thing she knew, time wasn't guaranteed. And Ben didn't have much left. He'd told her so last night. He'd said he could feel the days slipping away.

Chores done, for the morning at least, she retraced her path through the snow back to the house and was halfway up the porch stairs when she saw something from the corner of her eye. Someone coming up the road. Her brain registered who it was first, and then it registered with her heart. She grabbed the porch railing, her legs losing strength. She shook her head, unable to catch her breath.

In the moment Rand's arms came around her, she

knew it didn't matter whether death came suddenly, without warning, or whether it came slowly, giving you time to memorize the sound of its footsteps and the hollow cadence of its march. Whichever way death came, and however much she believed that the grave held no lasting victory, the same terrible rending tore down deep inside, severing what was from what would never be again.

At least, not here on this earth.

Lyda sat in the rocker, staring at the now-empty bed, weeping. Not in a wailing way, but in low, lonely sobs that were somehow even worse. Rachel set the cup of hot tea on the dresser beside her.

Rand had stopped by James and Molly's on the way out to her ranch and had told them about Ben's passing. James had been by some time ago and, with the help of Deputy Willis, moved Ben's body to Rand's clinic as Rand requested.

Rachel knelt and took hold of Lyda's hands. "I'll see to all the details. Don't you worry about a thing."

Lyda gestured. "His suit . . . It's in the chifforobe. And his tie is in the top drawer." Her eyes red-rimmed and swollen, she took a deep breath, held it for the longest time, and then gave it release. "One of the last things he said to me was . . ." She pressed her lips together, fresh tears coming. " 'I feel like there's a big surprise comin'.'" She said it the way Ben might have, then smiled softly. "I told him he was right, that there was. He asked me, 'Reckon what it might be?' And I said . . ." Her gaze lowered to the bed as though she could still see Ben lying there. "I said I couldn't tell him . . . or else it wouldn't be a surprise."

Rachel smiled, and held tighter to Lyda's hands.

Lyda dabbed her eyes with one of Ben's handkerchiefs. "I told him that . . ." She sniffed. "That when he saw Jesus, to run for Him with everything he had . . . and that I'd be right behind him . . . soon enough." She looked upward, another low sob breaking through. "And I think that's what he did."

Rachel laid her head in Lyda's lap. "I'm so sorry," she whispered, her chest tight with grief.

Lyda stroked her hair. "He's with them now. . . ."

Rachel nodded, knowing whom she meant.

"I like to think our sweet children were waitin' right there for him, for their papa, soon as he crossed over."

Rachel lifted her gaze. "I'm sure they were."

Lyda's expression held such tenderness. "Right beside your Thomas."

Rachel bowed her head and saw Lyda pull something from her pocket.

"Here," Lyda said softly, holding out her hand. "Ben wanted to have this buried with him."

Rachel took the suede pouch. She'd seen it

before and knew what it contained—the ball and jacks that had belonged to their son. Even now, Lyda fingered their daughter's hair ribbon in her hand.

"Reckon I'll save this," Lyda whispered, "and have it buried with me when my time comes."

Unable to answer, Rachel nodded.

For the longest moment, neither of them spoke. They sat together in the silence, each knowing what the other was feeling.

"I'm all alone now," Lyda whispered, her hands starting to tremble. She pressed a palm to her midsection. "My family's all gone. First our little Andrew and sweet Ellie Grace. And now Ben."

Rachel looked up. It had been years since she'd heard Lyda speak her son's and daughter's names aloud. She covered her hand. "You're not alone, Lyda. We'll be here for you—the boys and me. And I'll never forget Andrew and Ellie Grace. Or Ben. I'll remember them with you forever. I promise."

And then it occurred to her—Ben was home with Thomas now, and Ben had promised to give him her message. Which meant . . . without a doubt *now,* Thomas knew.

"I appreciate your help with this, James. I couldn't have done it without you." Rachel closed the door to the back room of the clinic and followed her brother down the hallway, hoping Rand would return before the undertaker arrived. He'd been gone all day. Sally Brewer's labor, her first, was apparently taking longer than they'd hoped.

"Thank you for asking me." Her brother's smile was typical James—warm, caring, ever strong. "I consider it an honor. Ben and Lyda have always seemed like family."

Rachel agreed, but she was glad to have this part behind them. She'd pressed Ben's suit and tie earlier that afternoon, as Lyda requested. And though they looked handsome on him, it just didn't look like Ben to her. She would always picture him with that white apron cinched about his waist, his winsome smile at the ready.

James ran a hand over the medicine chest they'd given Rand. "This looks good in here."

"Yes, it does. It's nice to see it being used again."

"And by another doctor, no less." A discerning look moved in behind his eyes, one she knew quite well.

Aware of how easily he read her, Rachel picked up a book Rand had left on the hearth and studied the cracked binding. *The Science of Cardiac Health and Healing.* The pages were dog-eared, notes scribbled in the margins. No telling how many times he'd read and reread this volume.

"He's not like our father," James said softly behind her. "But I'm sure you know that by now."

She thumbed the pages of the book, vowing to read it, and relishing the scent of aged ink and paper, and the fact that Rand had held it. "Yes, I do." She could ask James the reason behind his and Rand's meeting days back, but in her heart, she knew. And besides, James wouldn't divulge a thing. Honor was his middle name. She returned the book to its place.

"Rand Brookston is a fine man." She turned to face her brother. "He's kind and caring and intelligent, and a gifted physician. And while I truly appreciate what you're trying to do—"

"I'm not trying to do anything, Rachel. I promise." Sincerity marked his words. "I just want you to know where I stand where he's concerned. I loved Thomas like a brother. But I know he'd want you to be happy, and to move on. For your sake as much as the boys'. "

Rachel lowered her gaze, fingering the edge of her sleeve. "I realize that."

"No, I don't think you do. And I think that's part of your problem."

She lifted her head, surprised at the bluntness in his tone. "My *problem?*"

He gently tweaked the tip of her nose the way he'd done when they were younger. "That was a poor choice of words on my part. I apologize. I'm only saying what I think Thomas would want me to say, Rachel, if he were listening in on our conversation right now. And I think he'd want me to tell you that he wants you to be as happy as you can be on the road God's marked out for you . . .

which may look very different from the road you and Thomas were traveling together."

He pressed a quick kiss to her forehead, then ducked to be eye level with her. "Are we still on speaking terms?"

She smiled up at him, thanking God for such a wise brother. How would she and the boys have gotten through these past two and a half years without him? "Yes. But it's against my better judgment."

He grinned, then glanced at the clock, his expression sobering. "Want me to stay until Carnes gets here?"

Rachel pictured the town's undertaker—such an odd little man—and almost said yes, then thought of Molly back at the ranch with baby Jo, and Mitch and Kurt. "No, I'm fine. Rand should be back any time." And would be exhausted from no sleep last night and a full day of doctoring.

Once James left, she began straightening up. Heaven knew, there was plenty to clean in this place, though Rand wasn't at fault. Having witnessed his regimen for cleanliness, she understood that now. She found an old rag and began dusting, anything to keep busy.

She'd spent most of the day with Lyda, and seeing Lyda hurting the way she was brought back so many memories. None of them good. But instead of dwelling on that and on Ben being gone, Rachel determined to recall as many good memories of Ben as she could. That's what Ben would have wanted.

One immediately sprang to mind and she bit her lower lip, remembering the time Ben had traded out the jar of cherry jawbreakers for hot cinnamon ones. He'd laughed so hard when seeing the boys' eyes water and mouths pucker. . . . She smiled, teary at the memory.

She straightened a stack of books on an end table and dusted beneath them, then noticed Rand's Bible lying on the edge of the chair. An embroidered bookmark peeked from the pages, and she opened to the marked passage. Rand had bracketed a set of verses and written something in the margin. She recognized his handwriting. *Lord, grow within me such a faith.* Echoing that sentiment, she thumbed the pages of Scriptures and paused when one page in particular snagged her attention.

Its passages were underlined, some more than once, and the edges of the page were crinkled from repeated handling. She smiled when realizing what psalm it was. One of her favorites.

"Whither shall I go from thy spirit?" she read more from memory than from the printed text. *"Or whither shall I flee from thy presence? If I ascend up into heaven, thou art there: if I make my bed in hell, behold, thou art there. . . ."* Her eyes went to a portion of Scripture that Rand, she assumed, had underlined twice. *"If I say, Surely the darkness*

shall cover me; even the night shall be light about me. Yea, the darkness hideth not from—"

A knock sounded on the door.

Already knowing who it would be, she returned the Bible to its place and readied herself to face Mr. Carnes, the town's curious and socially awkward undertaker. She opened the door to a cold rush of wind and snow.

"Daniel!" She took a quick step back, holding the door steady in the wind. "W-what are you doing here?" She glanced past him, seeing Beau, his dog, but noticing Elizabeth wasn't with them. Elizabeth's absence meant no buffer between her and Daniel, a situation she tried to avoid at all costs. "Where's Elizabeth? Is she all right?"

"She's over at the store, with Lyda—and Dr. Brookston."

Shoulders hunched against the wind, Daniel seemed reluctant to meet her gaze. Common courtesy dictated she invite him inside, and it took every ounce of courtesy within her to oblige. She gestured, but he hesitated. As if seeking to make his decision easier, a gust of wind and snow barreled around the corner. Daniel stepped inside, Beau following, and Rachel closed the door.

Dressed in his customary buckskin, rifle in hand, Daniel seemed to fill the room. Rachel had forgotten that about him. He'd always had a powerful presence, even as a younger man.

"I was bringing Elizabeth into town to see the

421

doctor, but we met up with him on his way back from the Brewers'. He told us about Ben." Daniel shook his head. "I'm sorry, Rachel. I know how close you were to him."

Though she found it hard to look into his eyes, she forced herself and nodded. His eyes held such sincerity, such honesty. But after what he'd done to Thomas—his behavior had been so reckless, irresponsible. And had cost her so much. "Is Elizabeth sick? Is it something with the baby?"

"Dr. Brookston thinks everything is okay. But Elizabeth's been real tired. She fainted earlier today, and that's not like her at all, even since she's been with child." He removed his hat and held it in his hands. "Dr. Brookston sent me to get some medicine." He pulled a piece of paper from his pocket.

Reading what Rand had written, Rachel calmed. She recognized what he was likely treating Elizabeth for from the medicine he requested. "I know right where these things are. Wait here and I'll get them for you." She worked quickly, knowing the sooner she gave Daniel the medicine, the sooner he would leave.

It took her a few minutes, but Daniel didn't move an inch from his spot by the door. Nor did he speak.

"Here's everything Dr. Brookston requested." She handed him the cloth sack, glancing down at Beau, who stayed ever close by his master's side.

"I wrapped it twice, but try not to let it get wet."

He opened his jacket and tucked the bundle inside.

The moment lengthened, and Rachel grew antsy.

"Rachel, I . . ." He ran his tongue along the inside of his cheek, a nervous habit of his since childhood. "I just want to say that . . ." He paused and stared at her, eyes beseeching, no words coming, and she glimpsed the shy boy she'd grown up with. The boy who had taught her how to tell the difference between animals' tracks, who had shown her his best secret fishing holes, and the friend who had eaten at her and Thomas's table more times than she could count. The friend Thomas had loved. That *she* had loved. Just as Daniel loved them.

A frown creased his brow, but it wasn't anger or frustration she saw in Daniel's face. It was hurt. Hurt and regret layered so deep that the grief seemed to flow between them without need of words. Maybe it was Ben's passing and the reminder of the brevity of this life, maybe it was the long hours of day wearing thin into night, but she felt the barrier of blame and judgment she'd harbored and tended since Thomas's death begin to give way.

She scrambled to shore it up, reminded of the countless times she'd seen the look of yearning in Thomas's eyes when his own sons had scampered up to Daniel's lap, begging Uncle Daniel to tell them, one more time, about his latest adventure. If Daniel hadn't pushed Thomas to prove himself in front of his sons, then perhaps Thomas would still be—

The last words Thomas spoke to her came back in a rush. She could imagine him standing there in the doorway of their cabin, could still hear his voice. "Do you not think I can do this, Rachel?" He'd smiled, so kind-natured, loving, always so quick to forgive her—and everyone else. "Have a little more faith in me, honey." He'd winked. "I love you. I'll be home before dark."

And she never saw him alive again.

Staring into Daniel's eyes, reliving that scene, Rachel felt a weight inside her. A truth buried deep, unearthing itself, growing heavier by the second.

Daniel opened his mouth as if to say something, then swallowed. His lower lip trembled. "I-I'm sorry, Rachel. . . ." His eyes filled. "If I could go back and . . ." He gritted his teeth, the muscles in his jaw cording tight. "If I could go back and do things different, I would."

Oh, how many times she'd longed for that very thing.

Daniel studied the plank-wood floor beneath his boots, giving her time, she knew. But she couldn't think of anything to say and couldn't have spoken past the knot in her throat if she'd wanted to.

He slipped his hat on and opened the door,

turning his shoulder into the storm. "Dr. Brookston said he'd meet you here shortly." With one last look, he left.

But he took a piece of her heart with him—the jagged, razor-edged shard that had broken away the moment James had told her how Thomas had been killed. The shard that had lodged itself deep and impenetrable in her pride and in her desperation to blame someone else for something she'd done. Something she'd thought she could never undo.

But she'd been wrong. And Ben had helped her to see that.

33

Rand closed the clinic door behind him and set his bag on the table, relieved Rachel had left a couple of lamps burning. A fire crackled warm in the hearth and he heard footsteps in the back. Glad to discover she hadn't left, he saw further evidence of her presence in the clinic—bottles and tins perfectly straight on the shelf, all instruments washed and put away, surfaces wiped down, pristine.

He exhaled, weary, his eyes burning from too little sleep. Snow was still falling at a steady rate, and the night was frigid. He couldn't seem to shake this chill.

He raked a hand over his face and crossed to the

hearth, thinking of Ben and how brave a man he was, right until the very end. Which had come faster—mercifully so, one might argue—than any of them had expected.

Emotion tightened his throat, as it had at unexpected intervals throughout the day. Had he done everything he could for Ben? And to the best of his ability? The questions played over and over.

And again and again, the answer came back . . . yes.

He arched his back, stretching the tight muscles and reliving those last moments.

The chest pains that started without warning, Ben's heart rate escalating at an unnatural pace, the odd syncopated rhythms of his pulse. Rand closed his eyes. Witnessing the final moments of Ben's life, with Lyda by her husband's bedside, hearing their whispered *I love you*s, reminded him yet again of how precious time was and how quickly life passed.

"Rand . . ."

He looked up to see Rachel coming from the hallway.

"I'm glad you're back." Her smile faded slightly. "You look so tired."

Wishing he could cross the room and take her in his arms and hold her, just hold her, for a little while—or better, all night long—he drank in the sight of her instead. How quickly he'd grown accustomed to having her in his life, however impermanent the arrangement at present. Something he hoped to change.

"You've been busy." He glanced around the room. "Thank you for all you've done." He held her gaze, hoping she knew he was referring to more than just her cleaning.

Her expression warmed. "You're welcome. How is Lyda? And Elizabeth? Daniel said she'd fainted."

"Lyda's doing all right. I gave her something to help her sleep. And Elizabeth's fine." He stretched, his neck muscles tight. "She's suffering from anemia."

"Low iron."

He nodded. "Brought on by pregnancy. It's not serious, but it does mean I'll need to keep a closer eye on her during her remaining time. Lyda's invited the Ransletts to stay in her and Ben's home as long as they need to. They're staying with her at the store tonight. Lyda says she prefers to live there in the upstairs room rather than going home. At least for now."

Rachel nodded, understanding.

"Has Mr. Carnes come by yet?"

She shook her head, and he proceeded to take off his coat, knowing he still had a job to do before the undertaker arrived.

"Everything's taken care of, Rand," she said softly. "James came by earlier. . . . He helped me."

Rand knew it was probably a combination of

fatigue and overwork, but his throat tightened with emotion. "You're really special—you know that?" Her mouth tipped the slightest bit as she looked away. If he was reading her right, and he'd grown fairly adept at that, she was uncomfortable beneath the praise. "Is there anything else I need to do before Carnes arrives?"

She shook her head and picked up a lamp, motioning for him to follow. "I told Lyda I'd stop by and get her in the morning, for the funeral." She glanced back. "She's asked James to do the service."

Rand traced her steps down the dimly lit corridor to the storeroom. She opened the door and a cool rush of moist air hit him in the face. The wick of the oil lamp sputtered and teased, and the threat of darkness stopped him cold. Threadbare nerves went taut inside him and a light sweat broke out on his skin. His pulse kicked up a notch.

The flame flickered and struggled to full flame again—and Rand resumed breathing.

Rachel raised the lamp high. "Looks like it's about out of oil. But that's not a problem." She smiled softly. "You have enough oil stored up to light the entire town of Timber Ridge."

Rand was too focused on breathing to respond.

She preceded him into the room. "I pressed his suit and tie. It looks real nice, but I'll always picture him in that apron he used to wear. Lyda asked me to bury this with him." She held up a tiny pouch. Rand recognized it. Ben had shown it to him. "It belonged to their son. It was Andrew's—" She turned back. "Rand . . . is something wrong?"

Still standing in the hallway, he cleared his throat. "No . . ." His hands trembled. "Nothing's wrong." He would not do this again in front of her, lose control like he had that night at her cabin. The very thought that he might brought a rush of anger.

Trying not to focus on the nearly empty lamp in her grip, he forced one foot in front of the other until he was beside her, and then he looked down at Ben.

The lamplight was dim and the warm glow forgiving, but if he hadn't known better he might have thought Ben could awaken at any second.

A scene flashed in his mind, lightning quick and just as blinding. He heard the thud of Jessup Collum's shovel again and felt the wooden walls of the pine box pressing in. Closer, closer. He blinked, trying to dispel the image and his fears, knowing both were irrational.

He wasn't in the grave any longer. He was in the storeroom. With Rachel. And Ben was gone—he wasn't going to wake up. He'd held Ben's hand, felt the life drain away. He'd checked for a pulse, at least twenty times, just to be sure.

He heard Rachel's voice beside him, but his senses were honed in on the memory that had haunted him for the past twelve years, that had all but controlled him every time darkness fell.

429

A touch on his arm jolted him.

Rachel peered up, concern narrowing her eyes. "Are you all right? You're shaking."

He pulled away. *Oh, God, when will I conquer this? Will I ever?* "I'm fine!" His voice came out harsh, unrelenting, and he knew he deserved the bewildered look she gave him.

A distant knock sounded.

Rachel glanced down the hallway. "I'm guessing that's Mr. Carnes." Her voice was cool, and with good reason.

He followed her—and the light—down the corridor, but stopped her in the front room, hoping his voice was steadier than his nerves. "I th-think it would be best if I kept Ben's body here for the night."

She stared, her confusion evident. "But . . ." A discomfited look passed over her features. "Everything's done, Rand. Why would you—"

A second knock sounded.

She glanced at the door, then back at him. "I don't understand what just happened in there. Why you suddenly—"

"I'll explain," he said quickly, his temples throbbing. His fears were illogical, without foundation, yet he couldn't defy them. "Just let me handle this."

Questions weighted her expression, but it was the doubt in her eyes he found most cutting.

"Please, Rachel," he whispered. "Trust me."

When she didn't object, he opened the door and winter barged in. He gestured for Mr. Carnes and another man Rand knew by sight but not by name to step inside. Before he closed the door, he glimpsed the wagon pulled up along the boardwalk, a simple oblong pine box in the back.

Carnes shook the snow from his sleeves. "You ready for us, Doc?"

"Actually . . ." Rand shook his head, wishing they could have spoken outside, where Rachel couldn't hear. "I'm *not*. I'm sorry for the confusion, but I just got back here a few minutes ago. It's been a long day, and I still have some details to take care of. . . . I need to make final notations regarding Mr. Mullins's case." He looked at Carnes as though the man should know what he was referring to.

It took a second, but Carnes slowly nodded and leaned closer. "Does this have something to do with that surgery you did?"

Rand hesitated. "Something like that, yes."

"Good enough, then." Carnes reached for the door. "We'll be back first thing in the morning."

They left, and Rand turned to find Rachel standing exactly where he'd left her.

Skepticism lined her face. "What *details* are left?" she asked softly.

He took a step toward her, and though she didn't move an inch, he felt her retreat.

34

There *are* no details left, Rachel." Rand looked down, uncomfortable beneath her scrutiny, but even more with his own deceit. "I just said that so Carnes would leave."

"But . . . I don't understand. You're the one who asked him to come. What made you change your mind? And why did you lie?"

"I didn't change my mind. Not exactly. But I did lie. . . . And I'm sorry." He sighed, knowing there was no excuse. "I . . . panicked."

"Yes, I saw that. I'm still waiting to understand why."

"It's a long story. . . ."

"Then it's good that I have the time."

Dread filled him. He wished there were a way to explain his reactions that wouldn't leave him looking smaller in her eyes, foolish and weak. He motioned to one of the chairs before the hearth. "Would you sit with me? Please?"

She did as he asked.

He stoked the fire in the hearth and added more logs. Within minutes, the flames burned bright again, warming the front room of the clinic. He sat beside her and leaned forward, realizing where he needed to begin. "Do you remember that night at your cabin . . . when you found me on the porch?"

"Yes, I remember that night . . . quite well."

He shook his head. "Of course you do." He looked down at his hands. "I told you then that sometimes when I wake up at night, I start to feeling a little closed in." He winced. "That wasn't the entire truth."

When she didn't respond, he lifted his head. Her expression was inscrutable, guarded. But most of all watchful, waiting for the truth.

Memories stirred inside him, and unable to sit any longer, he rose. "Something happened to me the night I got shot."

"The night you got your scar. . . ."

He nodded, fingering the puckered flesh on his neck. "I'm not sure how long I lay there on the battlefield. Bullets zipping past me, hitting the ground on all sides . . . men falling, moaning, some crying out. But . . . I couldn't make a sound. I tried to draw breath, but my lungs felt like they were full of holes." He walked to the window and stared out into the night, the crackle of the fire in the hearth strangely reassuring.

"I must have passed out, because the next thing I remember . . . I woke up in the surgeon's tent. I saw a man . . . standing a few feet away. He never looked over at me, but his hands . . . they were stained with blood." He bowed his head. "It was all over the front of his apron and running down his arms."

He grimaced—the memory so clear in his mind, so vivid, even after so many years. He could still smell the chloroform, hear the battle raging outside the tent, and feel the earth tremble beneath each cannon blast.

"It was the surgeon?" Rachel whispered. "The man who sutured your neck?"

"Yes." He took a breath, hoping to cleanse his senses of the sounds and smells of war, but in vain. "After some time passed, and I was well enough, I went searching for him."

"You wanted to thank him," she said, her voice quiet.

He smiled. "Yes. I wanted to thank him. . . ." He turned to her. "But I also wanted to warn him."

She frowned. "Warn him . . . about what?"

Ignoring his instinct to look away, he held her gaze. "About the dangers of overdosing a patient by administering morphine and laudanum . . . with too much chloroform."

She stared. "But he saved your life." Incredulity colored her tone.

"Yes, he did. In more ways than one. And when I finally found him, I told him how grateful I was. But I also had to tell him . . ." Needing to feel a support beneath him, Rand sat down again. "I had to tell him about the mistake he'd made."

Her eyes narrowed. She watched him, her expression keen.

"Following the surgery, after he sutured my wound . . . I didn't wake up. And he never detected a heartbeat."

Her brow furrowed tight. She shook her head. "I don't understand. . . . He never detected a heartbeat?" Her laugh was brief, frustrated. "You're here. You're alive."

As delicately as he could, Rand searched for a way to fill in the missing piece for her. "He didn't send me to a hospital after the surgery, Rachel. He sent me to City Cemetery, there in Nashville."

Seconds passed, ponderous and heavy.

The subtlest of shadows crossed her expression. She blinked. Her lips moved before the words were formed. "Are y-you saying that . . ."

"I was buried on December seventeenth, just hours after the battle ended."

Her hand went to her stomach. "But . . ." She took a stuttered breath. "How is that possible?"

"A series of mistakes," he said quietly, having been over the reasons so many times, on so many nights. "The combination of medicines and the loss of blood slowed my heart rate to a point where it was no longer detectable. And the setting didn't help either. The surgical tents were chaotic. Too many men, too few doctors. The battle was still being fought all around, and the Federal Army bearing down hard on us."

Silent tears slipped down her cheeks. "You're excusing what that man did to you?"

"That man . . ." Rand warmed at her coming so quickly to his defense. "No, I'm not excusing what he did. And neither did he. I'm just allowing room

for understanding how the mistake was made. I guess that's been part of how I've dealt with it through the years."

For the longest time, she stared into the fire, her cheeks wet with tears. When she looked up again, the aversion and hesitance in her eyes revealed her question before she asked it. "How did they . . . find you?"

"The gravedigger, a man named Jessup Collum, had tended that cemetery for years. As he did right up until the day he died. . . ." Speaking of Jessup brought a tenderness despite the harshness of the accompanying memories. "People thought he was a little *touched* because he did some strange things at times, but he had a way about him."

Rand stared into the glow of the flame as Rachel listened, never interrupting. He spoke of that night, of Jessup telling him how he'd tied the string around his wrist, and of hearing the bell. He told her things he'd never told another soul, things he never thought he'd speak aloud. And when he finished, feeling strangely unburdened, he dried tears he hadn't realized he'd shed.

Moments passed.

Rachel didn't look at him, and he sensed the distance between them increasing. He bowed his head, counting the cost of having been so transparent, while trying not to imagine how he must look in her eyes.

Finally, he stood. It was late. He'd promised

James he'd see her safely home, and James was probably wondering where his little sister was about now. "The livery was closed, so I left my horse at James and Molly's," he said quietly, helping her slip her coat on. Then she turned to him.

She brought his hand to her lips and kissed it, much as he'd done to her that night at the resort. The warmth of her breath and the gentleness of her touch moved him. More than she likely realized.

"We're all afraid of something, Rand," she whispered, laying her hand on his chest. "And you have reason beyond anyone I've ever known."

He traced the curve of her lower lip with his thumb, her words—her acceptance—touching a place deep inside him. But they also stirred a question. One that he thought he already knew the answer to. But, he wondered . . . did she?

He framed her face with his hands, seeing the affection in her eyes while also feeling her tense the slightest bit. "Now you know my deepest fear . . . but what is yours?" He moved closer. "What are you most afraid of, Rachel?"

She tried to look away, but he gently coerced her focus back.

She covered his hands on her face. "I think you know what I'm afraid of," she whispered.

He drew closer, loving this woman with everything in him. "Tell me."

Tears rose in her eyes. "I'm afraid of . . ." A

frown pinched her brow. "Of going through what Lyda's going through right now, all over again. I've lived that before, Rand." She took a breath. "I don't ever want to hurt like that again."

"Who's to say that you will?"

She stepped back, and he let her go.

She pulled her coat closer about her. "You don't know what it's like. You've never been in that place before."

He couldn't argue that point. "You're right, I haven't. But I do know what it's like to sit by a couple's bed in their final moments together and to see them, to *hear* them . . . declaring their love for each other." His throat tightened. "If you were to ask them, in that moment, if they would undo all the years of being together, all the joy they've shared, in order to avoid the coming pain"—he leveled his gaze—"neither of them would say yes, Rachel. Neither of them," he whispered. "Including Lyda."

Her gaze lowered, and he could feel her thinking, turning things over in her mind. He also saw her hands, balled into tight fists, and that gave insight into her as well. He'd told her before that he was a patient man, and he was. But he had a feeling she might just put his patience to the test. Still, whatever it took to win this woman's heart, he was willing to do it.

He banked the fire and grabbed his duster from the coat hook, the lack of sleep catching up with him. "It's time I got you home."

She joined him by the door, then paused and looked up at him. Then, wordless, she retrieved an oil lamp from the table and disappeared with it down the hall, in the direction of the storeroom. She returned a moment later without the lamp, but with a smile lighting her eyes.

Realizing what she'd done, Rand leaned down and kissed her cheek. "Thank you," he whispered. He opened the door and offered his arm. She tucked her hand through.

More than eight inches of snow had fallen the previous night, and if the current rate of snow kept up, that much would likely fall again. A subtle wind blew down from the north, sending powdery white flakes wafting downward, shrouding the town and lending the night an uncanny resemblance to day. The streets were deserted and the jagged snow-dusted knife blades of the Rockies stood sentinel above the town like sleeping giants. Rand thanked God again for bringing him to this breathtaking country, and into the life of the woman walking beside him.

He slipped an arm about her waist as they climbed the icy stairs to James and Molly's home. He waited for her to produce the key, then slid it into the lock. "You stay inside. I'll get my horse and meet you back here."

Rachel stepped inside and paused, briefly bowing her head. "I want you to know that it's not because I don't care about you. I do." She smoothed a hand over his lapel. "Very much. There's a part of me that knows what you're saying is right, and I want to follow that voice. But there's another voice"—she shook her head, her face pale in the moonlight—"that's screaming inside . . . telling me to run. To hide."

"I have a solution," he said quietly, caressing her cheek. "Either go with the first option, or go with the second and run to me. I'll hide you and keep you safe."

She sighed, a tiny smile peeking through. "I wish I could make you understand what I'm feeling."

"I think I do understand, Rachel." He fingered a dark curl at her neckline, struggling with how to phrase his thoughts in a way that wouldn't leave them on the wrong footing. "I know you're afraid of opening your heart again, of losing someone . . . like you lost Thomas. And while I know life doesn't hold any guarantees, I've also learned that there's no joy in this life without pain. I'm willing to take some risks in order to have that kind of happiness. And, if you're willing"—he hoped he wasn't overstepping his bounds, pushing too hard, assuming too much—"I'd like to share that kind of happiness with you." The tender look in her eyes encouraged him. "Maybe together," he said, "we could help each other face our fears."

"Help each other face our fears," she repeated, her voice soft and her smile tentative, revealing both the hope she had, as well as the slenderest thread of lingering doubt. "That sounds so beautiful. . . . And so easy, the way you say it."

He brushed the hair back from her forehead and kissed her—once, twice . . . and a third time—hearing her quickening breaths, which only made him want to kiss her again. "I doubt it'll be easy, Rachel. But I promise you, it'll be worth it. Now"—not wanting to, he gave her a gentle nudge farther inside—"I'll be right back."

Half an hour later, he guided the mare up the mountain toward the Boyd ranch, the snow coming down heavy. Rachel sat sidesaddle in front of him, tucked warmly against his body, and he had a peace he hadn't felt in . . . well, that he couldn't remember ever feeling before. He glanced up at the stars, thinking of Ben, and wondering what heaven was like. He recalled something Ben had said to him once, some time back. *If this side of heaven's this pretty, Doc . . . just imagine what the other side must be like."*

Rand looked heavenward, thankful his eternity with Ben Mullins had started in Timber Ridge, and envying the fact that Ben didn't have to use his imagination anymore.

He guided the horse along the final curve to Rachel's cabin and pulled back on the reins, seeing someone riding straight for them.

Rachel straightened. "It's James," she whispered, concern in her voice.

James reined in sharp, his face half hidden beneath his hat. "I was just on my way to town to find you." His horse whinnied, struggling at the bit, and James pulled the reins taut. "I'm sorry, Rachel . . . it's the boys. Molly and I have looked everywhere for them. But they're gone."

35

An endless hour later, Rachel stood by the front window, her breath fogging the pane. Her throat ached with tears, both those shed and those she fought to hold back. The scene outside was disturbingly familiar. Torches dotted the perimeter of the yard, flaming bright despite the snowfall, and she counted at least thirty men grouped together, James and Rand at the center.

"I'm so sorry, Rachel."

Hearing Molly's fragile voice beside her, Rachel pulled her sister-in-law close. "It's not your fault," she whispered, knowing it wasn't. Molly had sent the boys down to the springhouse to get some meat for dinner, something she let them do all the time. Except this evening, the boys hadn't come back. When Mitch and Kurt hadn't returned after ten minutes, Molly had searched the barn and the surrounding woods while James scoured the hills above.

Nothing.

Rachel hugged herself, the ache inside nearly

causing her knees to buckle. *Please, Lord . . . not my sons.*

Any tracks Mitch and Kurt might have left had been lost to the wind and snow. She looked beyond the search parties forming in front of the barn and could hardly fathom that her boys were out there in the bitter cold and pressing darkness. Somewhere. Alone. Without her.

The crowd of men outside continued to grow. But one man was noticeably absent. The man who knew these mountains better than anyone. Who could track anything, over rock and creek, through rain or snow. She kept praying she would see him ride up. But he hadn't. And she couldn't blame him, after how she'd treated him. She took a breath and wiped her tears. She'd asked James to send for him. And when he came, *if* he came, she would ask his forgiveness, as she should have a few hours ago—as she wanted to . . . yet somehow couldn't. And she would beg him to find her sons.

Arms came around her from behind, and she wrapped her hands over Rand's.

He leaned close. "We're about to set out. Is there any other place you've thought of where they might have gone? James wanted me to ask."

She shook her head. "No . . . but I'm coming with you."

"I expected you to say that," he said softly. He turned her in his arms until she faced him. "And none of us will try to stop you if you honestly feel that's best. But . . ." He cradled her face in his hands, silencing the argument she was about to make. "We feel it would be best if you'd stay here. That way"—he spoke with gentle persuasion—"if the boys return to the house, you'll be here. And"—earnestness filled his eyes—"if somehow they've gotten separated and only one of them finds their way back here, it'll be good for you to be with him until we bring the other safely home."

Hot tears slipped down her cheeks. She saw the wisdom in what he said, but it didn't feel right. Just sitting here. Waiting. Not doing anything to help. "Do you know if James has heard anything back yet from—"

"Rachel?"

At the sound of the voice, she turned and breathed the name already poised on her lips, "Daniel?"

Her fragile composure gave way, and on legs that hardly held her, she crossed the room and reached to take hold of Daniel's hands. But he drew her into his arms. "I'm so sorry, Daniel," she whispered. "I'm so sorry for how I treated—"

"Shhh . . ." He spoke softly, holding her closer. His nearness brought a comfort she wanted to trust in so badly. "It's gonna be okay," he whispered. He stroked her hair, much like James might have, and a strangled sound rose in his throat.

After a moment, he drew back, eyes misty. "The doc and I are riding together. We'll find them,

Rachel. Your boys are smart. They've been raised in these mountains. They know to stay together. They know what to do."

She sniffed. "Because you taught them."

He shook his head. "Because their father and I taught them."

She hugged him again, wanting to say more to him, but knowing those things could wait. Once Daniel found Mitch and Kurt, and he would, she told herself, she knew her sons could be in no better hands than Rand's.

She spotted Lyda standing between Elizabeth and Molly, and felt their gentle yet strong-as-steel resolve and love.

"I already checked the area around the springhouse," Daniel continued. "I found some broken branches." He briefly looked away, and Rachel felt more than glimpsed something incongruent in his manner. "I can't be sure. . . . It could be from the storm or from an animal, maybe a moose or an elk. But my gut tells me the boys headed downslope a ways, so that's the direction four of the groups will be riding. Doc and I among them."

If she were going by his tone alone, she never would have questioned him. But whatever it was she'd sensed . . . "Daniel, if you know something, *please,* just say it. Don't keep it from me."

He leveled his gaze. "All right," he said quietly, and Rachel felt a shiver up her spine. He reached into his coat and pulled out something she didn't recognize—at first.

Oh, dear God . . . Her breath left her in a rush, and Rand's arms came around her, holding her up. In Daniel's hand was the shredded remains of what appeared to be brown wrapping paper. The paper used to wrap meat.

Lyda came along beside her. "They're going to find your sweet boys," she whispered, hugging Rachel tight. "And I'm going to be with you when they do. We all are." She indicated Molly and Elizabeth with a nod. "The same as you were there for me."

Mounted up, the search parties began heading out into the night. Their torches bobbed like writhing stars as the men fanned out in all directions from the house, calling the boys' names, until finally the flickering points of light disappeared beneath the canopy of snow-ladened evergreens.

Seeing Ranslett saddled up, Rand turned to do the same.

"Rand?"

He turned back to see Rachel standing on the edge of the porch, flanked by Lyda, Elizabeth, and Molly.

"Please . . . signal as soon as you can." A sob broke through her resolve. "Either way," she whispered.

He strode back through the snow and gathered

446

her into his arms. She was shaking. He held her tighter, willing her fear to subside, willing her to give him her burden. He drew back. "You listen for two shots, Rachel," he whispered, his voice rough with emotion. "For each boy. We'll be firing *two* shots." He hugged her to him, then kissed her. When he lifted his head, she still had that fear in her eyes, so he kissed her again, deeper this time, digging his hands into her hair. He could still taste the salt of her tears as he and Ranslett rode out.

36

A blanket of snow all but silenced the plod of horses' hooves as Rand and Daniel picked a path downslope of the springhouse. Tree limbs, burdened with ice and freshly fallen powder, cracked and popped around them. "Mitchell! Kurt!" Rand called out every few seconds. Ranslett joined him, and they took turns calling the boys' names as they rode on up the mountain.

With no pattern that Rand could detect, Ranslett would stop and dismount, check the branches or a spot where the snow might be marred or crushed, then he'd mount up and they'd ride on. A short while later, they arrived in a clearing and Daniel reined in.

Built on the highest peaks—north, south, east, and west—fires burned bright against the dark night sky. Flaming beacons lit in the hope that

Mitch and Kurt would see them and make their way to where help was waiting.

They rode for another hour, covering a treacherous stretch along Crowley's Ridge before picking their way back along a ravine that bordered Rachel's land. Rand called the boys' names, over and over, and could hear someone from another party just across the ridge doing the same. Every few feet, Ranslett stopped to examine the trail, or a tree, or a boulder, looking for a sign. Rand did likewise. Looking for anything that might indicate what path the boys had taken.

They circled back, retracing their path, checking every cave and crevice in the mountain, and Ranslett seemed to know them all.

Finally, they arrived at a bluff not far from Rachel's cabin. Feeling the night wear on, a fraction of the fear Rand had seen in Rachel's eyes seeped into his bones and began to take hold, threatening to extinguish his hope.

With the aid of his torch, he checked the time. Almost half past three.

The snow had tapered off. Little wind stirred, but the night was bitter cold. His hands were numb, despite his gloves, and his feet ached. He could only imagine how cold Mitch and Kurt must be right now, and what injuries they would suffer if made to endure an entire night in these conditions. Molly had said the boys left for the springhouse with only their jackets on. No hats. No gloves.

Frostbite would set in within hours, then confusion, disorientation. . . .

But that possibility, however difficult, was less brutal than the other. Rand pictured the brown wrapping paper, shredded into ribbons, and shut out the thought that followed.

Ranslett pulled up sharply and peered off to his right.

"You see something?" Rand whispered, trying to decipher whatever it was that had caught his attention. To him, the dark wooded hillsides looked much the same. But he trusted Ranslett's experience and skill, as did Rachel, obviously. He didn't know all the history between Rachel and Daniel, only that they'd grown up together and that, from what he'd noticed, she was uncomfortable in the man's presence. But whatever their differences were, he was grateful things seemed to be on the mend. Especially now.

Ranslett pointed. "See the lowest bough of that spruce? Just to the right of the largest boulder. About fifteen feet out."

Rand squinted, trying to distinguish which spruce he was referring to. There were about two hundred at a glance and all of them seemed to be situated right by a—Then he saw it, and hope sprang up inside him. "It's not covered in snow like the others."

"And it's sheltered from wind beneath the larger ones around it. The snow had to be knocked off.

And since most of the larger animals bed down for the night . . ." Ranslett dismounted, rifle in hand. "Let's go on foot from here."

Rand tethered his horse to a tree, grabbed his medical bag and rifle, and followed.

Ranslett pointed as he cut a path through the snow. "All along that ridge are caves. They're not deep, but they go back a good ways. Perfect place for cougar or bear." He gestured behind them. "Back up this hill, a couple hundred yards or so—"

"Is Rachel's springhouse," Rand said, having regained his bearings.

Ranslett nodded. "Imagine we're Mitch and Kurt, and we've just latched the door to the springhouse behind us. We've got the meat Molly told us to get, but then—"

"We hear something."

Ranslett nodded again, stepping over a fallen aspen. "We already know what it is from the sound, but we turn around anyway because instinct tells us to. And that's when we see the cougar. What do we do?"

"Why do you think it's a cougar?" Rand asked.

"Because a bear would've left more tracks, even with the snow. I've seen a cougar leap from rock to rock, at least twenty feet, then shoot straight up a lodgepole pine, never stopping, and hardly leaving a trace."

The mental image was chilling, especially when considering the chance two young boys would have against such an adversary. Back to Ranslett's initial question, Rand turned the possibilities over in his mind, trying to think like a ten- and eight-year-old boy might. "Kurt does whatever Mitch does, so—whatever they did—I think Mitch made the decision."

"Agreed." Ranslett knelt just shy of the spruce, then stood, walked a few paces, knelt again, and leaned close to the ground. "Mitch's first thought is going to be for—"

"His brother," Rand supplied, knowing without hesitation that it was true, and rushing the possible scenario through his mind, just as he imagined Ranslett was doing. Mitch and Kurt had been taught not to run from bears and mountain lions. But they'd be scared, and undoubtedly remembering what happened to their father. "Do you think Mitch might've thrown the meat to the animal right away?"

Ranslett shook his head. "A person's first instinct when seeing something like that is to run. And anyway, I found the bag farther down here." He pointed. "The cat could've carried it a distance, but I don't think so. Cougars are normally shy of people, unless they smell food. My guess is that it was more interested in the meat than in the boys."

Rand shook his head. "But Mitch and Kurt wouldn't necessarily have known that. I think Mitch just grabbed his little brother's hand, and they ran. He probably tossed the meat down without thinking the cougar would go for it first."

Ranslett nodded, adjusting the pack on his back. "I'm hoping that bought the boys a little time." He crept closer, his moves cautious, wary. He ducked to peer beneath the branch. "Doc . . . you need to come here."

Uncertain at Ranslett's tone and feeling as if someone had punched him in the gut, Rand readied himself. He knelt, praying . . . The snow beneath the tree had been scraped back from around the side of the trunk, creating a kind of wall. "They were here," he whispered, hope rekindling. "They tried to create a shelter."

"And did a pretty good job of it too," Ranslett said, voice soft.

Rand looked over at him. "Something you taught them?"

Ranslett nodded. "Something I showed Thomas when we were out hunting together one time. Then Thomas and I taught them together at Thanksgiving, four years ago. I can't believe they still remembered."

They rose and walked deeper into the foliage, the shadows richer beneath the snowy canopy, the pungent scent of evergreen overwhelming.

"There." Rand motioned, then headed toward what appeared to be a crevice in the side of the mountain. Not knowing how far back it went, he knew that if he were a boy seeking shelter from the snow, that was where he would have headed next.

But as he peered into a tunnel of endless dark, he knew it was the very last place *he,* as a grown man, would *ever* choose to go.

37

"Mitch! Kurt!" Rand leaned down and called into the mouth of the cave, hoping the boys would answer if they were inside, while in the same breath praying they'd found another place to hunker down for the night. Someplace less . . . dark. Less gravelike.

Staring into the fathomless absence of light, he already found it hard to breathe. He called the boys' names again, but no reply came.

Torch in hand, Ranslett stooped and entered the cave without a moment's hesitation. "Be sure and bring your bag, Doc, just in case they're inside."

"Will do." Rand pushed the words past the vise-grip around his throat. Panic gripped him, and the heat of shame tightened its hold. Hours earlier he'd told Rachel they would face their fears together, and yet here he was, hardly able to even look his in the eye.

He peered down the tunnel, watching Ranslett's torch grow smaller. He told himself to take a step, but his feet wouldn't move. He swallowed. *Jesus, help me do this.*

Summoning courage he didn't feel, he bent and

forced one foot in front of the other. The cloying smell of moist earth filled his nostrils. Ice and damp slicked the walls of the tunnel, and the air smelled faintly of time forgotten and of something long dead. About twenty feet in, a clammy wave of déjà vu moved through him, and he fought the sudden urge to turn back and run.

Mindful of the tremor deep within, he pictured Rachel and the boys, then trained his focus on the precious halo of light illuminating his path and moved on, drawing strength from Rachel's belief in him.

The shaft was riddled with rocks and he watched his step. He heard a noise, a low distant murmur. Or was it a rumble? He went stock-still. "Ranslett?" He heard the fear in his voice and hated himself for it. He peered down the tunnel. Ranslett was gone. He swallowed, his throat like sand. "Ranslett, are you there?" He closed his eyes. *Oh, God, don't think—*

"Doc Brookston?" came a weak voice.

Mitch . . . Rand's eyes stung with relief. Both from knowing Mitch was alive and from knowing he wasn't alone.

"Back here, Doc." Ranslett's voice sounded strangely hollow and small.

Rand navigated the tunnel, moving faster than he would have thought possible.

The light from his torch reflected off the end of the passageway to reveal another tunnel off to his left. He rounded the corner and found himself in a small chamber—not tall enough in which to stand upright but that allowed him to walk hunched over.

Mitch lay on the floor, crying. Ranslett was kneeling beside him.

Rand joined them and brushed a quick kiss to Mitch's forehead. "Hey, buddy, how are you doin'?"

Mitch squeezed his eyes tight, shivering. "I'm s-sorry."

Rand scanned the chamber, not seeing Kurt. He looked at Ranslett. "Where's Kurt?" he said low.

Ranslett shrugged. "I asked him, but he just started crying."

Rand leaned close again. "Mitchell . . . buddy. Look at me." He wedged his torch into a crevice in the wall and tugged off his gloves. He took hold of Mitch's hands. They were like ice. "Did Kurt come into the cave with you?"

Mitch shut his eyes. "I was h-holding his hand"—a strangled cry—"and then he slipped. I couldn't see, and he—" His sobs came harder. "H-he fell."

Rand's heart broke. Mitchell being the "man of the house" at ten was a burden a boy shouldn't be saddled with, and one he aimed to lift from Mitch's frail shoulders . . . starting now. "I'll take care of Kurt, Mitch. Just like—" His throat tightened. "Just like I'm going to take care of you." He glanced up at Ranslett, not having meant to exclude the man, but a knowing look resided in Ranslett's eyes, and he gave Rand an affirming nod, as if understanding.

Rand cradled Mitch's face and worked to keep the panic from his voice. "We just need to know one thing, Mitch. . . . Where did Kurt fall?"

Mitch pointed, and both men looked across the chamber. Rand's gut churned. There was a hole in the earthen floor of the cave.

Ranslett rose. "I'll go check it out."

Mind racing, possibilities colliding—none of them ones he wanted to take back to Rachel—Rand examined Mitch's head, then his neck and arms. "It's not your fault, son. You did well." He ran a hand along the boy's leg, and Mitch winced. "Your leg hurts?"

Mitch nodded, shivering. "I fell when we were running."

Rand couldn't feel a bone protruding, which was good. He took off his coat and tucked it around the boy.

"Doc?" Ranslett called, voice tense.

Laying a gentle hand on Mitch's forehead, Rand summoned calm he didn't possess. "I'll be right back. Everything's going to be all right, Mitch." *Lord, please, let everything be all right.*

He joined Ranslett, who shone the light from his torch into what appeared to be another shaft, a passage sloping downward, at least twenty feet, maybe more. The light from the torch flickered and danced off the walls, making it hard to see. But it looked as if something, or someone, lay at the bottom.

Kurt.

Rand called his name, but no response. And a cold shudder of reality moved through him as what he had to do became clear. He was a good twenty pounds lighter than Ranslett, but more importantly, he was the physician. If Kurt was hurt, if the boy had sustained a broken bone in the fall, it would need to be treated. Rand held his breath. So *he* was the one who needed to go down there.

Every muscle in his body tensed and the familiar tremor he loathed started again down deep inside. His thoughts sprinted in different directions, taking his imagination in places he didn't want to go, and he suddenly wondered if he had the strength to do this. He didn't think he did.

"Doc . . . you okay?"

Rand squeezed his eyes tight, feeling a hundred-pound weight pressing squarely on his chest.

"Doc . . ." Ranslett touched his arm. "You want me to go down?"

"No," Rand heard himself say, wishing he could catch his breath. If only he could feel that same profound stillness he'd felt before, instead of shaking in his boots. He reached for the rope in his pack. "I'll go."

Temples pounding, gut churning, he descended headfirst into the tunnel, the rope tied about his waist. For a moment, he was certain he was going to be sick. The wave of nausea slowly passed, but the trembling inside him fanned out.

He clenched his jaw, making his way downward until the faint flicker from Ranslett's torch above was swallowed by ravenous night.

Condensation slicked the sides of the passage and soaked through his shirtsleeves, bringing on a chill. He tried to recall the words of a psalm, anything to help him not dwell on how far he was descending inside the earth's belly. Verses came in broken, jumbled fragments, mirroring how he felt inside.

"If I take the wings of the morning . . . and dwell in the uttermost parts of the sea—" The tunnel suddenly narrowed. The nausea returned. *"Even there"*—he squeezed through—*"shall thy hand lead me . . ."* His memory seized, and for a moment the same darkness encompassing him without threatened to do the same within. Then another fragment of the passage surfaced. One he'd clung to many nights in recent years. " 'If I say, Surely the darkness shall cover me' "—he hardly recognized the rasp of his voice—" 'even the night shall be light about me . . .' " He kept crawling, inching his way forward. " 'The night shineth as the day . . . the darkness and the light are both alike to thee.' " *Oh, God, I wish they were the same for me.*

A cold rush of air hit him in the face, and nothing

had ever felt so good. He struggled to make out Kurt's body below, knowing how frightened the boy would be once he awakened—and he *would* awaken, *Lord, please.*

He crawled another few feet, then hauled himself from the tunnel, mindful of Kurt somewhere on the ground around him. Relief poured through him at being in an open space again—however large this chamber was, impossible to tell in the darkness—and he moved to one side, allowing the faint light from Ranslett's torch to reach past him.

Kurt lay on his side, unmoving.

Rand pressed his fingertips against the icy underside of the boy's throat. A thready heartbeat registered just seconds before Kurt drew a hiccuped breath. The pull of air into his lungs sounded overloud in the vast silence.

"Is he all right?" Ranslett yelled from above, his voice another world away.

"He's breathing," Rand answered, relief crowding his anxiety. From what he could determine, Kurt's arms and legs and collarbone were intact, no broken bones. "Kurt . . . can you hear me?" He located one small hand, the skin so cold. He covered it with his, calling Kurt's name again.

"Mama?" Kurt whispered, stirring.

Rand's heart warmed. Such love and trust wrapped in a single name. He wished Rachel could have heard it, and from this son in particular. "It's

Doc Brookston, Kurt. I'm right here with you, son."

Kurt's grip tightened, though not by much. "I can't see anything."

"I know. We're in a cave. It's dark. But don't worry. I'm going to get you out of here." He was grateful Kurt couldn't feel the anxious drum of his pulse. "Do you hurt anywhere?"

Kurt took a moment to answer. "No . . ." His voice was groggy. "I'm just cold . . . and sleepy."

"We'll get you warmed up real soon, I promise." Rand untethered the rope at his waist. "Just lie still. I'm going to tie this around you, and then we're going to haul you up. I'll be right behind you." The boy's body felt so fragile and thin in the dark. Rand tied an extra knot and pulled it taut, then helped Kurt sit up.

"Is Uncle Ben still here?" Kurt whispered.

Rand hesitated. Had Rachel not told the boys about Ben's passing yet? Debating, he decided a partial truth would suffice for now. "No, Kurt . . . he's not."

"Oh . . ." Kurt sighed. " 'Cuz he was just here. We been playin' jacks. He even let me win. I could tell because"—his head lolled against Rand's chest—"because of how he smiled."

Rand's heart ached at the love in Kurt's voice, and he gathered him close, knowing how much both boys were going to miss—

He stilled.

Sticky wetness covered the back of Kurt's skull,

and only then did Rand feel the gash. Warm blood slicked his hand. *Oh, God . . .* No wonder Kurt was acting so sleepy.

"Ranslett!" He tugged on the rope. "We've got to hurry!"

Rachel stood in the open doorway of the cabin and scanned the eastern horizon, willing the dusty pink of dawn to hasten the sun's journey, and its warmth. She felt as if she were coming out of her skin. "Why hasn't someone signaled?"

Lyda reached for her hand and held it between hers, saying nothing, and not needing to.

Rachel knew the answer. It was because no one had found her sons yet. *Oh, Lord, where are my boys?*

"Would you like some coffee?" Molly asked. "It'll help warm you."

Rachel shook her head, not wanting to be warm when her sons were likely freezing out there somewhere. Elizabeth sat on the edge of the couch, head bowed, lips moving in silent prayer.

In the past few hours, Rachel had sorted through every memory she could summon of her sons. The silly and the sweet, the precious and the frustrating. She'd thought of the countless nights she'd sat by their beds and watched them sleeping, when she'd prayed over their futures, of what they might grow up to be, and the young women they would hopefully one day marry.

461

For the past two and a half years, she'd done everything she could to give her sons the dream for their lives that she and Thomas had wanted. Only, the life she and the boys lived now hardly resembled that dream. She spent her days working sunup to sundown, never caught up, and was getting ready to secure another loan to purchase cattle that would help assure success for a ranch she didn't even want. And for what purpose?

To give her boys a *better life*. How had she been so foolish?

Nerves taut, she pulled her hand away from Lyda's. "I can't wait here like this anymore. I can't just stand here and do nothing. I—"

A single rifle shot split the night. Rachel nearly went to her knees, and would have if not for Lyda beside her, with Molly and Elizabeth.

"Hold on, Rachel, it's coming," Lyda whispered, eyes lifted heavenward. "It's coming. . . ."

Rachel waited, breath held, feeling her world tilt and her heart begin to fract—

A second shot sounded, shattering the silence, followed by a third, and a fourth. . . .

38

Are you certain you want to do this, Rachel? I'm sure there's someone else out there who'd be willing to—"

"Please, Rand, let me stay. Let me do this." She

brushed a kiss against Kurt's dirt-smudged cheek. Kurt didn't move. Not that she expected him to with the chloroform Rand had administered. "I want to be here. And anything you need, I can do. I give you my word."

He searched her eyes until he seemed satisfied. "All right." He picked up the needle from the table by her bedside, dawn streaming in through the window at his back. "I'm going to start at the base of the gash and suture upward. He won't feel a thing as long as you continue to administer the chloroform. I'll let you know when I'm almost done."

Rachel nodded, one hand cradling the top of Kurt's head, the other the chloroform-doused cloth. She shivered, still chilled to the bone from the long night of waiting outside on the porch, praying for her boys to come home. Kurt lay on his side on her bed, covered in a blanket, and Rand knelt behind him. She watched Rand work, as much as she could from her perspective, and prayed for them both, as well as for Mitchell, who was resting, warm and safe, in his bed down the hallway, cuts and bruises the worst of his injuries.

"Kurt called out for you," Rand said softly. "When we were in the cave."

Rachel's heart clenched tight. "Really?"

He nodded, his focus intent on his task. "Never doubt how much he loves you. Never . . ."

She brushed a lock of red hair from Kurt's

temple and felt his soft breath on her hand. There were so many questions she wanted to ask Rand about what had happened, but there hadn't been time. When he and Daniel had brought the boys back to the house, it was clear Kurt bore the most serious injury. She'd washed her hands, but his blood still stained the front of her dress.

From what little Daniel had told her, she'd learned that Rand had climbed down a tunnel into utter darkness in order to rescue her son. Entering the cave had to have been hard enough for him, but the tunnel . . . She couldn't imagine, not with what he'd been through.

She stared at him, watching his movements, watching his hands—hands crafted by God to do precisely what he was doing—and she couldn't deny her overwhelming love for him. *"Don't be afraid of being happy again, Rachel,"* Ben had said to her. And she wasn't. Not anymore.

"You're a brave man, Rand Brookston."

His eyes narrowed as he completed another suture. "You wouldn't be saying that if you could have felt my heart pounding. I was scared to death down there, Rachel."

"But you went anyway," she whispered, feeling the reprise of tears. "Which makes you even braver."

Though he said nothing, his expression reflected gratitude.

"You've given me my life back." She sighed. "In so many ways."

His attention still focused on his task, the smile ghosting the corners of his mouth said plenty.

She recognized the change in Kurt's breathing pattern and held the cloth lightly over his nose and mouth until it evened out again. In less than an hour, Rand had the wound sutured, and she helped him bandage it. Kurt looked especially small and fragile lying there on the bed, his head swathed in white.

Rand rinsed his hands in the basin of water on the dresser and reached for a towel. "He lost some blood but not as much as he might have, considering it's such a deep gash. His cooler body temperature actually worked for him in that regard, stemming the blood flow." He laid the towel aside. "He's going to be fine, Rachel. He's going to have a whopping headache for a few days, and a scar on the back of his head he can boast about to his children. But I see no evidence of injury that would cause any ongoing challenge to him. He's a resilient little boy. Very much like his mother."

Grateful beyond words, she placed another kiss on Kurt's forehead and then tucked the blanket around his shoulders, knowing it would be a while before he awakened. She took hold of Rand's offered hand and let him pull her up beside him. Not waiting, she went straight into his arms, and he held her.

"Tighter," she whispered into his ear, wanting him to chase away every chill, every uncertainty.

"With pleasure," he whispered, and obliged.

She held on to him, shivering, the warmth from his body seeping into hers. The flicker of desire he'd lit within her not long ago fanned into flame, and she drew back enough to see him. She cradled the side of his face. He pressed a kiss to her palm and she felt the sensation all the way to her toes.

"May I ask you a question?" she whispered, looking at his mouth, remembering what kissing him had been like.

"Anything."

"How can you be so warm when I'm still so cold?"

His subdued laugh held boldness. "I know one sure way to warm you up." He didn't hesitate in the least. Not this time. His lips moved over hers as if the two of them had done this together a thousand times before. Gentle, tender at first, he wasn't the least bit uncertain. And when he deepened the kiss, she couldn't resist a smile, and felt him do the same.

"I love you," he whispered, searching her eyes. "I have for a long time."

She ached inside for him. Not only with physical desire, but with the desire to give herself fully to him, as he wanted her to, as she wanted to, without the underlying fear of losing him someday. Of being left alone. He must have read the fear in her eyes because he kissed her again, so long and so thoroughly that when he finally broke the kiss, she was breathless and could hardly stand.

"I want to marry you, Rachel Boyd. I want to be a father to your sons. And I promise . . . I will never leave you. Not of my own will. I'll be here with you, beside you, for the rest of my life. Or for the rest of yours. . . ."

She read sincerity in his expression and understood what he was saying. And yet . . . "I love you too," she whispered, feeling the beat of her heart. And of his. "But . . ." She gave a little shrug. "I'm still scared."

A roguish smile tipped one side of his mouth. "Which, to use your logic, will just make you even braver, right?"

Smiling, she drew his face down to hers and kissed him, savoring the man he was and the gift she'd been given for the second time in her life.

His hands moved down her back, wonderfully possessive in their quest, and pressed her closer against him. "I'm going to take that as a yes to my proposal, Mrs. Boyd," he whispered.

"Did you know my papa, Doc Brookston?"

Rand stilled at Kurt's question, grateful they were almost done with the examination. He'd removed the sutures a month ago, and the wound on Kurt's head was healing nicely. Rand reached for the jar of sugar sticks on the shelf behind him. "No, Kurt, I didn't. Your papa was already in heaven when I came to Timber Ridge."

A look of consternation crossed Kurt's face.

Rand opened the jar and Kurt withdrew a piece of candy.

"Grape?" he asked.

Kurt nodded.

Rand chose the same. "Grape's my favorite too."

Kurt's smile was more easily won these days, but Rand still sensed there was something on the boy's mind, as he had during their last few visits. What was bothering Kurt, he didn't know. But he thought he'd narrowed it down. It had something to do with Thomas, he was almost certain, and he'd shared as much with Rachel. She'd dropped Kurt off earlier, saying she'd come back for him, but Rand arranged for her to meet them later, wanting this time together with Kurt. Alone.

"Ready to go?" he asked.

Kurt hopped off the table.

He let Kurt set the pace down the boardwalk, enjoying the warmth of a July sun.

Kurt peered up. "Is your papa in heaven too?"

"Yes, he is. He went to heaven several years ago. Before you were even born."

"Were you a boy, like me?"

Rand felt a tenderness inside at the question. "No, I was already grown up."

Kurt didn't say anything to that, but Rand could feel the boy's wheels spinning. With forethought, Rand steered their path toward Miss Clara's, where they claimed a table over on the side beneath the shade of the tree. Miss Clara brought them glasses of lemonade, cool and tart, and kept refilling them to the brim.

Rand watched as Kurt downed his third glass. "What do you remember about your papa, Kurt?"

Kurt wiped his mouth on his sleeve. "Mitch says Papa used to take us on picnics. Mama says my legs got tired and Papa had to carry me on his shoulders, but I think I walked. Like Mitch."

Rand leaned forward. "What else do you remember?"

The boy studied the tabletop for a moment, as though it might hold the answer. "Mitch has a hat that Papa used to wear. Mama gave it to him. And sometimes Mama wears his old trousers beneath her skirt." He grinned, but it was short-lived.

Rand scooted his chair a little closer. "What do *you* remember about your papa, Kurt? Not something that Mitch remembers, or that your mother remembers. But something that's all yours."

Kurt frowned. His lips pulled tight. And as hard as he seemed to try, he couldn't hold back the tear that eked out the corner of his eye. He swiped it away, an all-too-familiar scowl darkening his face.

His heart breaking, Rand grew more certain than ever about what troubled this little boy. "It's not your fault that you don't remember anything about your papa. You were too young, Kurt. It doesn't mean you loved him less just because you can't remember things about him."

"But Mama and Mitch . . . *they* both remember. They talk about him sometimes, and . . ."

"And it makes you feel bad that you can't remember the same stories."

Kurt's brows pinched together. "Mama acts like I should remember. She's even said I should. But I don't." A single, begrudging tear rolled down his cheek. "I can't e-even remember what his face looked like."

Rand knelt before him. "Is that why you sometimes misbehave? Because you're angry that you can't remember? And maybe you're even a little angry with your mama for making you feel as if you should?"

Kurt studied him as though trying to gauge whether or not he was being tricked. Then he gave a little shrug, so reminiscent of his mother. Finally, he nodded and bowed his head.

Rand urged his face back up. "Can I tell you something, Kurt? Something that I know for sure?"

Kurt blinked, eyes wide and watchful.

"I know for a fact that your mama loves you and that your papa loved you very much too. And your mama would never want you to feel bad for not remembering him. Just like your papa wouldn't. Do you believe me?"

Again, Kurt stared, then nodded, his little chin quivering before giving way to the tears he fought to hold back.

Rand hugged him, and to his joy, Kurt's arms came tight about his neck. "Let me tell you something else, son," Rand whispered. "We're going to make lots of new memories together. You and me, and your mama and Mitch."

Kurt drew back. " 'Cuz you're gonna be my new papa."

They'd talked about this before, so Rand knew he wasn't asking a question. "Yes, I am. And I can hardly wait for us to go fishing and to catch bugs, and—"

"And look at them under your microscope?"

Rand tousled his red hair. "You bet we will. I give you my word on that."

After considering for a moment, Kurt nodded and dried his eyes with his sleeve.

They finished their lemonade, and as they headed toward the store, their steps lighter, Rand saw Rachel coming up the street. Her bright expression said she'd already spotted them and— guessing by her smile—she had news of some kind. Apparently good news.

"Mama, Doc Brookston and I had lemonade. At Miss Clara's. Just us!"

She brushed a kiss to his forehead, and Rand was pleased when Kurt didn't pull away. Rachel shot him a secretive look saying she was too. "That's wonderful. And I've got another treat. . . . Aunt Lyda's waiting for you inside with Mitch. She has a cookie for you, if you're still hungry."

"Cookies too?" Kurt ran on ahead.

Rachel followed him with her gaze. "I take it you two had a good time together?"

"Very. I'll tell you about it in a minute, but first give me your news."

She eyed him. "Who said I have news?"

He gave her a droll look. "We may not be married quite yet, but I know when you've got something up your sleeve."

"Oh, all right." She smiled and pulled an envelope from her reticule. "Mr. Westin gave me this just a few minutes ago. It's from the files of the Union Pacific Railroad. As he said, I think it explains a lot."

Rand opened it and read the letter. It took a moment for the information to sink in. "No wonder Charlie's name sounded familiar to him. Have you shown this to Charlie yet?"

She shook her head. "I wanted us to go together. I know he's at the store right now. I just saw him."

"Let's go, then. This kind of news can't wait."

She tucked her hand into the crook of his arm. "Did you have a chance to meet with Mr. Tolliver this morning?"

"I did."

"And?"

Rand smiled. "And you're now looking at the *former* not-so-prestigious physician for the Colorado Hot Springs Resort."

Rachel squeezed his arm, grinning. "How did you finally manage that?"

"It seems Brandon Tolliver is suffering from a severe sore throat and is in need of medical attention."

"And since you're the only doctor within a fifty-seven-mile radius . . ."

He grinned. "We'll be operating on him next week."

She came to a halt. "No . . ." Humor laced her voice. "You're kidding me."

He laughed. "I'm not. We're performing our first tonsillectomy together. And the best thing is . . . Brandon Tolliver won't be able to say a word for at least a week."

They found Charlie in the back room of the store, unloading a wagon. Rachel glanced at the storeroom as they passed, and remembered Ben. So much had happened since that day. . . . She pulled the envelope from her reticule and wondered, as she had when first reading its contents, if Ben was somehow assisting God in orchestrating this moment for Charlie Daggett. And for her too.

"Miss Rachel." Charlie hefted an oversized crate off his shoulder and onto the floor with a thud, then wiped the sweat from his brow. "Doc." He nodded, glancing between the two of them. "If it's medicine you're here for, Doc—" He pointed. "It's right here. Just unloaded it."

Rand ran a hand over the box. "Thanks, Charlie. But Rachel and I are here to speak with you about something else." He motioned to some chairs outside the back door, where a cool breeze issued. "If you have the time."

Looking between them, curiosity evident, Charlie lumbered out the back door and claimed a chair. He reached into his coat pocket for something—Rachel could easily guess what—then glanced at her and seemed to think better of it.

"Charlie," she began softly, having discussed with Rand how best to approach the topic. "Do you remember the day when Edward Westin told you that he thought your name sounded familiar to him?"

Fear crept into Charlie's expression, just as Rand said it would.

Charlie's eyes narrowed. He shook his head. "I don't know that man. And he don't know me."

He started to rise, but Rachel took hold of his hand and urged him back down. "There's a reason your name sounded familiar to him. It's because he'd heard your name before. Many years ago. When he worked at the railroad."

"The same railroad you worked at, Charlie . . ." Rand laid a gentle hand on Charlie's arm. "Where you were employed as a brakeman . . . the night the accident happened."

Charlie's breathing grew heavy. He looked first at Rachel, then at Rand. "H-he . . . told you?" His lips formed a thin, guilty line. "You know what I done?"

Rachel withdrew the letter from the envelope. "Mr. Westin gave this to me just this morning. He wanted to speak to you himself about it, but thought it would be better coming from us."

Charlie glanced at the piece of paper, then bent forward, forearms resting on his knees. "I'm sorry," he whispered. "I've asked God a thousand times over to forgive me." He stared at his hands. "But I know He can't. Not after what happened. All those people . . . all those lives . . ."

Rachel held out the letter. "You need to read this, Charlie. It will make things a lot clearer for you."

Charlie just stared ahead, as though seeing something she couldn't. "Things are already clear enough, Miss Rachel. I remember every face. Every name. I still hear the sounds of the railroad cars plowin' into each other." His jaw tightened, but his mouth still trembled. "I carry that night around inside me. I always will. It's my punishment."

Rachel started to urge the letter in front of him again, but Rand caught her eye.

He shook his head and took the letter from her hand. "Would you permit me to read this to you, Charlie?"

And then it struck her. . . . Rachel winced at her own thoughtlessness. Charlie Daggett didn't know how to read. No wonder he'd never read about the account of events in the newspapers.

"The letter's addressed to you, Charlie. . . . To Mr. Charles Wesley Daggett. It's dated November 26, 1868."

Charlie bowed his head as though about to receive a life sentence.

"'On behalf of the Union Pacific Railroad,'" Rand continued, "'I wish to convey our deepest apologies and most sincere regrets over any anguish we have caused you since the railroad incident that occurred last fall.'"

Charlie's head stayed bowed, but Rachel sensed a keenness in his attention.

"'After a thorough investigation of the accident, we have concluded that the events leading to the accident on the night of December 15, 1867, were due in total to faulty equipment in the braking system, and not in any part, as was previously judged, to your personal error.'"

Charlie drew in a sharp breath.

Rand paused in the reading. "The letter goes on, Charlie, explaining what they found wrong with the braking system, but what they're saying . . . what they ruled all those years ago, was that accident wasn't your fault. In no way were you responsible for the deaths of those sixty-eight people. You did everything right that night. It was the people who designed the braking system who made the mistake, however unintentional. Not you. You are not at fault. You were never at fault."

Charlie's massive shoulders shook for a full

476

moment before deep sobs finally broke through. Rachel held him on one side, while Rand sat close on the other, and as if looking into a mirror, she saw herself and the needless guilt she'd carried after Thomas's passing. Much like the burden Charlie had been carrying within himself. But for years now, what a price he'd paid. . . .

Edward Westin had asked to meet with Charlie after they were done, to tell him about the financial settlement the railroad had offered to him after he'd been unjustly accused and fired from his job. Mr. Westin had been in contact with railroad officials and had arranged for interest to be added to the tidy sum indicated in the letter that Rand had yet to finish. Money wouldn't come close to alleviating the pain Charlie had been through, but it *would* help in rebuilding his future.

She and Rand sat with him for the next hour, talking, praying, and she felt God pouring a balm of grace over Charlie's wound that ran over into her own, bringing healing and hope.

The night before Ben died, she'd asked him to tell Thomas that she was sorry for what she'd said to him their last morning together, before he'd left to go hunting. She hadn't known it at the time, but Rand overheard a part of that conversation. When he'd asked her about it and she explained, Rand had echoed Ben's sentiments—that he knew Thomas had already forgiven her. "But how can you be so sure?" she'd asked. He'd taken her hand

and pressed it against his heart. "Because I know the kind of woman you are. A man couldn't love you like I do, and like I believe Thomas did . . . and not know what's within your heart."

Watching Rand now, thinking of the days ahead, working alongside one another, his being a father to her boys, she grew to love him, her future husband and partner, in every way, even more.

EPILOGUE

SEPTEMBER 17, 1877

Rachel checked her reflection in the hallway mirror, knowing it was almost time. She was more nervous about today than she knew she should be. For Rand as well as herself. Her gaze lowered to the table beside her, and she fingered the delicate curves of the crystal vase he had given her last night. An early wedding present, he'd said, to replace the one he'd broken. It was exquisite, and so like the one from her mother.

She peeked out the front windows of the newly refurbished lobby and saw only a smattering of people milling about outside, despite the invitation she and Rand had extended to the entire town. She had hoped more people would come. But if not today, perhaps eventually.

She glanced down the hall. "Are all my boys ready?"

"We are," Rand said, appearing in the arched doorway, Mitch and Kurt in tow. Rand looked handsome in his pressed suit and tie, and the boys equally dashing in their starched white-collared shirts and new trousers.

She gave an approving nod, pleased with the outcome. "You all look good enough to eat."

Kurt giggled. "Don't try to take a bite of me!"

Rachel tried to do just that, which sent both boys running for the next room.

Rand, however, held his ground, invitation written all over his face. "I wouldn't mind if you tried taking a nibble or two."

She leaned in and gave him a kiss, smoothing a hand over his shirt. "How can you be so calm?"

He shrugged. "One thing I've learned in recent months . . . if I'm not a little scared inside, then I'm probably not where God wants me to be."

Rachel knew that to be true, having evidenced it in her own life.

Exactly one week from today, she would walk down the aisle, her hand tucked in the crook of James's arm, and would publicly pledge her heart to this man. She had no misgivings about her love for Rand, or his for her, but she couldn't deny that she'd be shaking in her boots as she took that first step toward her new future.

Since God had given her sons back to her—that's how she thought of the night when Rand and Daniel found the boys in the cave—she viewed life differently. Things she'd once considered so very important didn't consume her as they once had. Yes, the bills still needed to be paid, and on occasion, she still found herself worrying about how that would happen. Especially now.

But each time she caught herself not trusting the Lord, whether about money, or the boys, or Rand and his practice, or the ranch, or one of so many other uncertainties, she took herself back to that night, and she remembered waiting to hear the successive gunshots. Then she relived the night years earlier when she'd waited beside Lyda—and they hadn't heard. Hearing the gunshots or not, Thomas being killed or not, didn't change the eternal truth that God was sovereign, that His provision was unfailing, and that His love was perfect. She knew that. But believing it was easier when God said yes. It was when He said no, or didn't even give you a chance to voice your plea, that trusting oftentimes became painful acceptance, excruciating surrender. And yet, though she hadn't been aware of if then, those were all times she'd taken a step closer to Christ.

Edward Westin peered around the corner. "We're about ready to begin. If you two are."

Rand nodded and gave her one last hug. "Here we go. . . ." He smiled.

She followed him toward the front of the building, thinking of all that had gone into making this moment, this dream, come to fruition. Lyda waited for them in the lobby, and Rachel took hold of her hand.

"I'm so nervous," Lyda said, reaching for the shawl that had slipped from her shoulders. But Edward Westin beat her to it. Lyda thanked him with a smile. "I hope I don't embarrass us all."

"That's not possible, Mrs. Mullins," Mr. Westin said. "I assure you."

Rachel hugged her. "Ben would be so proud. As would Evelyn, I'm certain."

Rand reached for the double front doors, and even before he could pull them completely open, applause broke out. Rachel walked beside him and the boys, followed by Lyda and Mr. Westin, onto the front porch, overwhelmed at the size of the crowd gathered.

The streets and boardwalks brimmed with people. It looked as if half the town was crowded around the building.

Rand stepped forward, and as the applause subsided, he greeted everyone. "We appreciate all of you coming out today to help us celebrate the opening of the new clinic." The applause rose again. "This clinic exists to serve the entire community of Timber Ridge, and many of you have contributed your time and money to make this day and to make this—"

Rachel heard the catch in Rand's throat and felt one in hers.

"—and to make this facility possible. On behalf

of myself and my beautiful soon-to-be wife, Mrs. Rachel Boyd"—he winked at her, and whoops and hollers went up in the crowd—"we thank you for your trust and generosity."

Rachel clapped along with everyone else and spotted Paige Foster and her family off to her left. She returned their waves and blew a kiss to James and Molly, who stood toward the very front. She still had trouble believing that James had lost the sheriff's election to his deputy. She couldn't remember her older brother having lost at anything before in his life. But though his suspicions about people's still-tentative acceptance of Molly had proven true, she'd never seen James more at peace or excited about the future.

To Rachel's delight, James and Molly had purchased a share of the ranch, including the Scottish Highlanders now grazing in the upper pasture. They were living at the ranch now while she and the boys were staying with Daniel and Elizabeth in Ben and Lyda's house in town. She'd had the name of the ranch officially changed to the Boyd-McPherson Ranch to reflect the family partnership, and somehow she knew Thomas would have approved.

She no longer thought so much about what Thomas's dream had been for their boys, or even what her dream was for them. All she wanted for their sons, all she and Rand wanted together for them, was God's will for their lives. Whatever that entailed, wherever it took them. Be it to the ranch their father had started with such hope for the future . . . or for Mitch, following Rand into the medical field . . . or for Kurt . . . Rachel smiled, wondering if a job existed that called for expertise in bug collecting.

Whatever they chose to do, she wanted her sons to be centered in the middle of God's will for their lives, whatever that meant. The same for her and Rand.

Rand motioned for Mr. Westin to join him. "As many of you may know, Mr. Edward Westin is a relative newcomer to Timber Ridge, and he's largely responsible for the renovation of this hotel, as is another cherished member of our community whom I'll present to you in a moment. But first, Mr. Westin, a former executive with . . ."

Rachel searched the crowd, seeing lots of people she knew and plenty of folks she didn't. But the person who stood out most was Charlie Daggett. He stood front and center, clapping the hardest, smiling the biggest, and with Lori Beth Matthews close at his side. As Mr. Westin spoke, Rachel marveled at how God intertwined people's lives. Oftentimes without them ever knowing. But sometimes, like today, she glimpsed His handiwork, the attention He paid to the tiniest details in people's lives, and it gave her fresh hope, fresh courage. And made walking into the unknown a little less frightening knowing He was waiting there for her. For them all.

She spotted Daniel and Elizabeth standing off to the side and winked in their direction. His arm around his very pregnant wife, Daniel returned the gesture, and Rachel felt a warmth of love and gratitude for him. For them both. An entire group of townspeople from Little Italy were grouped farther back on the boardwalk, and Angelo was grinning from ear to ear.

But whom she saw next nearly made her chuckle out loud. Miss Judith Stafford stood near the front, hand tucked into the crook of Brandon Tolliver's arm. Rachel shook her head. After learning of Miss Stafford's interest in Rand and of her rather *bold* ways of expressing it, Rachel felt confident that at least a margin of the young teacher's coolness toward her of late was due to her upcoming marriage to Rand. But still . . . Brandon Tolliver? She hoped the young woman knew what she was doing. Yet wondered in the same breath if the two might not deserve each other.

"And now," Rand continued, "I'd like to ask Mrs. Lyda Mullins to step forward. Mrs. Mullins, along with her late husband, Ben, has served this community for almost twenty years. And she has quietly and most generously worked alongside us to bring this dream to light."

Lyda moved closer to the draped sign affixed to a column at the edge of the porch, watching for Rand's cue.

"We've asked Mrs. Mullins to read the dedication."

Lyda cleared her throat and glanced at the paper in her hand. "Before I read this, I'd like to personally extend my thanks to Dr. Brookston, not only for the honor of dedicating this clinic today, but"—she looked in Rand's direction—"for the care he gave my late husband in Ben's last days. I also want to thank him for leaving behind what I'm sure would have been a mighty fancy career back east to come and care for all of us out west."

"Let's hear it for Dr. Brookston!" Charlie called out. "Hip, hip—"

"Hooray!" the crowd countered, applauding and cheering.

Lyda waited until things grew quiet, then started to read. "We come together today, September seventeenth, the year of our Lord eighteen hundred and seventy-seven, to dedicate this clinic and everyone who works within it to the task of providing comfort and care to all residents of Timber Ridge, both now and in the years to come."

She reached for the drape covering the dedication sign, and a hush fell over the gathering. "In loving memory of Benjamin Everett Mullins—" she bit her lower lip and took a deep breath—"and Evelyn Grace Westin . . ." She cast a glance toward Edward Westin, and Rachel saw a shimmer in his eyes, same as was in Lyda's. "I'm honored to present"—Lyda's voice carried strong and clear in the silence—"the Timber Ridge Rocky Mountain Health Center." She removed the drape with a flourish.

The crowd responded with thunderous applause, and Rachel joined them, honoring not only the purpose for this clinic but also the man behind it, who not only taught her to open her heart to love again, but also taught her that joy costs pain. Life was full of risks, and, as Rand had told her just last night, that first step of faith was often taken neck-deep in fear.

Rand chose that moment to look at her, and Rachel knew that whatever pain and loss they would experience in their lives together, the love they shared would far outweigh it all in the end. And even as wonderful as that promised to be, she knew in her heart that it was still only a shadow of what was yet to come.

A NOTE FROM TAMERA

Dear Reader,

So far, all of my stories have grown out of struggles I'm having in my own faith walk or from questions I'm wrestling with at the time, and the story in these pages is no exception. I began writing *Within My Heart* in the fall of 2008 with the goal of finishing the first draft by late spring of '09. However, with no warning, life changed, as life often does, and I had to put this book on hold for a while. My publisher graciously extended my deadline, and I took a hiatus from writing and spent the last few precious months of my mother's life by her bedside.

Mom was diagnosed with gallbladder cancer in February 2009 and went home to be with the Lord on August 17. Six all-too-short and painful months . . . yet they were full of blessing. Mom faced the road that God asked her to walk with bravery, courage, and grace, and when my time comes to cross over from this life to the next, I'll do a better job of it because of watching her go before me.

Many of the conversations between the characters in this story had their seeds in conversations she and I shared during those final days. Upon learning that the chemotherapy was having no effect on the cancer, which had already spread to Mom's liver by the time it was diagnosed, Mom made the decision to spend her remaining time at home, surrounded by family in the sunroom she so enjoyed. With the assistance of hospice—for whom I'll be eternally grateful—we made the transition and brought Mom home. We thought (hoped) we had weeks left together, but ten days after coming home she breathed her last here on earth. And as her lungs filled with the sweetness of heaven's breath, Dad, my older brother, Doug, and I stood by her bedside as she stepped into her loving Savior's waiting arms.

Losing Mom was painful, but we shared some humorous moments in our journey too. On her first oncology visit, I went with her and Dad, and as we were waiting on the doctor, the nurse came in and asked some preliminary questions, then asked if Mom would take some deep breaths. Seconds passed, and Mom and I looked at each other, hearing "deep breaths" coming from someone else other than Mom. It was *Dad,* sitting in the chair beside her, taking breaths for her, not even aware of what he was doing. We got so tickled. I told them I thought that was taking the "oneness in marriage" thing a little too far. We laughed about that many times, but it's always been that way for them. They truly were *one.*

Days before Mom passed, I was getting ready for the hospice aid to arrive when I saw Kenny Chesney singing on TV. I'd muted the TV during a commercial, since Mom was resting. Yet knowing how she *loved* Kenny, I turned up the volume. She immediately started shimmying from side to side in bed, just smiling. I asked her, "What on earth are you doing?" She smiled that sweet smile of hers and said, "I'm bed dancin'. " We laughed and danced together for a minute. She was such a hoot and such fun. She always was. That's one thing I love most about the relationship we shared . . . we loved to laugh together, and laughed together a lot. And will again. Someday.

Closer to her passing, Mom awakened from a nap and with anticipation in her eyes, she told me and Dad, "I feel like a big surprise is coming!" She giggled, and wriggled her eyebrows. We told her, "Well, there *is* a big surprise coming." "When is it coming?" she asked. We responded (much as Lyda did with Ben), "If we told you . . . then it wouldn't be a surprise." I've no doubt that her anticipation was spurred on by her desire to see her Lord and to be with Him in her *forever home,* cancer-free.

Two dear friends, Judy McMahan and Eva Lyn Frieden, who have already lost their precious mothers, walked this road with me as I walked it with Mom. Early on, they both told me that the person dying gets to choose . . . that when "hope for healing" gives way to "good-bye for now," the person making the journey home should get to make the final choices. I took that advice to heart, and it made such a difference in the final weeks and days with Mom. It gave me a peace and a "release" in that my role was to aid her in her journey that God was leading her on, not to help determine the path she would take. God was already working in her to lead her steps on that path. My role became to help her take those steps, and at times when she could no longer take them on her own, quite literally.

I treasure every moment with her, every overnight hospital stay, every "early wee hours of the morning" chat when she couldn't sleep and we'd sit up and talk. Every one of those times is written on my heart and has changed me and my view of this life. I think for the better. Though I miss her in a profound way, and know I will for the rest of my life here, knowing she's in the presence of Jesus brings such a measure of peace and joy.

Many of you wrote to me during this past year and shared words of comfort and hope. Every note felt like a hug. Thank you. I especially appreciate your overwhelming excitement for this story, and for your patience as Rand and Rachel's journey finally took shape and found its way onto the page and into your hands. Rand and Rachel each took steps of faith into the life God was calling them to, though they couldn't see what that life would look like. Because, like us, if they could see, then it wouldn't be faith.

When thinking of great faith, we rarely think of great fear. But the Bible shows repeatedly that people of great faith also trembled in their boots as they took that first step in following God's will for their lives. Nevertheless, they took it, trusting Him and then running for Him with everything they had.

May we do no less.

I'm already hard at work on a new three-book historical series, with the first book scheduled for release in 2011. These new characters and their stories have captured my heart, as I hope they will yours. For more information on upcoming books and to stay in touch, visit my Web site (*www.tameraalexander.com*) or my blog (*www.tameraalexander@blogspot.com*).

Until next time,
Tamera

ACKNOWLEDGMENTS

There were moments when writing this book that I doubted whether I'd ever reach "the end." But God provided the perfect encouragement (and firm nudges) exactly when I needed them, and I'm so grateful. . . .

To Jesus, for holding my hand as we continue to take steps of faith together. Thanks for never complaining when I squeeze a tad too hard and for taking me places I'd never have the courage to go without you.

To Joe, Kelsey, and Kurt, for your acceptance, your laughter, your love, and for making my world complete.

To Dad, for your steadfast faith and courage. This past year has been the most difficult of your life, I know. But remember, the best is *still* yet to come. Our home is richer for having you in it, and I look forward to sharing the years ahead.

To Doug, my older brother, for sharing your strength during this past year. You spoke so beautifully at Mom's Celebration Service. I was so proud of you then, just as I've always been.

To Dr. Fred Alexander, my favorite father-in-law, for seeing what others miss.

To Deborah Raney, my writing critique partner, for sharing your enormous talent and for always being just a click (and peanut butter twist) away.

493

To my agent, Natasha Kern, for doing what you do so very well.

To the Coeur d'Alene women, for our summer retreats full of plotting and playing. Who knew *work* could be such fun?

To Karen Schurrer, Helen Motter, Charlene Patterson, Sharon Asmus, Ann Parrish, my editors at Bethany House, and to Raela Schoenherr, an early reader, for your suggestions and catches. We all know what my writing is like without you. So bless you, dear friends!

To Judy McMahan (AKA: *Mouth of the South*) and Eva Lyn Frieden, for helping me walk Mom home. You were Jesus in the flesh to me during those excruciating yet oh so precious days, and I'm so grateful God brought you into my life, and Mom's, all those years ago.

To Sunni Jeffers, for sharing your knowledge of cattle and ranching.

And to my readers, for your continual support and e-mails asking, "When is *Within My Heart* going to be ready?" You'll never know how much your excitement to read Rand and Rachel's story helped me through a dark time. Next time we're together, please grab me. I've got a hug with your name on it!

TAMERA ALEXANDER is a bestselling novelist whose deeply drawn characters, thought-provoking plots, and poignant prose resonate with readers worldwide. Having lived in Colorado for seventeen years, she and her husband now make their home in Nashville, Tennessee, where they enjoy life with Tamera's father, Doug, and with their two adult children, Kelsey and Kurt. And last but not least, a precious—and precocious—silky terrier named Jack.

Tamera invites you to visit her Web site at
www.tameraalexander.com
or write her at the following postal address:

Tamera Alexander
P.O. Box 871
Brentwood, TN 37024

Center Point Publishing
600 Brooks Road ● PO Box 1
Thorndike ME 04986-0001 USA

(207) 568-3717

US & Canada:
1 800 929-9108
www.centerpointlargeprint.com

98

X

FOR WITHDRAWN LIBRARY

Rm

H